BOOK ONE: THE MERCHANT OF DEATH

PENDRAGON
GRAPHIC NOVEL

D.J. MACHALE

Adapted and illustrated by
Carla Speed McNeil

ALADDIN PAPERBACKS
New York London Toronto Sydney

For Patrick, Courtney, and Shannon (the real ones) —D. J. M.

To A. S.: I know how it is. —C. S. M.

This book is a work of fiction. Any references to historical events, real people, or real locales are used fictitiously. Other names, characters, places, and incidents are the product of the author's imagination, and any resemblance to actual events or locales or persons, living or dead, is entirely coincidental.

ALADDIN PAPERBACKS
An imprint of Simon & Schuster Children's Publishing Division
1230 Avenue of the Americas, New York, NY 10020

Designed by Sammy Yuen
Manufactured in the United States of America
First Aladdin Paperbacks edition May 2008
10 9 8 7 6 5 4 3 2 1
Library of Congress Control Number 2007937920
ISBN-13: 978-1-4169-5080-6
ISBN-10: 1-4169-5080-X

F·OREWORD

When writing a Pendragon novel, I feel as if I'm going on Bobby's adventure with him. The way I write is to imagine the characters and the settings and the action in my head, then describe it all with words. I'm often asked what my favorite Pendragon book is. My answer is always the same: It's the book I happen to be writing at the time, because I'm in the thick of the action and discovering things right along with the characters. So you can imagine how fun it was for me to actually see Bobby's adventure unfold visually in this, the first of the graphic novel series. Carla Speed McNeil did an awesome job capturing the essence of the characters, story, and action of *The Merchant of Death*.

The graphic novel form is new to me. I haven't read anything like it since I collected Superman and Batman comics when I was a kid. (My all-time favorite comic character? Mr. Mxyzptlk. Is he still around?) So I was surprised at how fast-paced the story is. It was a real education for me. So much is conveyed through expression, body language, and of course action. When I saw rough sketches during the adapting process, there were a few times when I was concerned that a key story point wasn't getting across. Those with more experience assured me that I was crazy. In the end I think they're right. The devil, as they say, is in the details. It's all there. And I am crazy. But that's another story.

Transforming a novel into a graphic novel is a formidable challenge. Speed did a great job of depicting the essence of the book while adding her own storytelling style to make it work best visually. To do that, she had to change some small points while still holding true to the original plot and characters. And as all Pendragon readers know, there are elements set up in *The Merchant of Death* that play out over several novels, so Speed had to learn about things that won't happen until much later in the overall story. For example, it's a tricky thing to depict somebody traveling through a flume and arriving at a gate. This may be my story, but an artist has their own vision and interpretation of what they think things should look like, just as every reader has their own vision. So while depicting the gates and the flumes in the first story, Speed had to take into account specific action that takes place at the gates in later novels. Which means she had to learn so much more about Bobby and the Travelers than is contained in *The Merchant of Death*. And it's a pretty big story. Sorry Speed! At least that means creating the future graphic novels will be that much easier.

In the end, I think the result is fantastic. I hope that it's not only fun for all Pendragon readers, but will also open up Bobby's world to a whole 'nother group of readers who enjoy graphic novels.

Now I can't wait to see what Speed comes up with for Cloral. That ought to be good.

Hobey ho,
D. J. MacHale

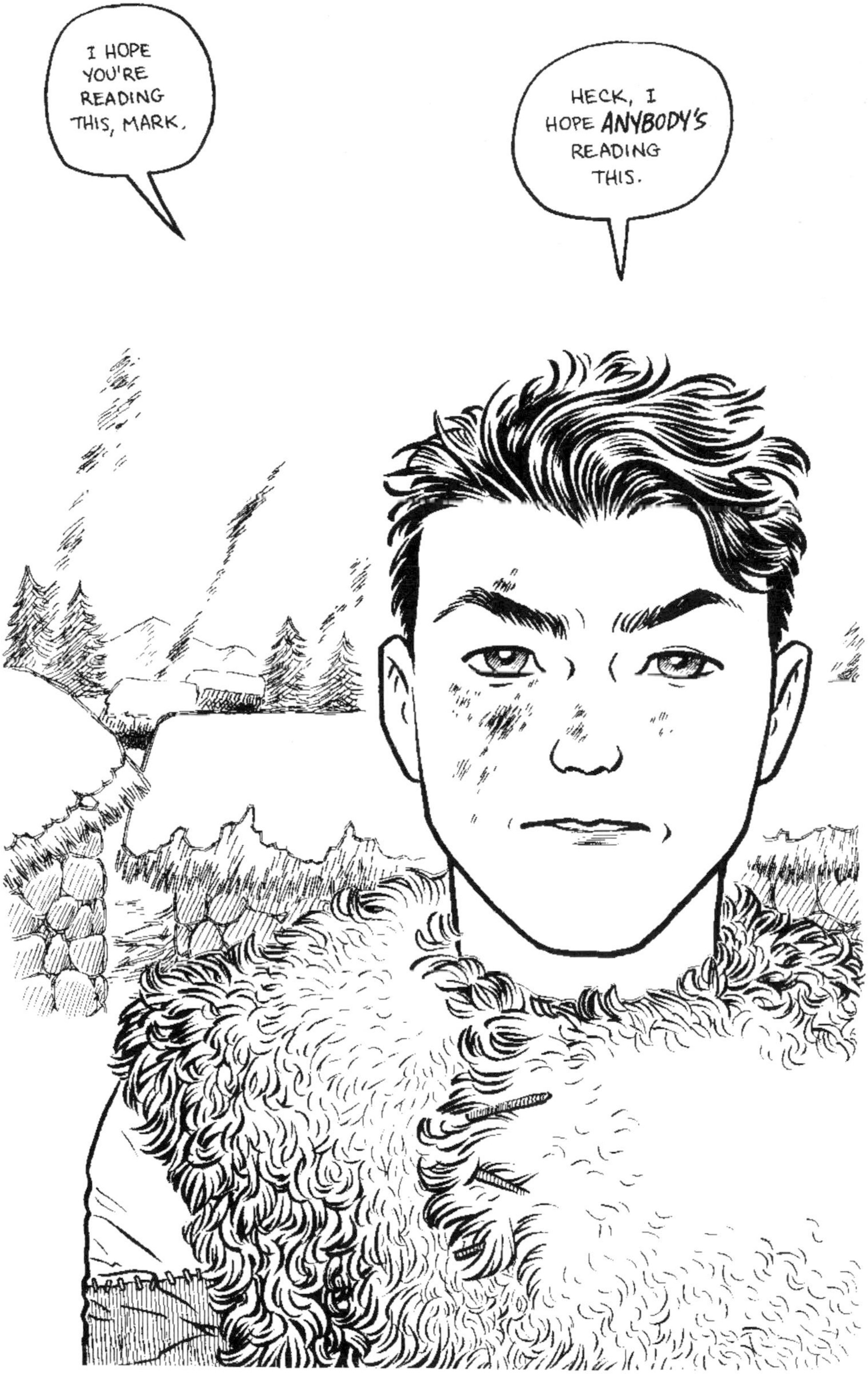
I HOPE YOU'RE READING THIS, MARK.
HECK, I HOPE ANYBODY'S READING THIS.

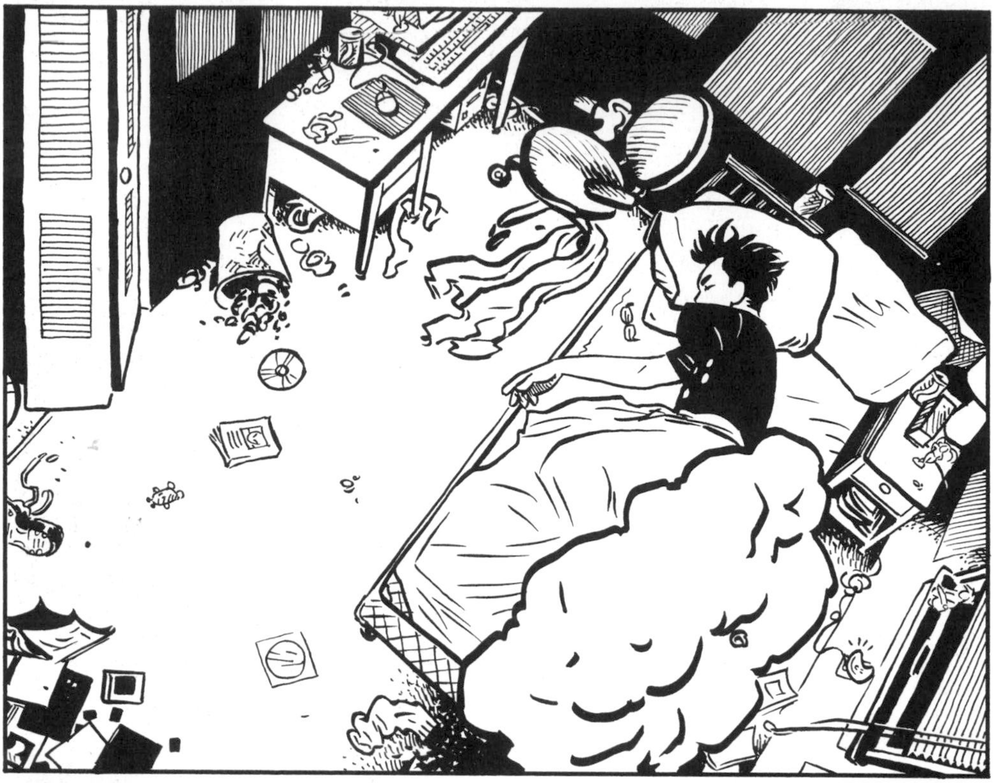

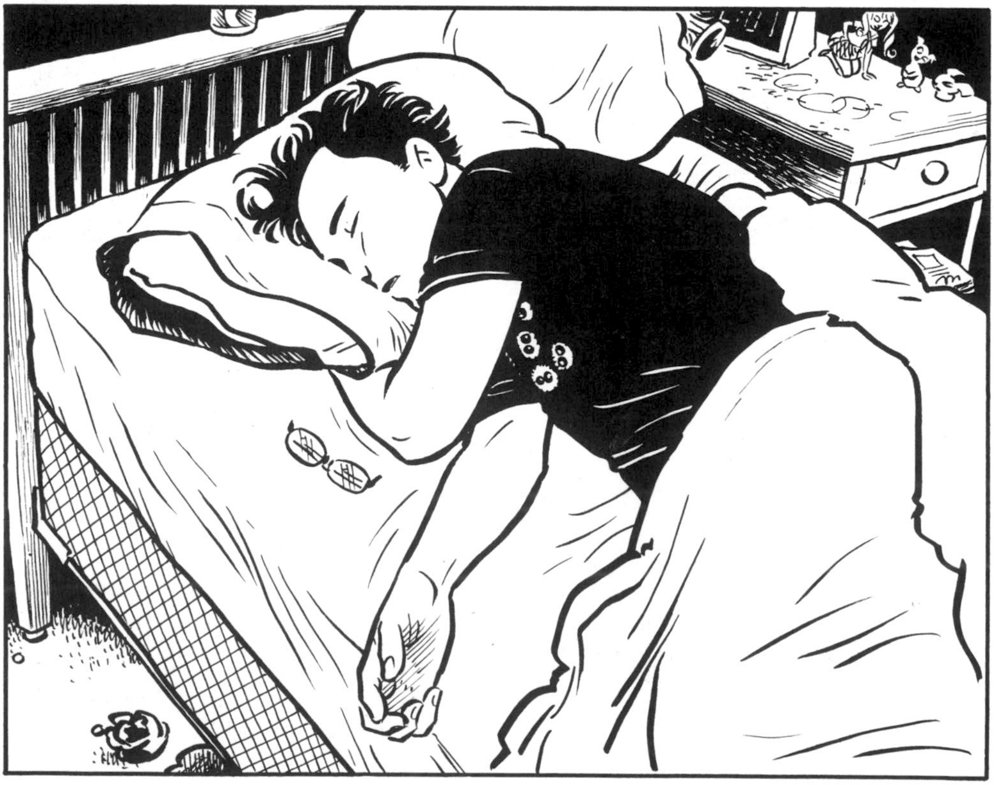

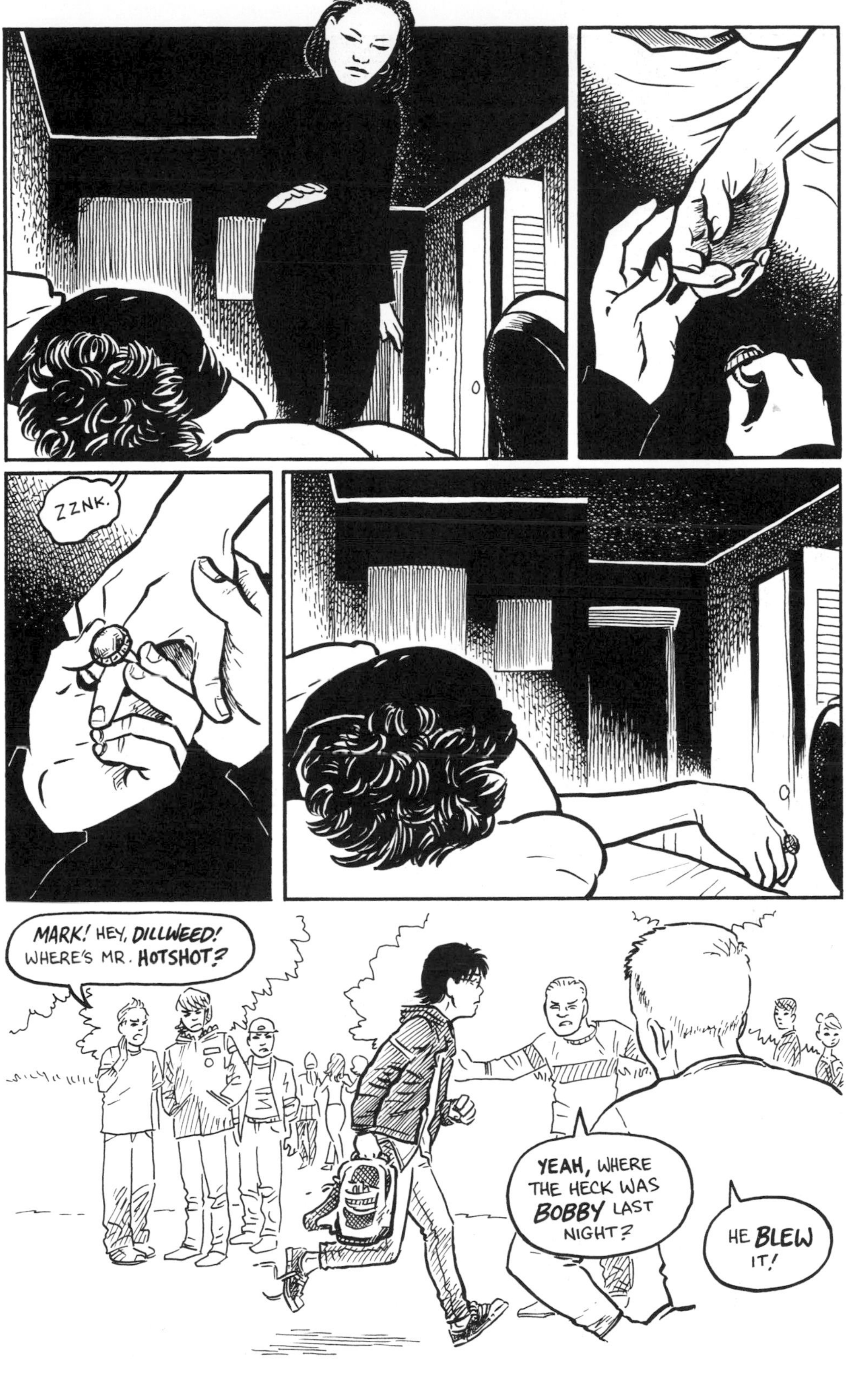
ZZNK.
MARK! HEY, DILLWEED! WHERE'S MR. HOTSHOT?
YEAH, WHERE THE HECK WAS BOBBY LAST NIGHT?
HE BLEW IT!

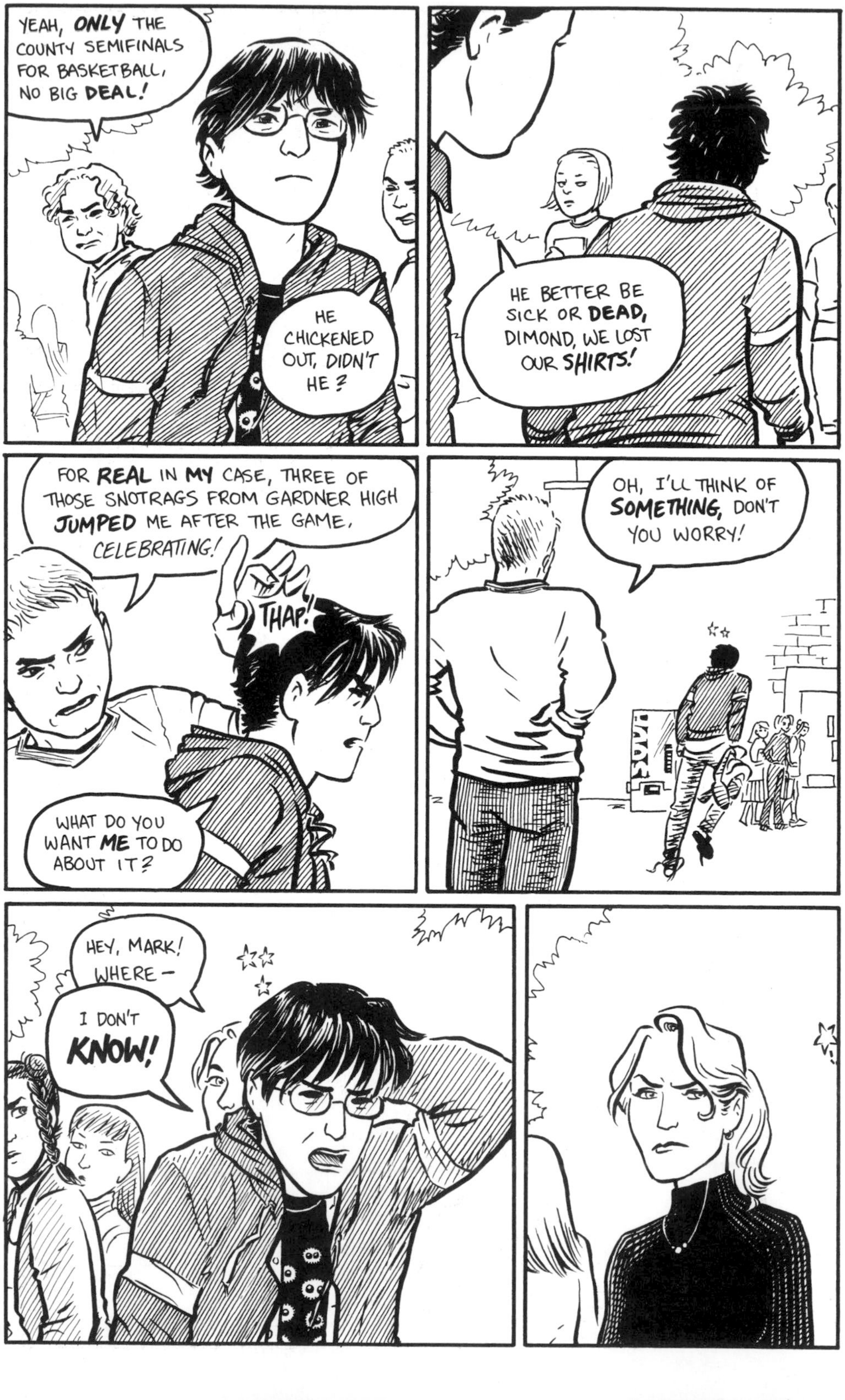
YEAH, ONLY THE COUNTY SEMIFINALS FOR BASKETBALL, NO BIG DEAL!
HE CHICKENED OUT, DIDN'T HE?
HE BETTER BE SICK OR DEAD, DIMOND, WE LOST OUR SHIRTS!
FOR REAL IN MY CASE, THREE OF THOSE SNOTRAGS FROM GARDNER HIGH JUMPED ME AFTER THE GAME, CELEBRATING!
THAP!
WHAT DO YOU WANT ME TO DO ABOUT IT?
OH, I'LL THINK OF SOMETHING, DON'T YOU WORRY!
HEY, MARK! WHERE—
I DON'T KNOW!

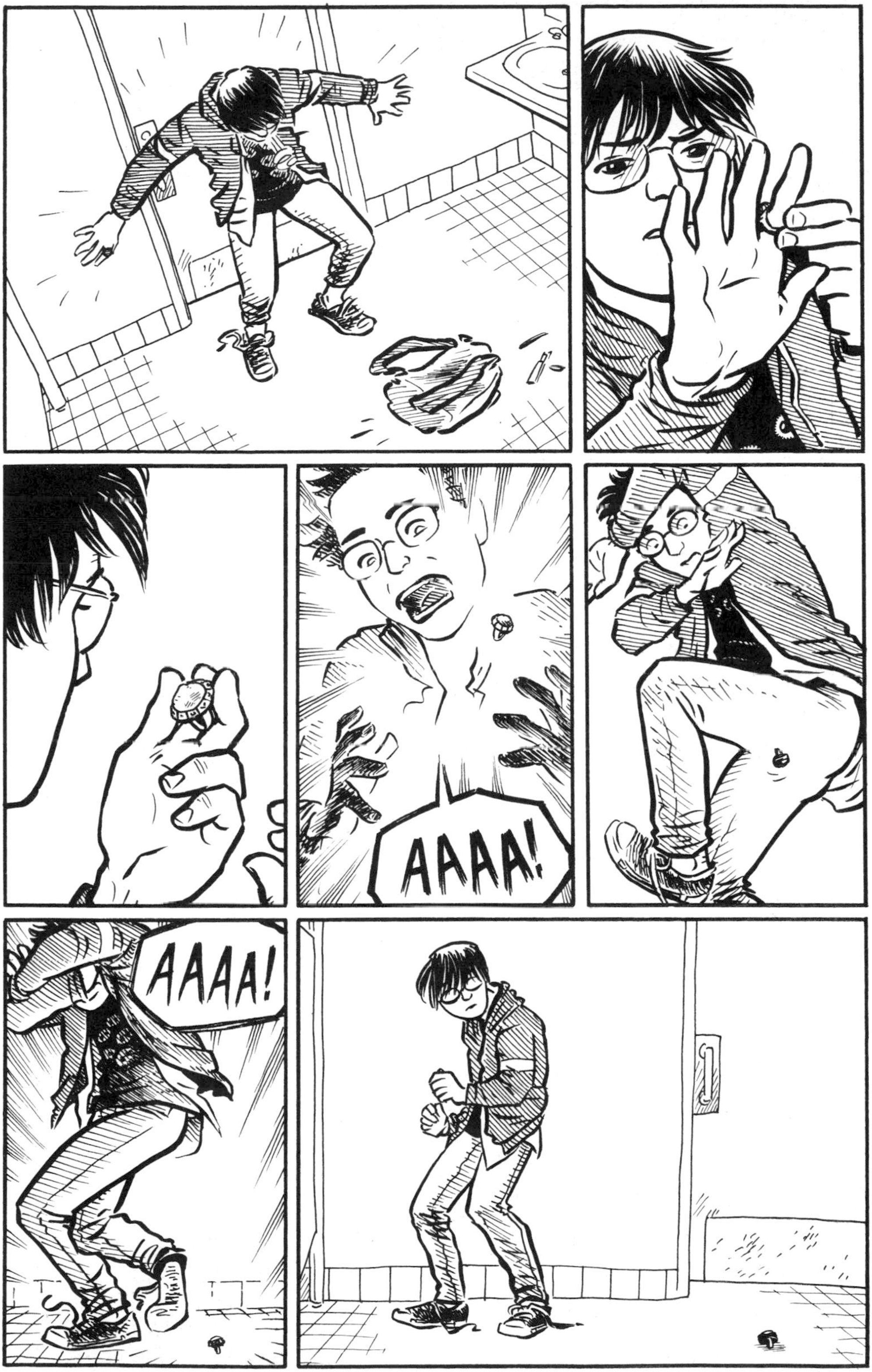
AAAA!
AAAA!

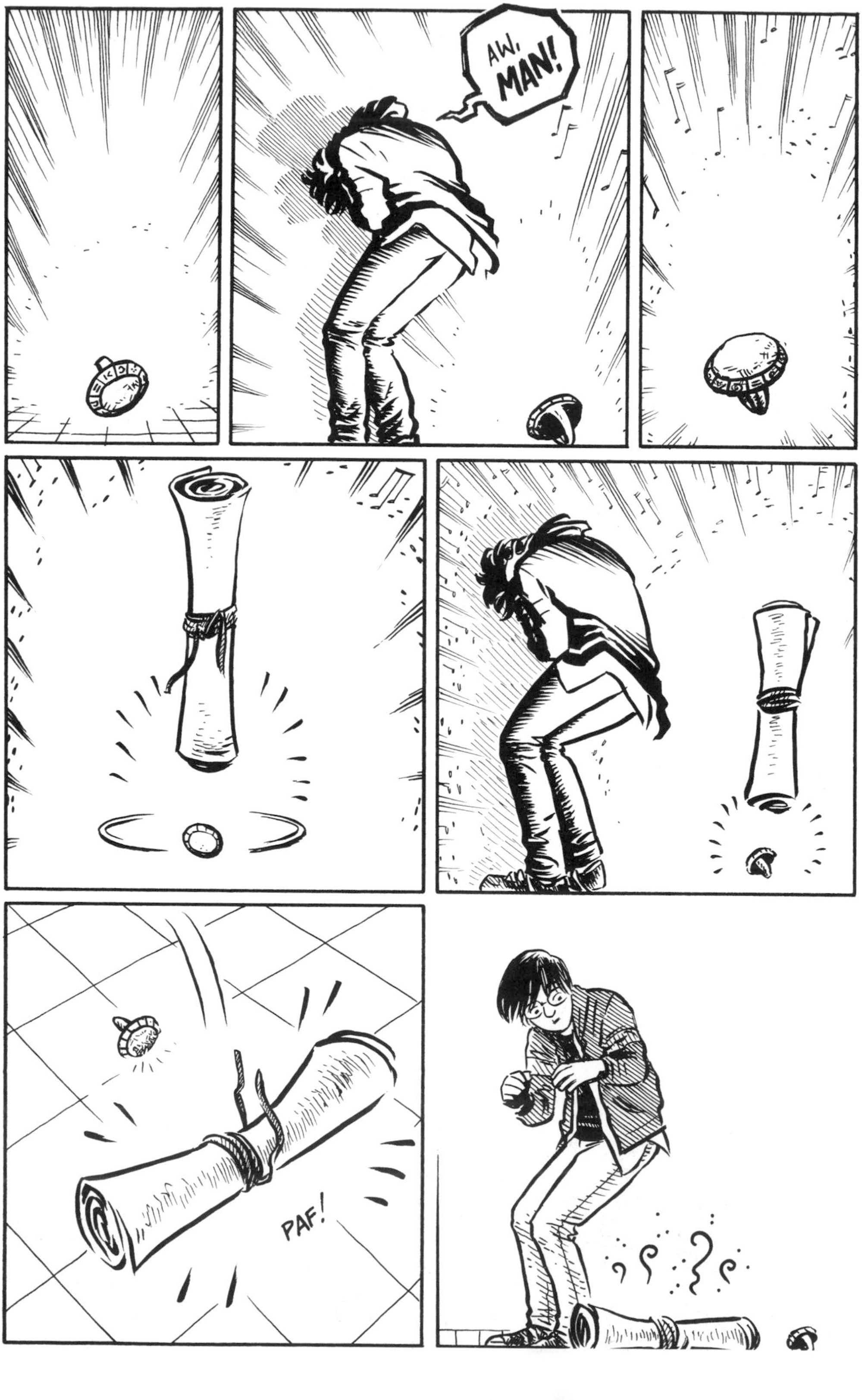
AW, MAN!
PAF!

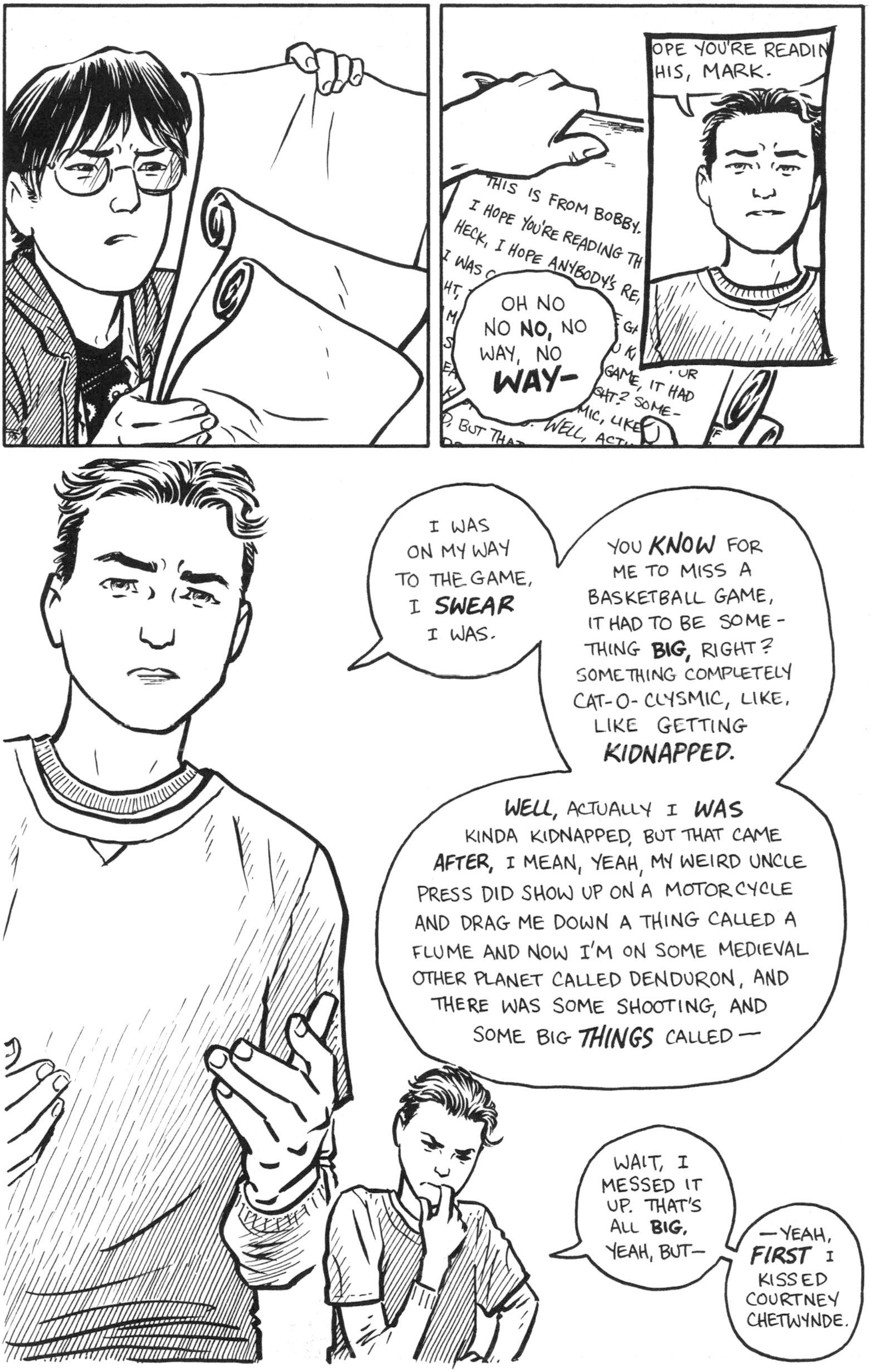
OPE YOU'RE READIN
HIS, MARK.
THIS IS FROM BOBBY.
I HOPE YOU'RE READING TH
HECK, I HOPE ANYBODY'S RE
OH NO NO NO, NO WAY, NO WAY-
I WAS ON MY WAY TO THE GAME, I SWEAR I WAS.
YOU KNOW FOR ME TO MISS A BASKETBALL GAME, IT HAD TO BE SOME-THING BIG, RIGHT? SOMETHING COMPLETELY CAT-O-CLYSMIC, LIKE, LIKE GETTING KIDNAPPED.
WELL, ACTUALLY I WAS KINDA KIDNAPPED, BUT THAT CAME AFTER, I MEAN, YEAH, MY WEIRD UNCLE PRESS DID SHOW UP ON A MOTORCYCLE AND DRAG ME DOWN A THING CALLED A FLUME AND NOW I'M ON SOME MEDIEVAL OTHER PLANET CALLED DENDURON, AND THERE WAS SOME SHOOTING, AND SOME BIG THINGS CALLED—
WAIT, I MESSED IT UP. THAT'S ALL BIG, YEAH, BUT—
—YEAH, FIRST I KISSED COURTNEY CHETWYNDE.

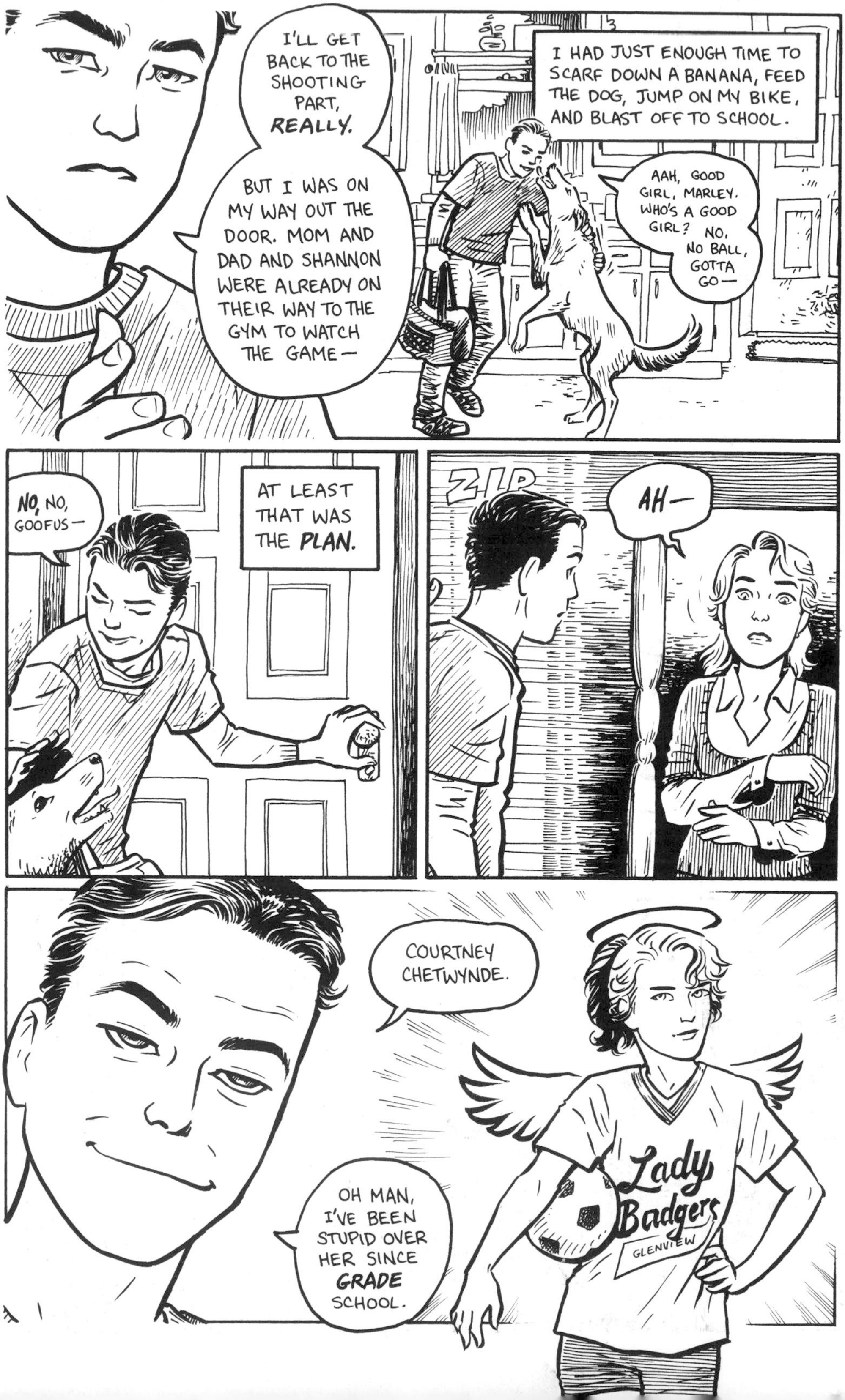
I'LL GET BACK TO THE SHOOTING PART, **REALLY**.
BUT I WAS ON MY WAY OUT THE DOOR. MOM AND DAD AND SHANNON WERE ALREADY ON THEIR WAY TO THE GYM TO WATCH THE GAME—
I HAD JUST ENOUGH TIME TO SCARF DOWN A BANANA, FEED THE DOG, JUMP ON MY BIKE, AND BLAST OFF TO SCHOOL.
AAH, GOOD GIRL, MARLEY. WHO'S A GOOD GIRL? NO, NO BALL, GOTTA GO—
NO, NO, GOOFUS—
AT LEAST THAT WAS THE **PLAN**.
ZIP
AH—
COURTNEY CHETWYNDE.
Lady Badgers
GLENVIEW
OH MAN, I'VE BEEN STUPID OVER HER SINCE **GRADE** SCHOOL.

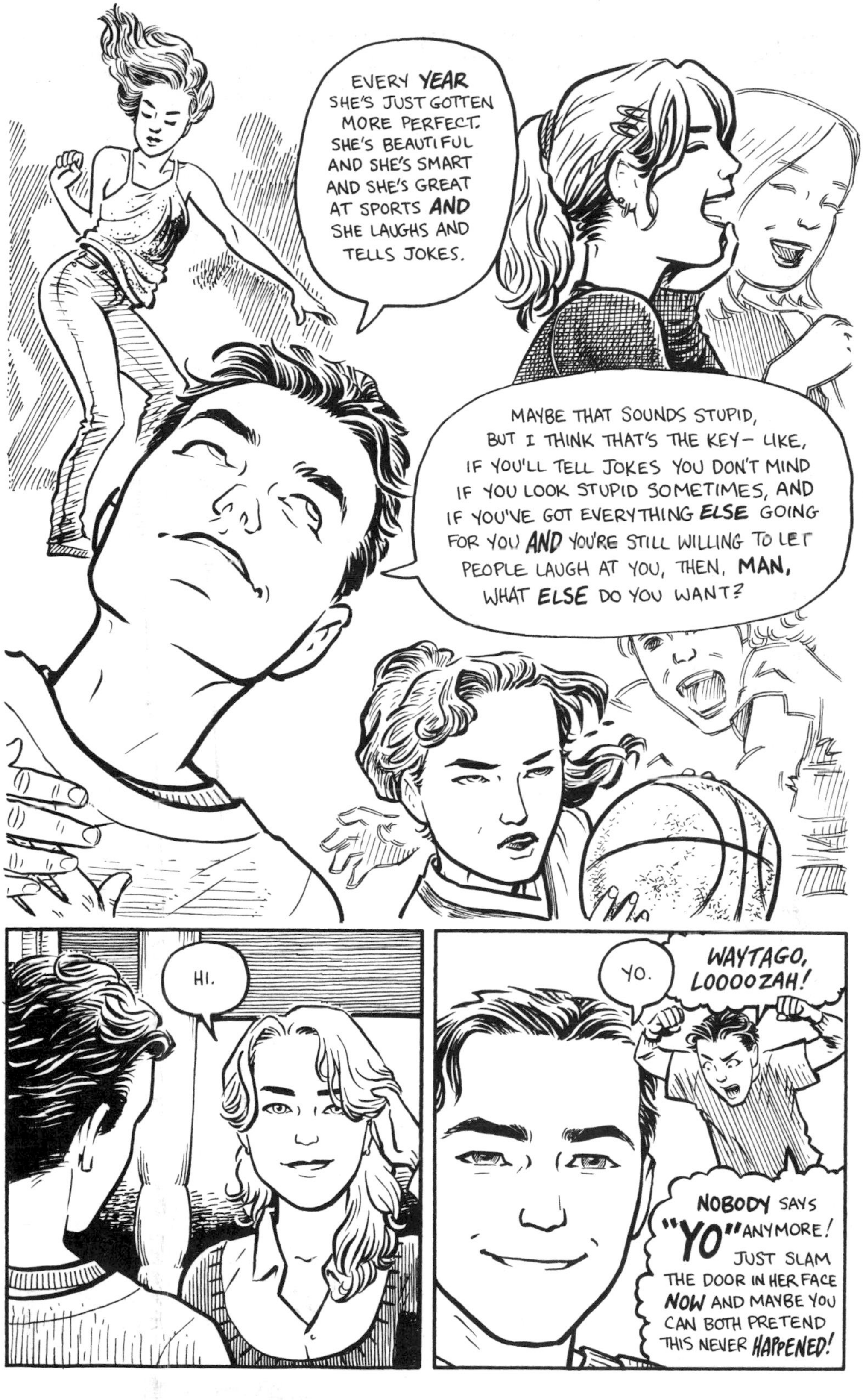
EVERY YEAR SHE'S JUST GOTTEN MORE PERFECT. SHE'S BEAUTIFUL AND SHE'S SMART AND SHE'S GREAT AT SPORTS AND SHE LAUGHS AND TELLS JOKES.
MAYBE THAT SOUNDS STUPID, BUT I THINK THAT'S THE KEY– LIKE, IF YOU'LL TELL JOKES YOU DON'T MIND IF YOU LOOK STUPID SOMETIMES, AND IF YOU'VE GOT EVERYTHING ELSE GOING FOR YOU AND YOU'RE STILL WILLING TO LET PEOPLE LAUGH AT YOU, THEN, MAN, WHAT ELSE DO YOU WANT?
HI.
YO.
WAYTAGO, LOOOOZAH!
NOBODY SAYS "YO" ANYMORE! JUST SLAM THE DOOR IN HER FACE NOW AND MAYBE YOU CAN BOTH PRETEND THIS NEVER HAPPENED!

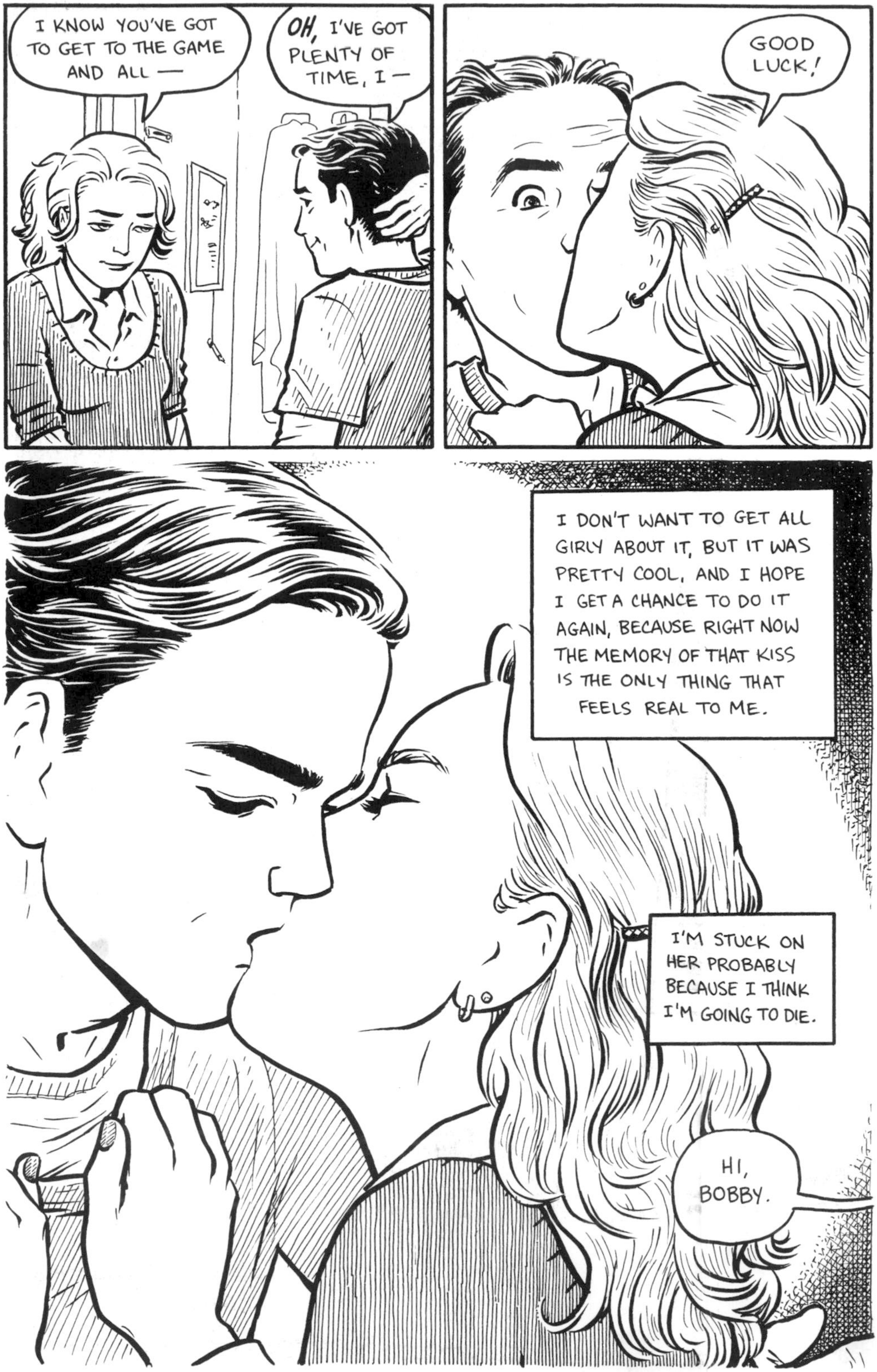
I KNOW YOU'VE GOT TO GET TO THE GAME AND ALL —
OH, I'VE GOT PLENTY OF TIME, I —
GOOD LUCK!
I DON'T WANT TO GET ALL GIRLY ABOUT IT, BUT IT WAS PRETTY COOL, AND I HOPE I GET A CHANCE TO DO IT AGAIN, BECAUSE RIGHT NOW THE MEMORY OF THAT KISS IS THE ONLY THING THAT FEELS REAL TO ME.
I'M STUCK ON HER PROBABLY BECAUSE I THINK I'M GOING TO DIE.
HI, BOBBY.

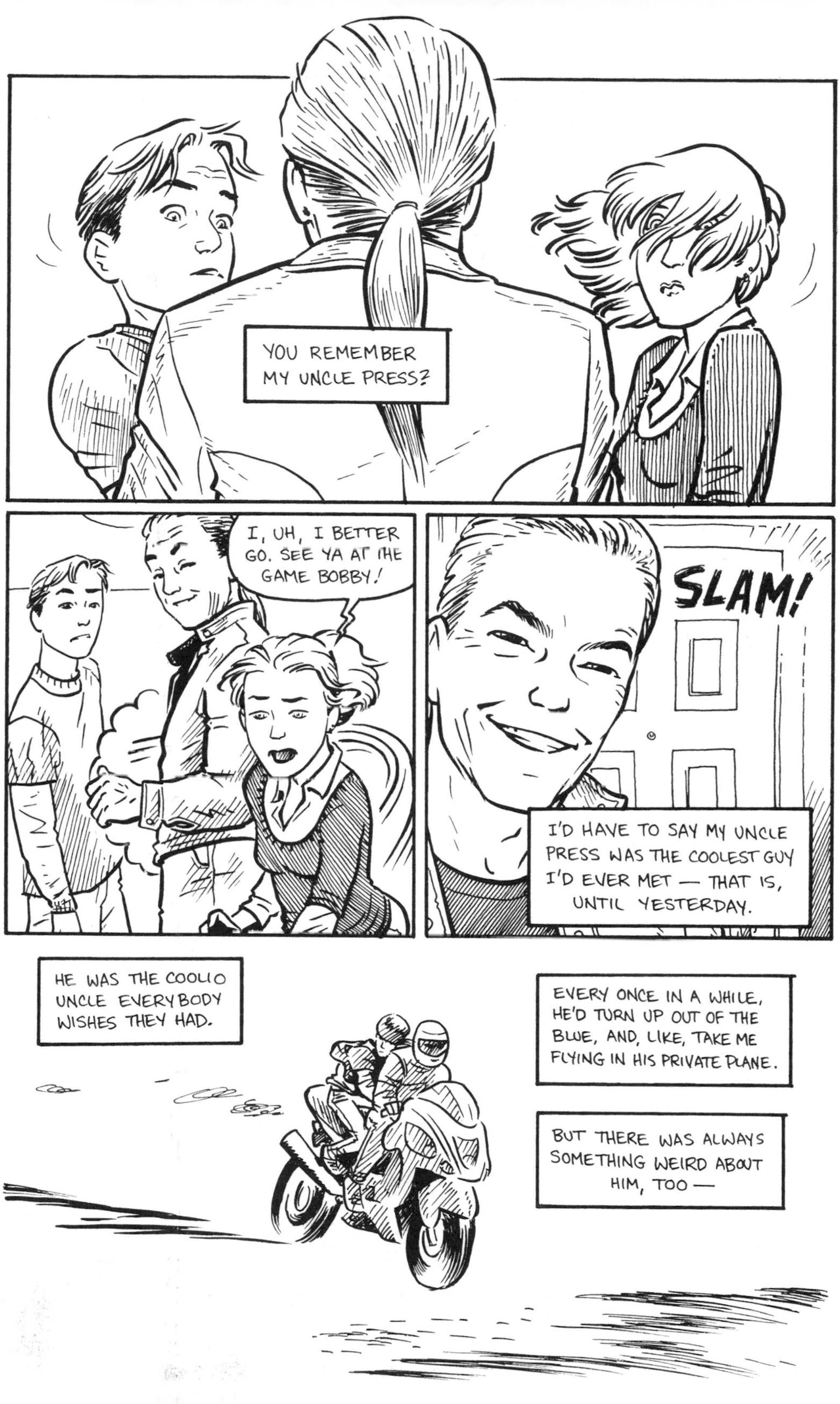

YOU REMEMBER MY UNCLE PRESS?
I, UH, I BETTER GO. SEE YA AT THE GAME BOBBY!
SLAM!
I'D HAVE TO SAY MY UNCLE PRESS WAS THE COOLEST GUY I'D EVER MET — THAT IS, UNTIL YESTERDAY.
HE WAS THE COOLIO UNCLE EVERYBODY WISHES THEY HAD.
EVERY ONCE IN A WHILE, HE'D TURN UP OUT OF THE BLUE, AND, LIKE, TAKE ME FLYING IN HIS PRIVATE PLANE.
BUT THERE WAS ALWAYS SOMETHING WEIRD ABOUT HIM, TOO —

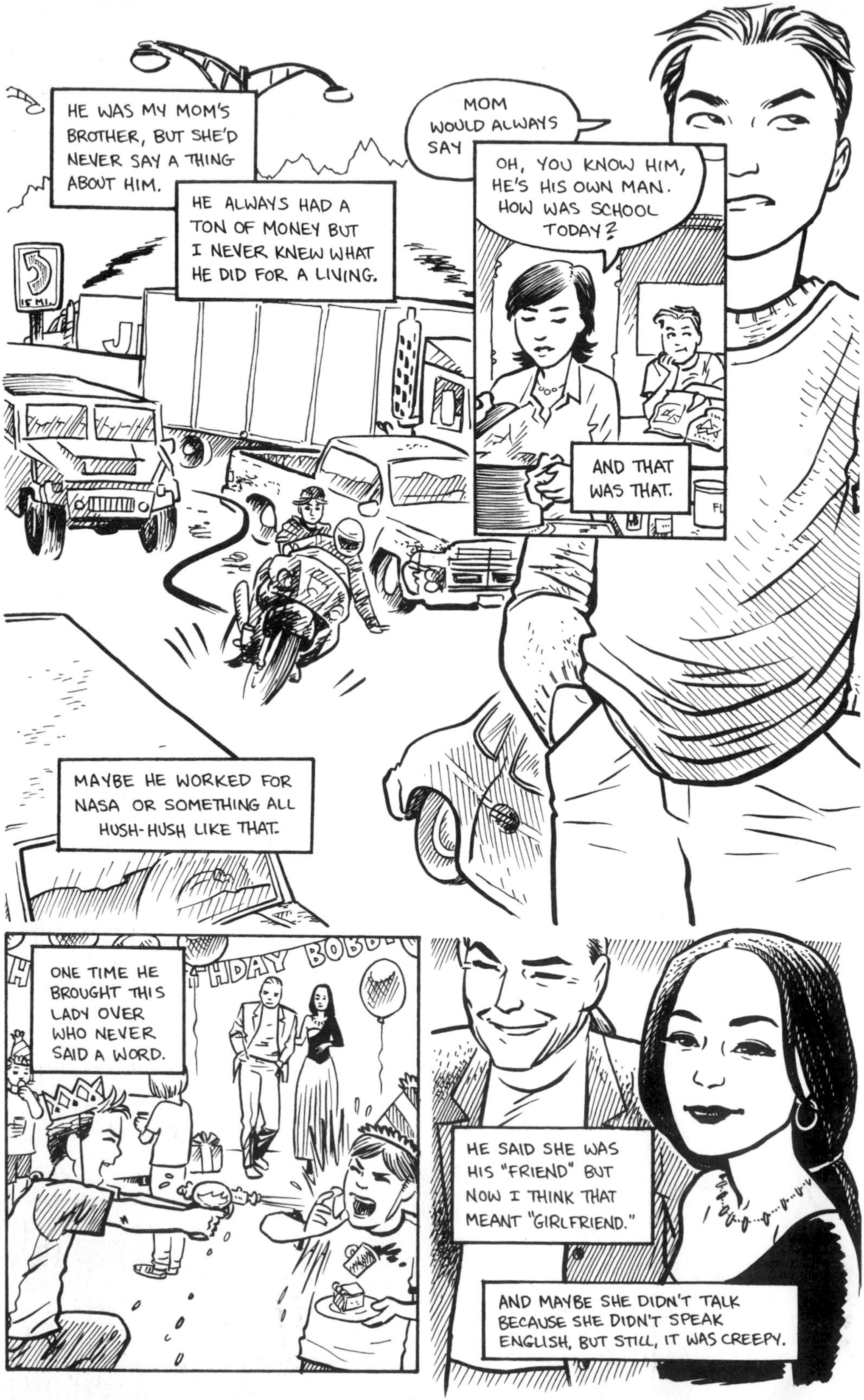
HE WAS MY MOM'S BROTHER, BUT SHE'D NEVER SAY A THING ABOUT HIM.
HE ALWAYS HAD A TON OF MONEY BUT I NEVER KNEW WHAT HE DID FOR A LIVING.
MOM WOULD ALWAYS SAY
OH, YOU KNOW HIM, HE'S HIS OWN MAN. HOW WAS SCHOOL TODAY?
AND THAT WAS THAT.
MAYBE HE WORKED FOR NASA OR SOMETHING ALL HUSH-HUSH LIKE THAT.
ONE TIME HE BROUGHT THIS LADY OVER WHO NEVER SAID A WORD.
HE SAID SHE WAS HIS "FRIEND" BUT NOW I THINK THAT MEANT "GIRLFRIEND."
AND MAYBE SHE DIDN'T TALK BECAUSE SHE DIDN'T SPEAK ENGLISH, BUT STILL, IT WAS CREEPY.

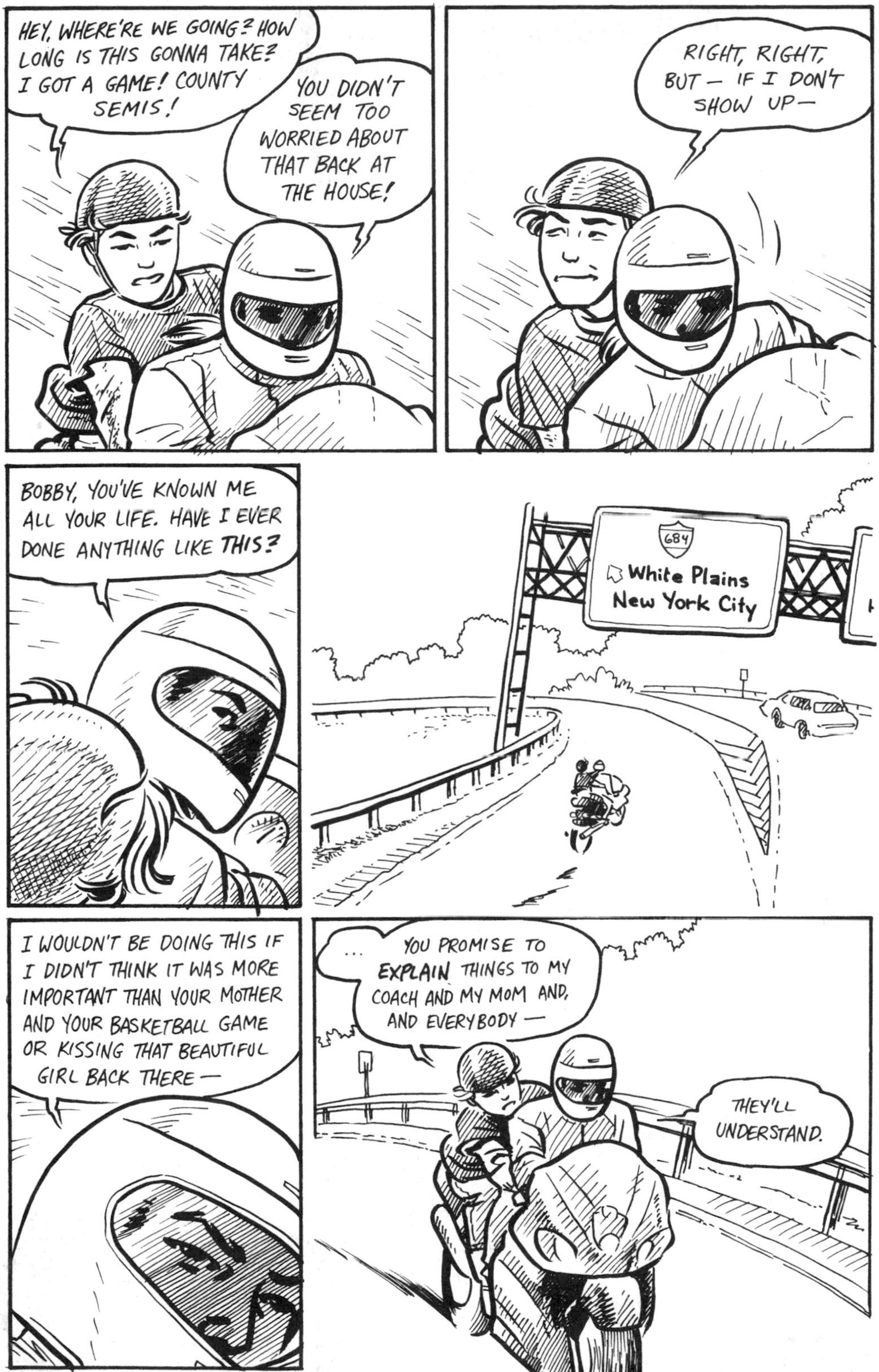
HEY, WHERE'RE WE GOING? HOW LONG IS THIS GONNA TAKE? I GOT A GAME! COUNTY SEMIS!
YOU DIDN'T SEEM TOO WORRIED ABOUT THAT BACK AT THE HOUSE!
RIGHT, RIGHT, BUT — IF I DON'T SHOW UP —
BOBBY, YOU'VE KNOWN ME ALL YOUR LIFE. HAVE I EVER DONE ANYTHING LIKE THIS?
684
White Plains
New York City
I WOULDN'T BE DOING THIS IF I DIDN'T THINK IT WAS MORE IMPORTANT THAN YOUR MOTHER AND YOUR BASKETBALL GAME OR KISSING THAT BEAUTIFUL GIRL BACK THERE —
... YOU PROMISE TO EXPLAIN THINGS TO MY COACH AND MY MOM AND, AND EVERYBODY —
THEY'LL UNDERSTAND.

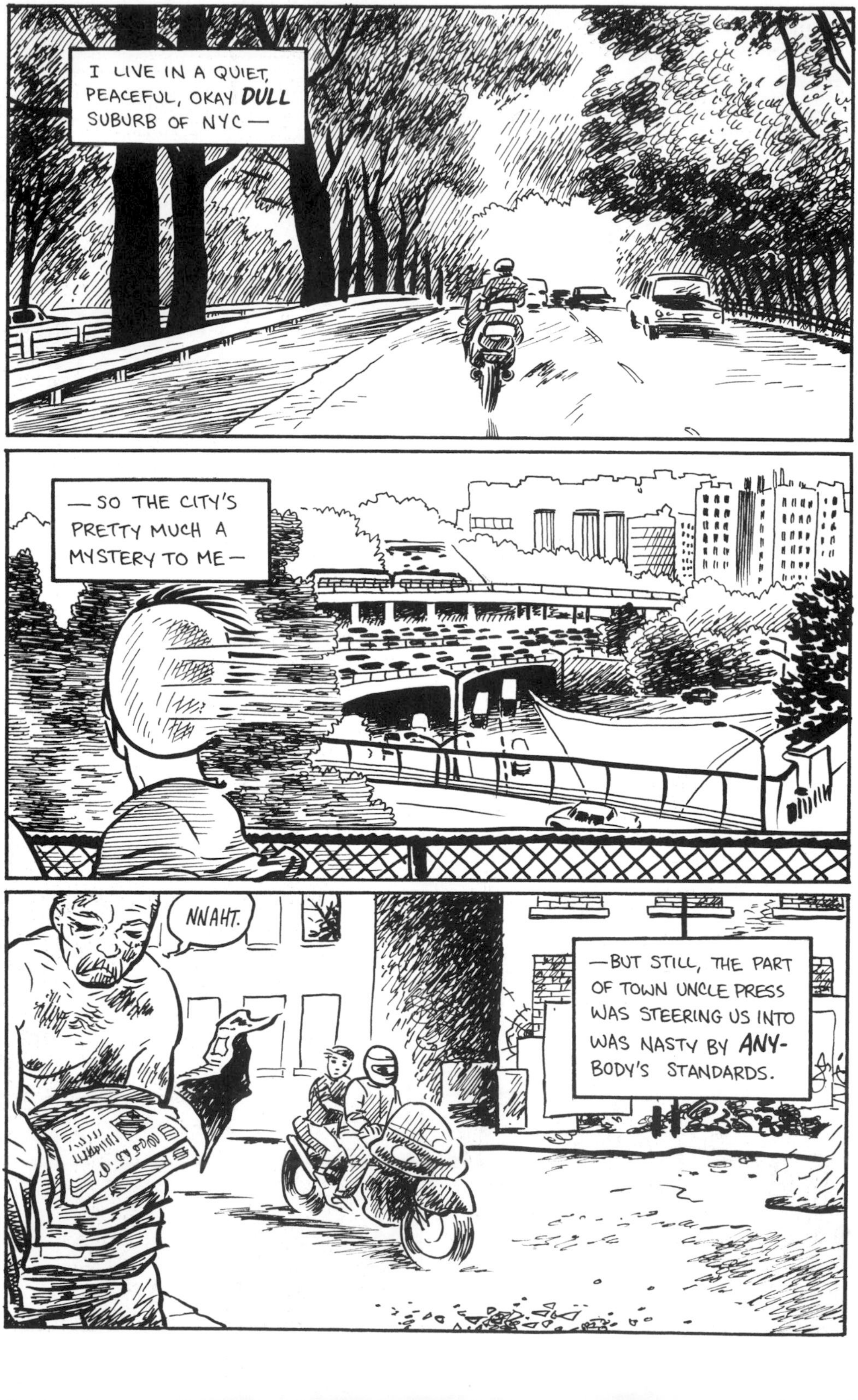
I LIVE IN A QUIET, PEACEFUL, OKAY **DULL** SUBURB OF NYC—
—SO THE CITY'S PRETTY MUCH A MYSTERY TO ME—
NNAHT.
—BUT STILL, THE PART OF TOWN UNCLE PRESS WAS STEERING US INTO WAS NASTY BY **ANY**-BODY'S STANDARDS.

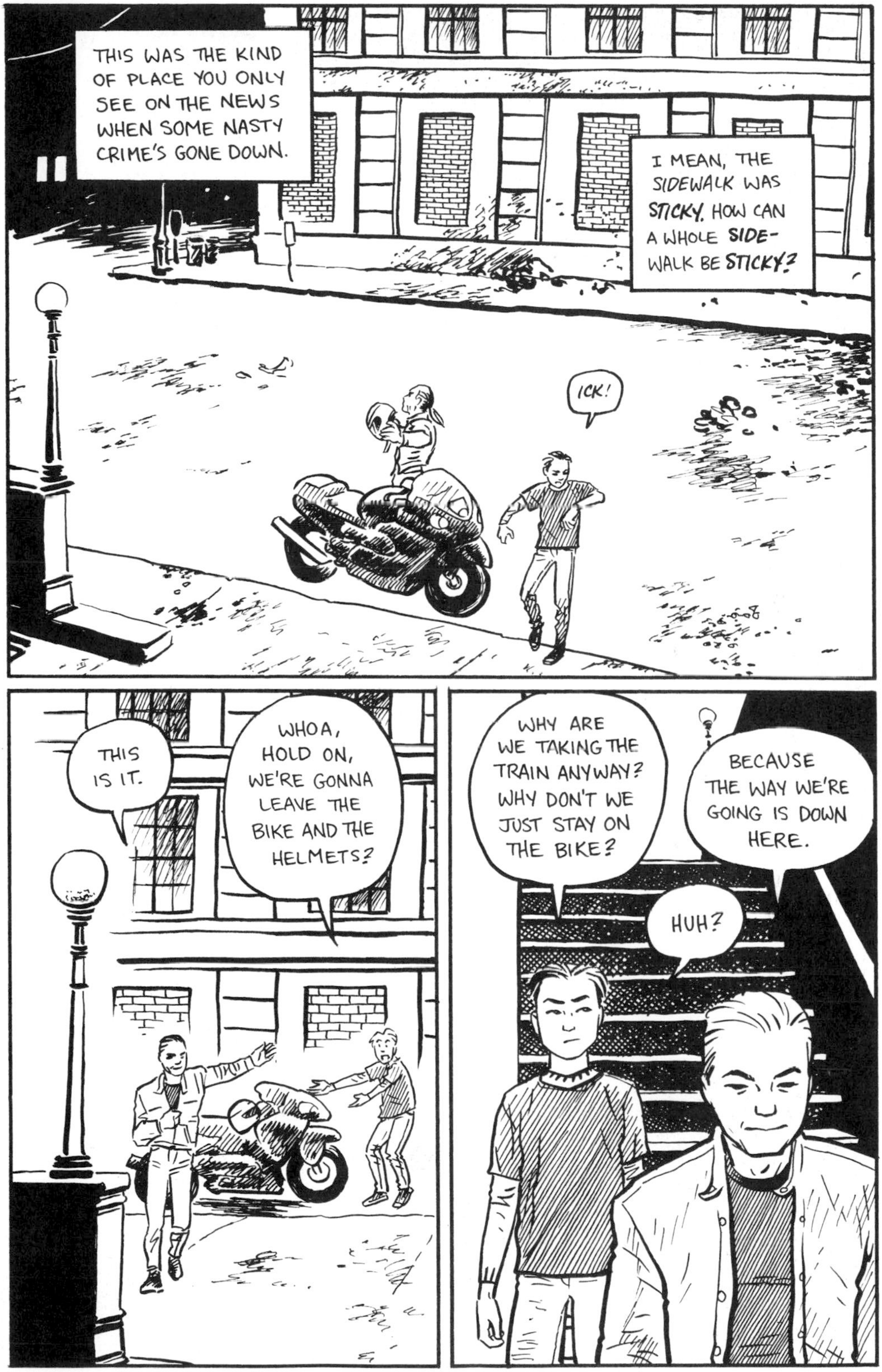
THIS WAS THE KIND OF PLACE YOU ONLY SEE ON THE NEWS WHEN SOME NASTY CRIME'S GONE DOWN.
I MEAN, THE SIDEWALK WAS STICKY. HOW CAN A WHOLE SIDE-WALK BE STICKY?
ICK!
THIS IS IT.
WHOA, HOLD ON, WE'RE GONNA LEAVE THE BIKE AND THE HELMETS?
WHY ARE WE TAKING THE TRAIN ANYWAY? WHY DON'T WE JUST STAY ON THE BIKE?
BECAUSE THE WAY WE'RE GOING IS DOWN HERE.
HUH?

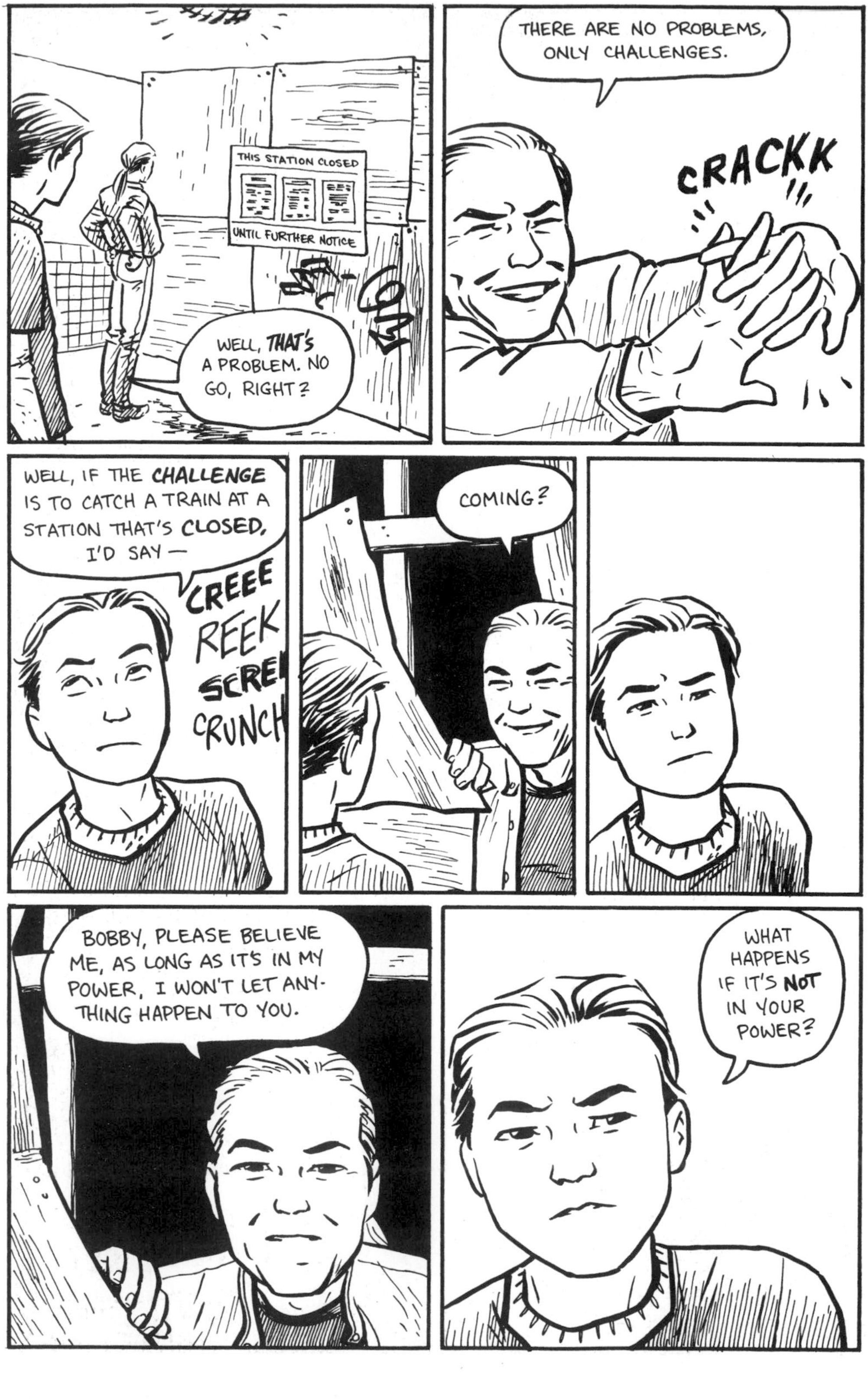
THIS STATION CLOSED
UNTIL FURTHER NOTICE
WELL, THAT'S A PROBLEM. NO GO, RIGHT?
THERE ARE NO PROBLEMS, ONLY CHALLENGES.
CRACKK
WELL, IF THE CHALLENGE IS TO CATCH A TRAIN AT A STATION THAT'S CLOSED, I'D SAY —
CREEE
REEK
SCREE
CRUNCH
COMING?
BOBBY, PLEASE BELIEVE ME, AS LONG AS IT'S IN MY POWER, I WON'T LET ANYTHING HAPPEN TO YOU.
WHAT HAPPENS IF IT'S NOT IN YOUR POWER?

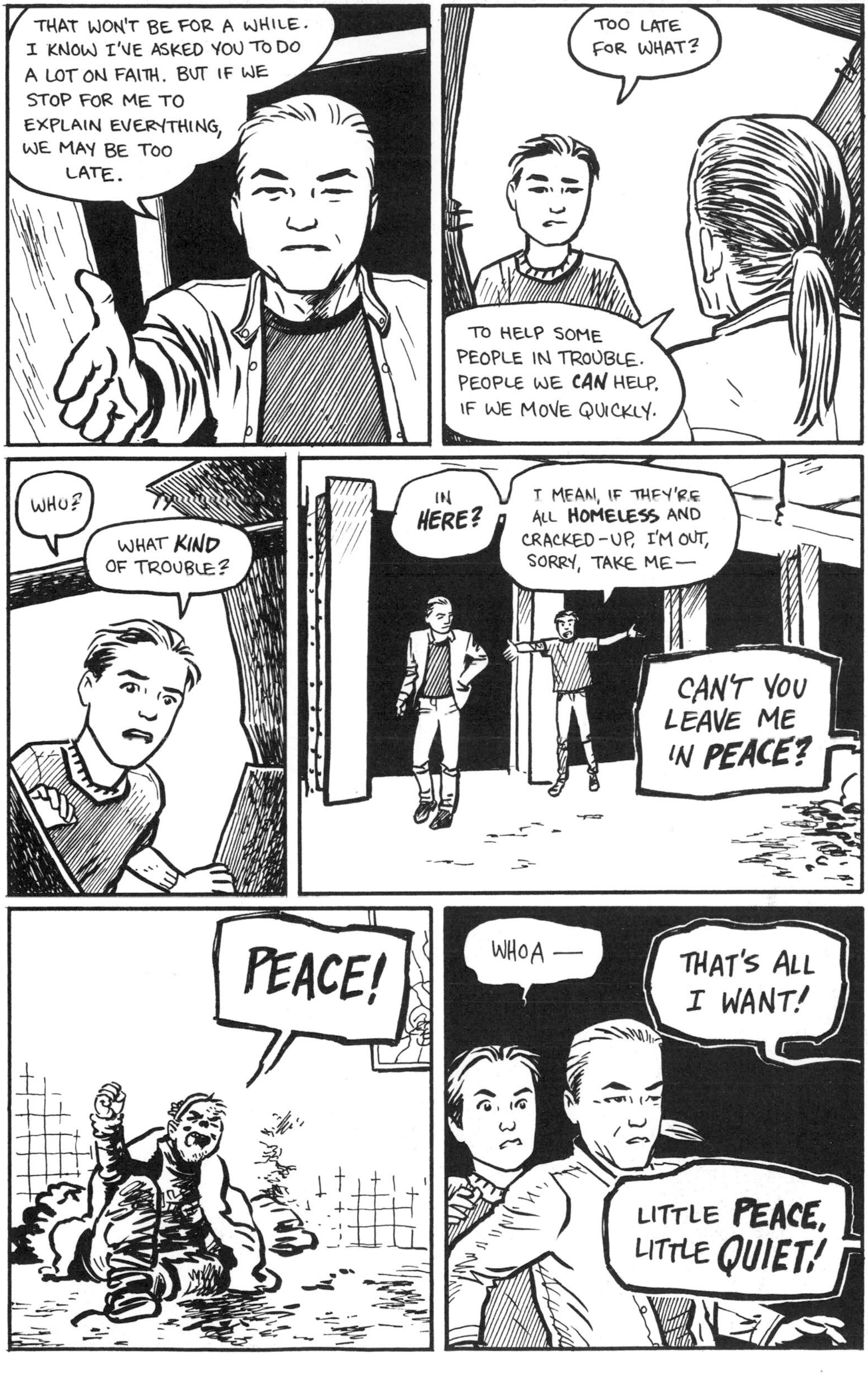

THAT WON'T BE FOR A WHILE. I KNOW I'VE ASKED YOU TO DO A LOT ON FAITH. BUT IF WE STOP FOR ME TO EXPLAIN EVERYTHING, WE MAY BE TOO LATE.
TOO LATE FOR WHAT?
TO HELP SOME PEOPLE IN TROUBLE. PEOPLE WE **CAN** HELP. IF WE MOVE QUICKLY.
WHO?
WHAT **KIND** OF TROUBLE?
IN **HERE?**
I MEAN, IF THEY'RE ALL **HOMELESS** AND CRACKED-UP, I'M OUT, SORRY, TAKE ME—
CAN'T YOU LEAVE ME IN **PEACE?**
PEACE!
WHOA —
THAT'S ALL I WANT!
LITTLE **PEACE,** LITTLE **QUIET!**

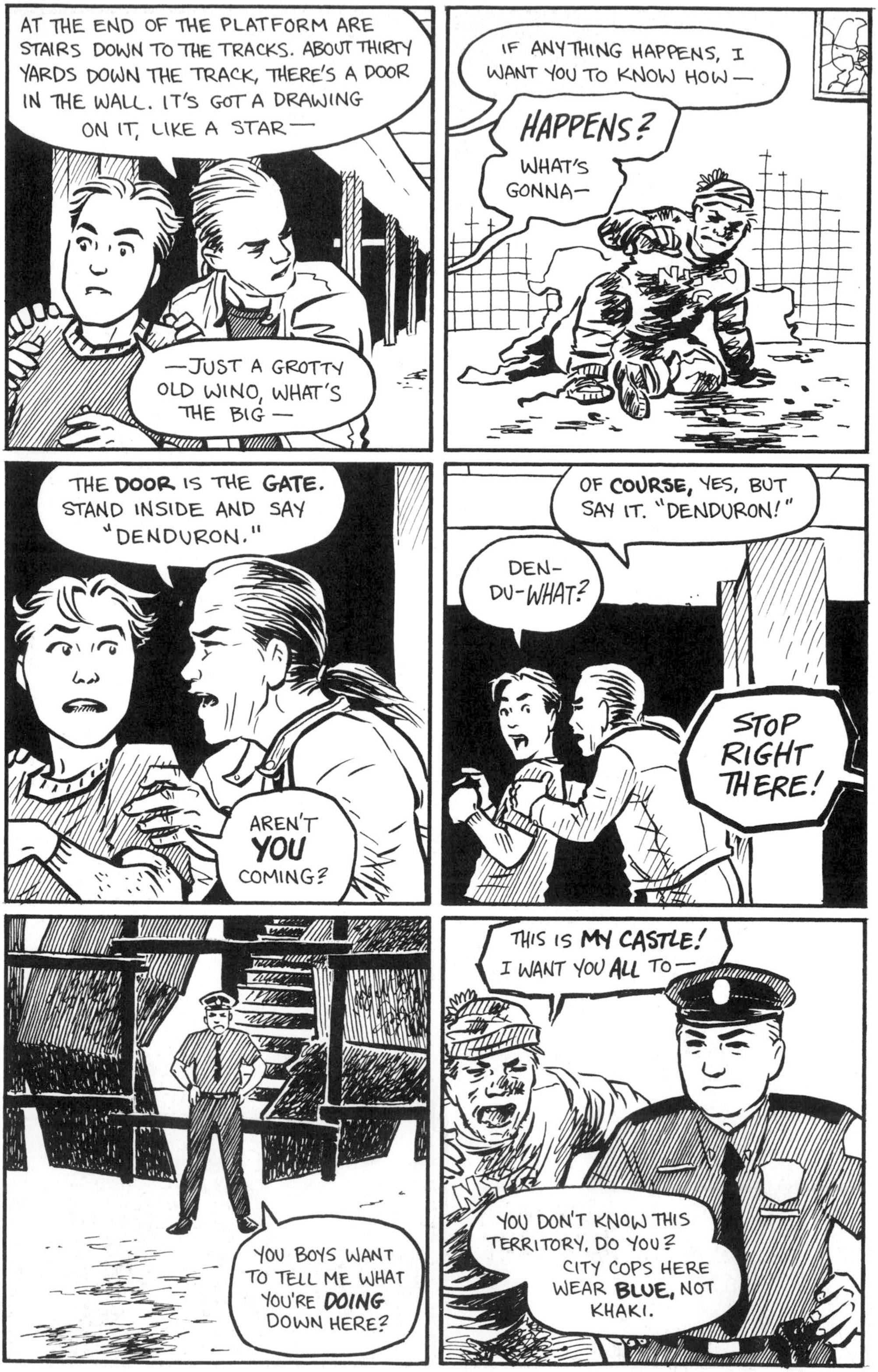
AT THE END OF THE PLATFORM ARE STAIRS DOWN TO THE TRACKS. ABOUT THIRTY YARDS DOWN THE TRACK, THERE'S A DOOR IN THE WALL. IT'S GOT A DRAWING ON IT, LIKE A STAR—
—JUST A GROTTY OLD WINO, WHAT'S THE BIG—
IF ANYTHING HAPPENS, I WANT YOU TO KNOW HOW—
HAPPENS? WHAT'S GONNA—
THE **DOOR** IS THE **GATE**. STAND INSIDE AND SAY "DENDURON."
AREN'T **YOU** COMING?
OF **COURSE**, YES, BUT SAY IT. "DENDURON!"
DEN-DU-WHAT?
STOP RIGHT THERE!
YOU BOYS WANT TO TELL ME WHAT YOU'RE **DOING** DOWN HERE?
THIS IS **MY CASTLE!** I WANT YOU **ALL** TO—
YOU DON'T KNOW THIS TERRITORY, DO YOU?
CITY COPS HERE WEAR **BLUE**, NOT KHAKI.

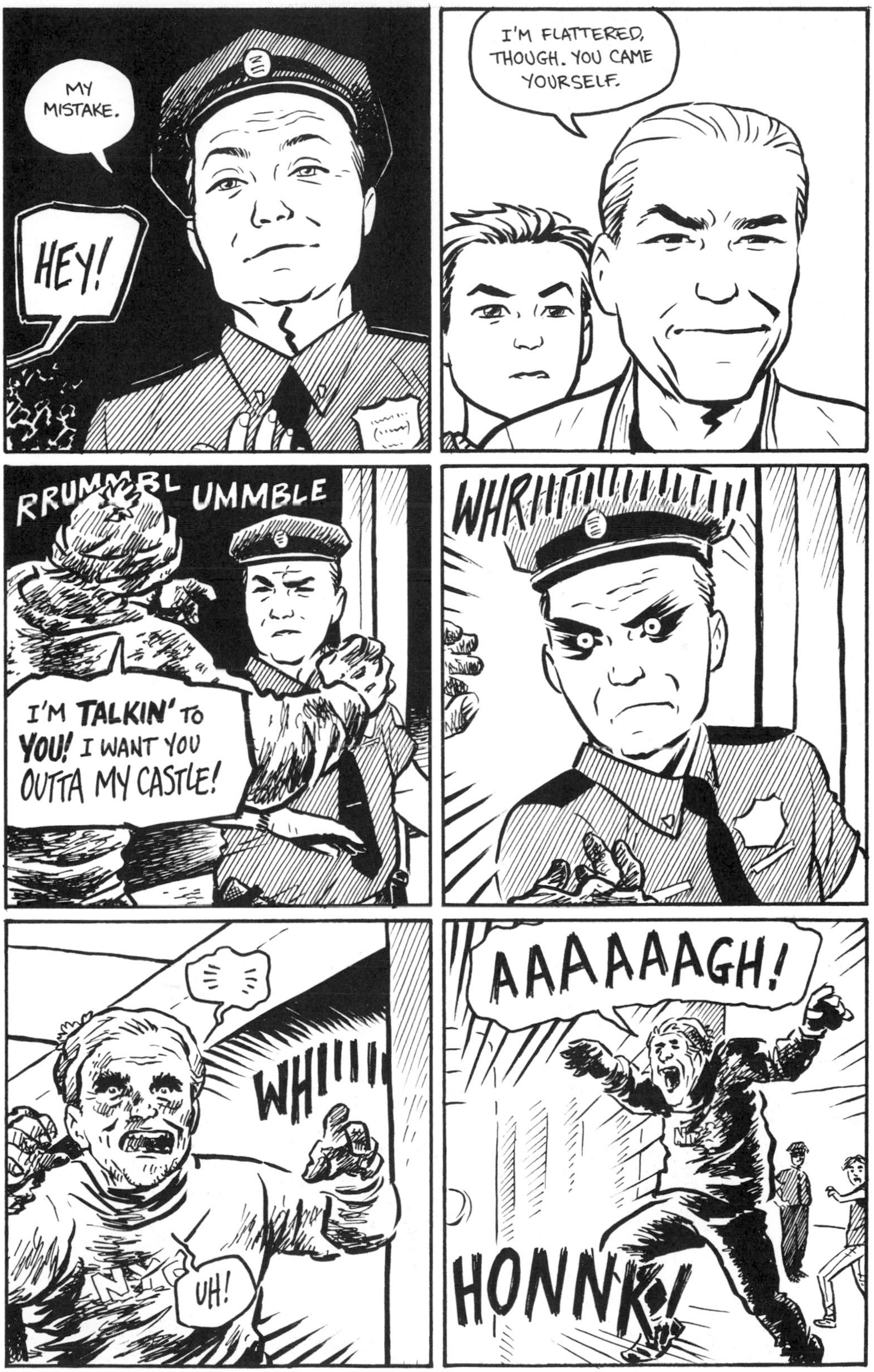
HEY!
MY MISTAKE.
I'M FLATTERED, THOUGH. YOU CAME YOURSELF.
RRUMMBL UMMBLE
I'M TALKIN' TO YOU! I WANT YOU OUTTA MY CASTLE!
WHRIIIIIIIIIII
WHIIIII
UH!
AAAAAAGH!
HONNK!

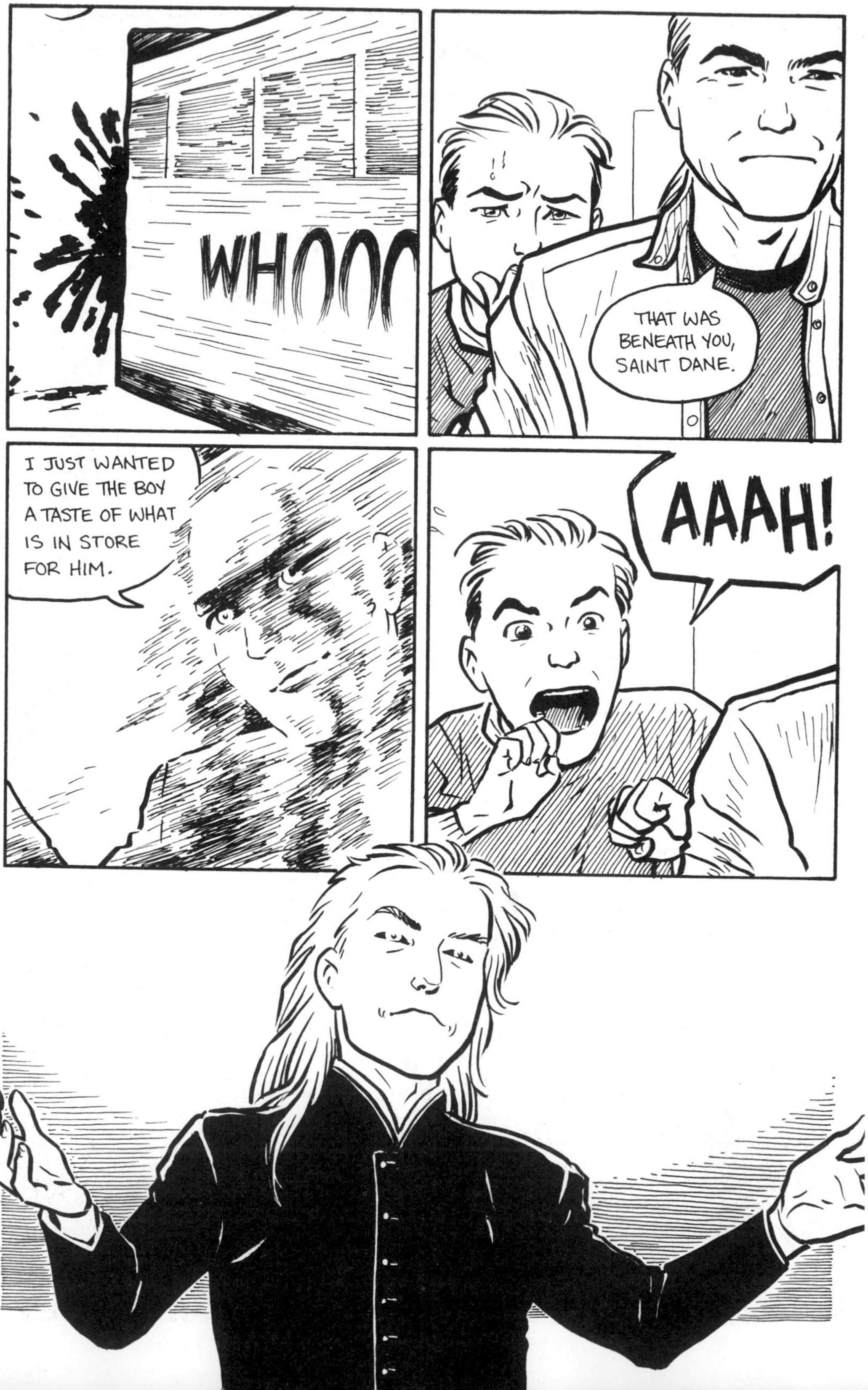
WHOO
THAT WAS BENEATH YOU, SAINT DANE.
I JUST WANTED TO GIVE THE BOY A TASTE OF WHAT IS IN STORE FOR HIM.
AAAH!

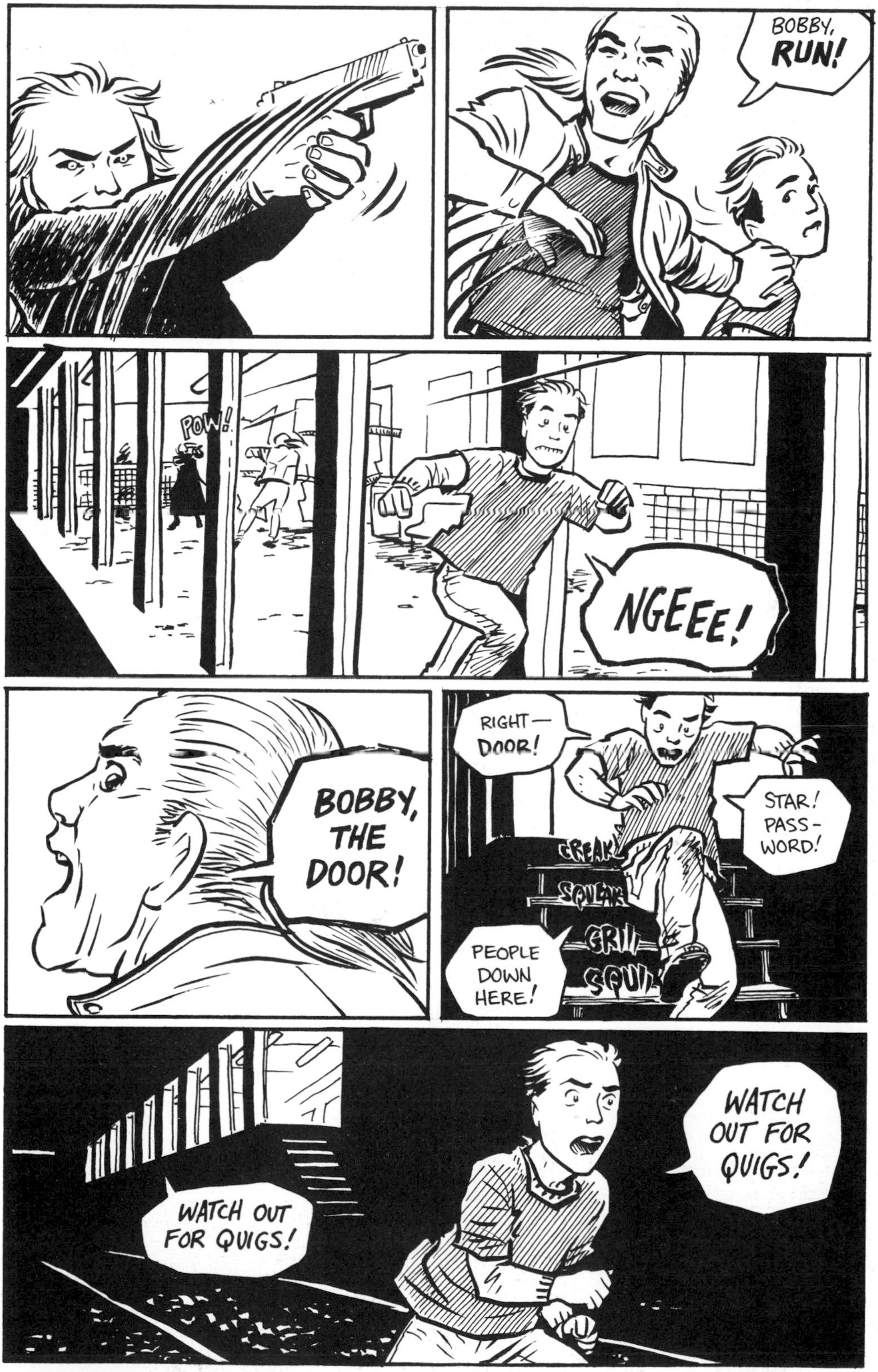
BOBBY, RUN!
POW!
NGEEE!
BOBBY, THE DOOR!
RIGHT— DOOR!
STAR! PASS- WORD!
CREAK
SQUEAK
PEOPLE DOWN HERE!
WATCH OUT FOR QUIGS!
WATCH OUT FOR QUIGS!

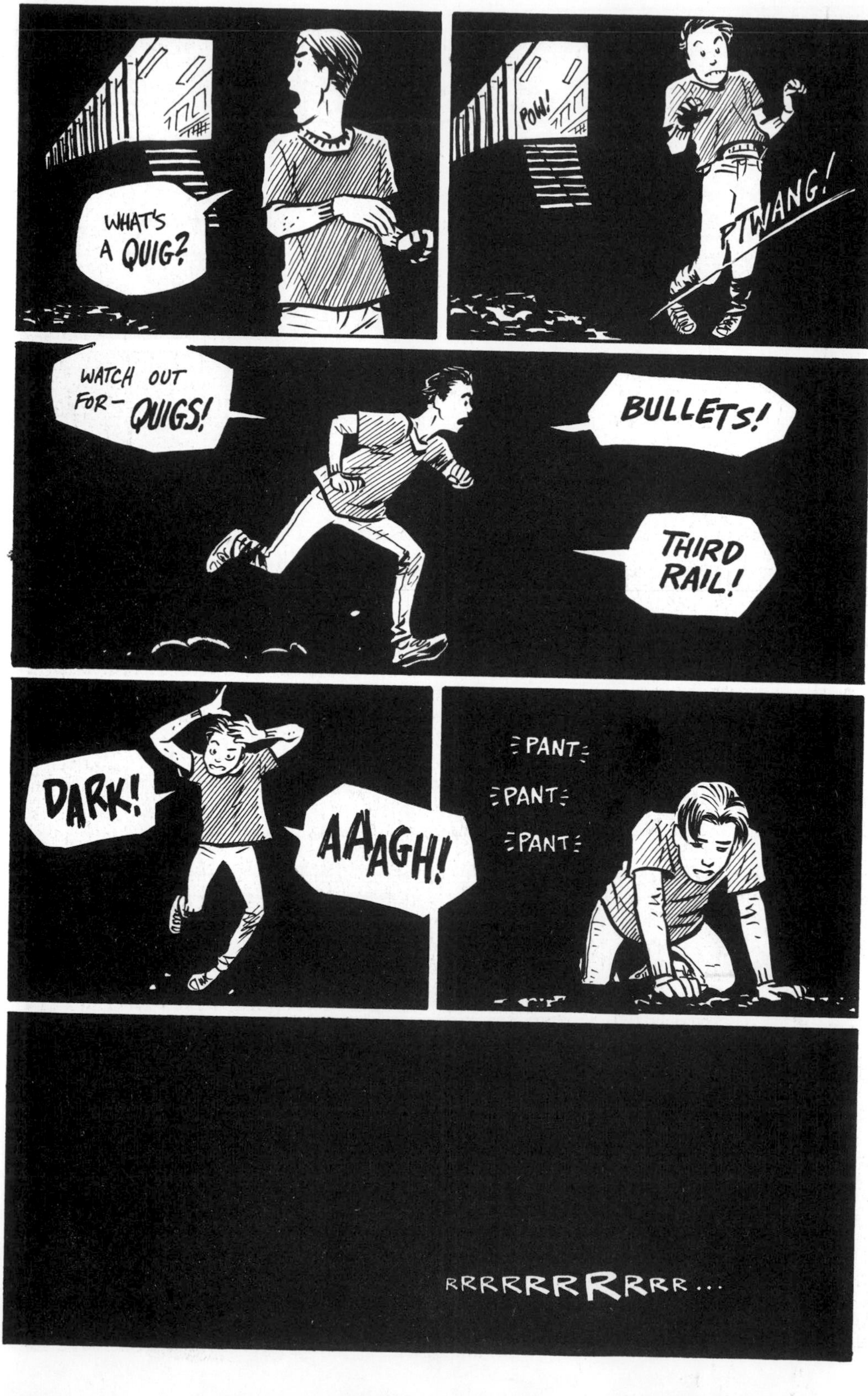
WHAT'S A QUIG?
POW!
PTWANG!
WATCH OUT FOR— QUIGS!
BULLETS!
THIRD RAIL!
DARK!
AAAGH!
PANT
PANT
PANT
RRRRRRRRRRR...

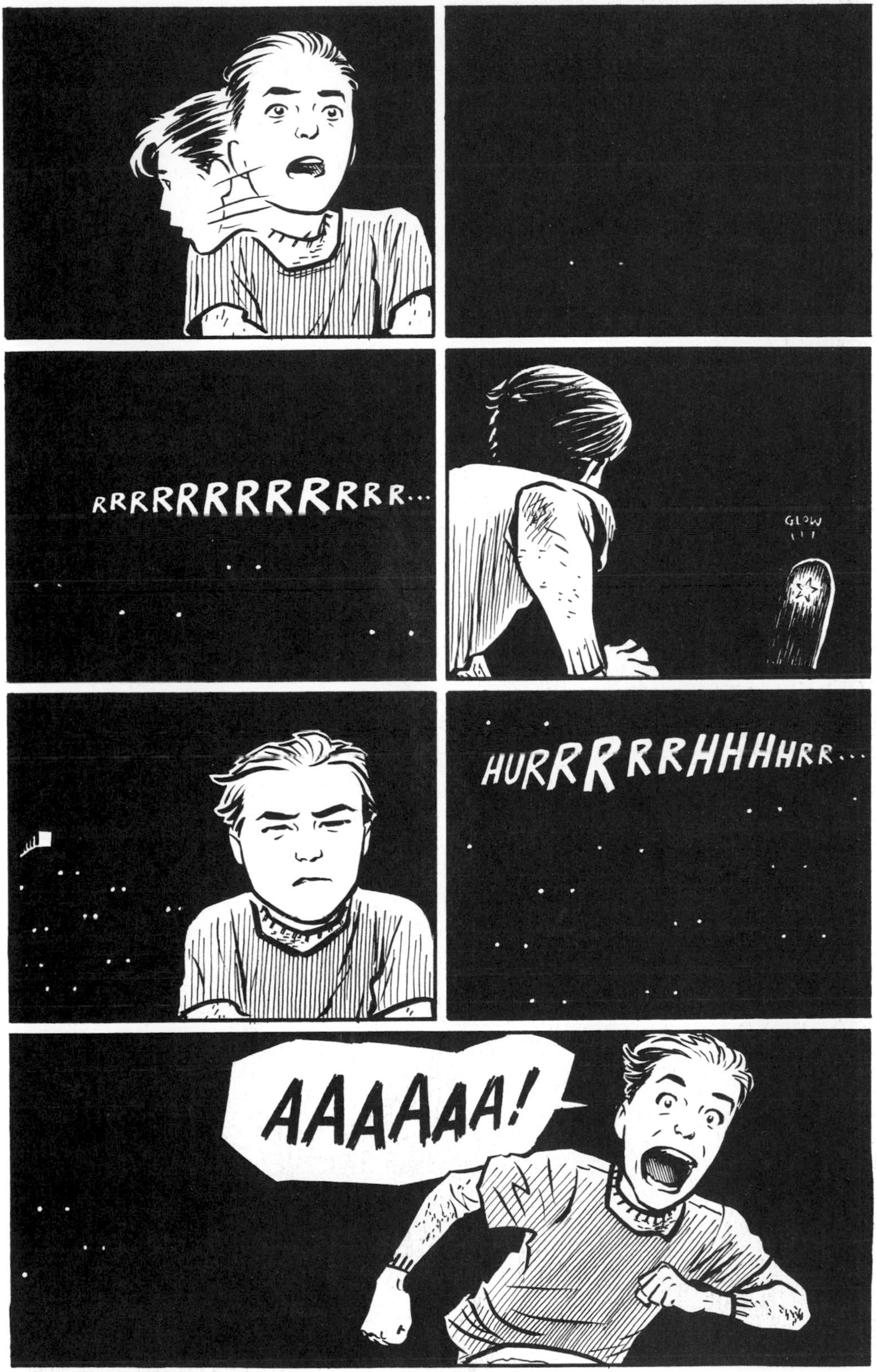
RRRRRRRRRRRRR...
GLOW
HURRRRRHHHHRR...
AAAAAA!

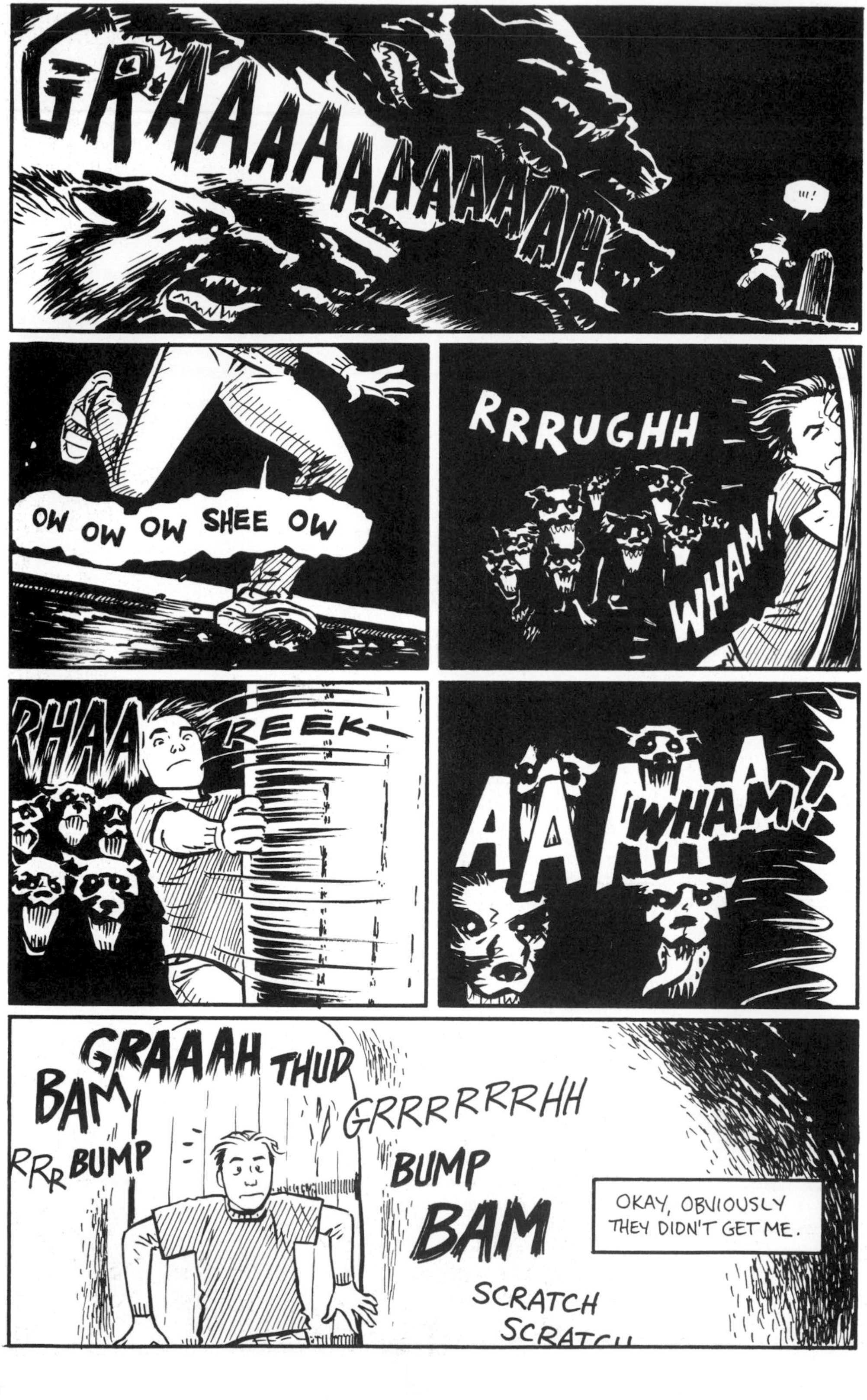
GRAAAAAAAAAAH
!!!!
OW OW OW SHEE OW
RRRUGHH
WHAM!
RHAA
REEK
AA
WHAM!
GRAAAH
THUD
BAM
GRRRRRRRHH
RRR BUMP
BUMP
BAM
OKAY, OBVIOUSLY THEY DIDN'T GET ME.
SCRATCH
SCRATCH

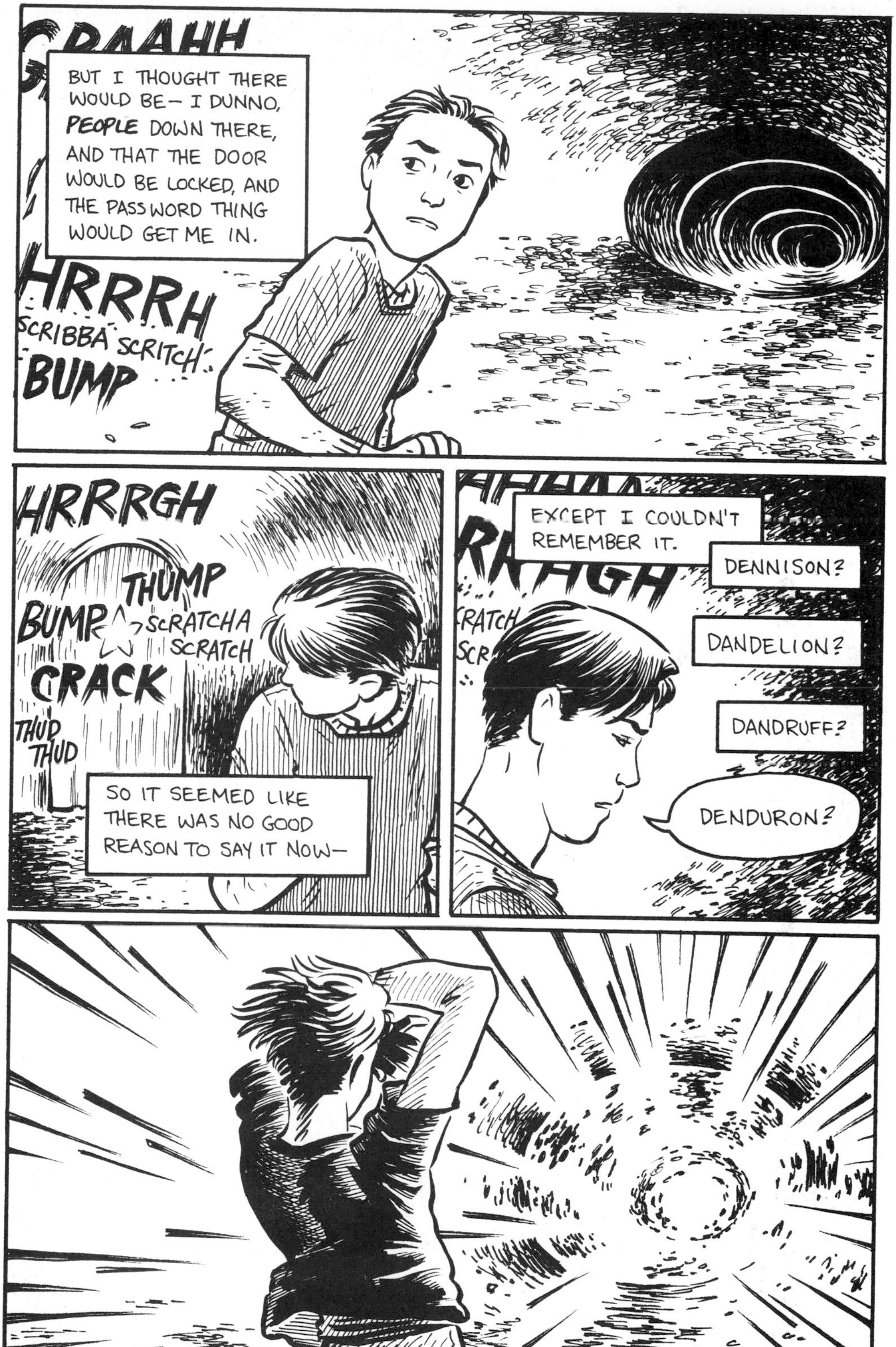
BUT I THOUGHT THERE WOULD BE— I DUNNO, **PEOPLE** DOWN THERE, AND THAT THE DOOR WOULD BE LOCKED, AND THE PASSWORD THING WOULD GET ME IN.
HRRRH
SCRIBBA SCRITCH
BUMP
HRRRGH
THUMP
BUMP
SCRATCHA SCRATCH
CRACK
THUD THUD
SO IT SEEMED LIKE THERE WAS NO GOOD REASON TO SAY IT NOW—
EXCEPT I COULDN'T REMEMBER IT.
DENNISON?
DANDELION?
DANDRUFF?
DENDURON?

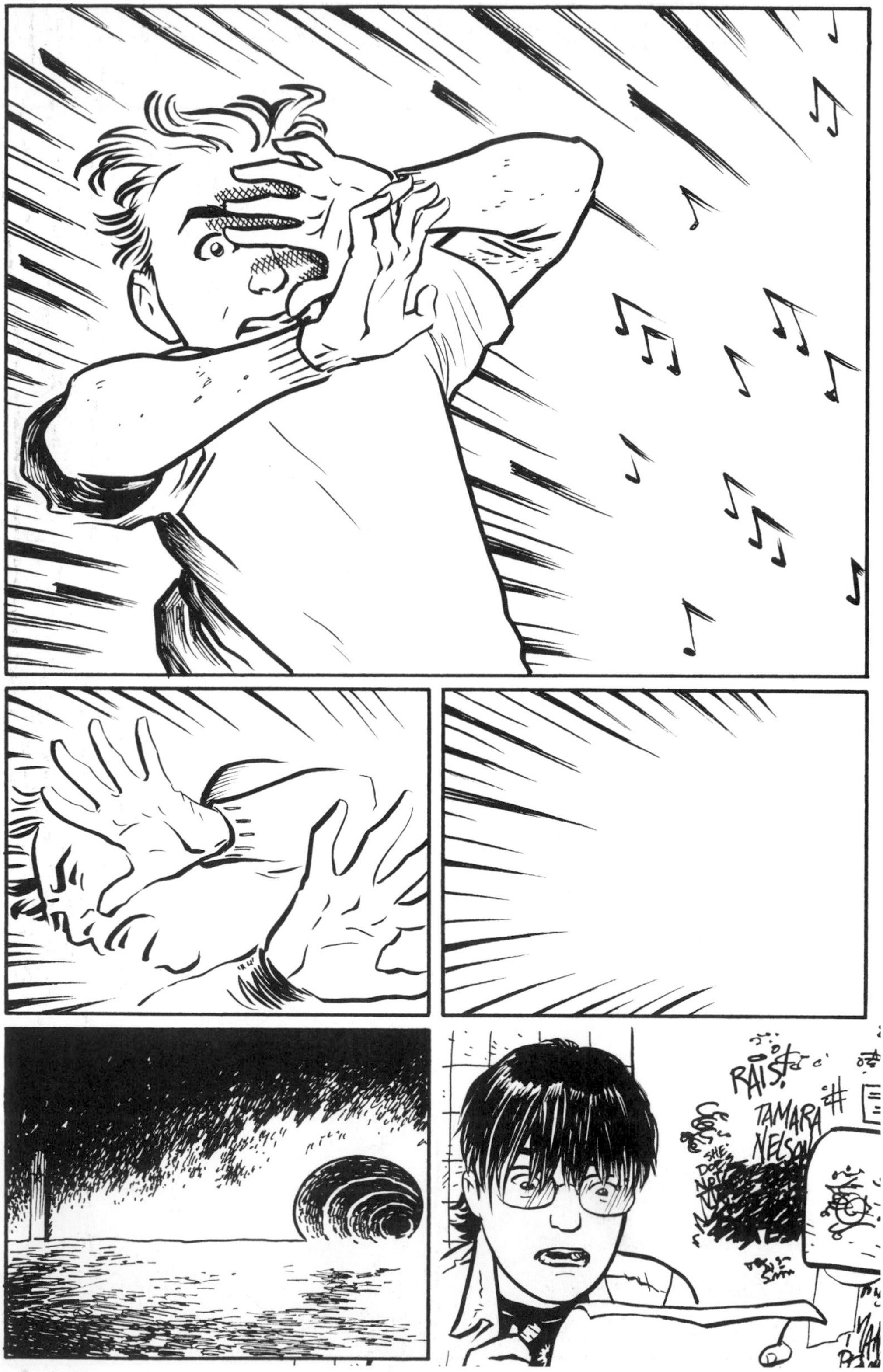
RAIS!
TAMARA
NELSON

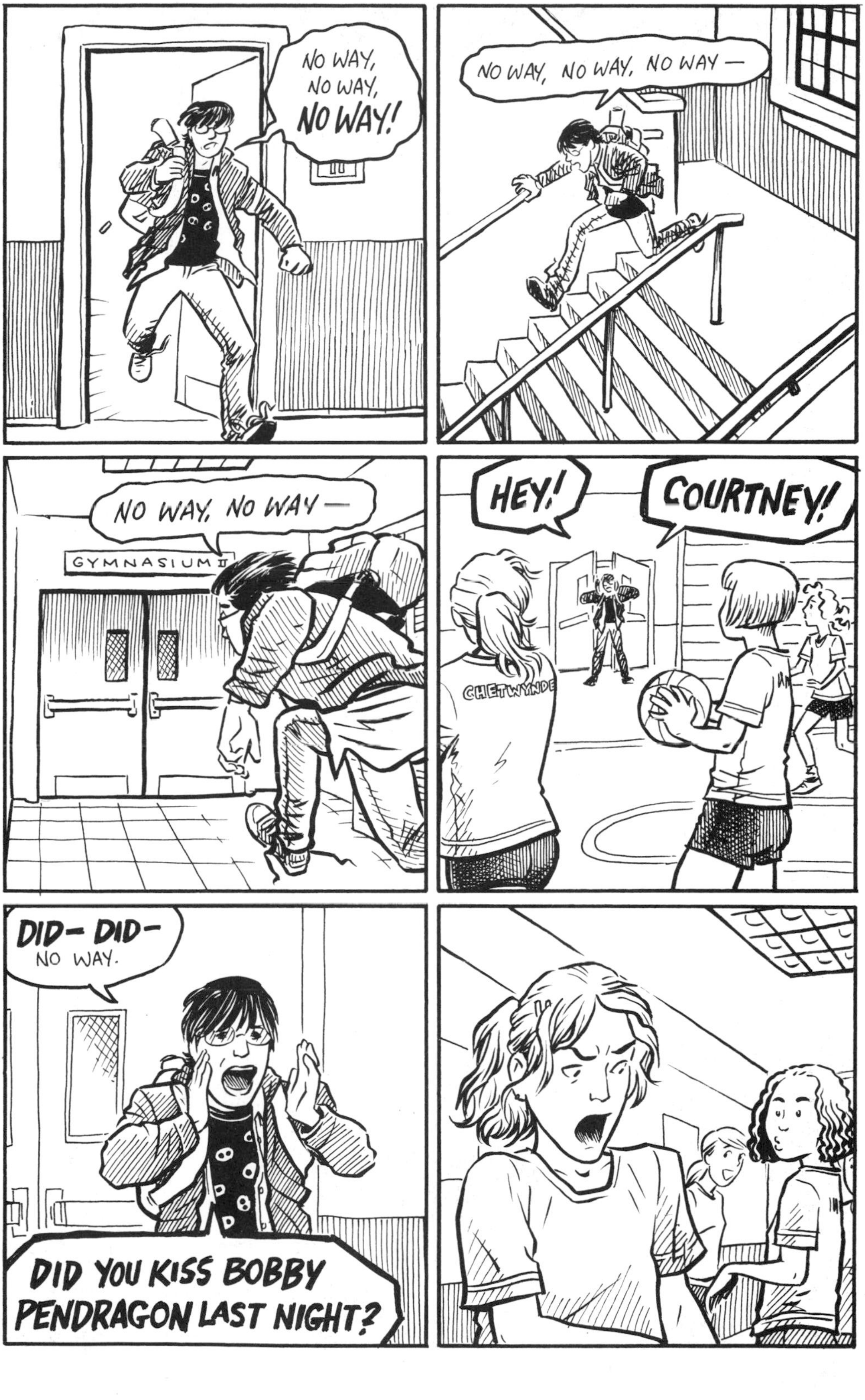
NO WAY, NO WAY, NO WAY!
NO WAY, NO WAY, NO WAY —
NO WAY, NO WAY —
GYMNASIUM II
HEY!
COURTNEY!
CHETWYNDE
DID— DID— NO WAY.
DID YOU KISS BOBBY PENDRAGON LAST NIGHT?

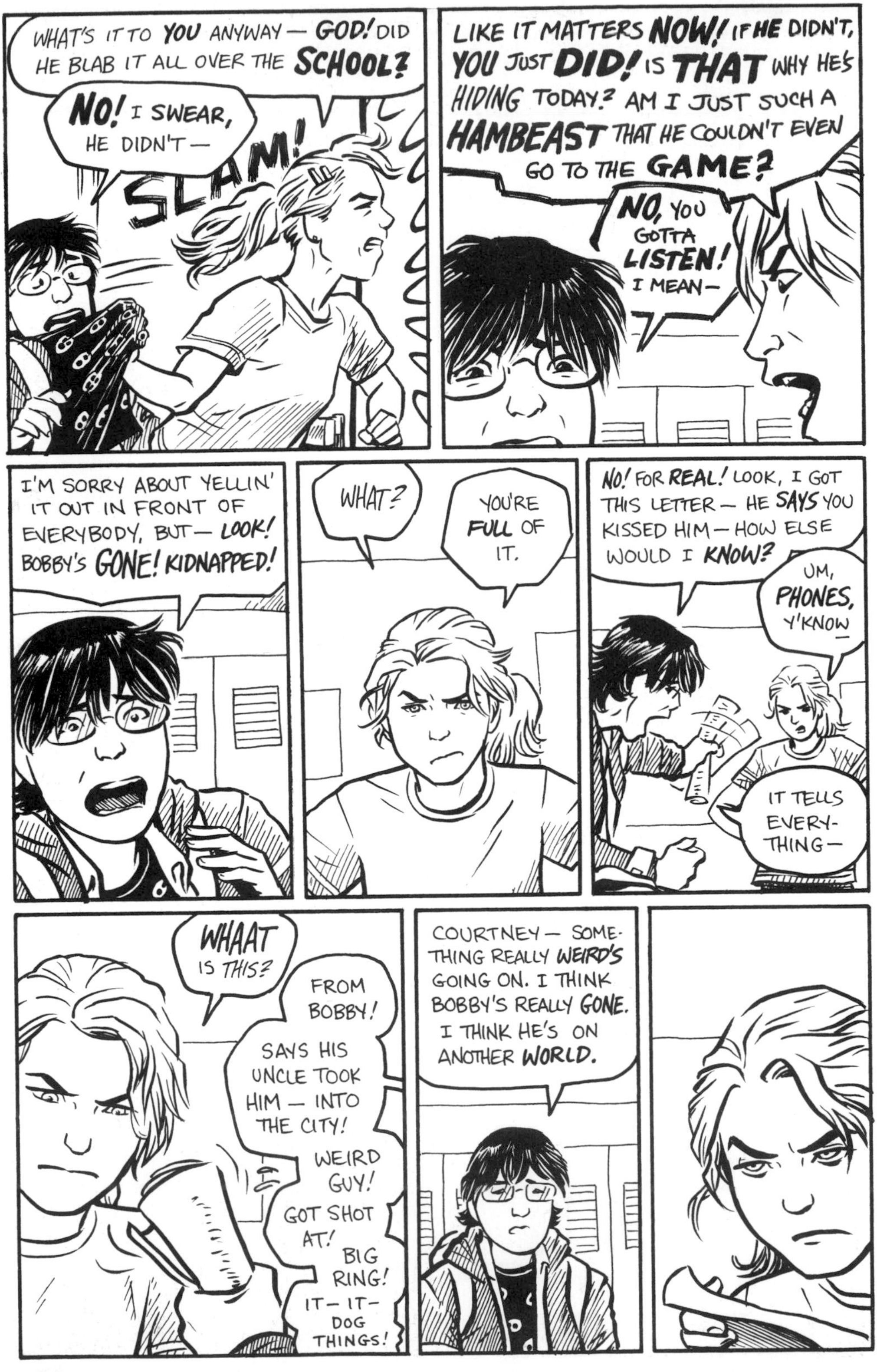
WHAT'S IT TO YOU ANYWAY — GOD! DID HE BLAB IT ALL OVER THE SCHOOL?
NO! I SWEAR, HE DIDN'T —
SLAM!
LIKE IT MATTERS NOW! IF HE DIDN'T, YOU JUST DID! IS THAT WHY HE'S HIDING TODAY? AM I JUST SUCH A HAMBEAST THAT HE COULDN'T EVEN GO TO THE GAME?
NO, YOU GOTTA LISTEN! I MEAN—
I'M SORRY ABOUT YELLIN' IT OUT IN FRONT OF EVERYBODY, BUT— LOOK! BOBBY'S GONE! KIDNAPPED!
WHAT?
YOU'RE FULL OF IT.
NO! FOR REAL! LOOK, I GOT THIS LETTER — HE SAYS YOU KISSED HIM — HOW ELSE WOULD I KNOW?
UM, PHONES, Y'KNOW
IT TELLS EVERY-THING—
WHAAT IS THIS?
FROM BOBBY!
SAYS HIS UNCLE TOOK HIM — INTO THE CITY!
WEIRD GUY!
GOT SHOT AT!
BIG RING!
IT— IT— DOG THINGS!
COURTNEY— SOME-THING REALLY WEIRD'S GOING ON. I THINK BOBBY'S REALLY GONE. I THINK HE'S ON ANOTHER WORLD.

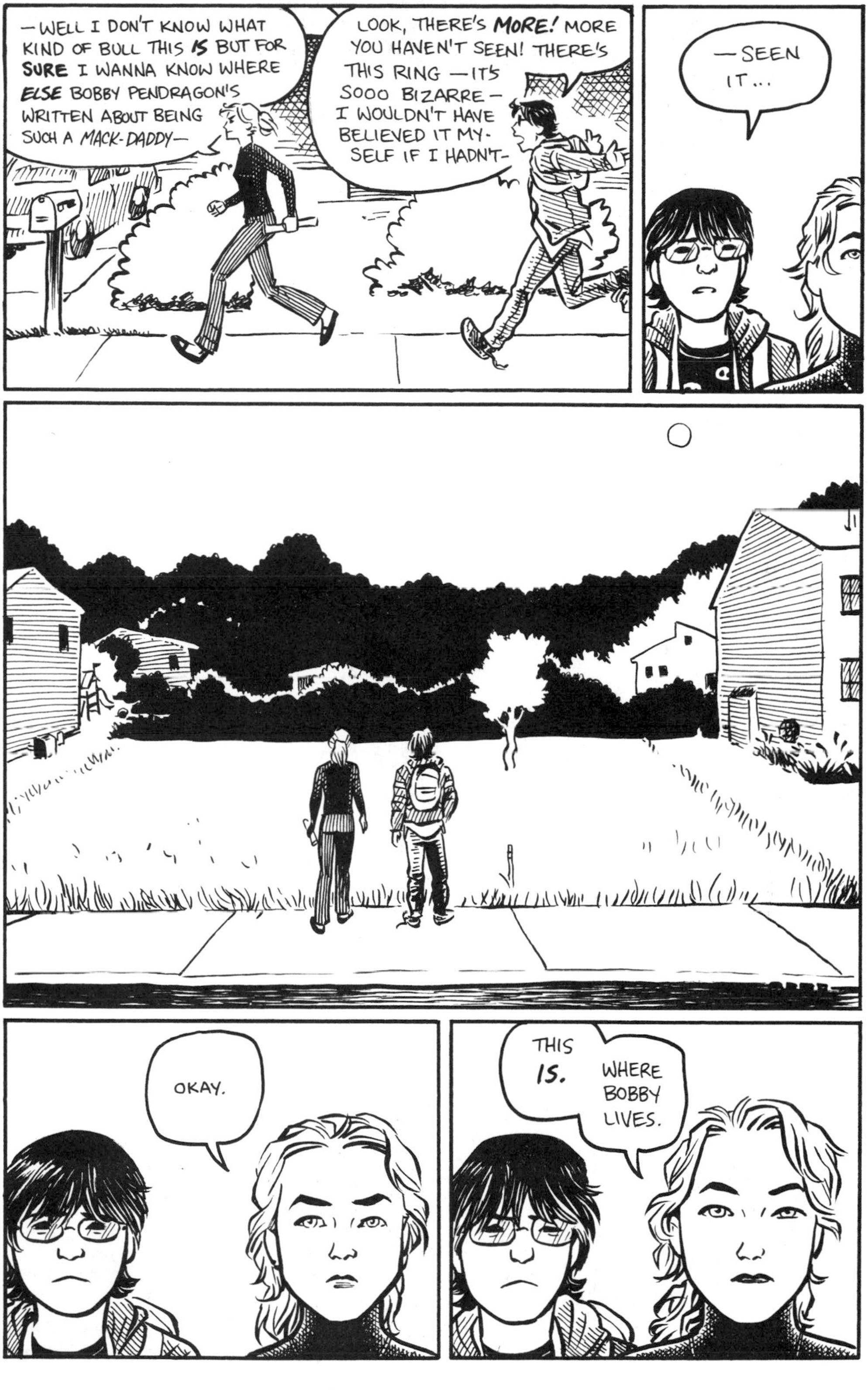

—WELL I DON'T KNOW WHAT KIND OF BULL THIS IS BUT FOR SURE I WANNA KNOW WHERE ELSE BOBBY PENDRAGON'S WRITTEN ABOUT BEING SUCH A MACK-DADDY—
LOOK, THERE'S MORE! MORE YOU HAVEN'T SEEN! THERE'S THIS RING —IT'S SOOO BIZARRE— I WOULDN'T HAVE BELIEVED IT MY-SELF IF I HADN'T-
—SEEN IT...
OKAY.
THIS IS.
WHERE BOBBY LIVES.

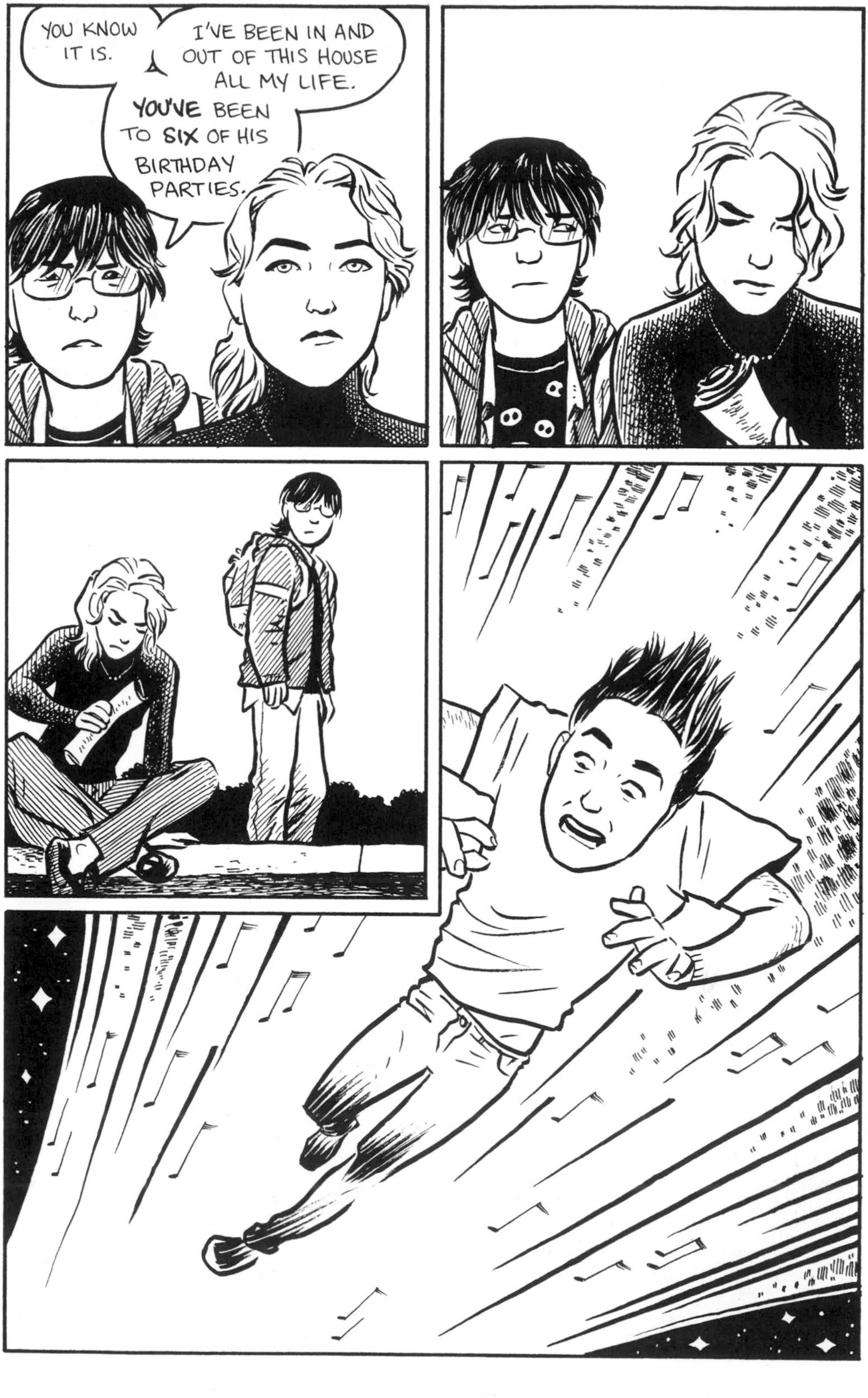
YOU KNOW IT IS.
I'VE BEEN IN AND OUT OF THIS HOUSE ALL MY LIFE.
YOU'VE BEEN TO SIX OF HIS BIRTHDAY PARTIES.

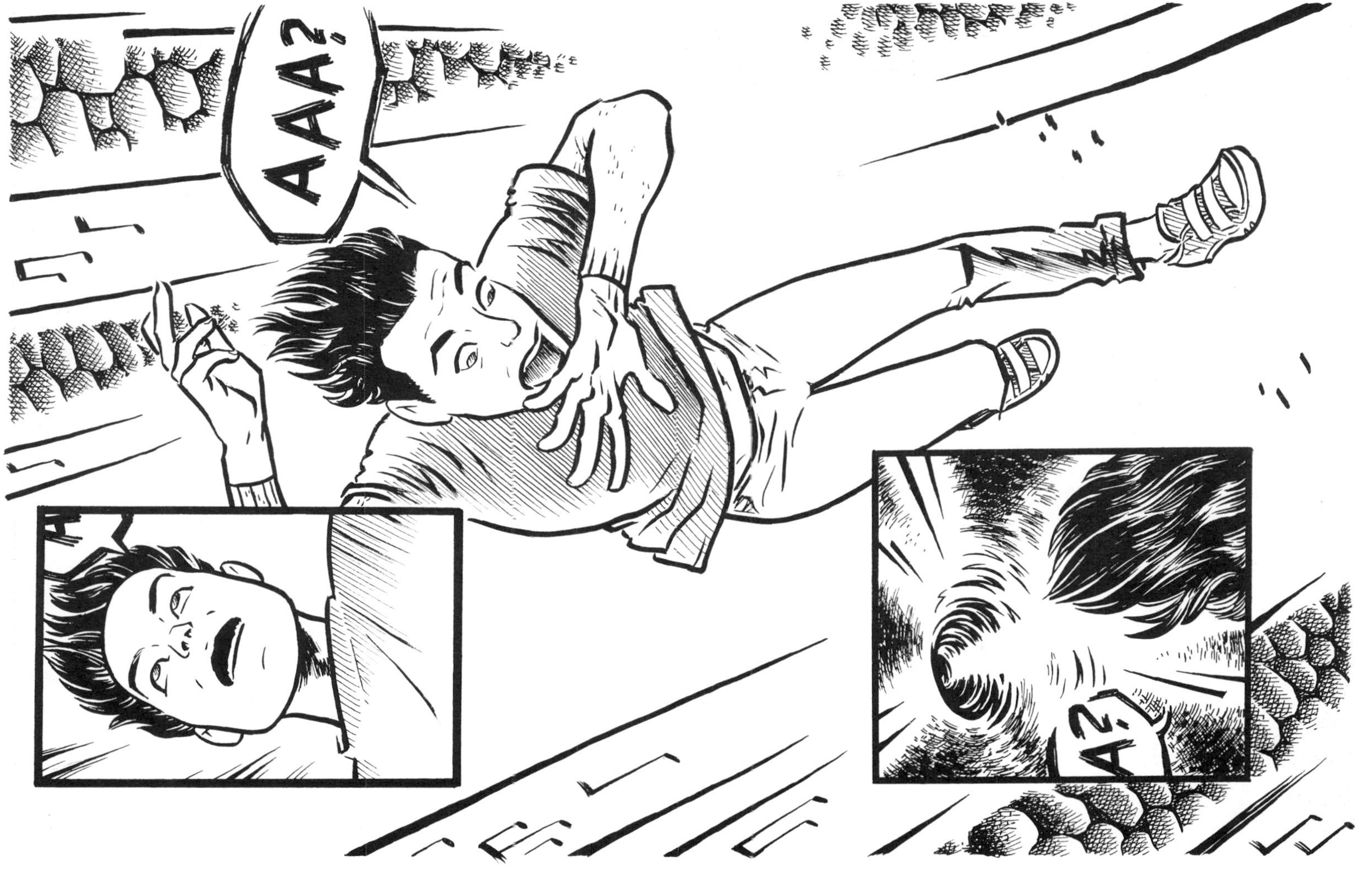
AAA?
A?

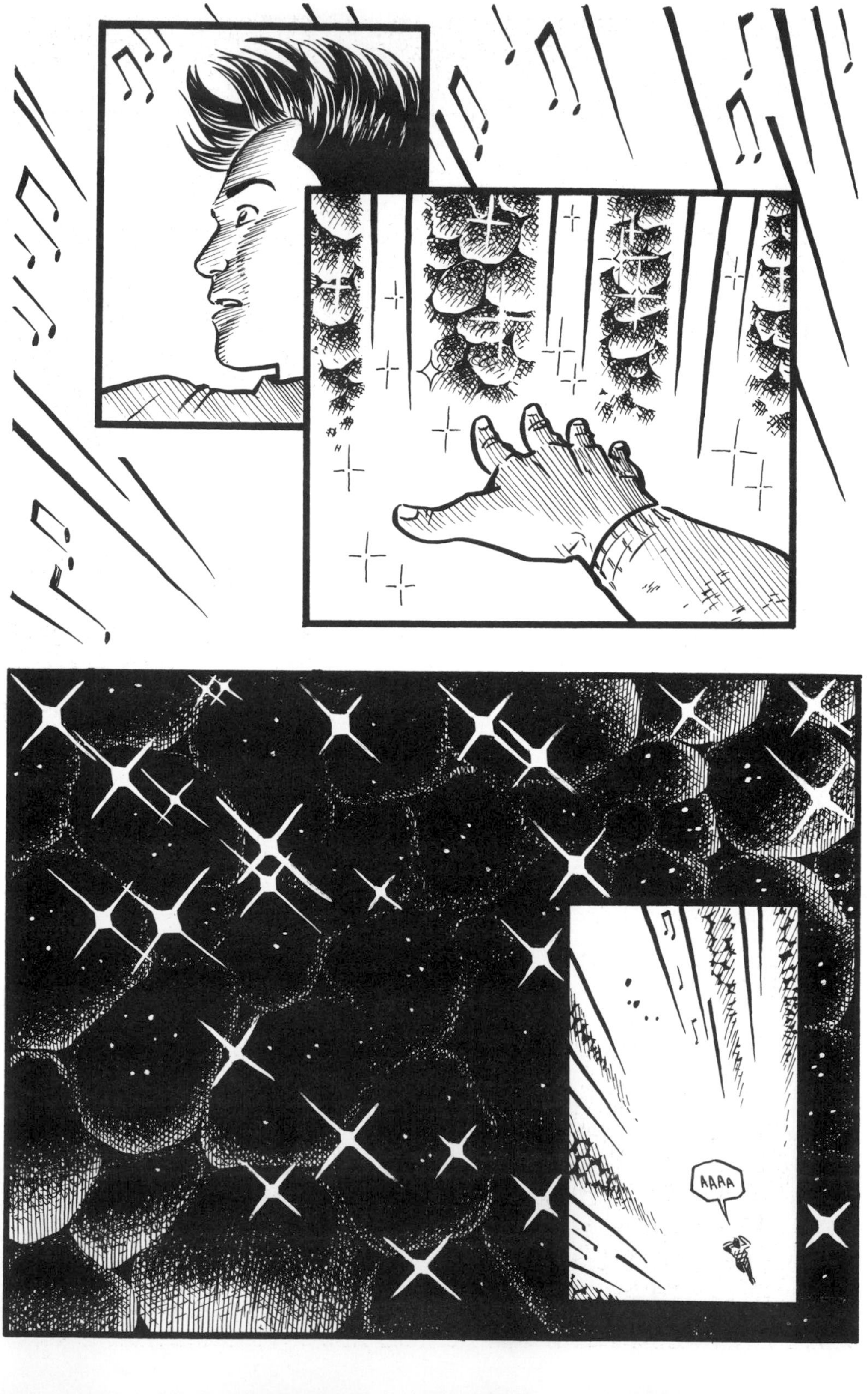
AAAA

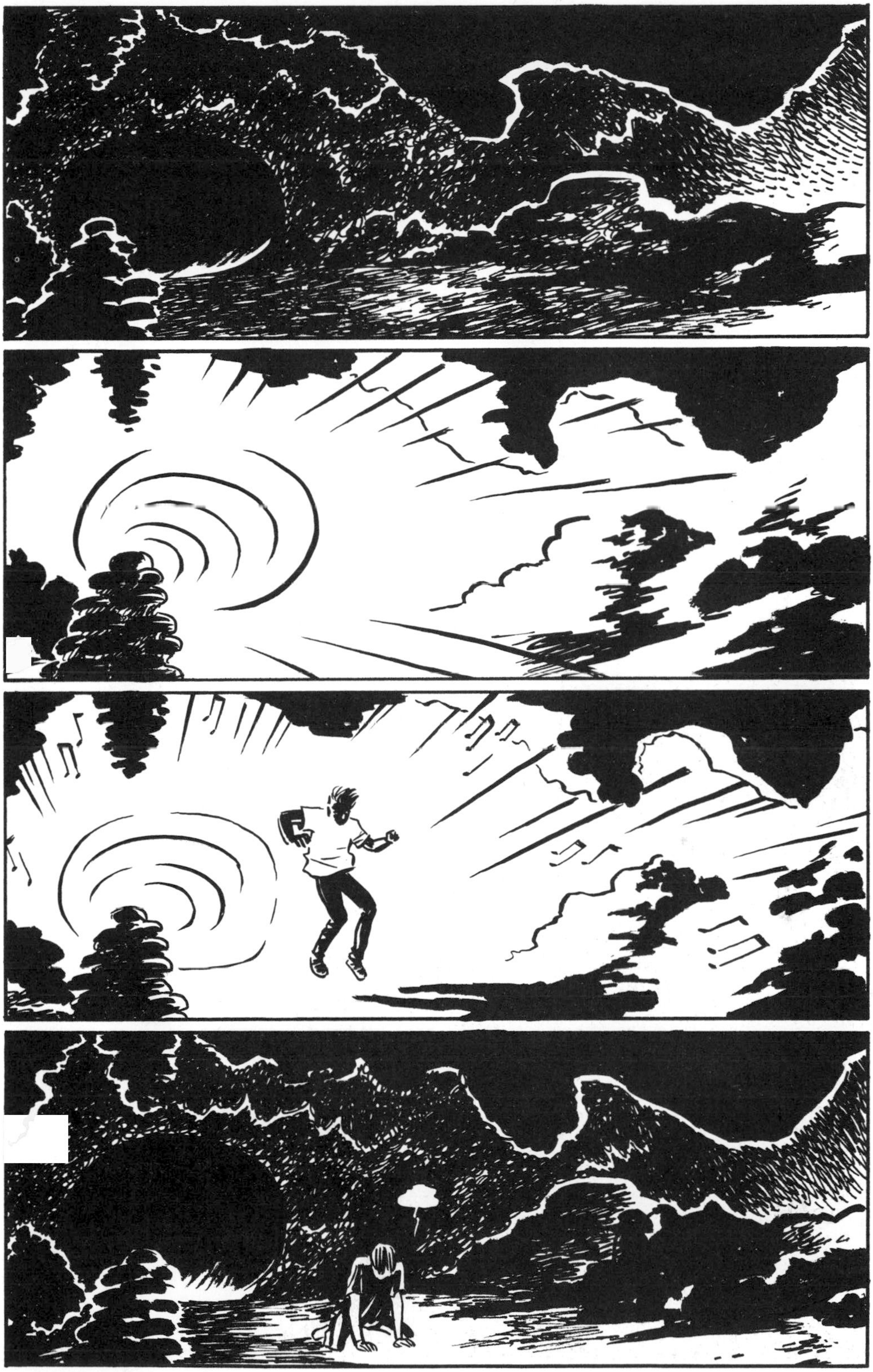

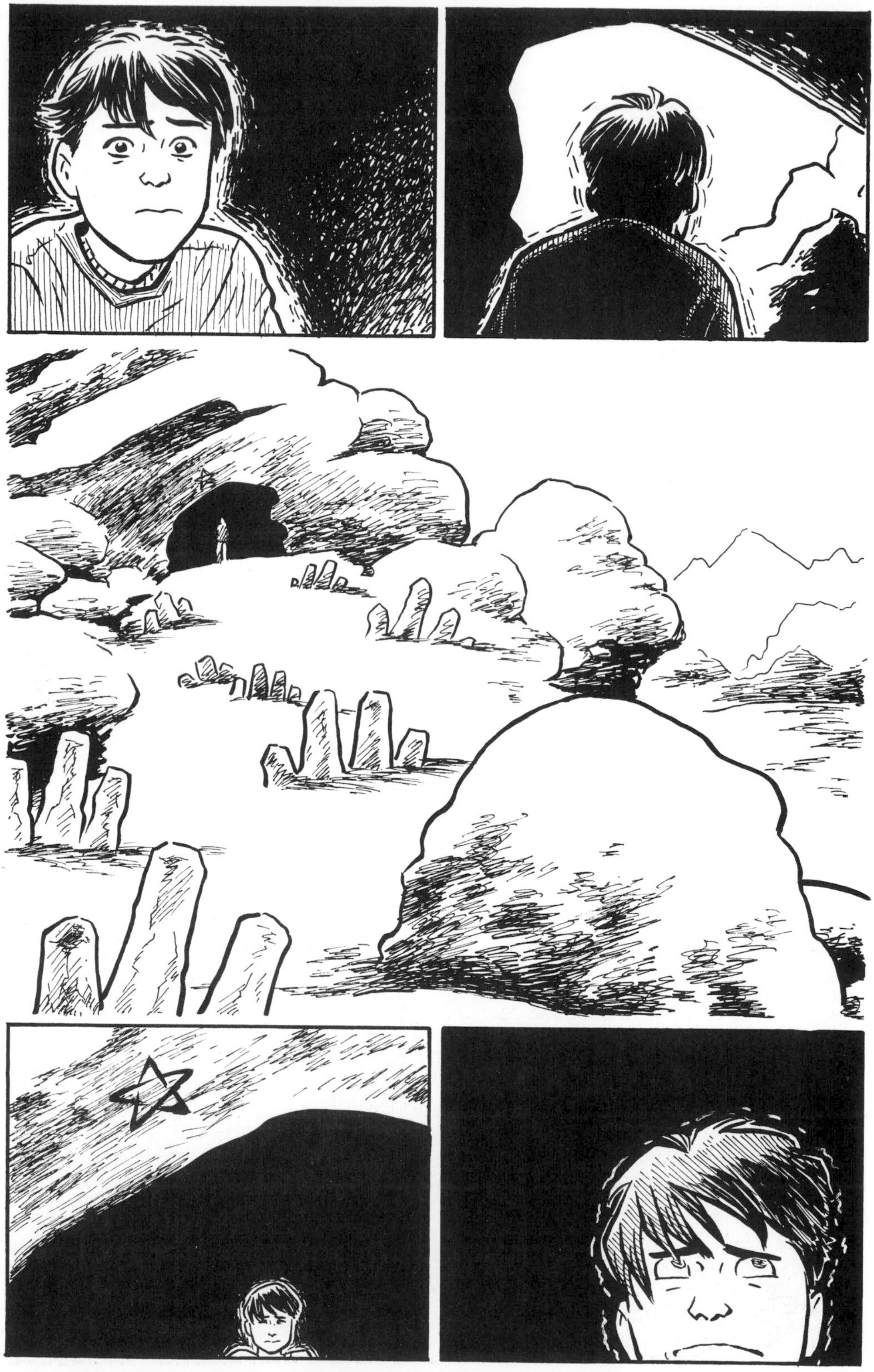

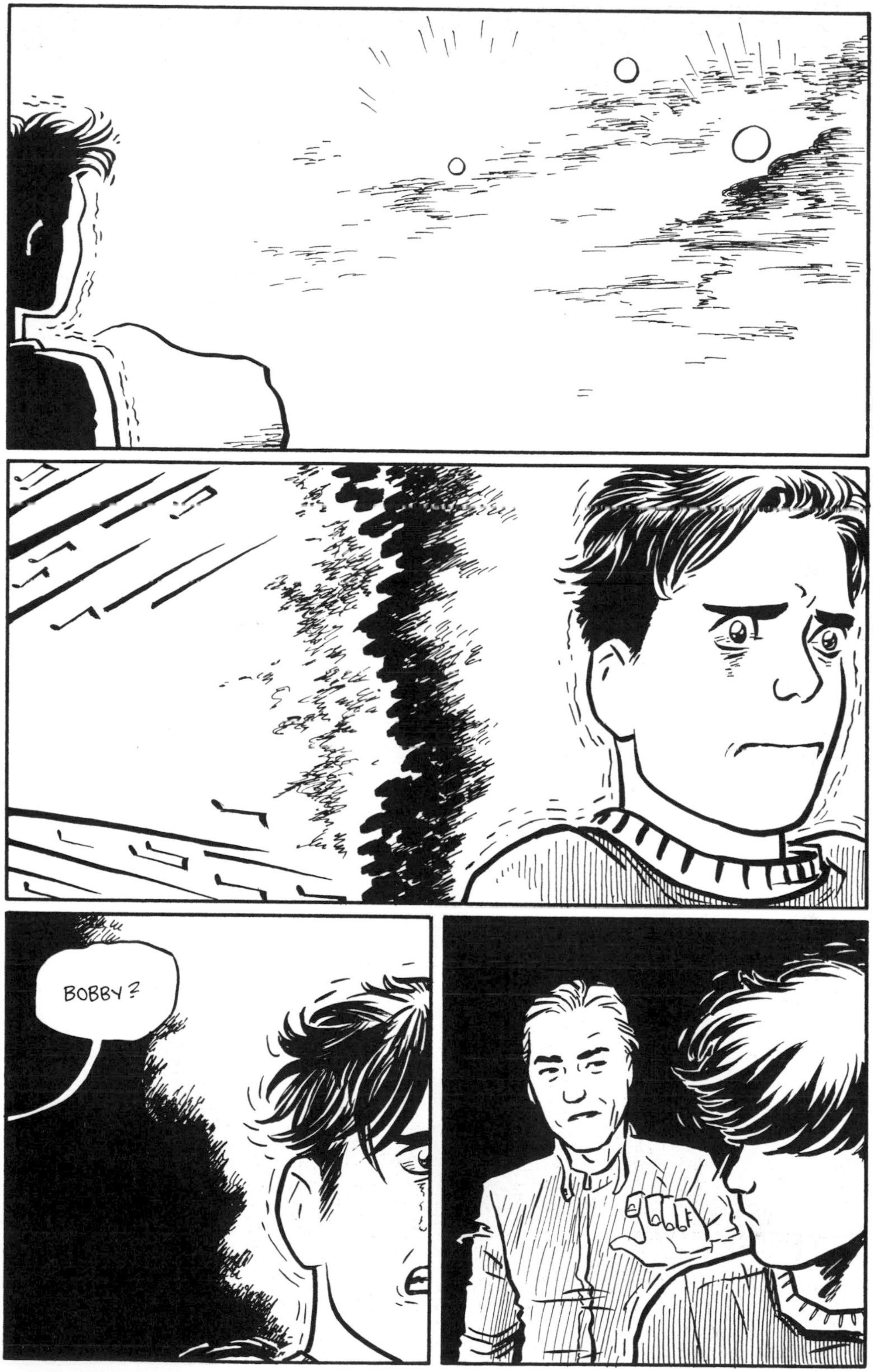
BOBBY?

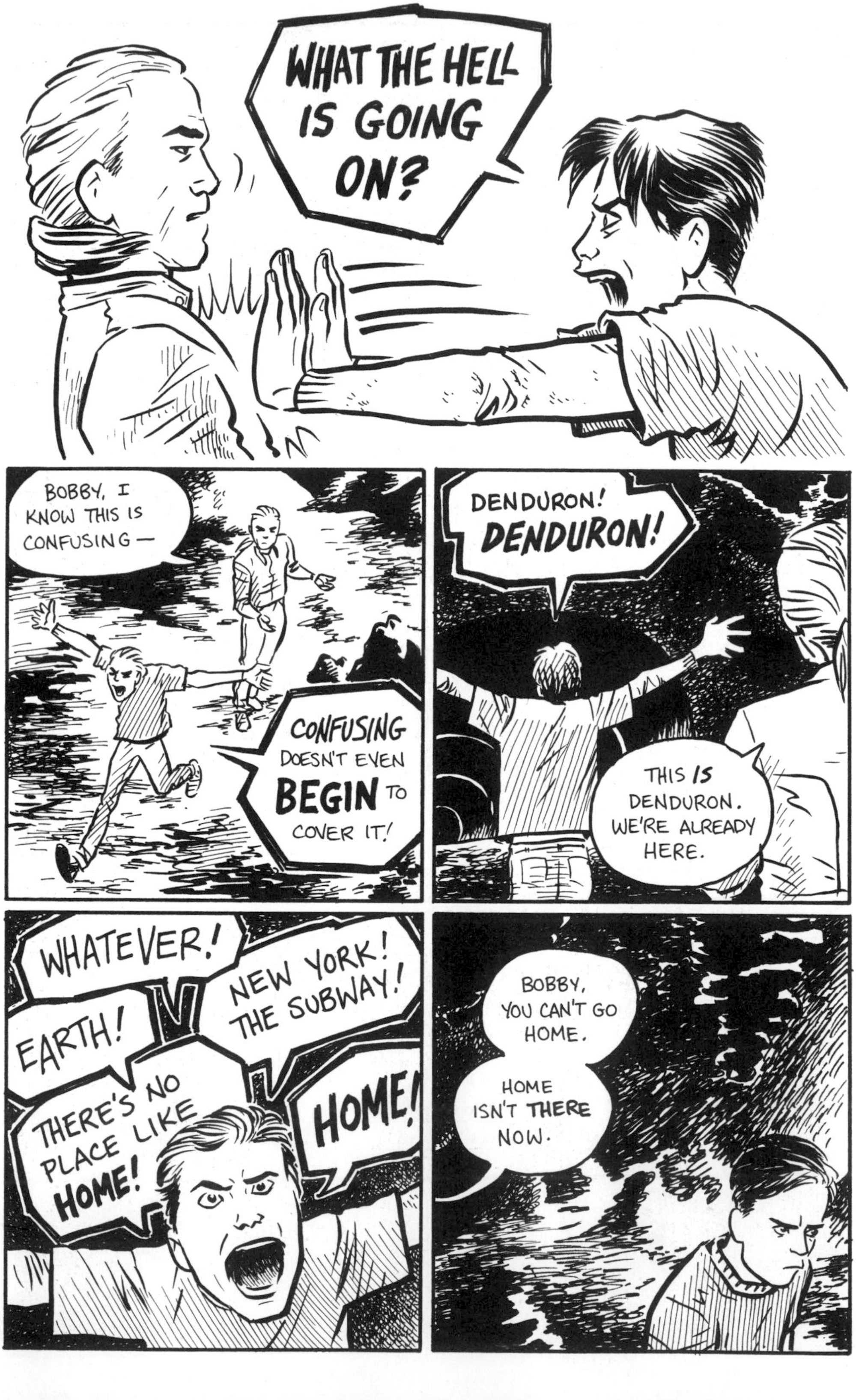
WHAT THE HELL IS GOING ON?
BOBBY, I KNOW THIS IS CONFUSING—
CONFUSING DOESN'T EVEN BEGIN TO COVER IT!
DENDURON! DENDURON!
THIS IS DENDURON. WE'RE ALREADY HERE.
WHATEVER!
EARTH!
NEW YORK! THE SUBWAY!
THERE'S NO PLACE LIKE HOME!
HOME!
BOBBY, YOU CAN'T GO HOME.
HOME ISN'T THERE NOW.

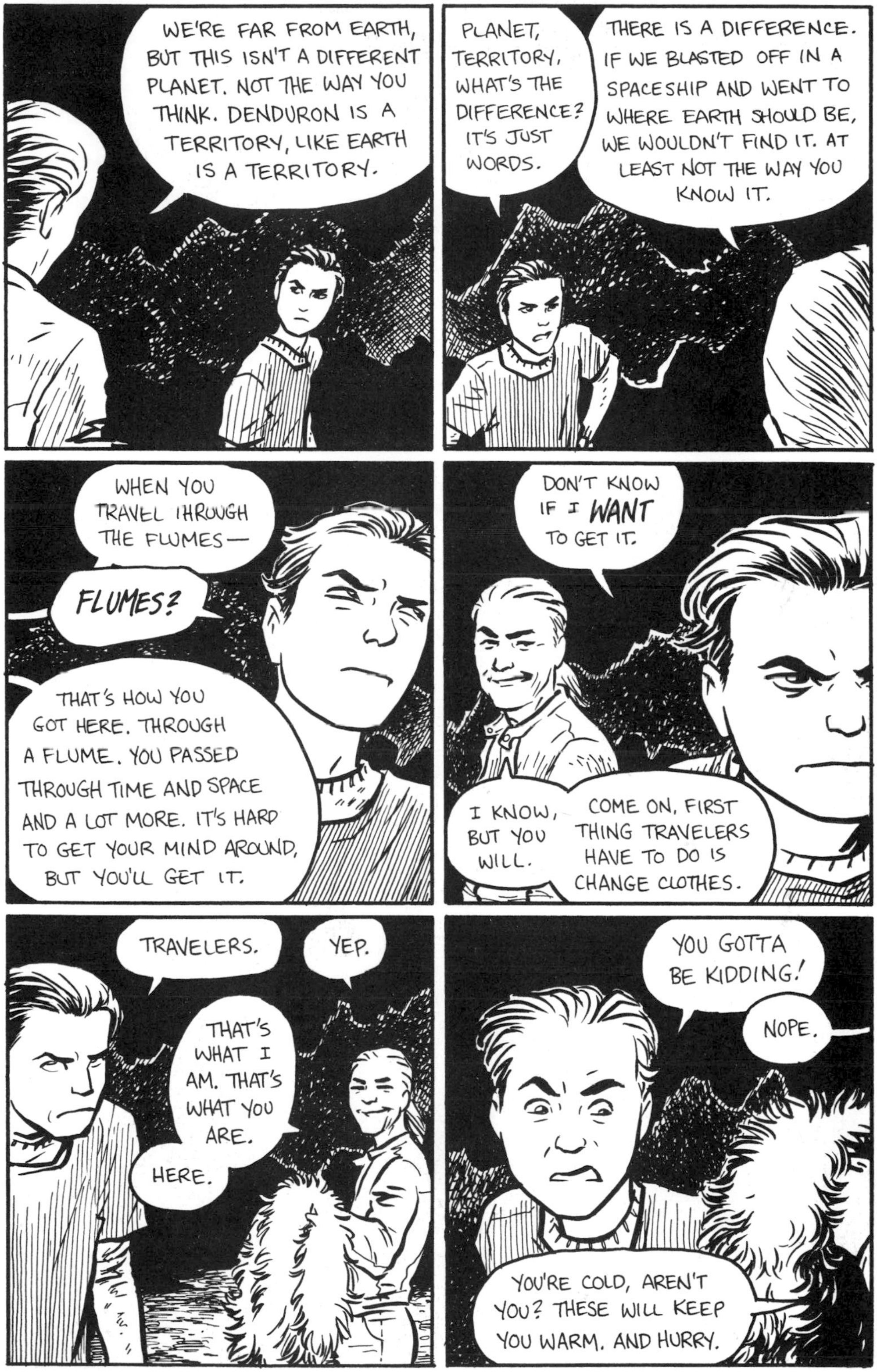
WE'RE FAR FROM EARTH, BUT THIS ISN'T A DIFFERENT PLANET. NOT THE WAY YOU THINK. DENDURON IS A TERRITORY, LIKE EARTH IS A TERRITORY.
PLANET, TERRITORY, WHAT'S THE DIFFERENCE? IT'S JUST WORDS.
THERE IS A DIFFERENCE. IF WE BLASTED OFF IN A SPACESHIP AND WENT TO WHERE EARTH SHOULD BE, WE WOULDN'T FIND IT. AT LEAST NOT THE WAY YOU KNOW IT.
WHEN YOU TRAVEL THROUGH THE FLUMES—
FLUMES?
THAT'S HOW YOU GOT HERE. THROUGH A FLUME. YOU PASSED THROUGH TIME AND SPACE AND A LOT MORE. IT'S HARD TO GET YOUR MIND AROUND, BUT YOU'LL GET IT.
DON'T KNOW IF I WANT TO GET IT.
I KNOW, BUT YOU WILL.
COME ON. FIRST THING TRAVELERS HAVE TO DO IS CHANGE CLOTHES.
TRAVELERS.
YEP.
THAT'S WHAT I AM. THAT'S WHAT YOU ARE.
HERE.
YOU GOTTA BE KIDDING!
NOPE.
YOU'RE COLD, AREN'T YOU? THESE WILL KEEP YOU WARM. AND HURRY.

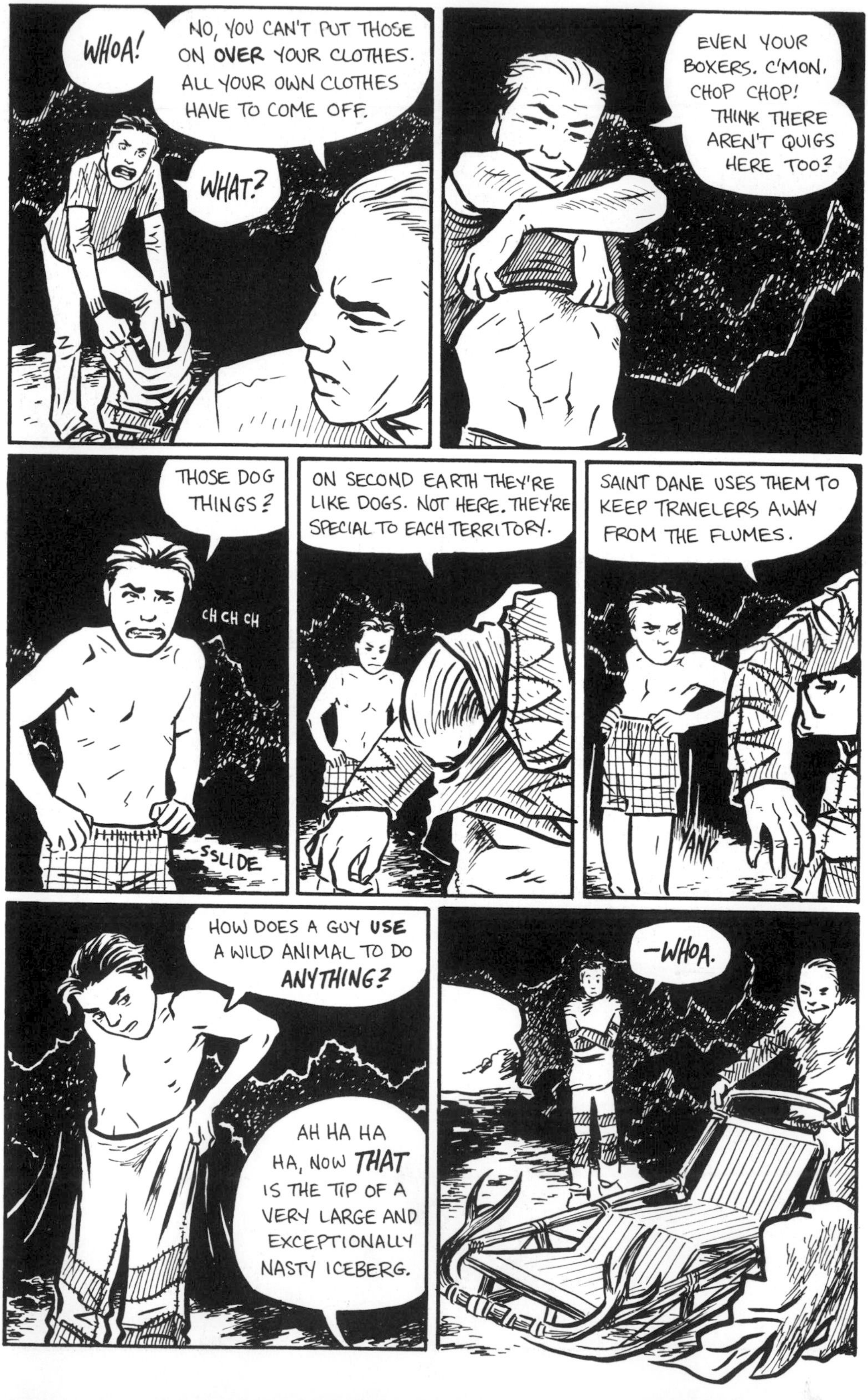
WHOA!
NO, YOU CAN'T PUT THOSE ON **OVER** YOUR CLOTHES. ALL YOUR OWN CLOTHES HAVE TO COME OFF.
WHAT?
EVEN YOUR BOXERS. C'MON, CHOP CHOP! THINK THERE AREN'T QUIGS HERE TOO?
THOSE DOG THINGS?
CH CH CH
SSLIDE
ON SECOND EARTH THEY'RE LIKE DOGS. NOT HERE. THEY'RE SPECIAL TO EACH TERRITORY.
SAINT DANE USES THEM TO KEEP TRAVELERS AWAY FROM THE FLUMES.
YANK
HOW DOES A GUY **USE** A WILD ANIMAL TO DO **ANYTHING?**
AH HA HA HA, NOW **THAT** IS THE TIP OF A VERY LARGE AND EXCEPTIONALLY NASTY ICEBERG.
—WHOA.

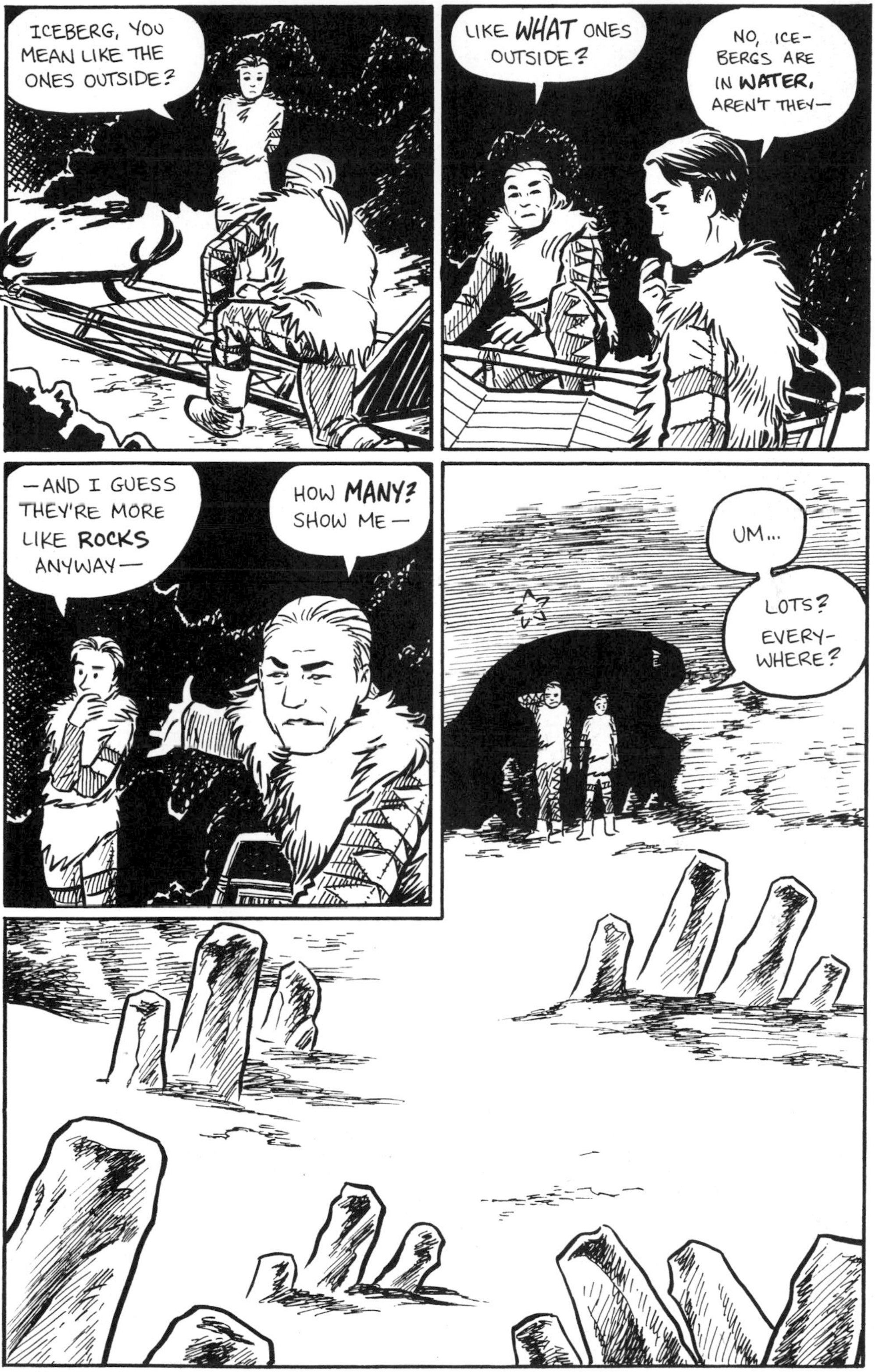
ICEBERG, YOU MEAN LIKE THE ONES OUTSIDE?
LIKE WHAT ONES OUTSIDE?
NO, ICE-BERGS ARE IN WATER, AREN'T THEY—
—AND I GUESS THEY'RE MORE LIKE ROCKS ANYWAY—
HOW MANY? SHOW ME—
UM...
LOTS? EVERY-WHERE?

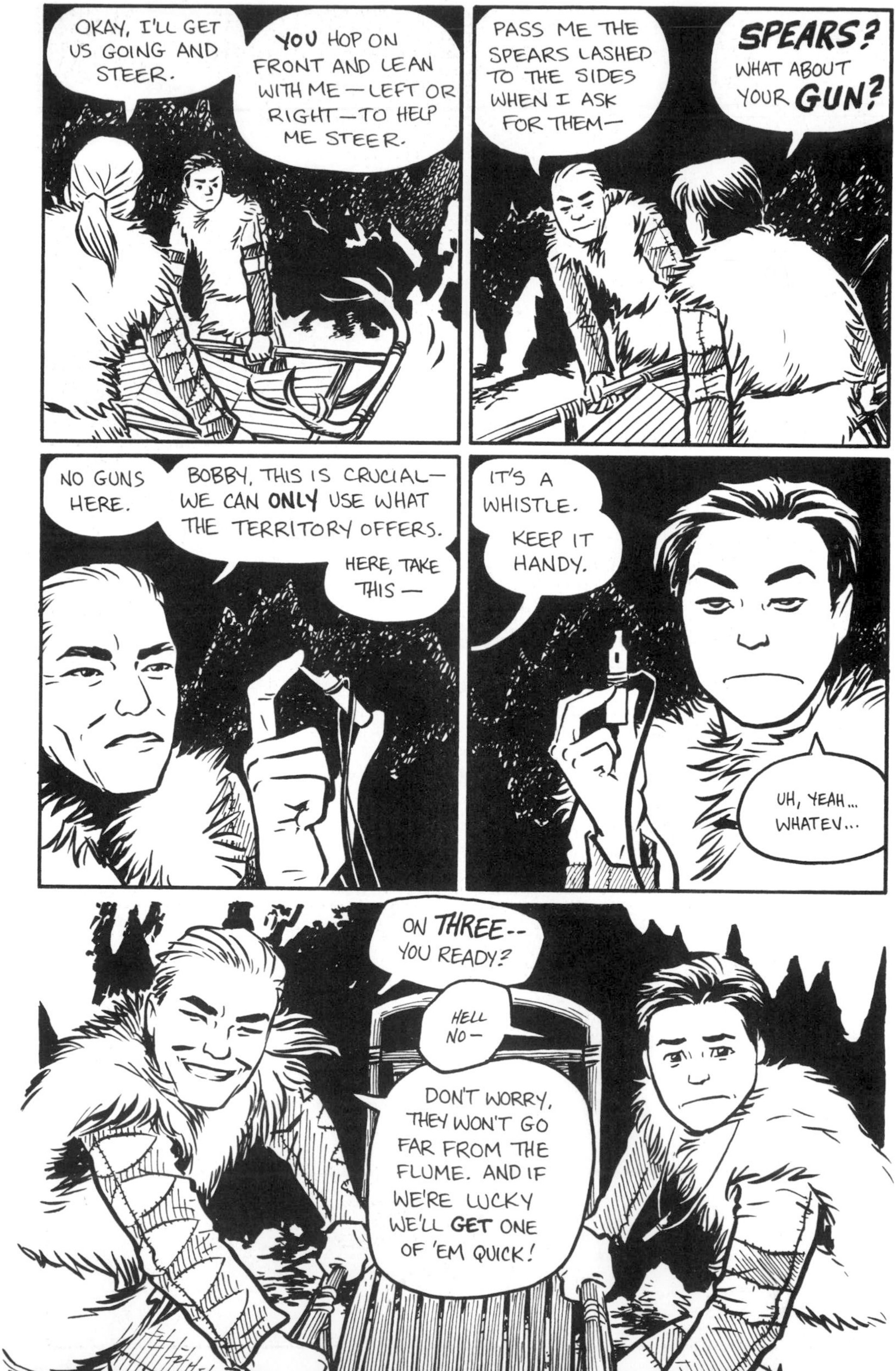
OKAY, I'LL GET US GOING AND STEER.
YOU HOP ON FRONT AND LEAN WITH ME—LEFT OR RIGHT—TO HELP ME STEER.
PASS ME THE SPEARS LASHED TO THE SIDES WHEN I ASK FOR THEM—
SPEARS? WHAT ABOUT YOUR GUN?
NO GUNS HERE.
BOBBY, THIS IS CRUCIAL—WE CAN ONLY USE WHAT THE TERRITORY OFFERS.
HERE, TAKE THIS—
IT'S A WHISTLE.
KEEP IT HANDY.
UH, YEAH... WHATEV...
ON THREE-- YOU READY?
HELL NO—
DON'T WORRY, THEY WON'T GO FAR FROM THE FLUME. AND IF WE'RE LUCKY WE'LL GET ONE OF 'EM QUICK!

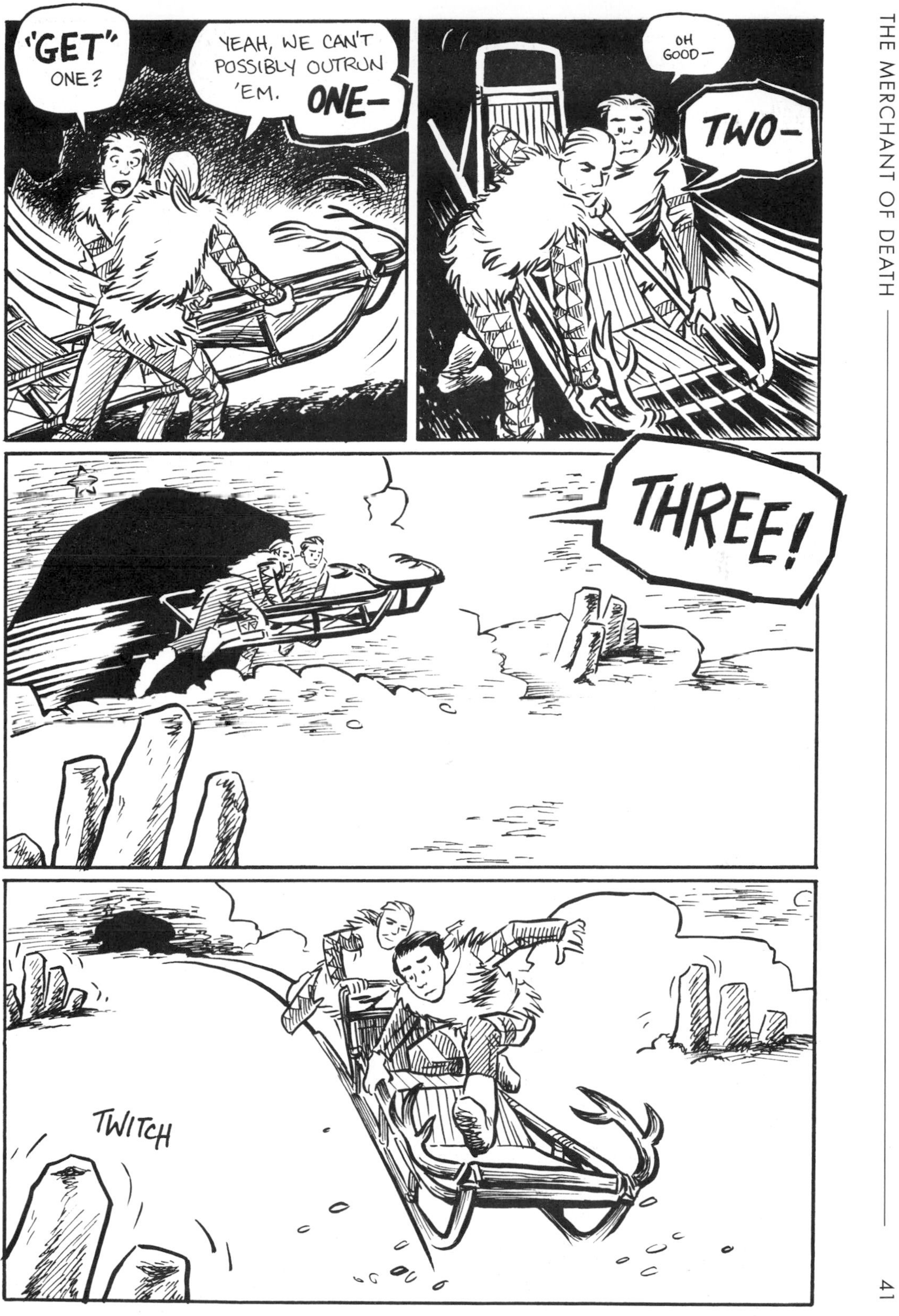
"GET" ONE?
YEAH, WE CAN'T POSSIBLY OUTRUN 'EM.
ONE–
OH GOOD–
TWO–
THREE!
TWITCH

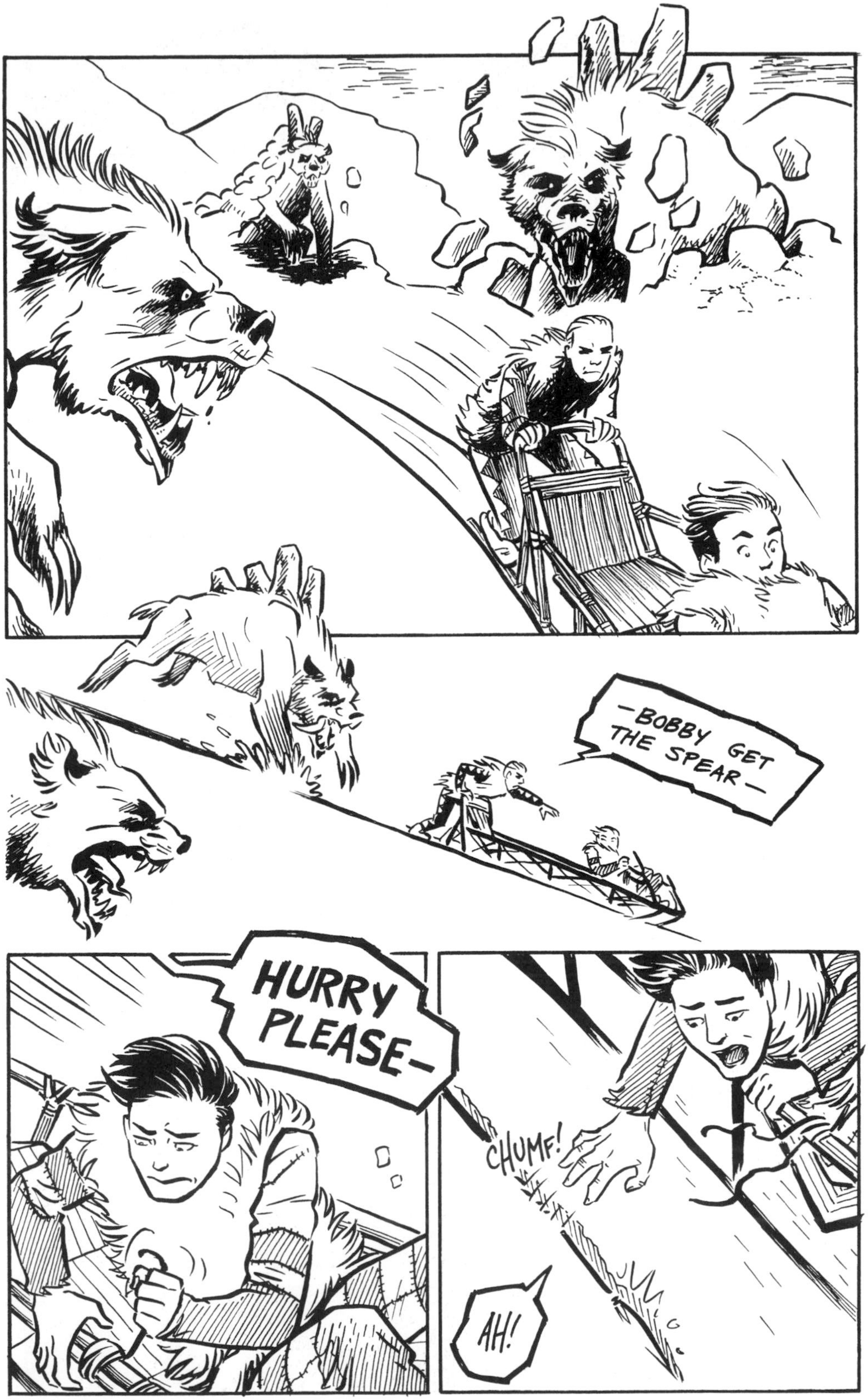
—BOBBY GET THE SPEAR—
HURRY PLEASE—
CHUMF!
AH!

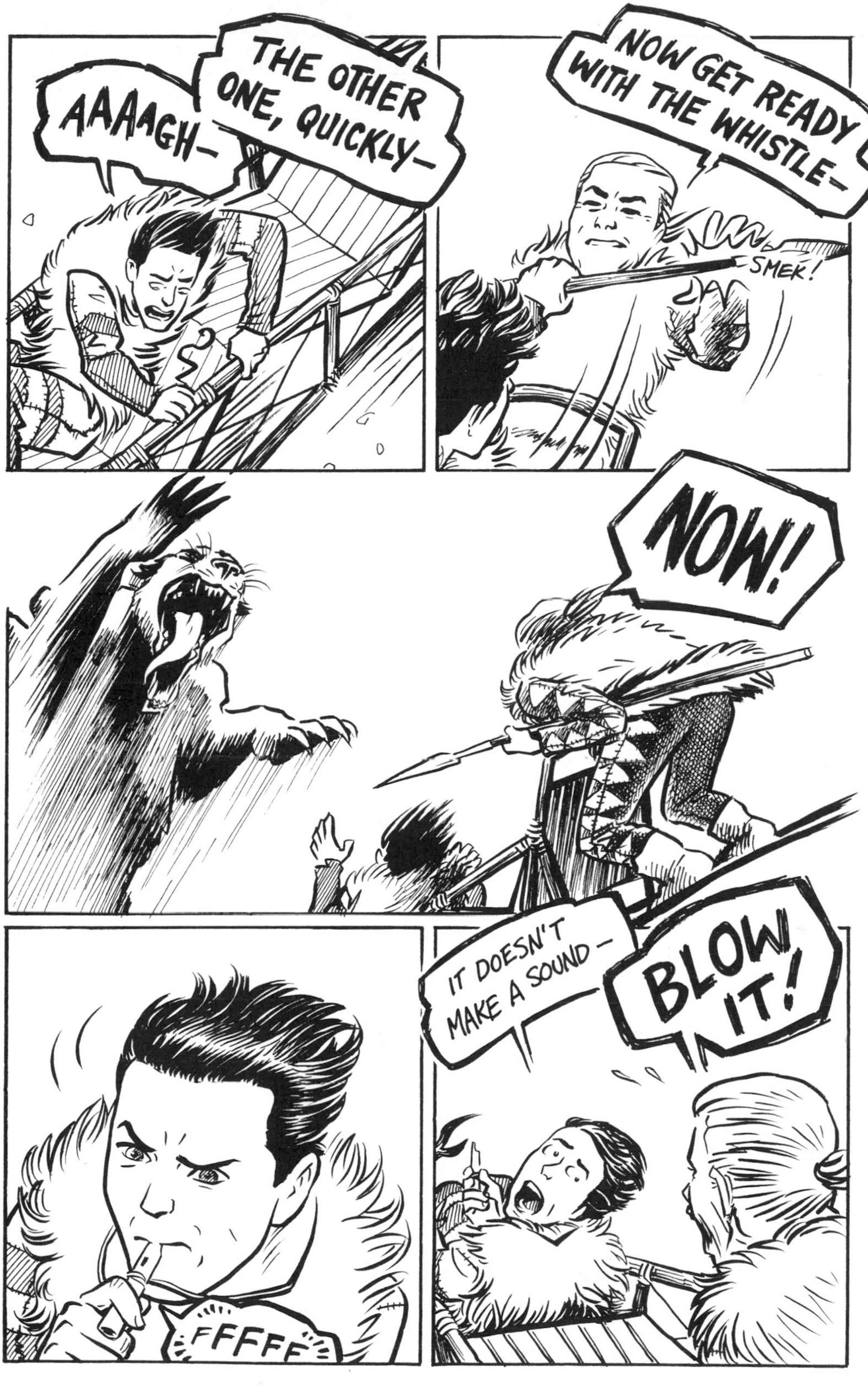
AAAAGH—
THE OTHER ONE, QUICKLY—
NOW GET READY WITH THE WHISTLE—
SMEK!
NOW!
IT DOESN'T MAKE A SOUND—
BLOW IT!
FFFFF

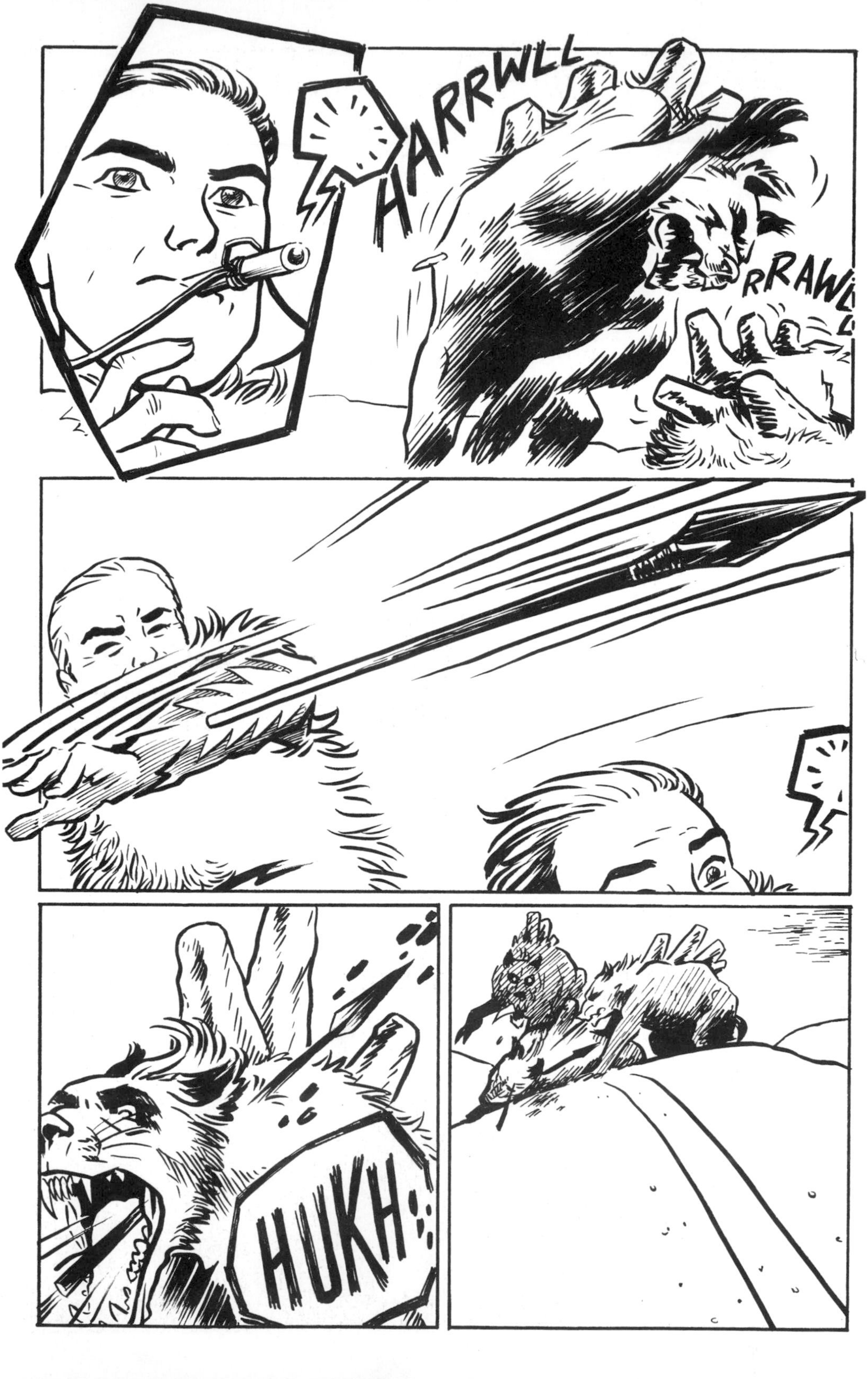
HARRWLL
RRAWL
HUKH

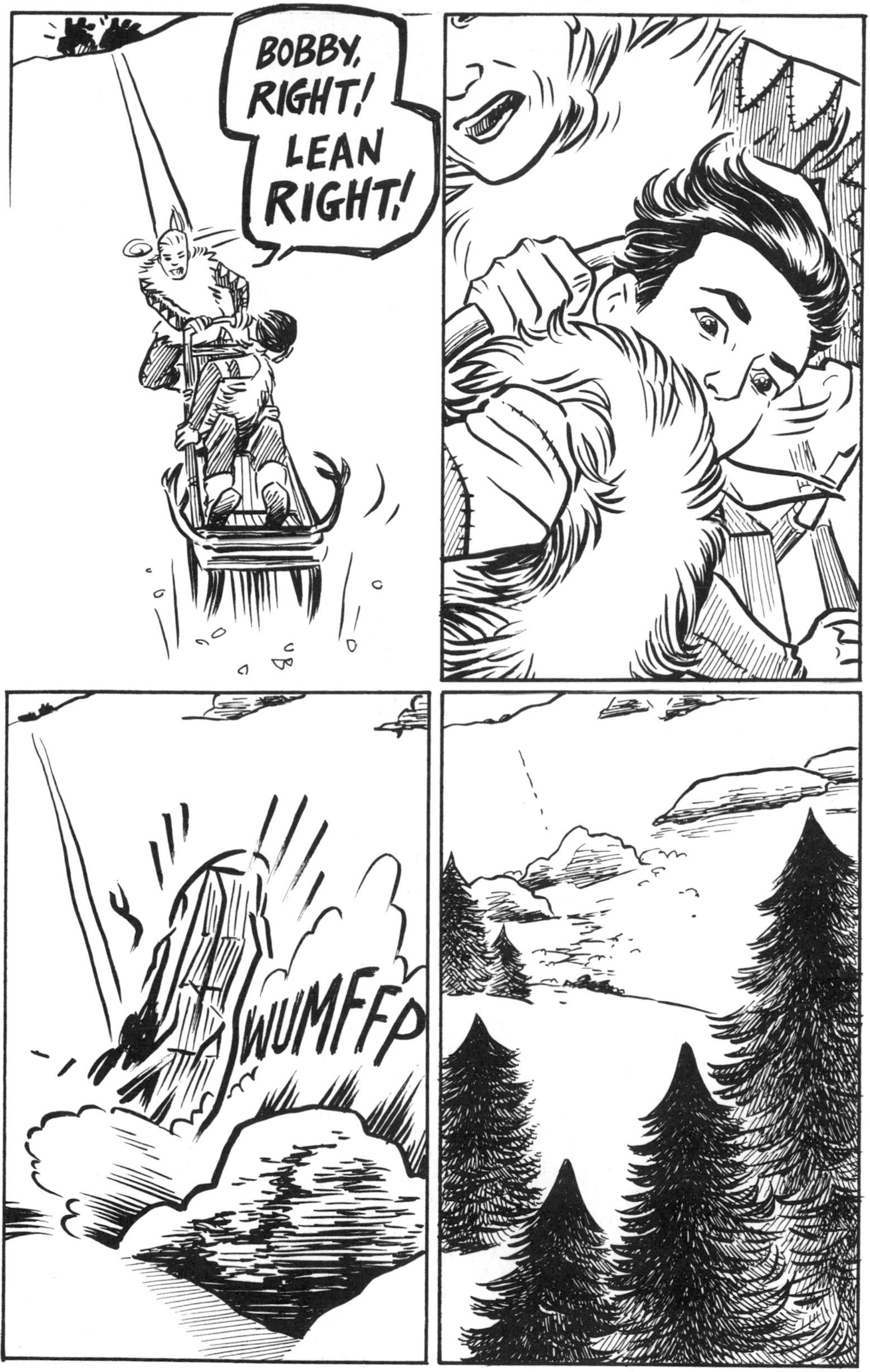
BOBBY, RIGHT! LEAN RIGHT!
WUMFFP

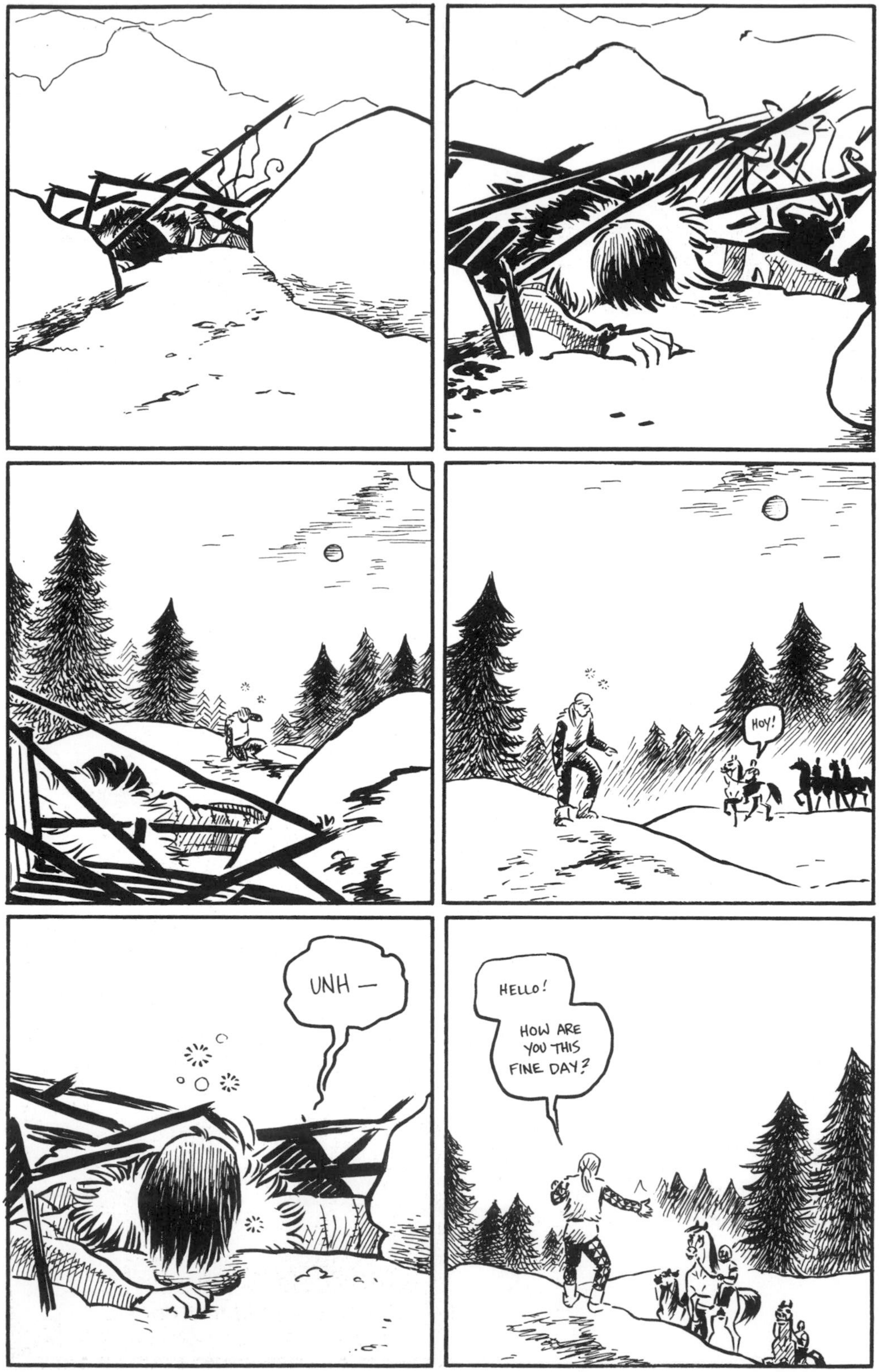
HOY!
UNH —
HELLO!
HOW ARE YOU THIS FINE DAY?

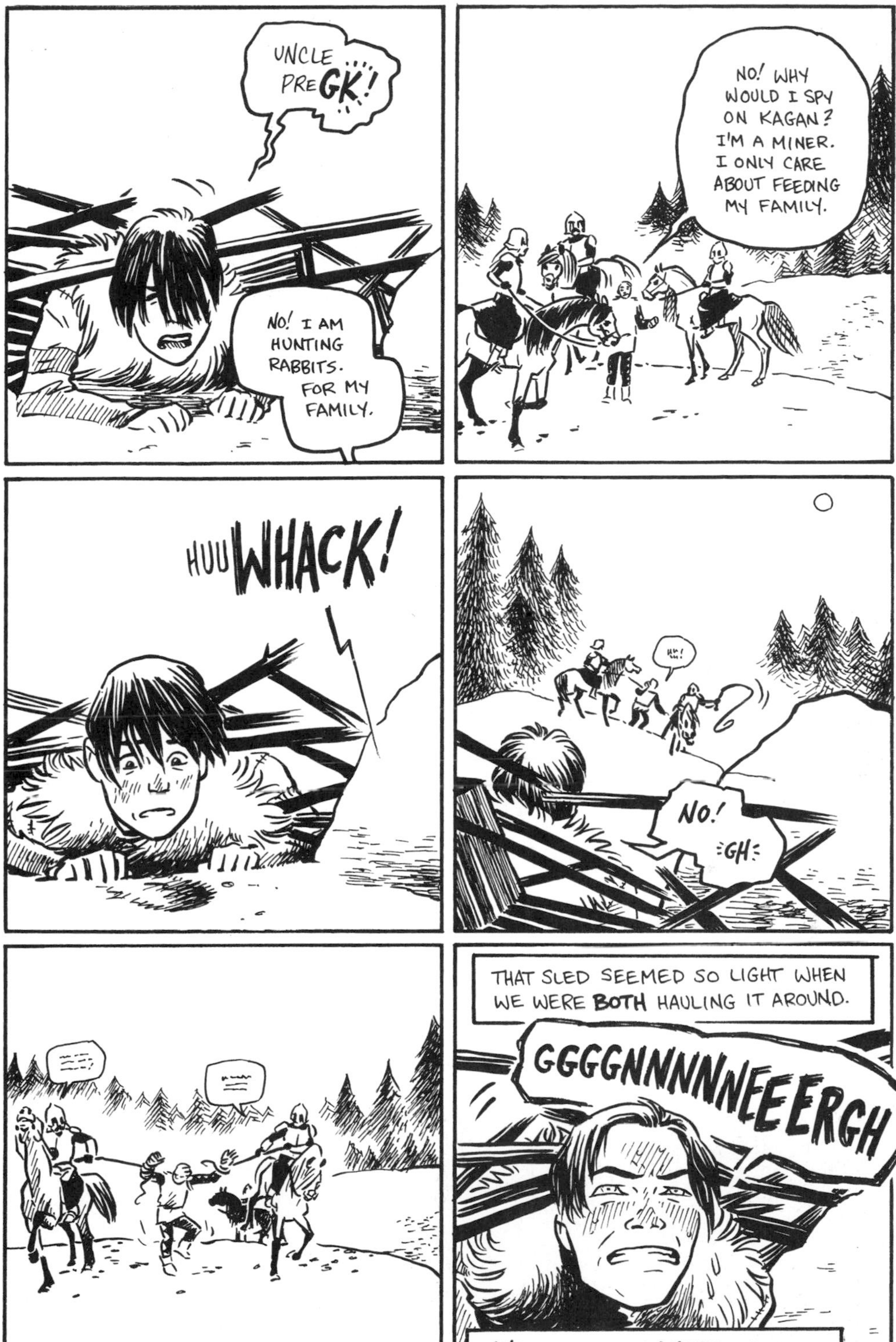
UNCLE PREGK!
NO! I AM HUNTING RABBITS. FOR MY FAMILY.
NO! WHY WOULD I SPY ON KAGAN? I'M A MINER. I ONLY CARE ABOUT FEEDING MY FAMILY.
HUUWHACK!
NO!
GH
THAT SLED SEEMED SO LIGHT WHEN WE WERE BOTH HAULING IT AROUND.
GGGGNNNNNNEEERGH
AND BEFORE IT LANDED ON ME, I HEAVED FOR ALL I WAS WORTH.

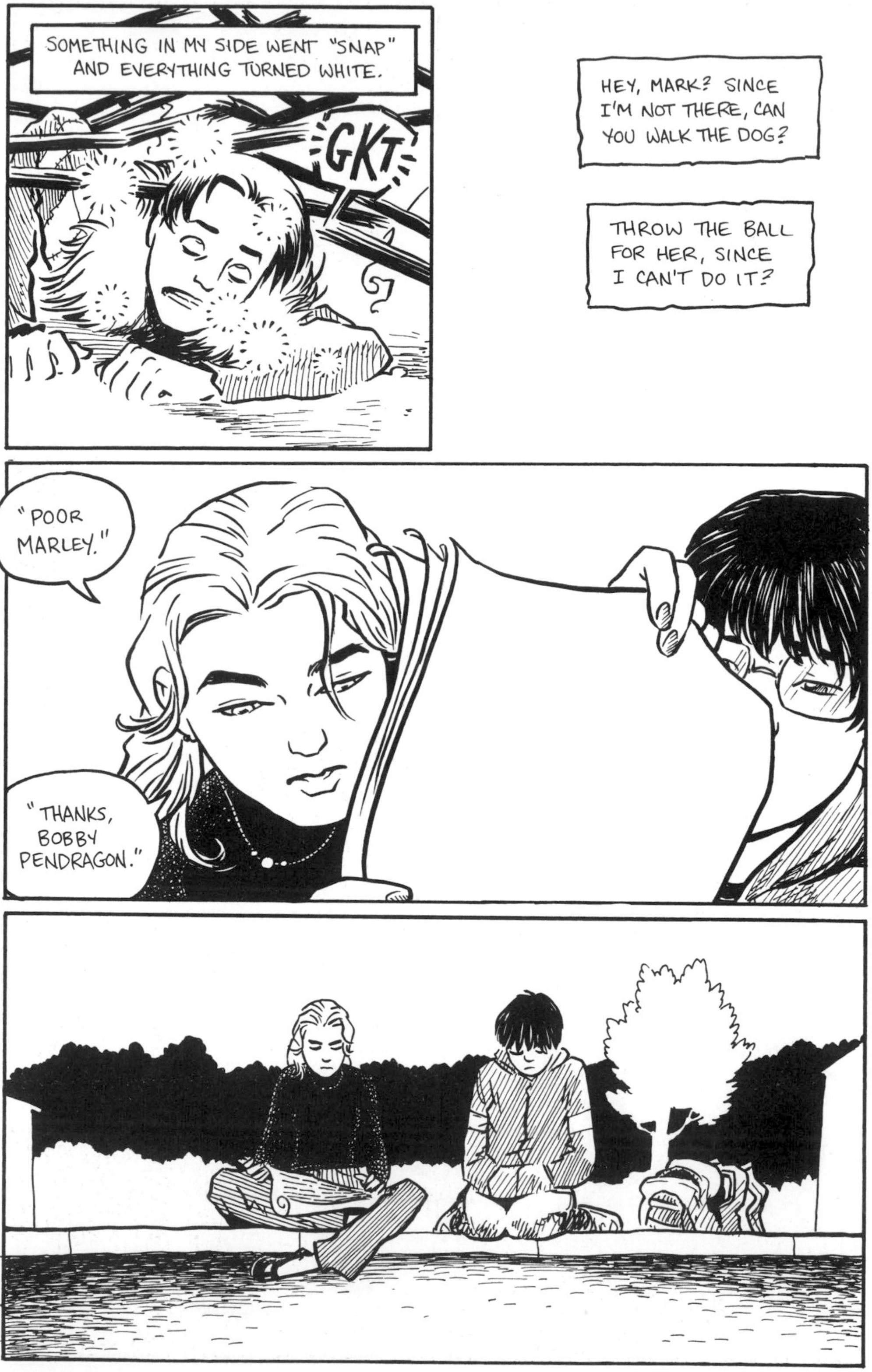
SOMETHING IN MY SIDE WENT "SNAP" AND EVERYTHING TURNED WHITE.
GKT
HEY, MARK? SINCE I'M NOT THERE, CAN YOU WALK THE DOG?
THROW THE BALL FOR HER, SINCE I CAN'T DO IT?
"POOR MARLEY."
"THANKS, BOBBY PENDRAGON."

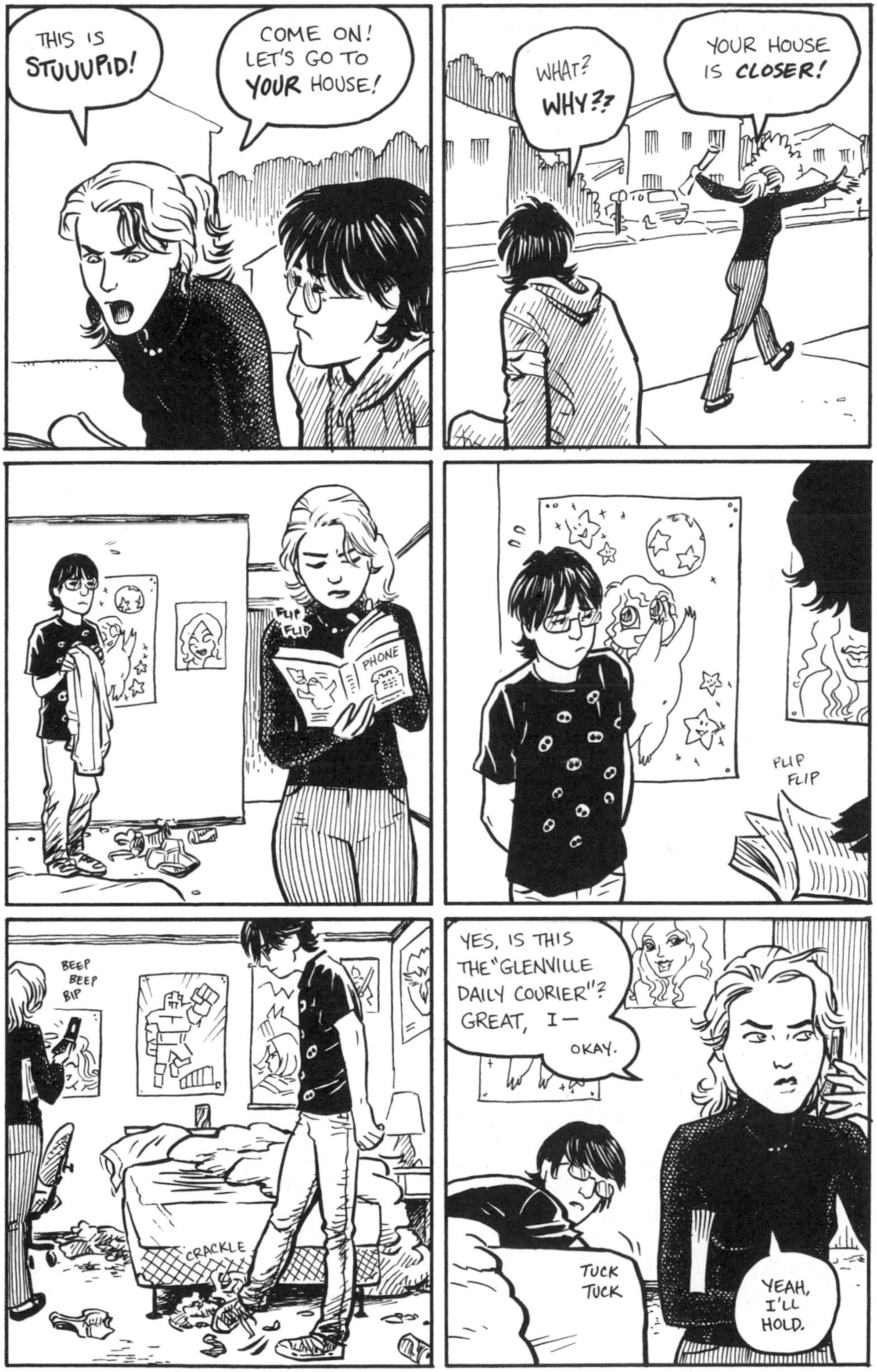

THIS IS STUUUPID!
COME ON! LET'S GO TO YOUR HOUSE!
WHAT? WHY??
YOUR HOUSE IS CLOSER!
FLIP FLIP
PHONE
FLIP FLIP
BEEP BEEP BIP
CRACKLE
YES, IS THIS THE "GLENVILLE DAILY COURIER"? GREAT, I—
OKAY.
TUCK TUCK
YEAH, I'LL HOLD.

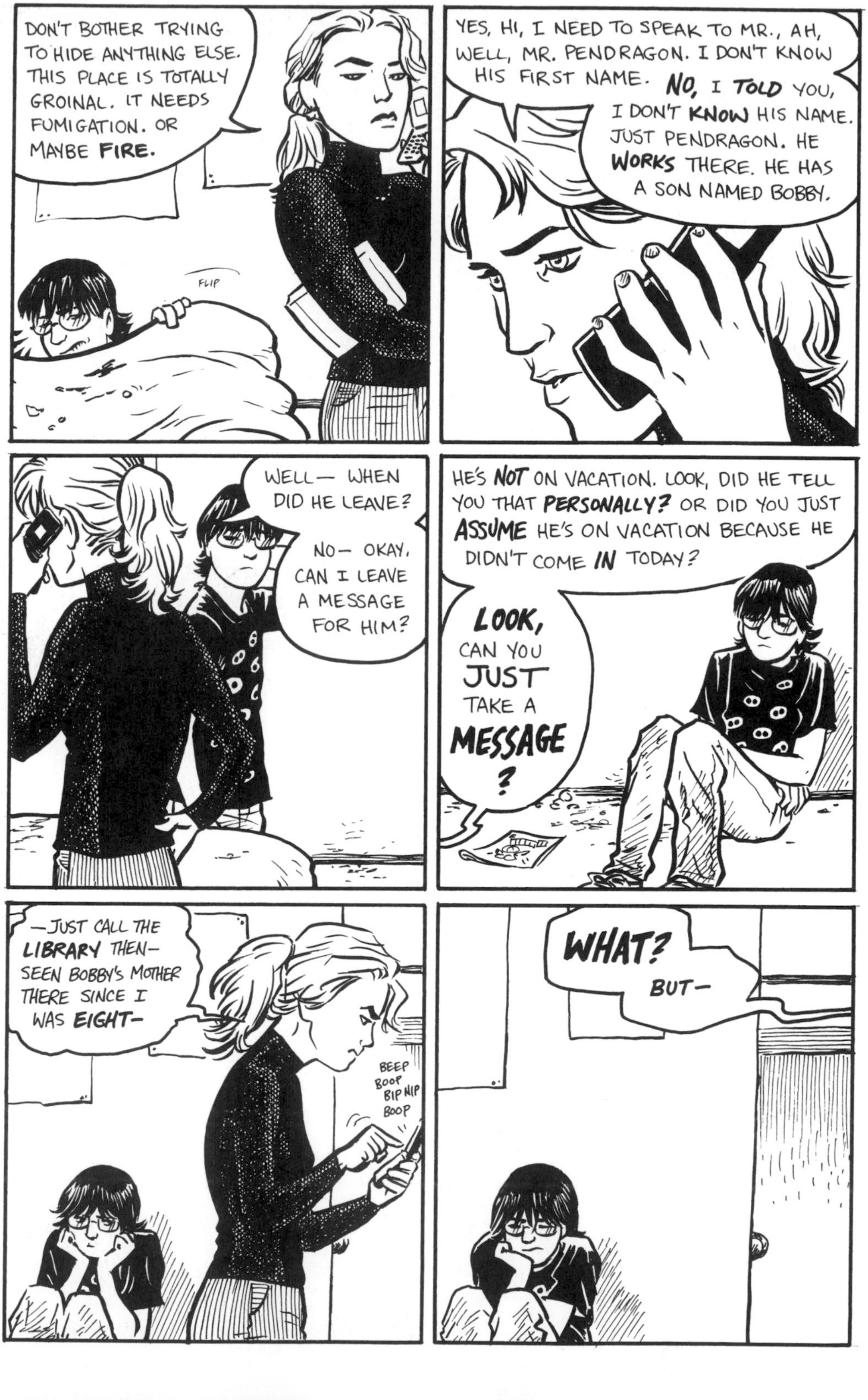
DON'T BOTHER TRYING TO HIDE ANYTHING ELSE. THIS PLACE IS TOTALLY GROINAL. IT NEEDS FUMIGATION. OR MAYBE **FIRE.**
FLIP
YES, HI, I NEED TO SPEAK TO MR., AH, WELL, MR. PENDRAGON. I DON'T KNOW HIS FIRST NAME. **NO,** I **TOLD** YOU, I DON'T **KNOW** HIS NAME. JUST PENDRAGON. HE **WORKS** THERE. HE HAS A SON NAMED BOBBY.
WELL— WHEN DID HE LEAVE?
NO— OKAY. CAN I LEAVE A MESSAGE FOR HIM?
HE'S **NOT** ON VACATION. LOOK, DID HE TELL YOU THAT **PERSONALLY?** OR DID YOU JUST **ASSUME** HE'S ON VACATION BECAUSE HE DIDN'T COME **IN** TODAY?
LOOK, CAN YOU JUST TAKE A **MESSAGE ?**
—JUST CALL THE **LIBRARY** THEN— SEEN BOBBY'S MOTHER THERE SINCE I WAS **EIGHT—**
BEEP BOOP BIP NIP BOOP
WHAT? BUT—

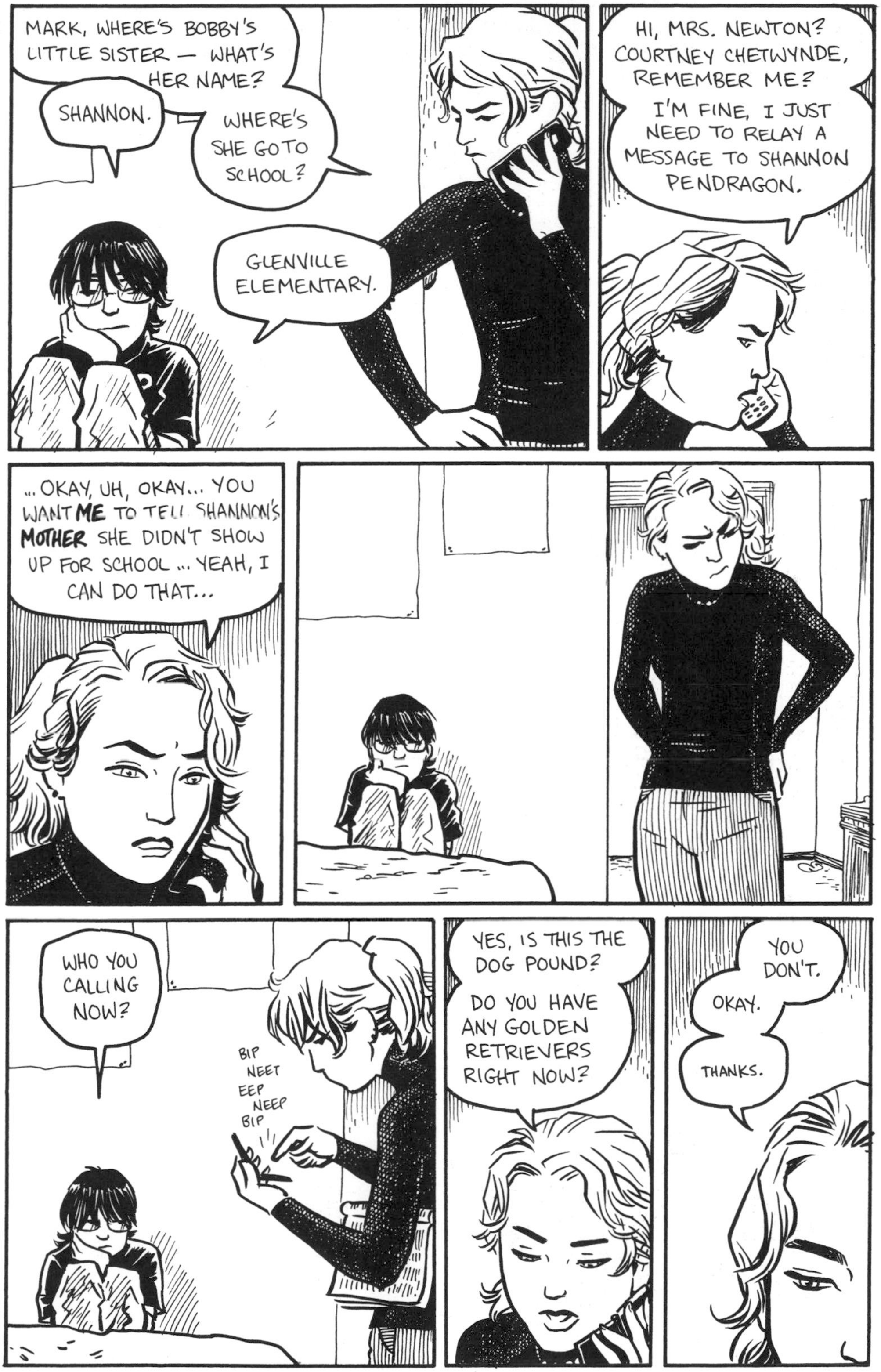
MARK, WHERE'S BOBBY'S LITTLE SISTER — WHAT'S HER NAME?
SHANNON.
WHERE'S SHE GO TO SCHOOL?
GLENVILLE ELEMENTARY.
HI, MRS. NEWTON? COURTNEY CHETWYNDE, REMEMBER ME?
I'M FINE, I JUST NEED TO RELAY A MESSAGE TO SHANNON PENDRAGON.
... OKAY, UH, OKAY... YOU WANT **ME** TO TELL SHANNON'S **MOTHER** SHE DIDN'T SHOW UP FOR SCHOOL ... YEAH, I CAN DO THAT...
WHO YOU CALLING NOW?
BIP
NEET
EEP
NEEP
BIP
YES, IS THIS THE DOG POUND?
DO YOU HAVE ANY GOLDEN RETRIEVERS RIGHT NOW?
YOU DON'T.
OKAY.
THANKS.

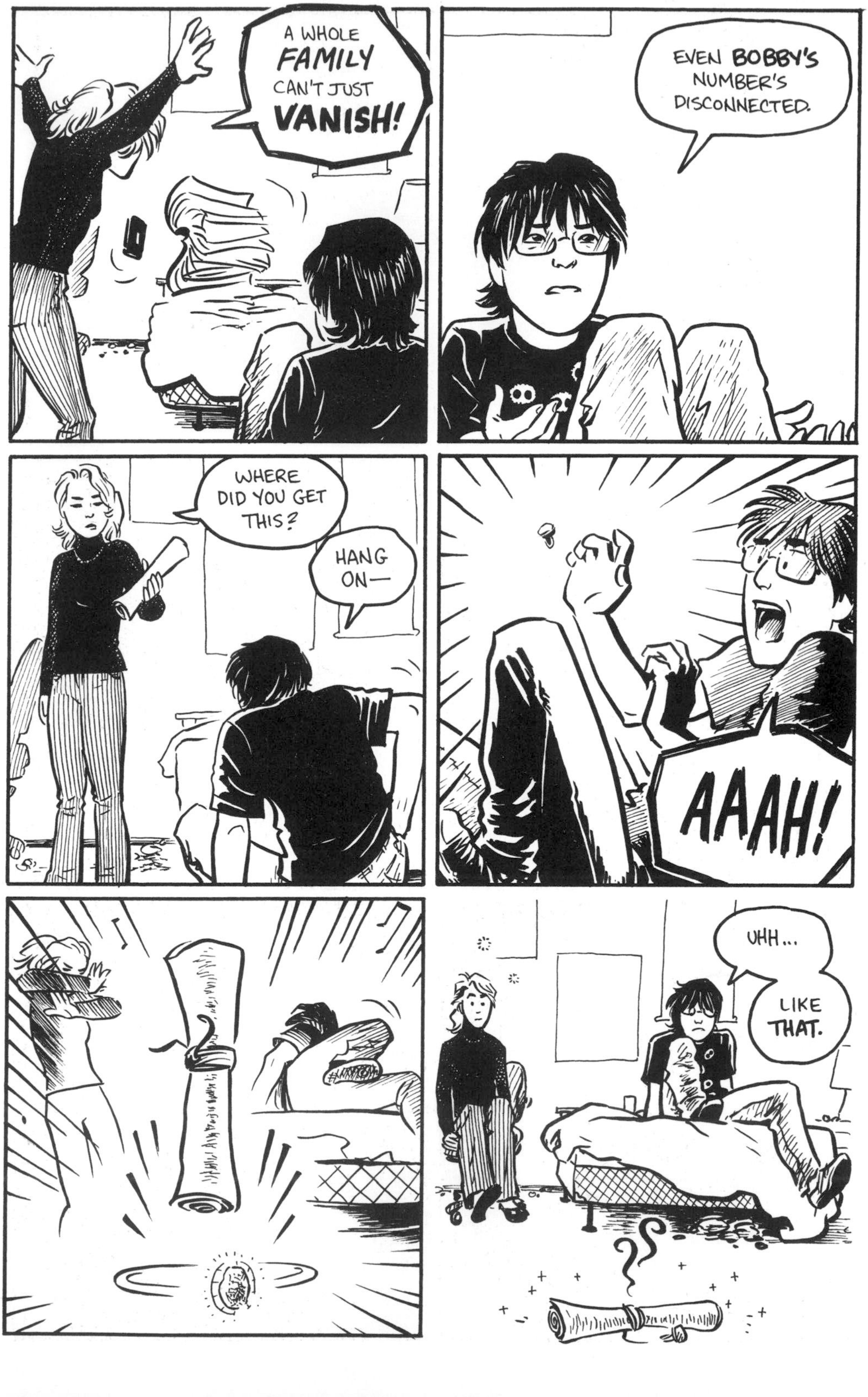
A WHOLE FAMILY CAN'T JUST VANISH!
EVEN BOBBY'S NUMBER'S DISCONNECTED.
WHERE DID YOU GET THIS?
HANG ON—
AAAH!
UHH...
LIKE THAT.

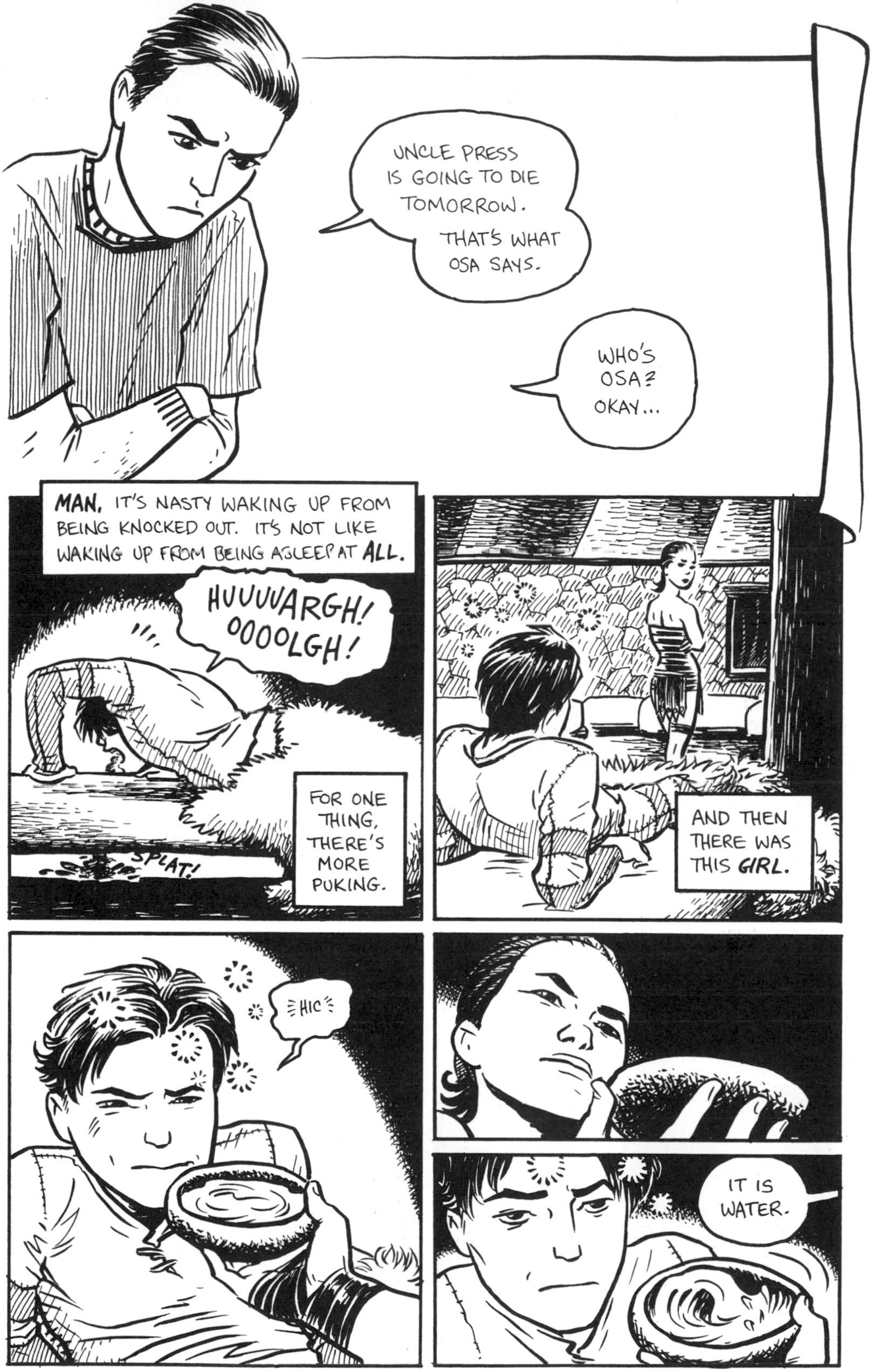
UNCLE PRESS IS GOING TO DIE TOMORROW.
THAT'S WHAT OSA SAYS.
WHO'S OSA? OKAY...
MAN, IT'S NASTY WAKING UP FROM BEING KNOCKED OUT. IT'S NOT LIKE WAKING UP FROM BEING ASLEEP AT ALL.
HUUUVARGH! OOOOLGH!
SPLAT!
FOR ONE THING, THERE'S MORE PUKING.
AND THEN THERE WAS THIS GIRL.
HIC
IT IS WATER.

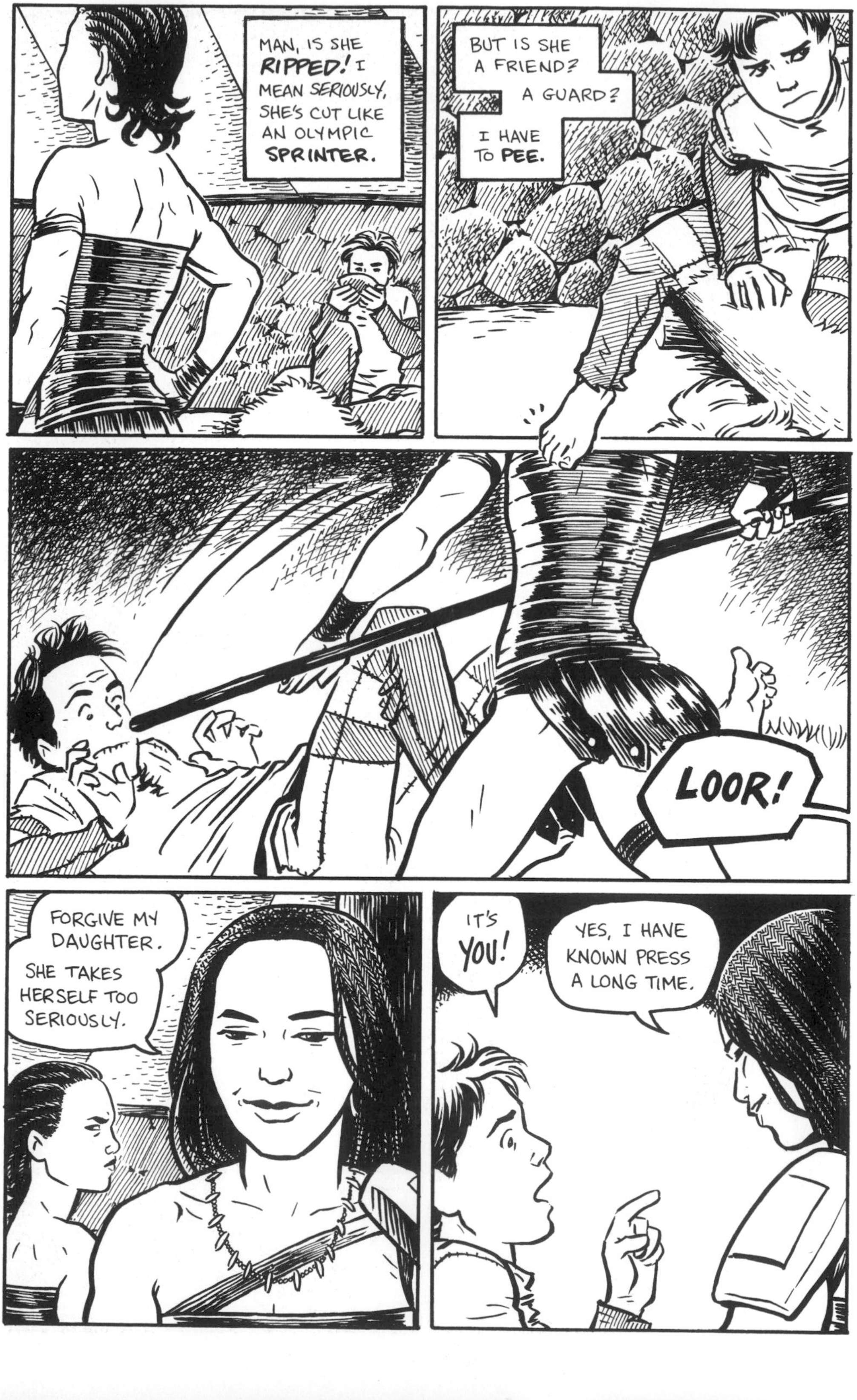
MAN, IS SHE RIPPED! I MEAN SERIOUSLY, SHE'S CUT LIKE AN OLYMPIC SPRINTER.
BUT IS SHE A FRIEND?
A GUARD?
I HAVE TO PEE.
LOOR!
FORGIVE MY DAUGHTER.
SHE TAKES HERSELF TOO SERIOUSLY.
IT'S YOU!
YES, I HAVE KNOWN PRESS A LONG TIME.

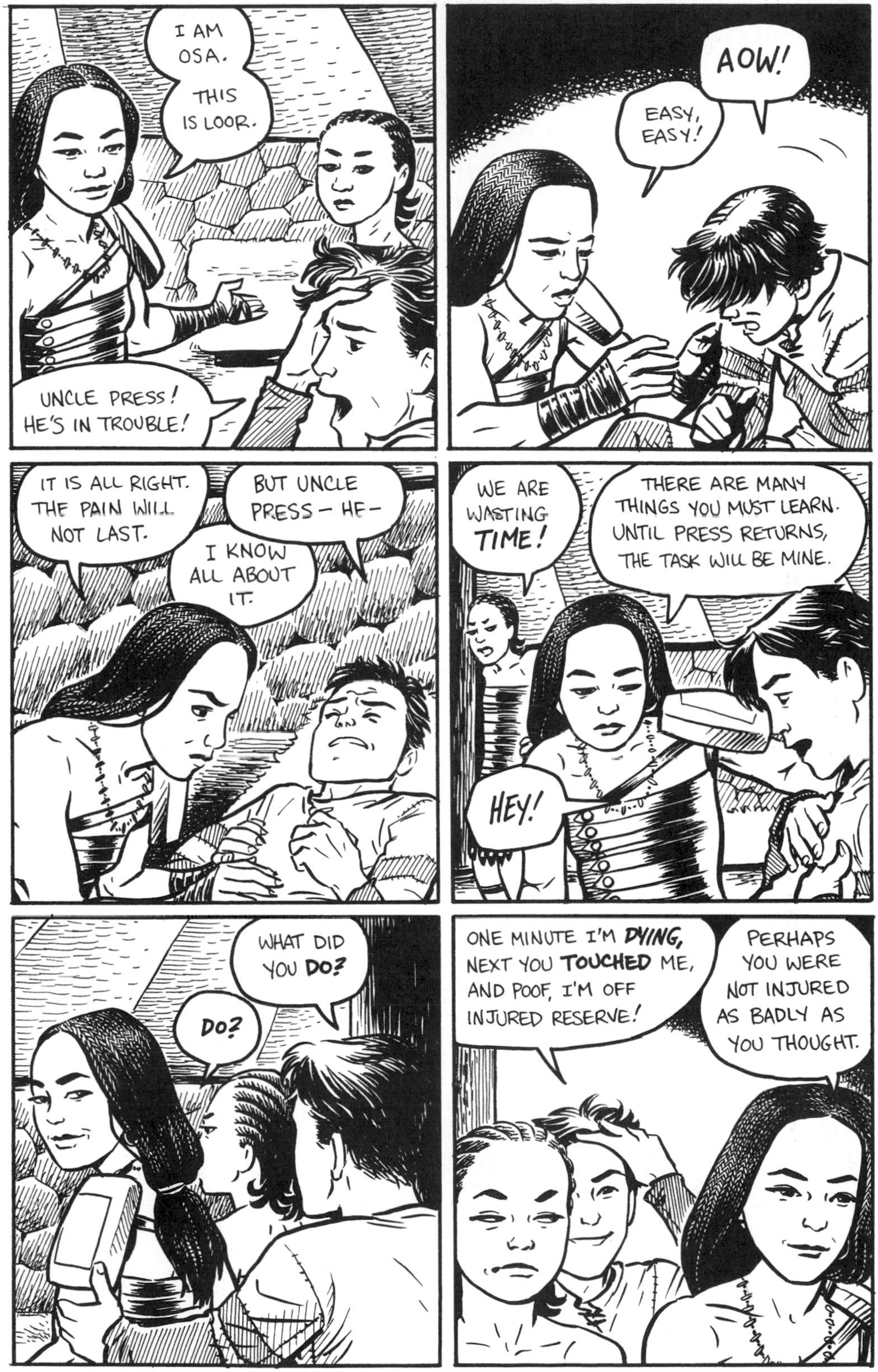
I AM OSA.
THIS IS LOOR.
UNCLE PRESS! HE'S IN TROUBLE!
EASY, EASY!
AOW!
IT IS ALL RIGHT. THE PAIN WILL NOT LAST.
BUT UNCLE PRESS—HE—
I KNOW ALL ABOUT IT.
WE ARE WASTING TIME!
THERE ARE MANY THINGS YOU MUST LEARN. UNTIL PRESS RETURNS, THE TASK WILL BE MINE.
HEY!
WHAT DID YOU DO?
DO?
ONE MINUTE I'M DYING, NEXT YOU TOUCHED ME, AND POOF, I'M OFF INJURED RESERVE!
PERHAPS YOU WERE NOT INJURED AS BADLY AS YOU THOUGHT.

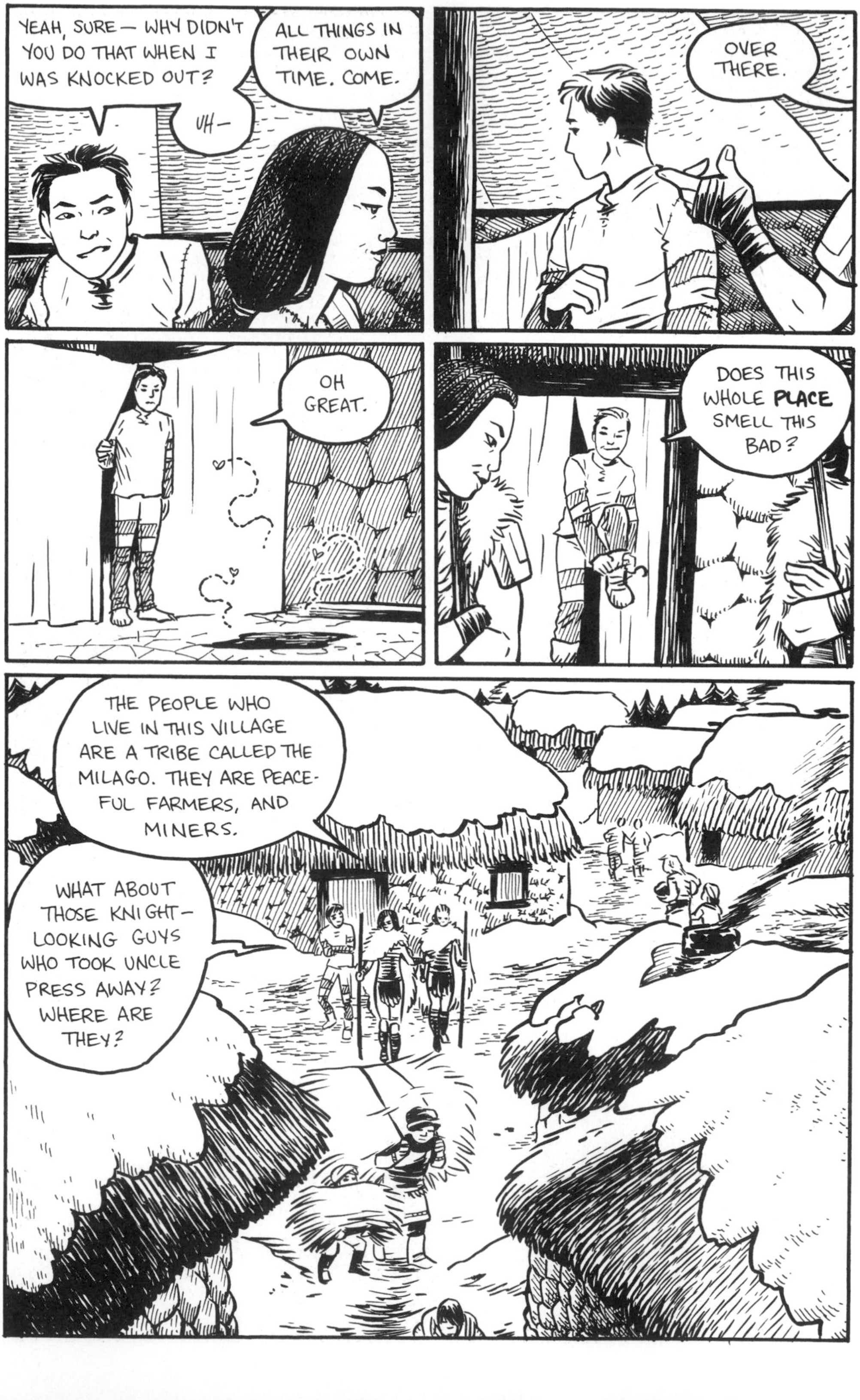
YEAH, SURE — WHY DIDN'T YOU DO THAT WHEN I WAS KNOCKED OUT?
UH—
ALL THINGS IN THEIR OWN TIME. COME.
OVER THERE.
OH GREAT.
DOES THIS WHOLE PLACE SMELL THIS BAD?
THE PEOPLE WHO LIVE IN THIS VILLAGE ARE A TRIBE CALLED THE MILAGO. THEY ARE PEACE-FUL FARMERS, AND MINERS.
WHAT ABOUT THOSE KNIGHT-LOOKING GUYS WHO TOOK UNCLE PRESS AWAY? WHERE ARE THEY?

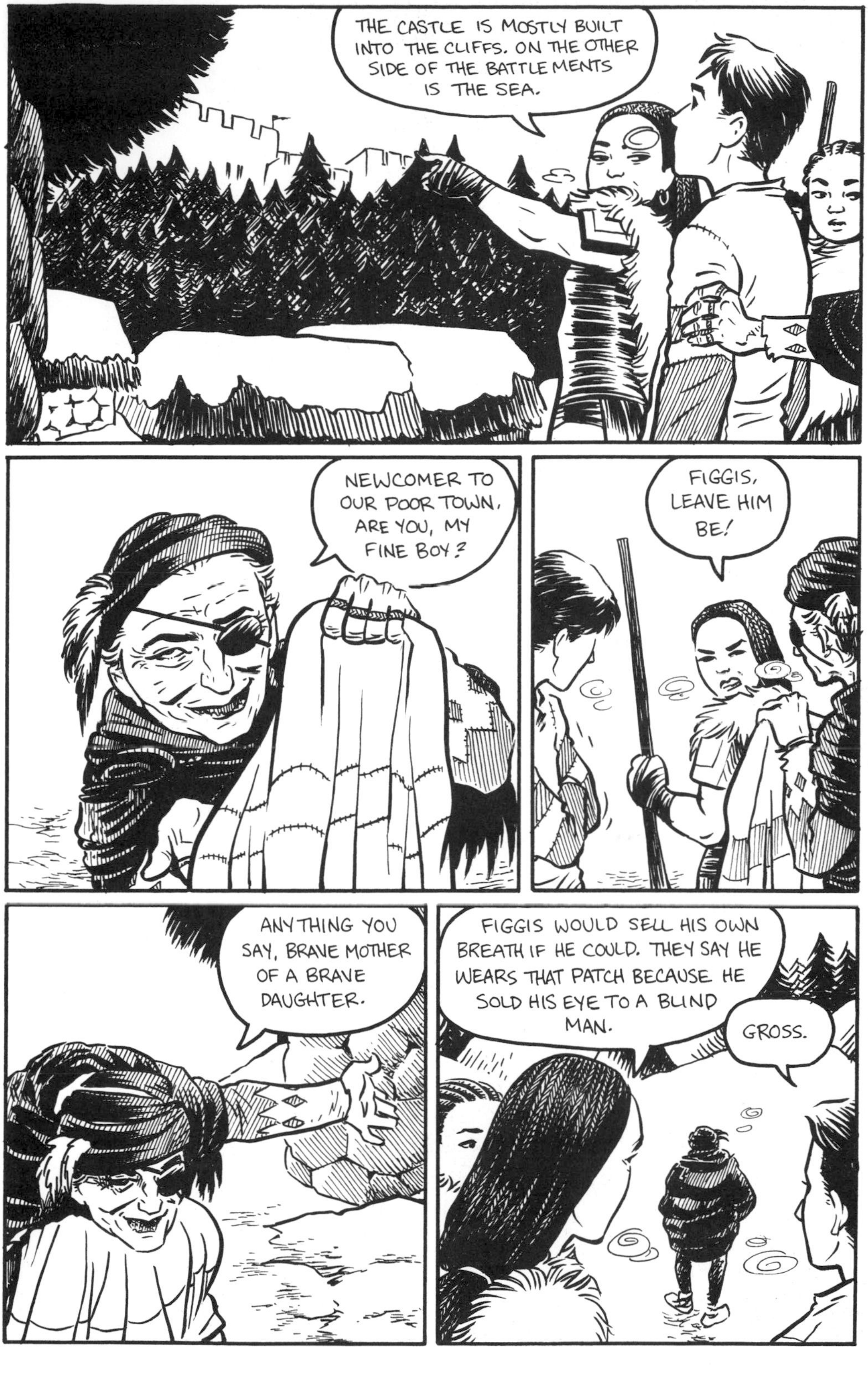
THE CASTLE IS MOSTLY BUILT INTO THE CLIFFS. ON THE OTHER SIDE OF THE BATTLEMENTS IS THE SEA.
NEWCOMER TO OUR POOR TOWN, ARE YOU, MY FINE BOY?
FIGGIS, LEAVE HIM BE!
ANYTHING YOU SAY, BRAVE MOTHER OF A BRAVE DAUGHTER.
FIGGIS WOULD SELL HIS OWN BREATH IF HE COULD. THEY SAY HE WEARS THAT PATCH BECAUSE HE SOLD HIS EYE TO A BLIND MAN.
GROSS.

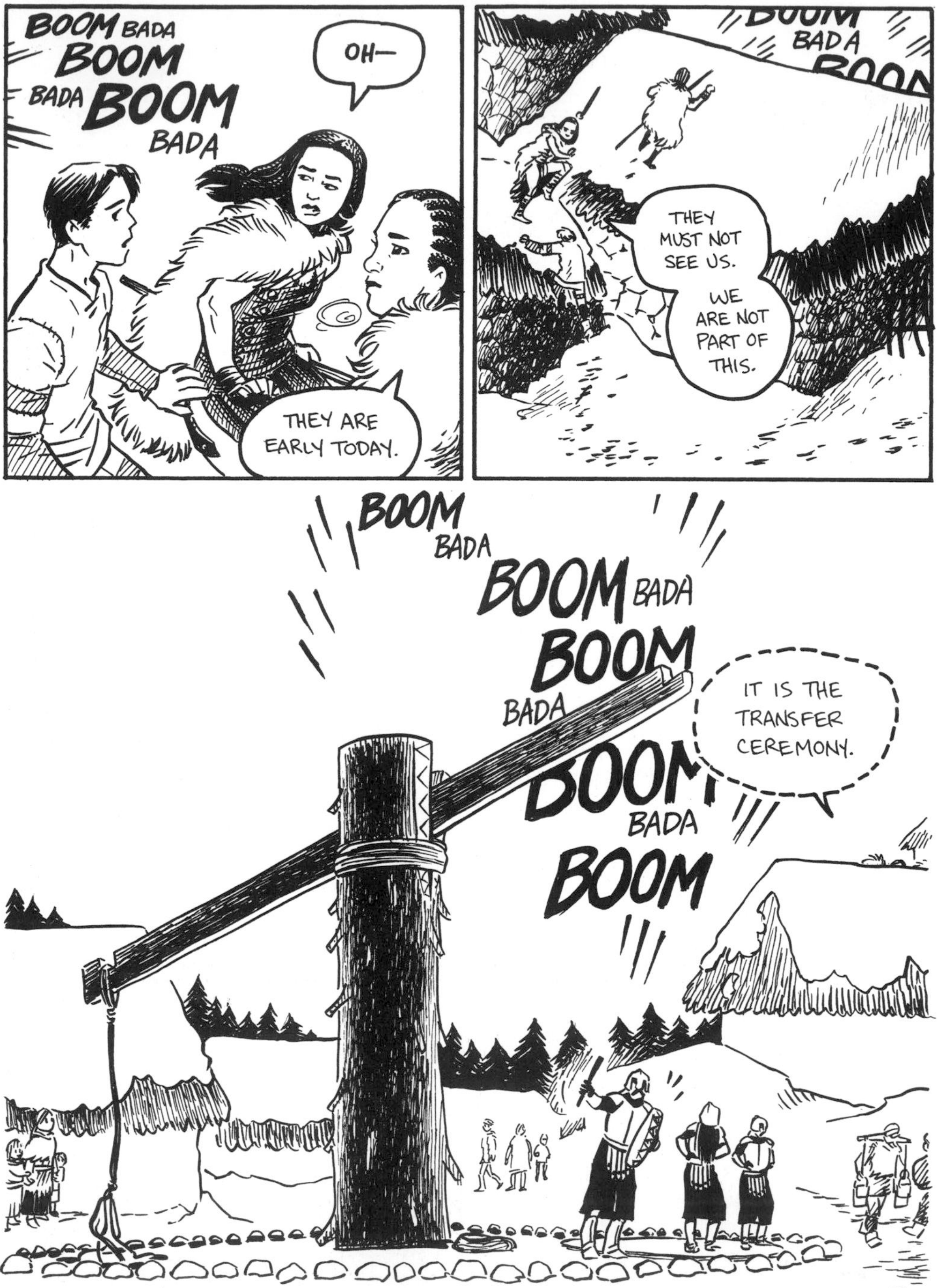
BOOM BADA BOOM BADA BOOM BADA
OH—
THEY ARE EARLY TODAY.
BADA
THEY MUST NOT SEE US.
WE ARE NOT PART OF THIS.
BOOM BADA BOOM BADA BOOM BADA BOOM BADA BOOM
IT IS THE TRANSFER CEREMONY.

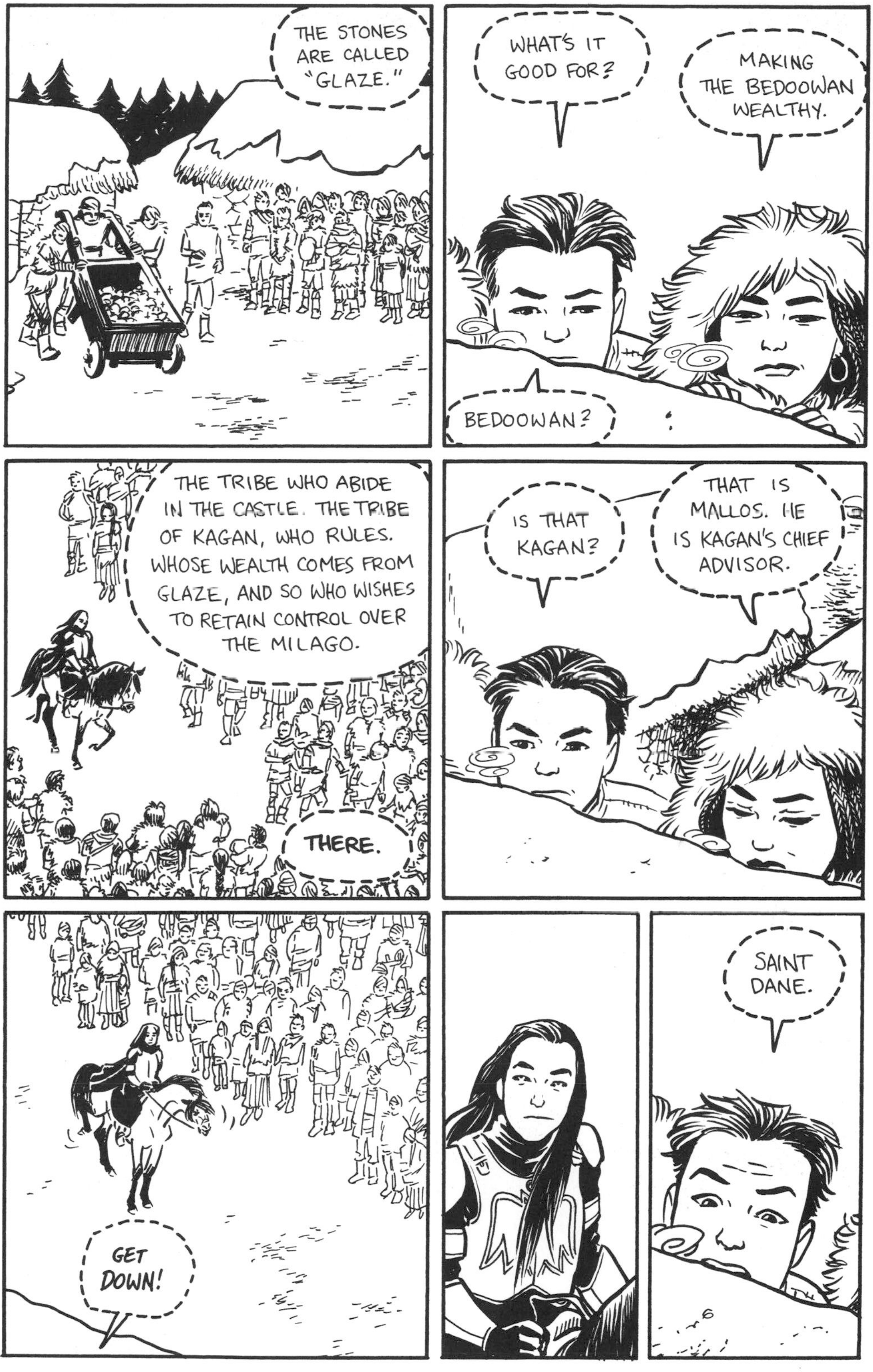
THE STONES ARE CALLED "GLAZE."
WHAT'S IT GOOD FOR?
MAKING THE BEDOOWAN WEALTHY.
BEDOOWAN?
THE TRIBE WHO ABIDE IN THE CASTLE. THE TRIBE OF KAGAN, WHO RULES. WHOSE WEALTH COMES FROM GLAZE, AND SO WHO WISHES TO RETAIN CONTROL OVER THE MILAGO.
THERE.
IS THAT KAGAN?
THAT IS MALLOS. HE IS KAGAN'S CHIEF ADVISOR.
GET DOWN!
SAINT DANE.

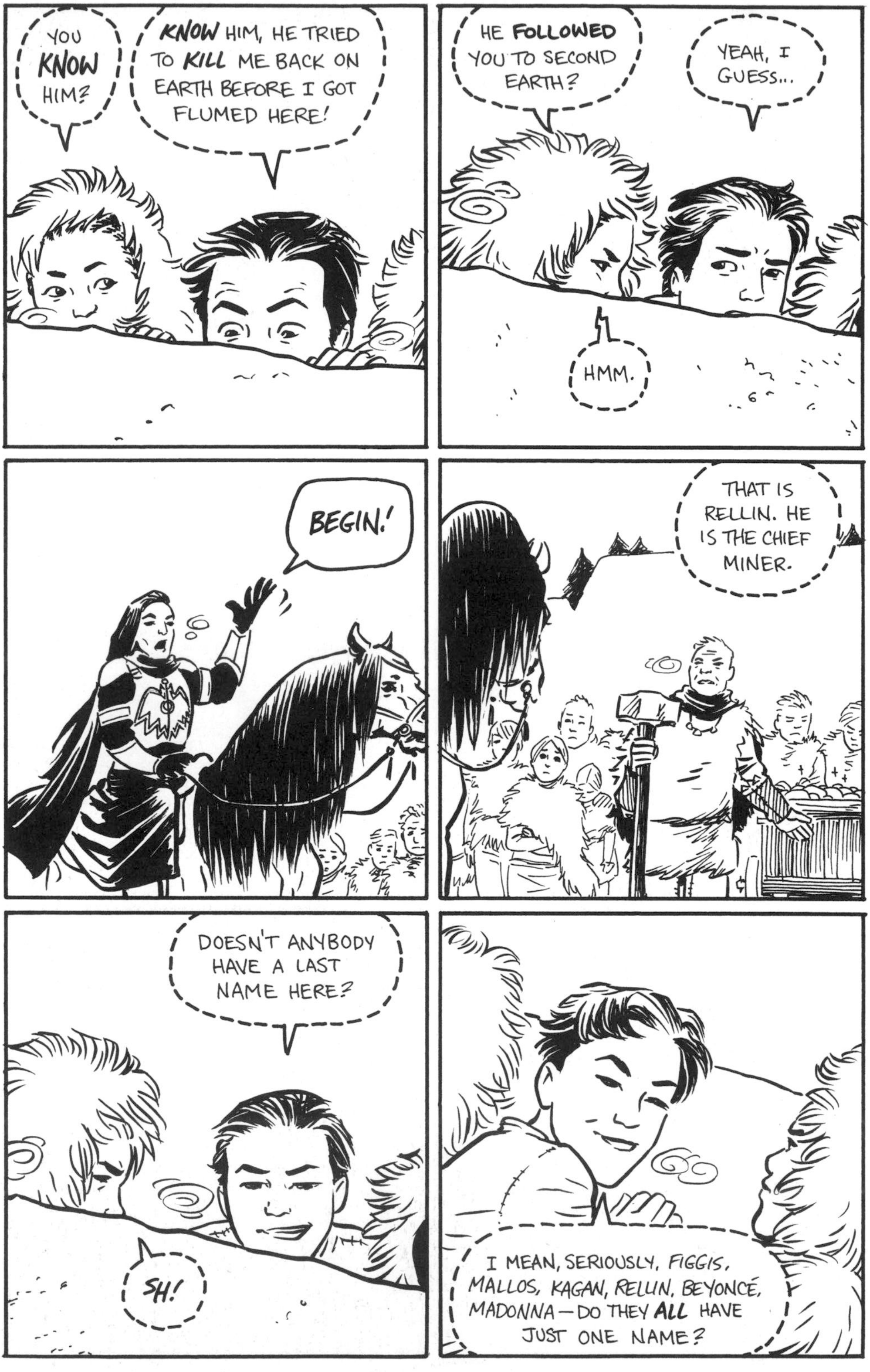
YOU KNOW HIM?
KNOW HIM, HE TRIED TO KILL ME BACK ON EARTH BEFORE I GOT FLUMED HERE!
HE FOLLOWED YOU TO SECOND EARTH?
YEAH, I GUESS...
HMM.
BEGIN!
THAT IS RELLIN. HE IS THE CHIEF MINER.
DOESN'T ANYBODY HAVE A LAST NAME HERE?
SH!
I MEAN, SERIOUSLY. FIGGIS, MALLOS, KAGAN, RELLIN, BEYONCÉ, MADONNA—DO THEY ALL HAVE JUST ONE NAME?

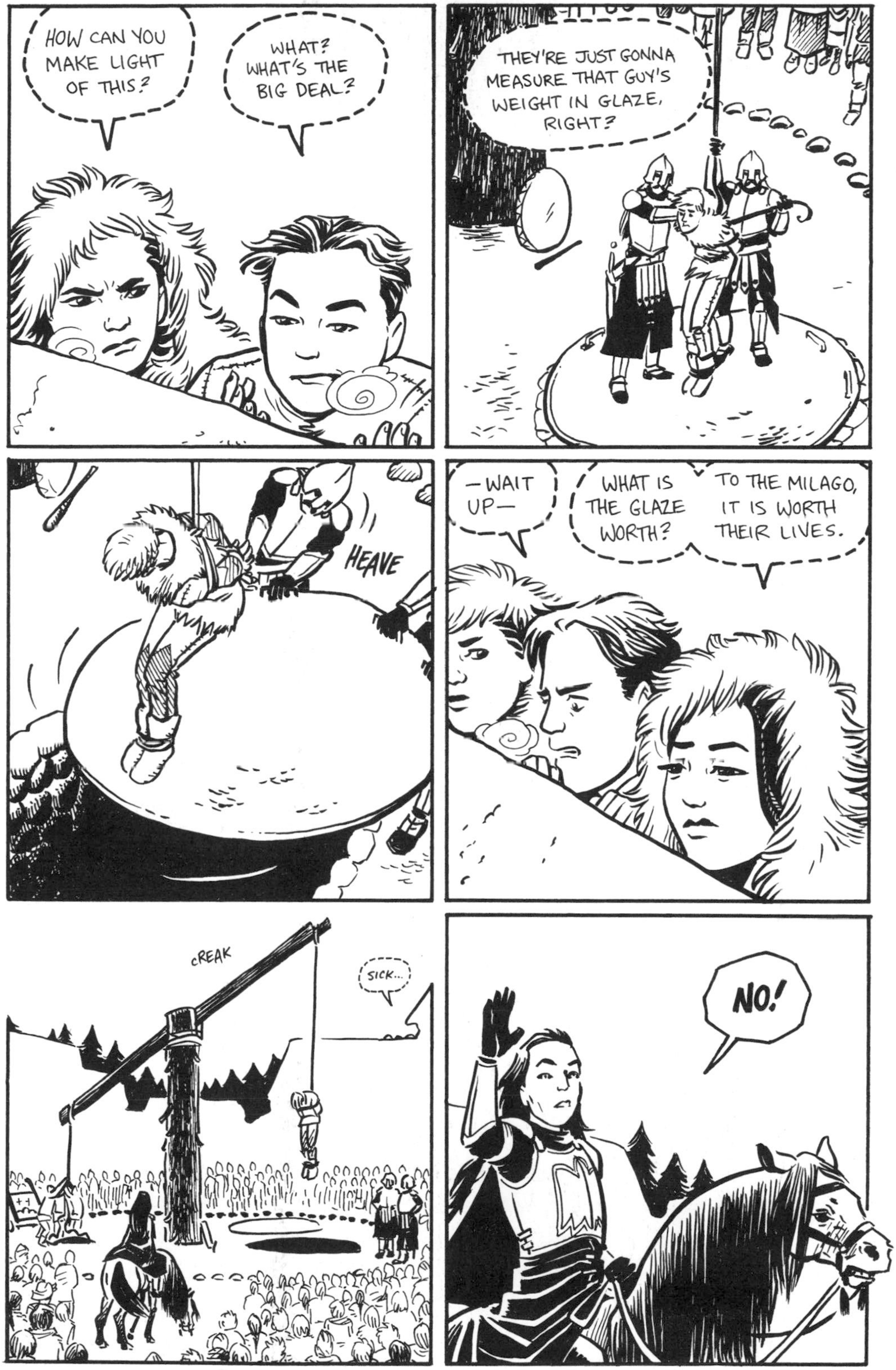
HOW CAN YOU MAKE LIGHT OF THIS?
WHAT? WHAT'S THE BIG DEAL?
THEY'RE JUST GONNA MEASURE THAT GUY'S WEIGHT IN GLAZE, RIGHT?
HEAVE
—WAIT UP—
WHAT IS THE GLAZE WORTH?
TO THE MILAGO, IT IS WORTH THEIR LIVES.
CREAK
SICK...
NO!

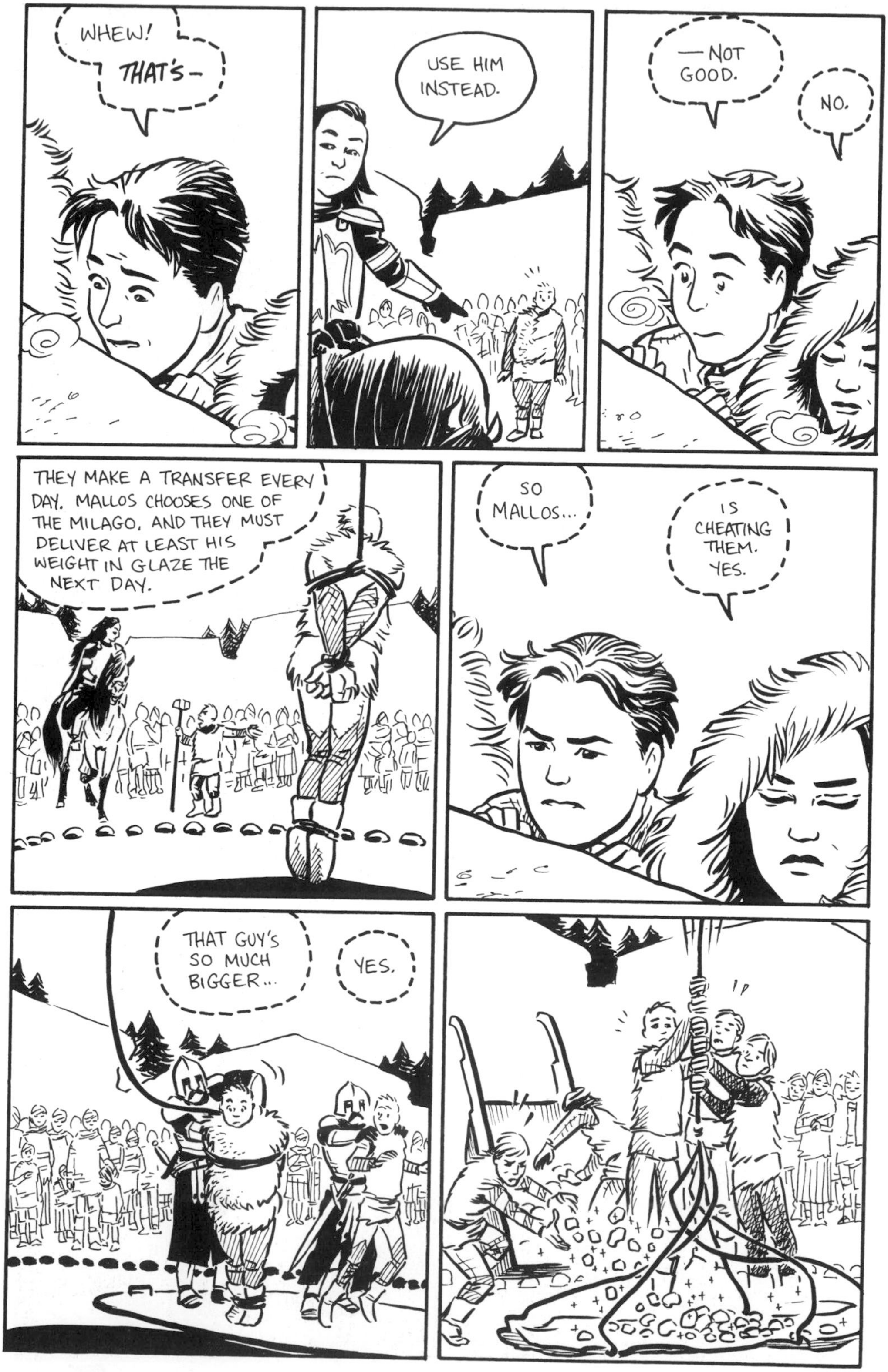
WHEW!
THAT'S—
USE HIM INSTEAD.
—NOT GOOD.
NO.
THEY MAKE A TRANSFER EVERY DAY. MALLOS CHOOSES ONE OF THE MILAGO, AND THEY MUST DELIVER AT LEAST HIS WEIGHT IN GLAZE THE NEXT DAY.
SO MALLOS...
IS CHEATING THEM. YES.
THAT GUY'S SO MUCH BIGGER...
YES.

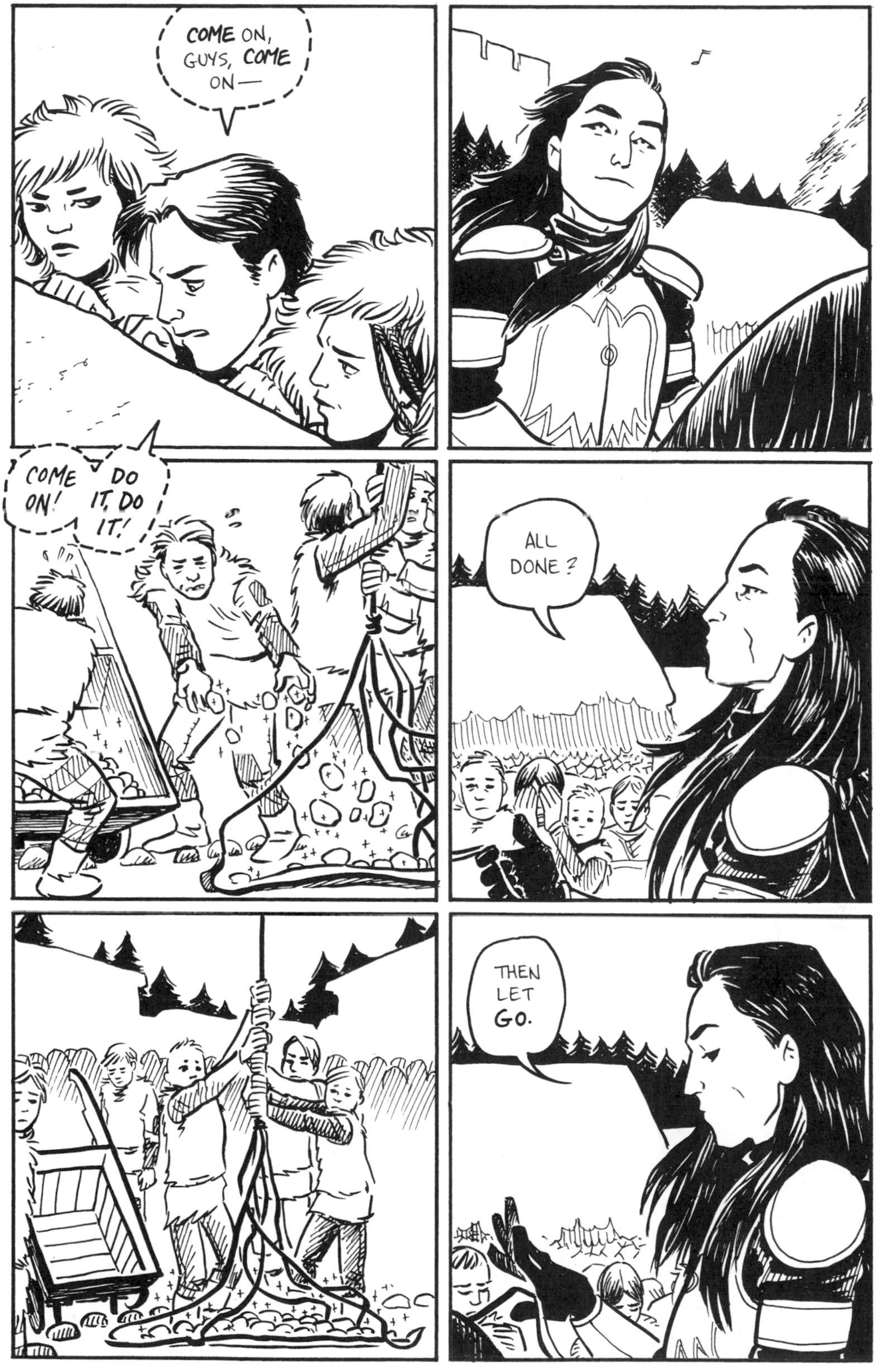
COME ON, GUYS, COME ON—
COME ON!
DO IT, DO IT!
ALL DONE?
THEN LET GO.

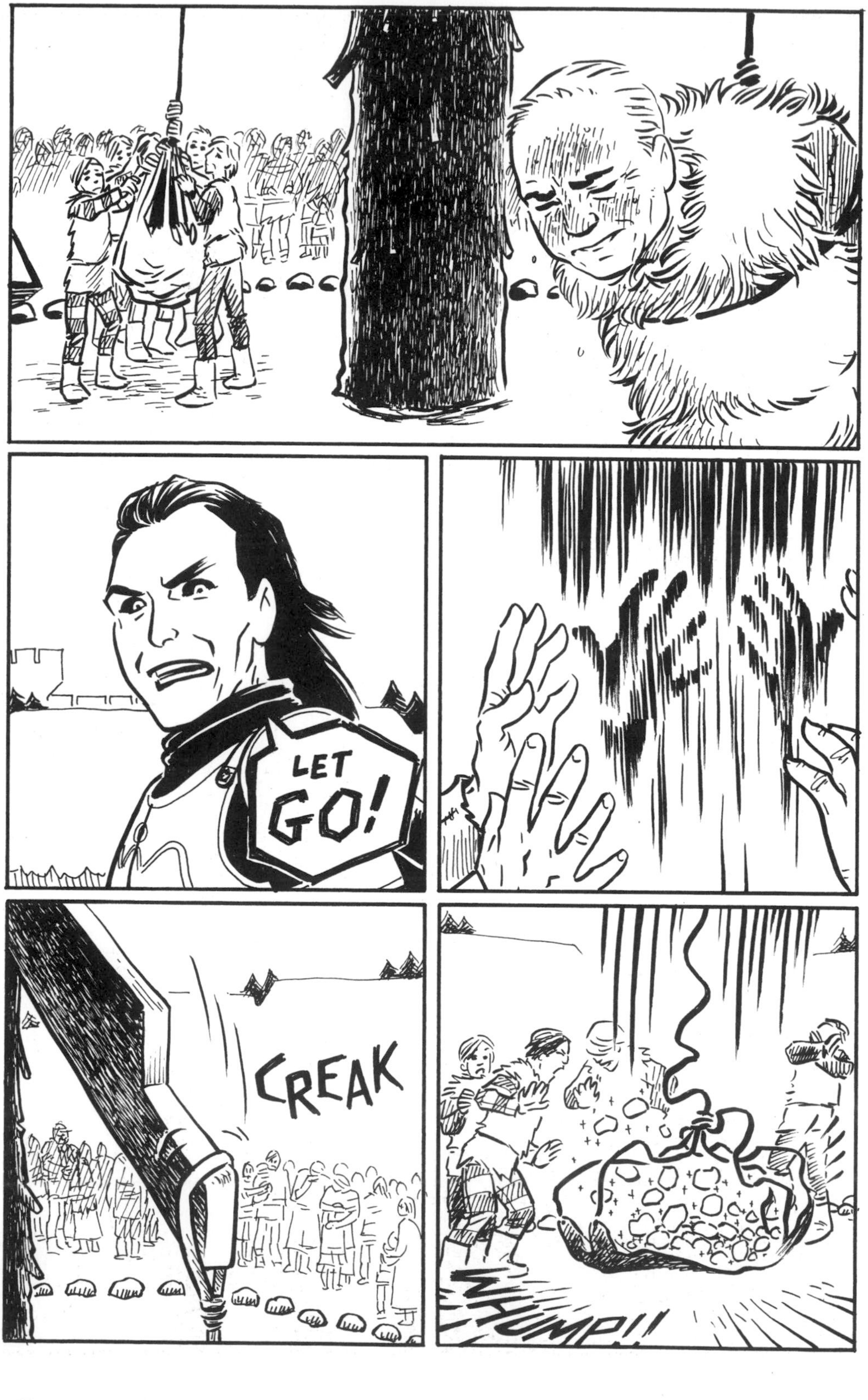
LET GO!
CREAK
WHUMP!!

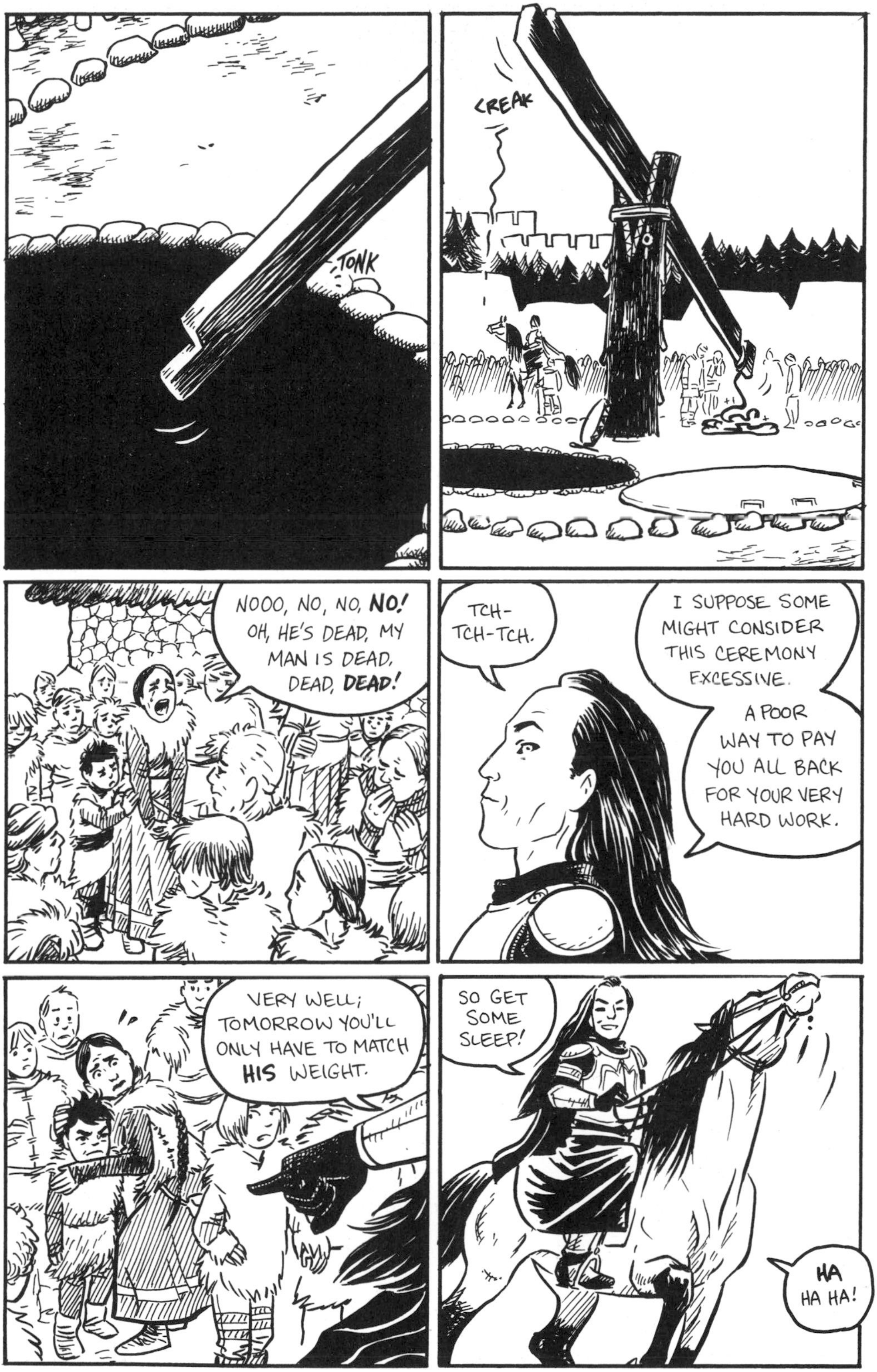
TONK
CREAK
NOOO, NO, NO, NO! OH, HE'S DEAD, MY MAN IS DEAD, DEAD, DEAD!
TCH-TCH-TCH.
I SUPPOSE SOME MIGHT CONSIDER THIS CEREMONY EXCESSIVE.
A POOR WAY TO PAY YOU ALL BACK FOR YOUR VERY HARD WORK.
VERY WELL; TOMORROW YOU'LL ONLY HAVE TO MATCH HIS WEIGHT.
SO GET SOME SLEEP!
HA HA HA!

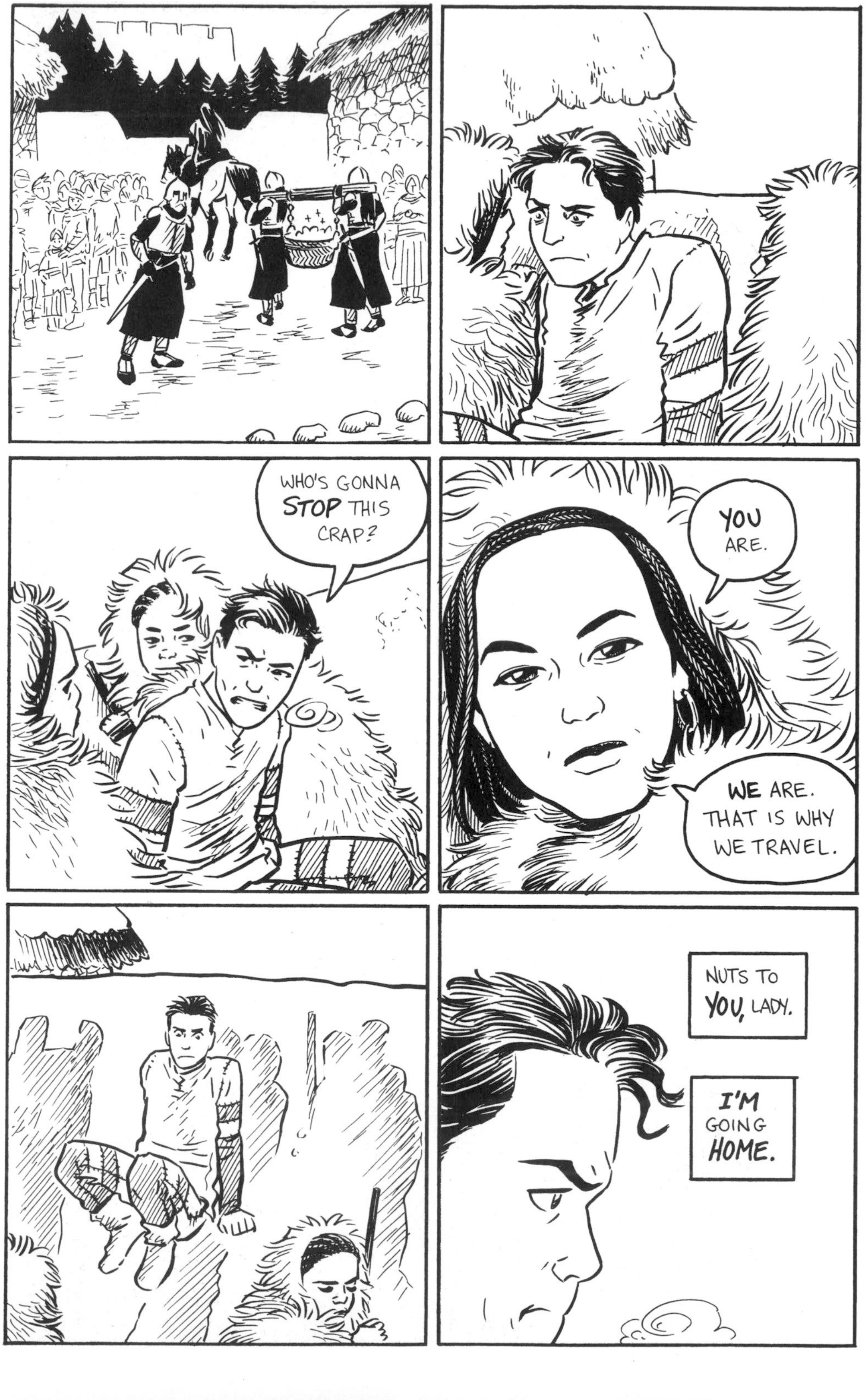
WHO'S GONNA STOP THIS CRAP?
YOU ARE.
WE ARE. THAT IS WHY WE TRAVEL.
NUTS TO YOU, LADY.
I'M GOING HOME.

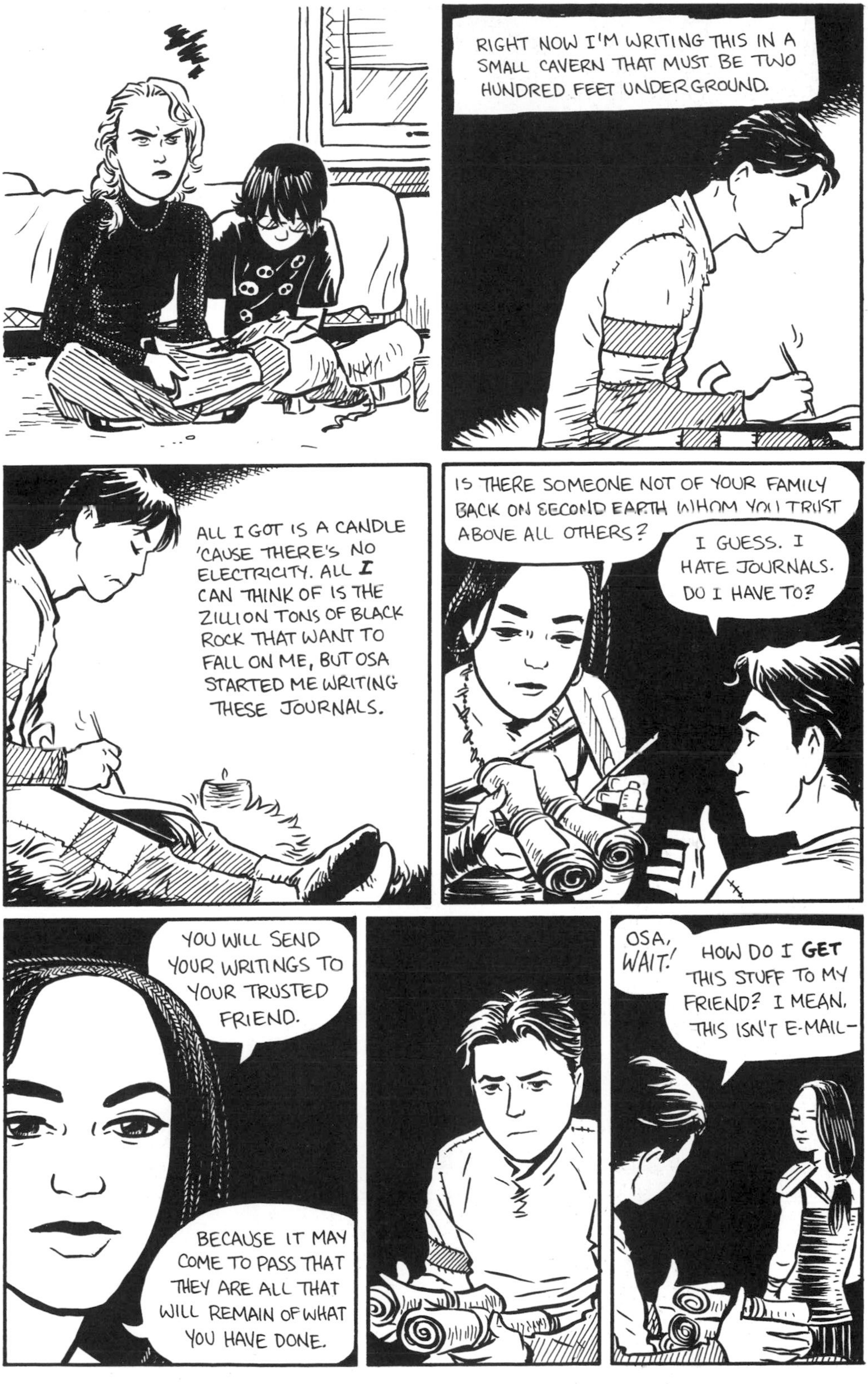
RIGHT NOW I'M WRITING THIS IN A SMALL CAVERN THAT MUST BE TWO HUNDRED FEET UNDERGROUND.
ALL I GOT IS A CANDLE 'CAUSE THERE'S NO ELECTRICITY. ALL I CAN THINK OF IS THE ZILLION TONS OF BLACK ROCK THAT WANT TO FALL ON ME, BUT OSA STARTED ME WRITING THESE JOURNALS.
IS THERE SOMEONE NOT OF YOUR FAMILY BACK ON SECOND EARTH WHOM YOU TRUST ABOVE ALL OTHERS?
I GUESS. I HATE JOURNALS. DO I HAVE TO?
YOU WILL SEND YOUR WRITINGS TO YOUR TRUSTED FRIEND.
BECAUSE IT MAY COME TO PASS THAT THEY ARE ALL THAT WILL REMAIN OF WHAT YOU HAVE DONE.
OSA, WAIT!
HOW DO I GET THIS STUFF TO MY FRIEND? I MEAN, THIS ISN'T E-MAIL—

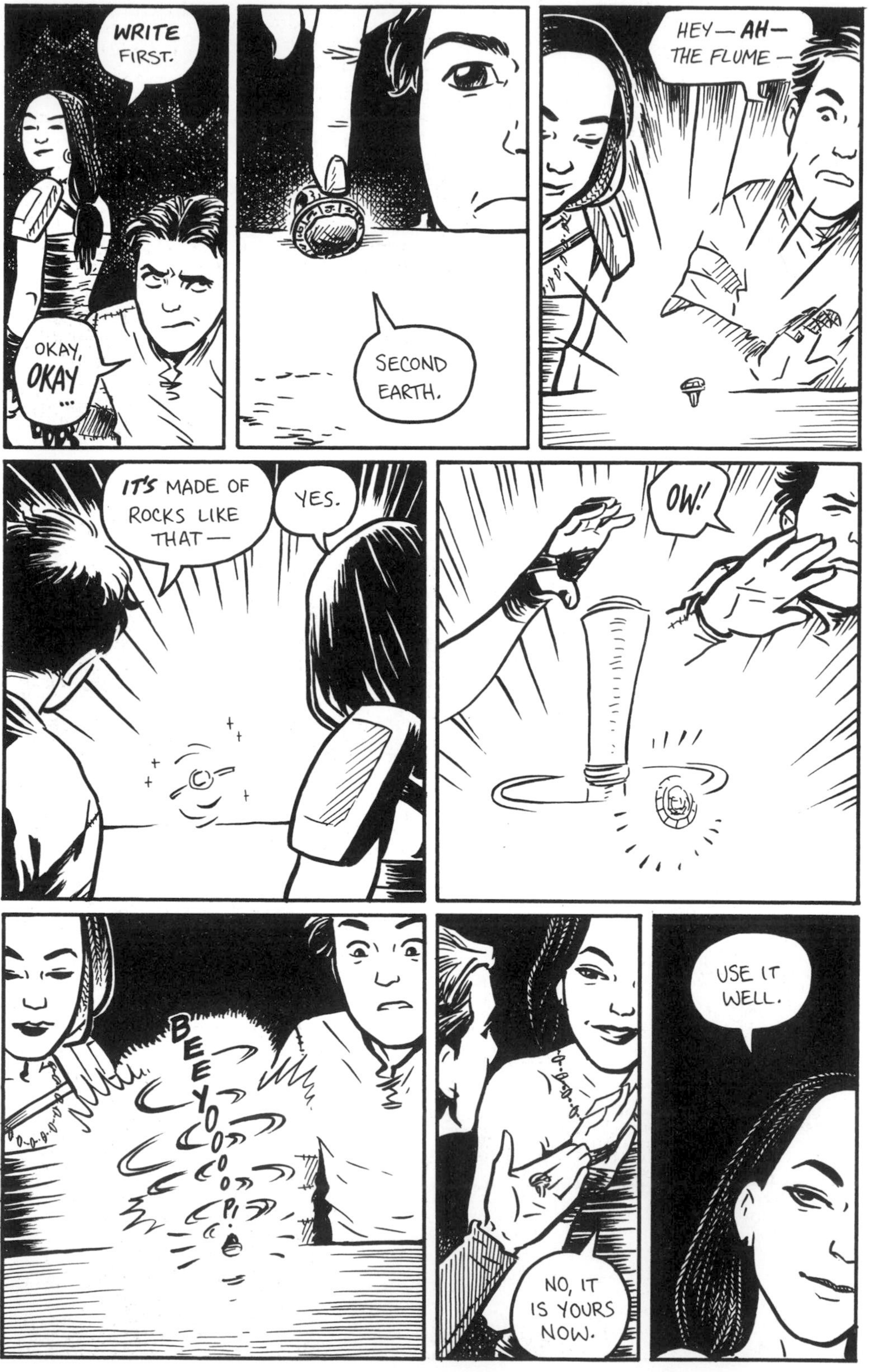
WRITE FIRST.
OKAY, OKAY ...
SECOND EARTH.
HEY— AH— THE FLUME—
IT'S MADE OF ROCKS LIKE THAT—
YES.
OW!
BEEYOOOOOOOP!
NO, IT IS YOURS NOW.
USE IT WELL.

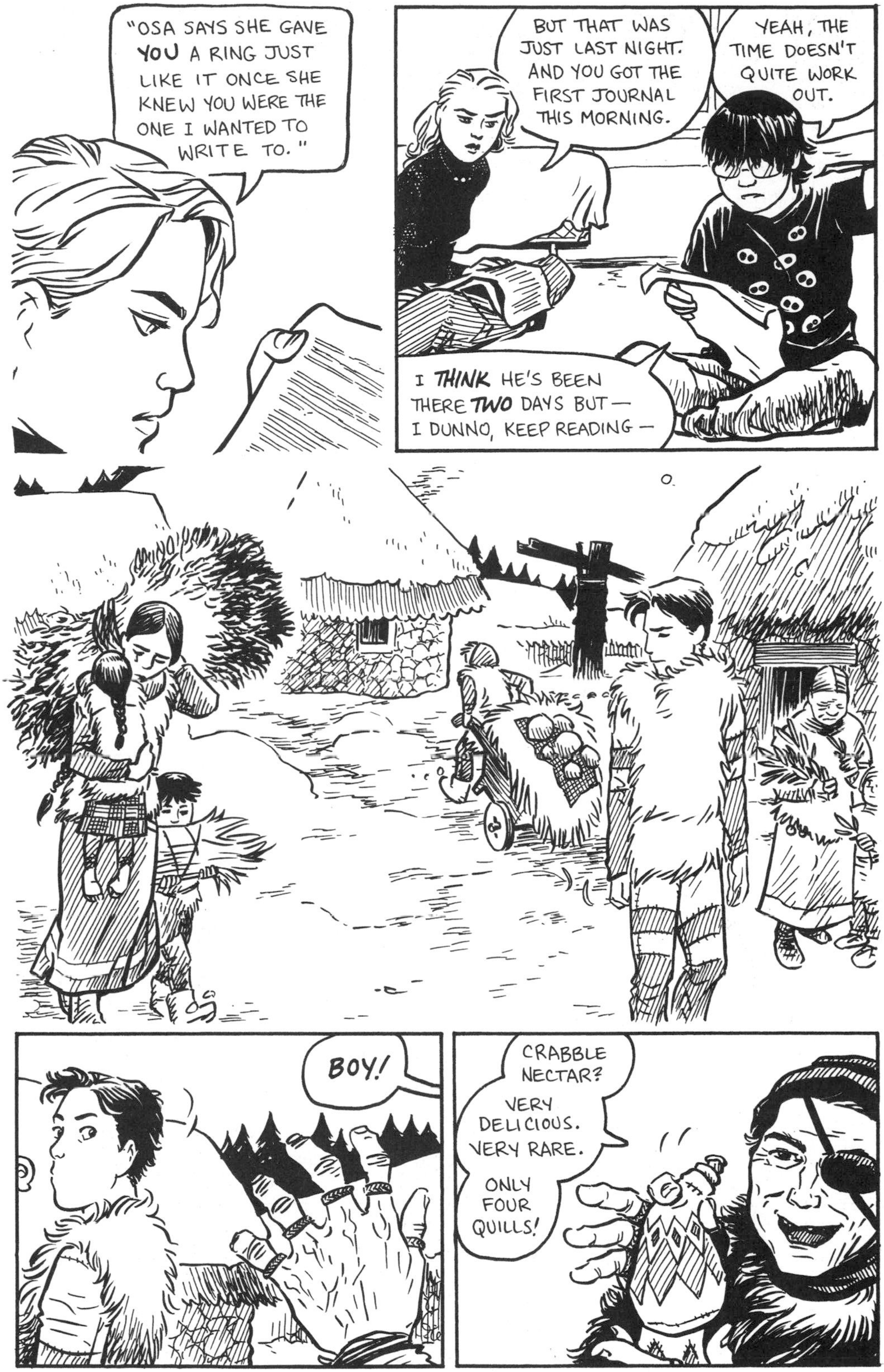
"OSA SAYS SHE GAVE YOU A RING JUST LIKE IT ONCE SHE KNEW YOU WERE THE ONE I WANTED TO WRITE TO."
BUT THAT WAS JUST LAST NIGHT. AND YOU GOT THE FIRST JOURNAL THIS MORNING.
YEAH, THE TIME DOESN'T QUITE WORK OUT.
I THINK HE'S BEEN THERE TWO DAYS BUT— I DUNNO, KEEP READING—
BOY!
CRABBLE NECTAR?
VERY DELICIOUS. VERY RARE.
ONLY FOUR QUILLS!

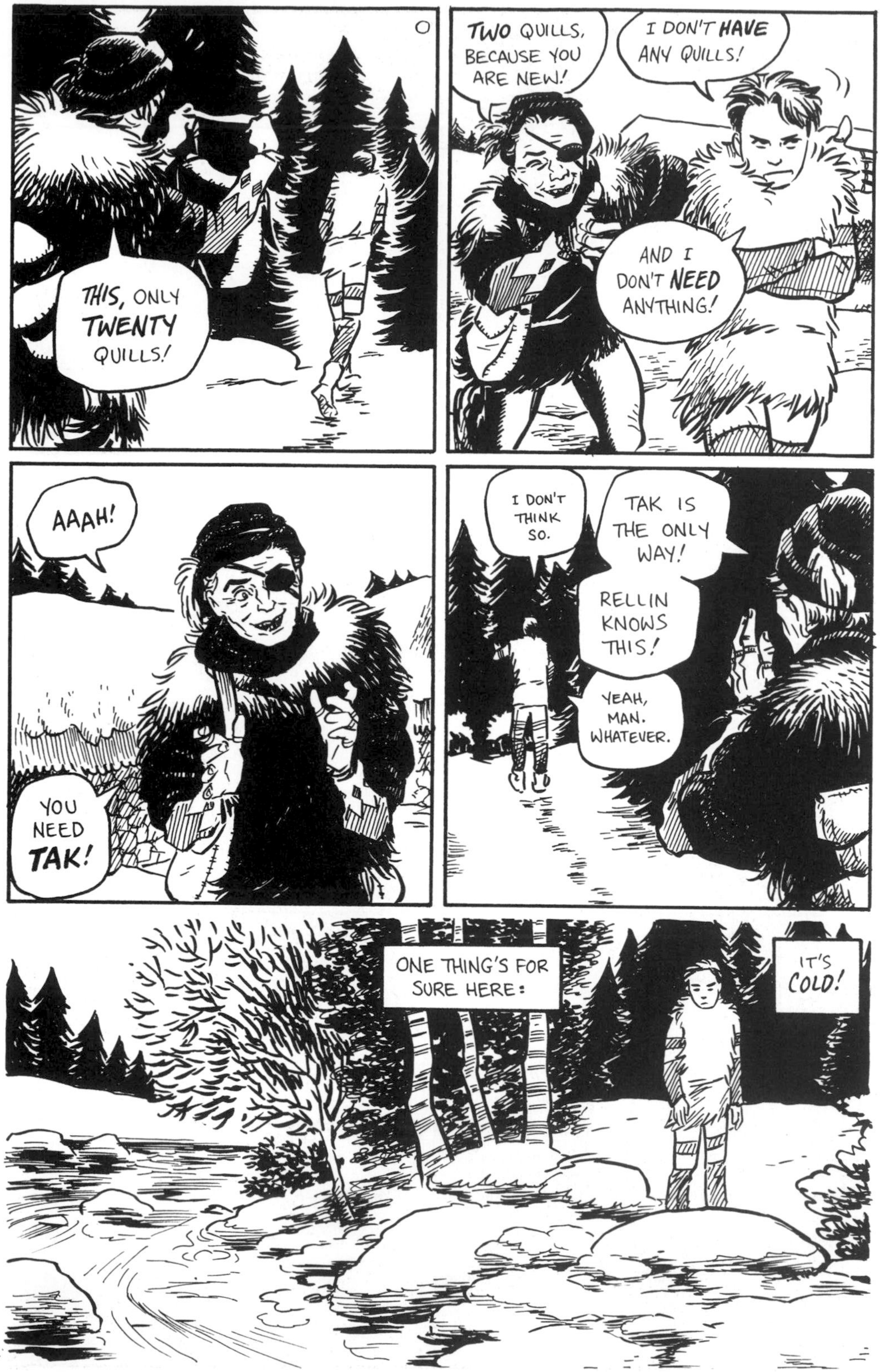
THIS, ONLY TWENTY QUILLS!
TWO QUILLS, BECAUSE YOU ARE NEW!
I DON'T HAVE ANY QUILLS!
AND I DON'T NEED ANYTHING!
AAAH!
YOU NEED TAK!
I DON'T THINK SO.
TAK IS THE ONLY WAY!
RELLIN KNOWS THIS!
YEAH, MAN. WHATEVER.
ONE THING'S FOR SURE HERE:
IT'S COLD!

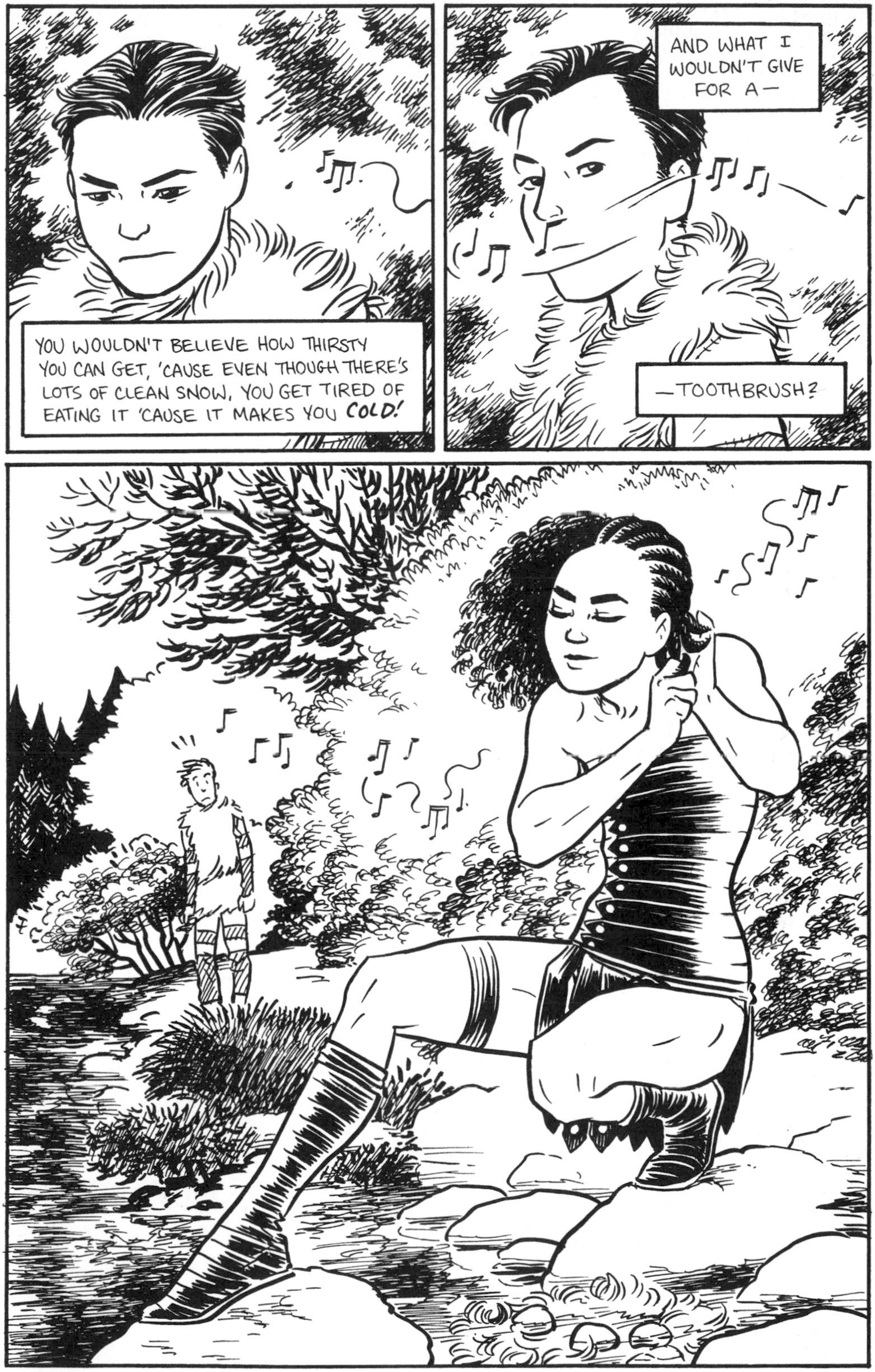
YOU WOULDN'T BELIEVE HOW THIRSTY YOU CAN GET, 'CAUSE EVEN THOUGH THERE'S LOTS OF CLEAN SNOW, YOU GET TIRED OF EATING IT 'CAUSE IT MAKES YOU COLD!
AND WHAT I WOULDN'T GIVE FOR A—
—TOOTHBRUSH?

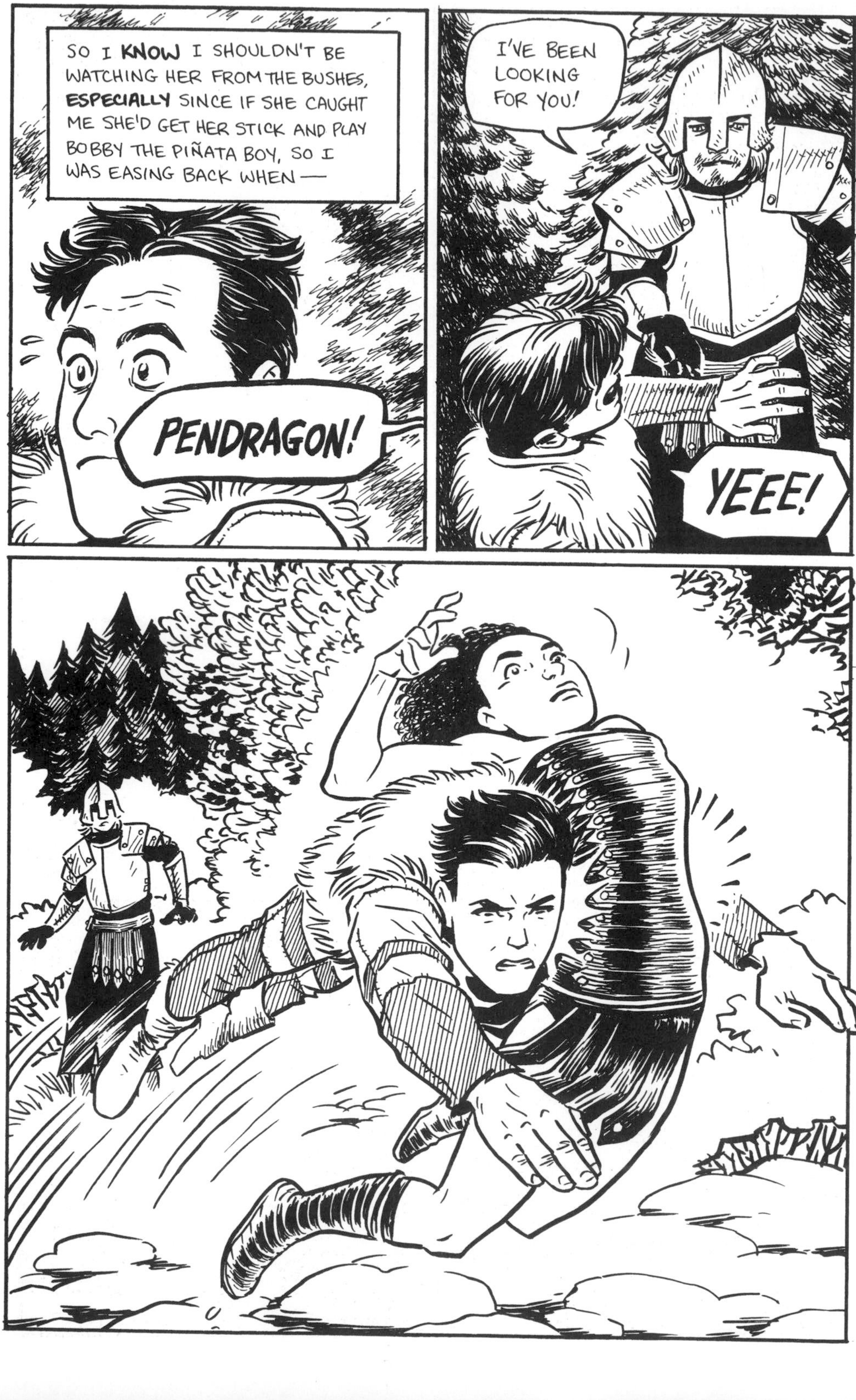
SO I **KNOW** I SHOULDN'T BE WATCHING HER FROM THE BUSHES, **ESPECIALLY** SINCE IF SHE CAUGHT ME SHE'D GET HER STICK AND PLAY BOBBY THE PIÑATA BOY, SO I WAS EASING BACK WHEN —
PENDRAGON!
I'VE BEEN LOOKING FOR YOU!
YEEE!

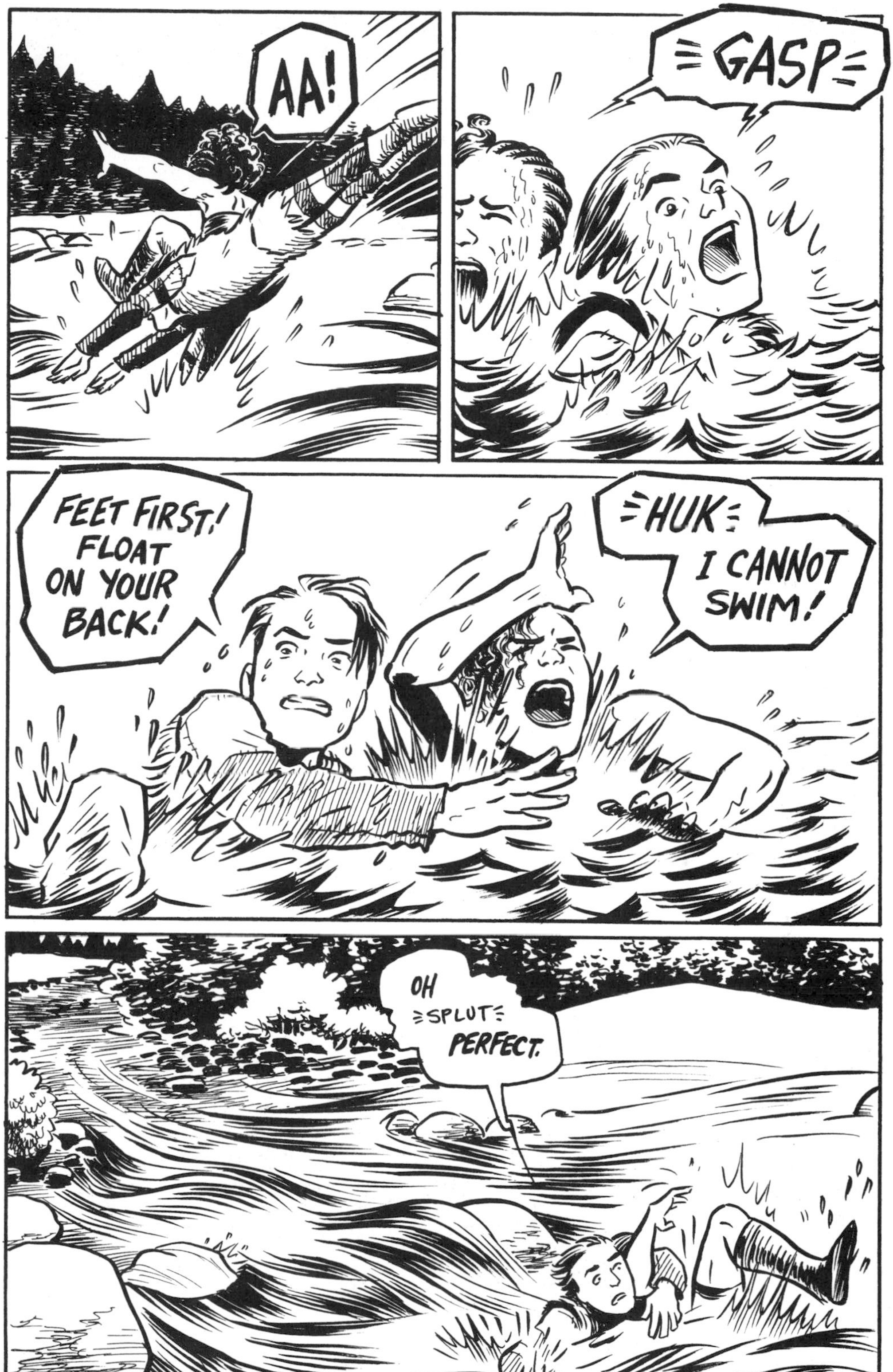
AA!
GASP
FEET FIRST! FLOAT ON YOUR BACK!
HUK I CANNOT SWIM!
OH SPLUT PERFECT.

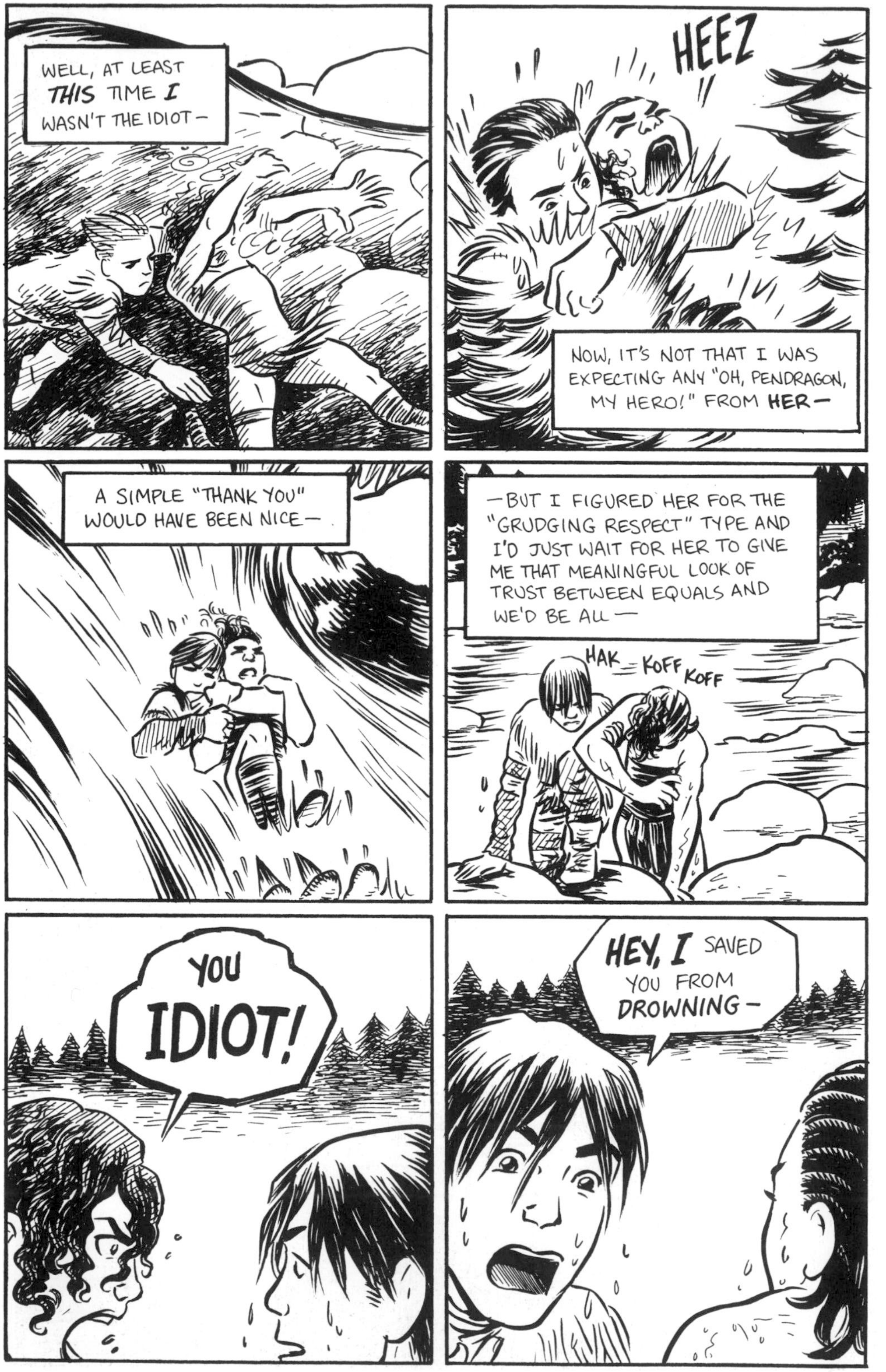
WELL, AT LEAST THIS TIME I WASN'T THE IDIOT—
HEEZ
NOW, IT'S NOT THAT I WAS EXPECTING ANY "OH, PENDRAGON, MY HERO!" FROM HER—
A SIMPLE "THANK YOU" WOULD HAVE BEEN NICE—
—BUT I FIGURED HER FOR THE "GRUDGING RESPECT" TYPE AND I'D JUST WAIT FOR HER TO GIVE ME THAT MEANINGFUL LOOK OF TRUST BETWEEN EQUALS AND WE'D BE ALL—
HAK—KOFF KOFF
YOU IDIOT!
HEY, I SAVED YOU FROM DROWNING—

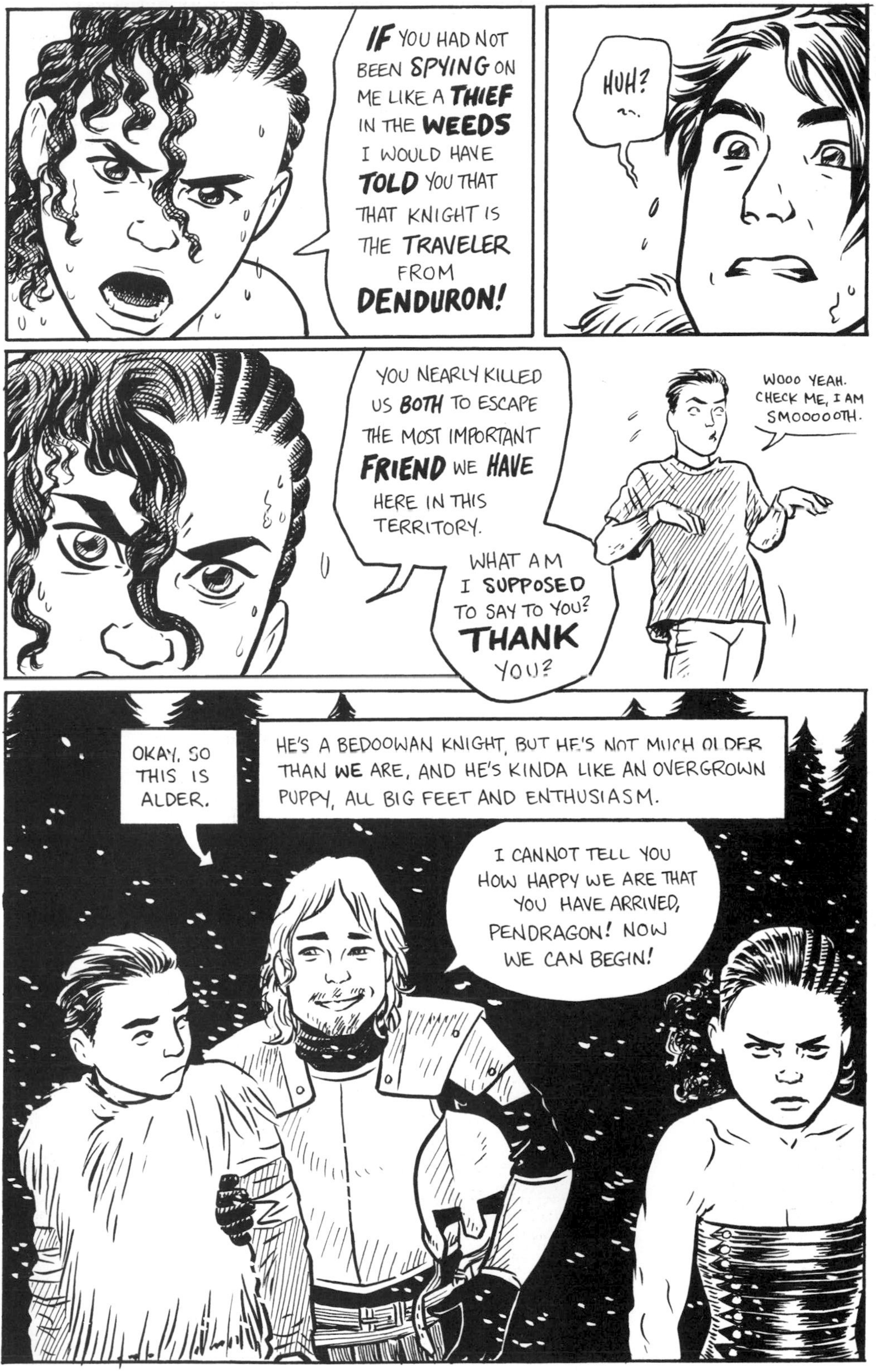
IF YOU HAD NOT BEEN SPYING ON ME LIKE A THIEF IN THE WEEDS I WOULD HAVE TOLD YOU THAT THAT KNIGHT IS THE TRAVELER FROM DENDURON!
HUH?
YOU NEARLY KILLED US BOTH TO ESCAPE THE MOST IMPORTANT FRIEND WE HAVE HERE IN THIS TERRITORY.
WHAT AM I SUPPOSED TO SAY TO YOU? THANK YOU?
WOOO YEAH. CHECK ME, I AM SMOOOOOTH.
OKAY, SO THIS IS ALDER.
HE'S A BEDOOWAN KNIGHT, BUT HE'S NOT MUCH OLDER THAN WE ARE, AND HE'S KINDA LIKE AN OVERGROWN PUPPY, ALL BIG FEET AND ENTHUSIASM.
I CANNOT TELL YOU HOW HAPPY WE ARE THAT YOU HAVE ARRIVED, PENDRAGON! NOW WE CAN BEGIN!

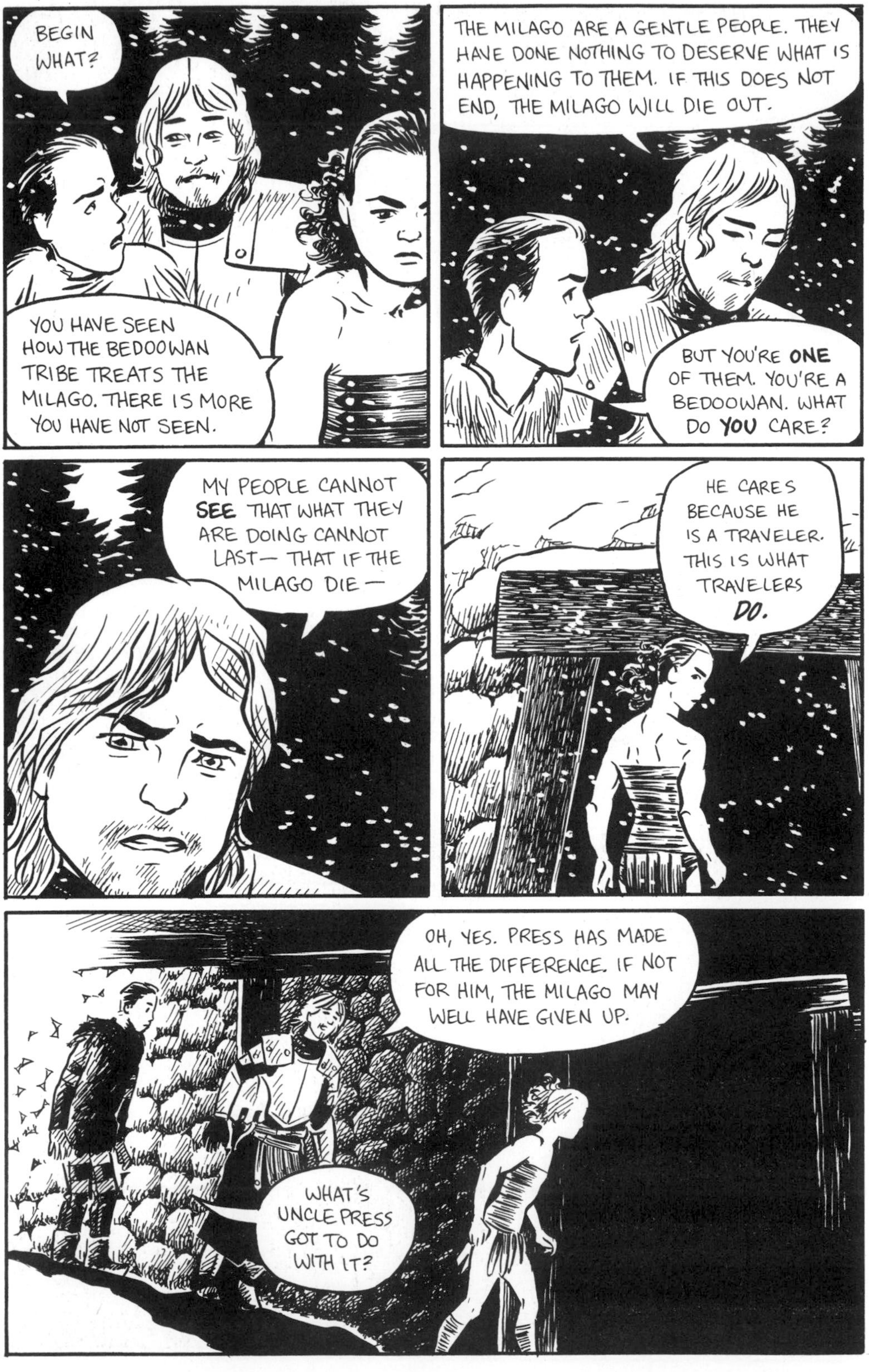
BEGIN WHAT?
YOU HAVE SEEN HOW THE BEDOOWAN TRIBE TREATS THE MILAGO. THERE IS MORE YOU HAVE NOT SEEN.
THE MILAGO ARE A GENTLE PEOPLE. THEY HAVE DONE NOTHING TO DESERVE WHAT IS HAPPENING TO THEM. IF THIS DOES NOT END, THE MILAGO WILL DIE OUT.
BUT YOU'RE ONE OF THEM. YOU'RE A BEDOOWAN. WHAT DO YOU CARE?
MY PEOPLE CANNOT SEE THAT WHAT THEY ARE DOING CANNOT LAST— THAT IF THE MILAGO DIE—
HE CARES BECAUSE HE IS A TRAVELER. THIS IS WHAT TRAVELERS DO.
OH, YES. PRESS HAS MADE ALL THE DIFFERENCE. IF NOT FOR HIM, THE MILAGO MAY WELL HAVE GIVEN UP.
WHAT'S UNCLE PRESS GOT TO DO WITH IT?

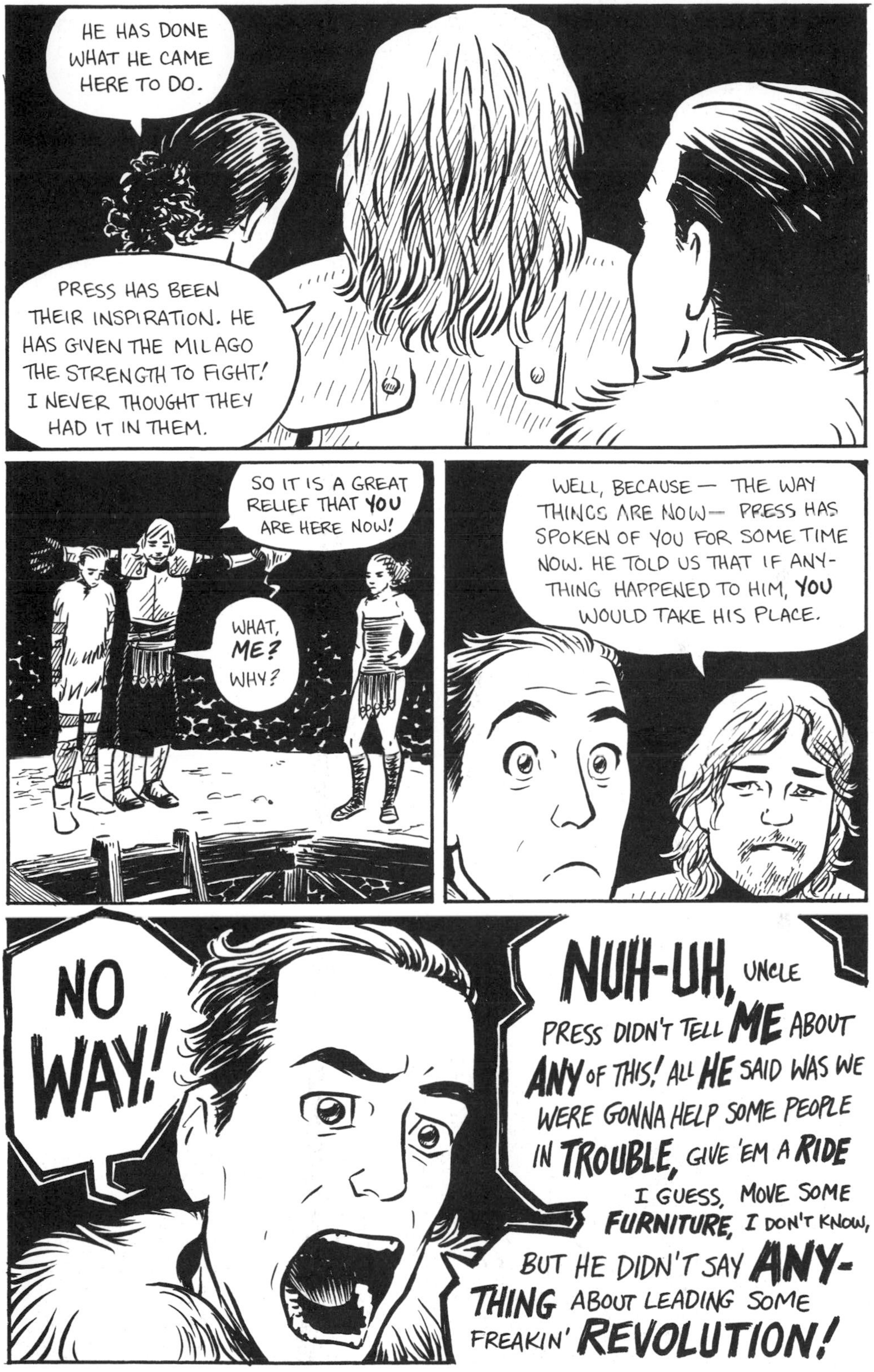
HE HAS DONE WHAT HE CAME HERE TO DO.
PRESS HAS BEEN THEIR INSPIRATION. HE HAS GIVEN THE MILAGO THE STRENGTH TO FIGHT! I NEVER THOUGHT THEY HAD IT IN THEM.
SO IT IS A GREAT RELIEF THAT YOU ARE HERE NOW!
WHAT, ME? WHY?
WELL, BECAUSE— THE WAY THINGS ARE NOW— PRESS HAS SPOKEN OF YOU FOR SOME TIME NOW. HE TOLD US THAT IF ANY-THING HAPPENED TO HIM, YOU WOULD TAKE HIS PLACE.
NO WAY!
NUH-UH, UNCLE PRESS DIDN'T TELL ME ABOUT ANY OF THIS! ALL HE SAID WAS WE WERE GONNA HELP SOME PEOPLE IN TROUBLE, GIVE 'EM A RIDE I GUESS, MOVE SOME FURNITURE, I DON'T KNOW, BUT HE DIDN'T SAY ANY-THING ABOUT LEADING SOME FREAKIN' REVOLUTION!

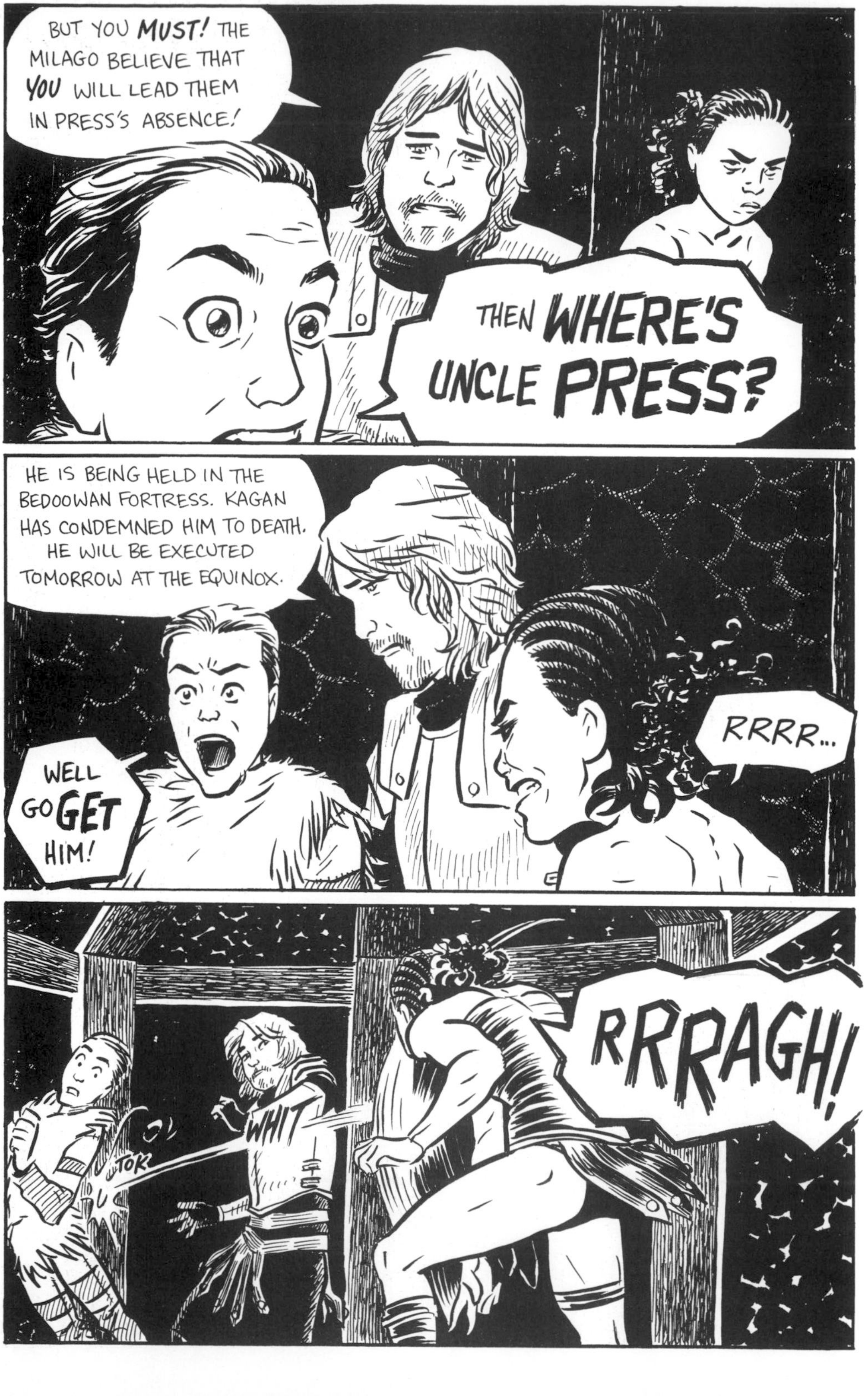
BUT YOU MUST! THE MILAGO BELIEVE THAT YOU WILL LEAD THEM IN PRESS'S ABSENCE!
THEN WHERE'S UNCLE PRESS?
HE IS BEING HELD IN THE BEDOOWAN FORTRESS. KAGAN HAS CONDEMNED HIM TO DEATH. HE WILL BE EXECUTED TOMORROW AT THE EQUINOX.
WELL GO GET HIM!
RRRR...
RRRAGH!
WHIT
TOK

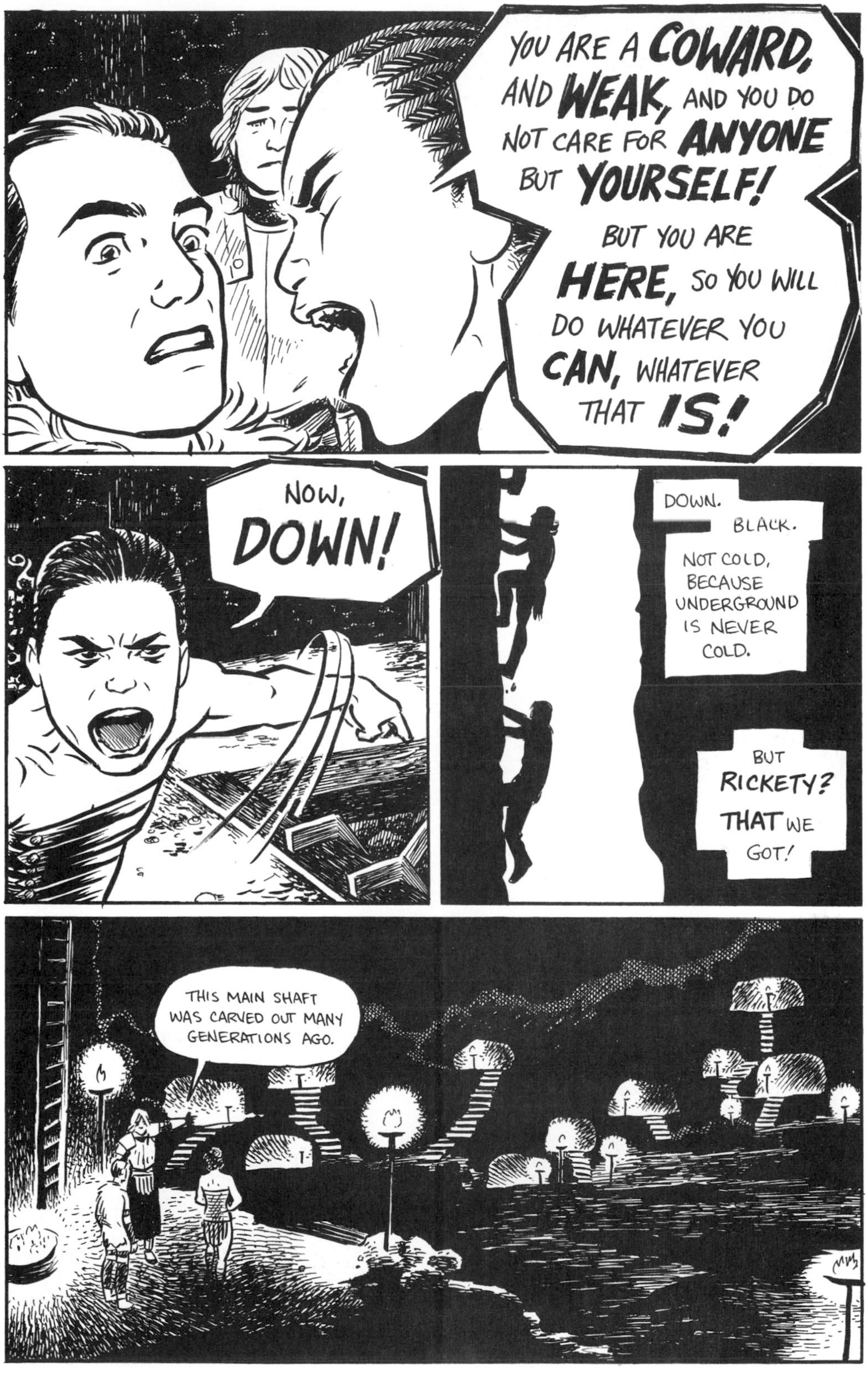
YOU ARE A COWARD, AND WEAK, AND YOU DO NOT CARE FOR ANYONE BUT YOURSELF! BUT YOU ARE HERE, SO YOU WILL DO WHATEVER YOU CAN, WHATEVER THAT IS!
NOW, DOWN!
DOWN.
BLACK.
NOT COLD, BECAUSE UNDERGROUND IS NEVER COLD.
BUT RICKETY? THAT WE GOT!
THIS MAIN SHAFT WAS CARVED OUT MANY GENERATIONS AGO.

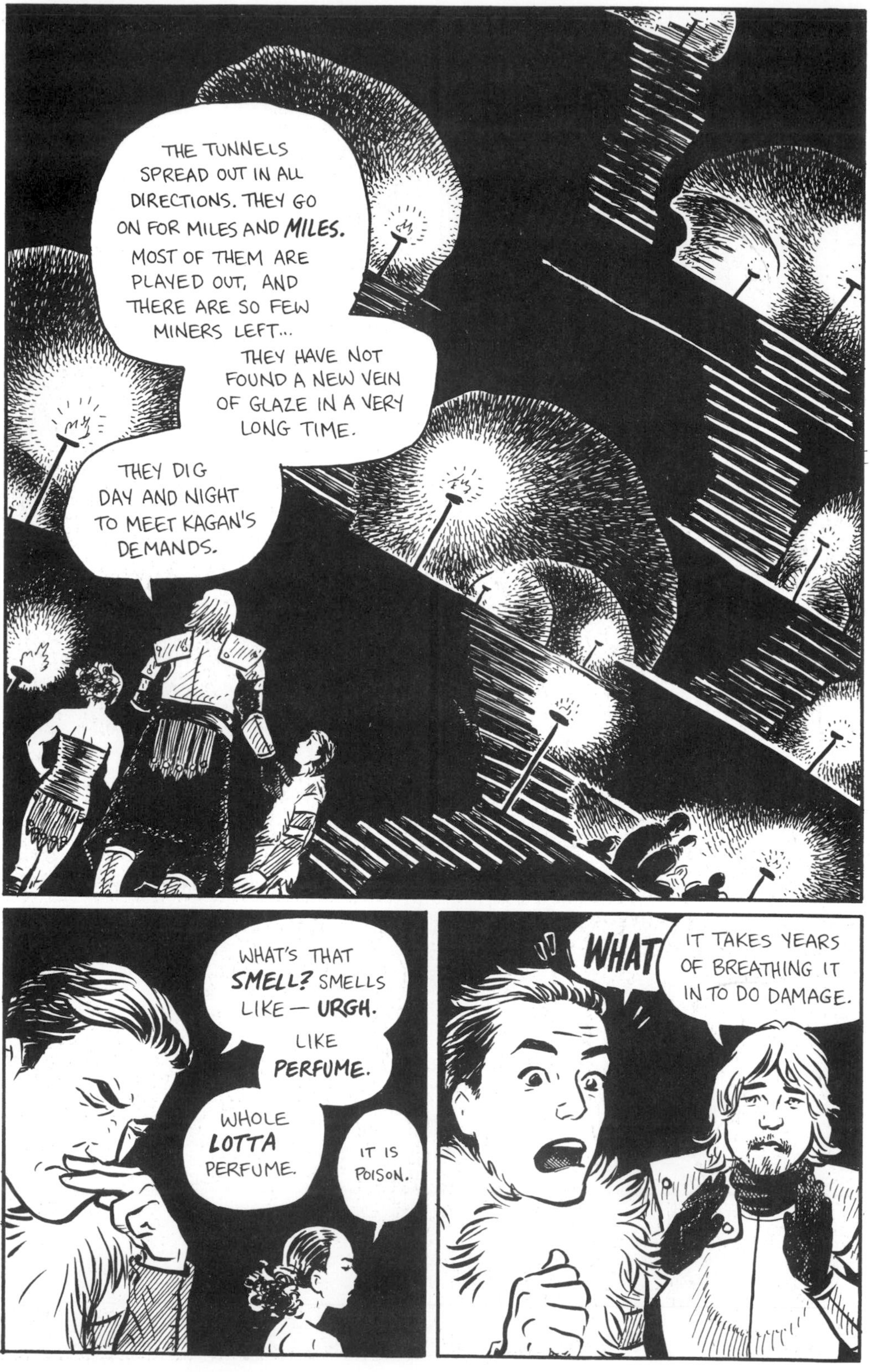
THE TUNNELS SPREAD OUT IN ALL DIRECTIONS. THEY GO ON FOR MILES AND MILES. MOST OF THEM ARE PLAYED OUT, AND THERE ARE SO FEW MINERS LEFT...
THEY HAVE NOT FOUND A NEW VEIN OF GLAZE IN A VERY LONG TIME.
THEY DIG DAY AND NIGHT TO MEET KAGAN'S DEMANDS.
WHAT'S THAT SMELL? SMELLS LIKE — URGH.
LIKE PERFUME.
WHOLE LOTTA PERFUME.
IT IS POISON.
WHAT
IT TAKES YEARS OF BREATHING IT IN TO DO DAMAGE.

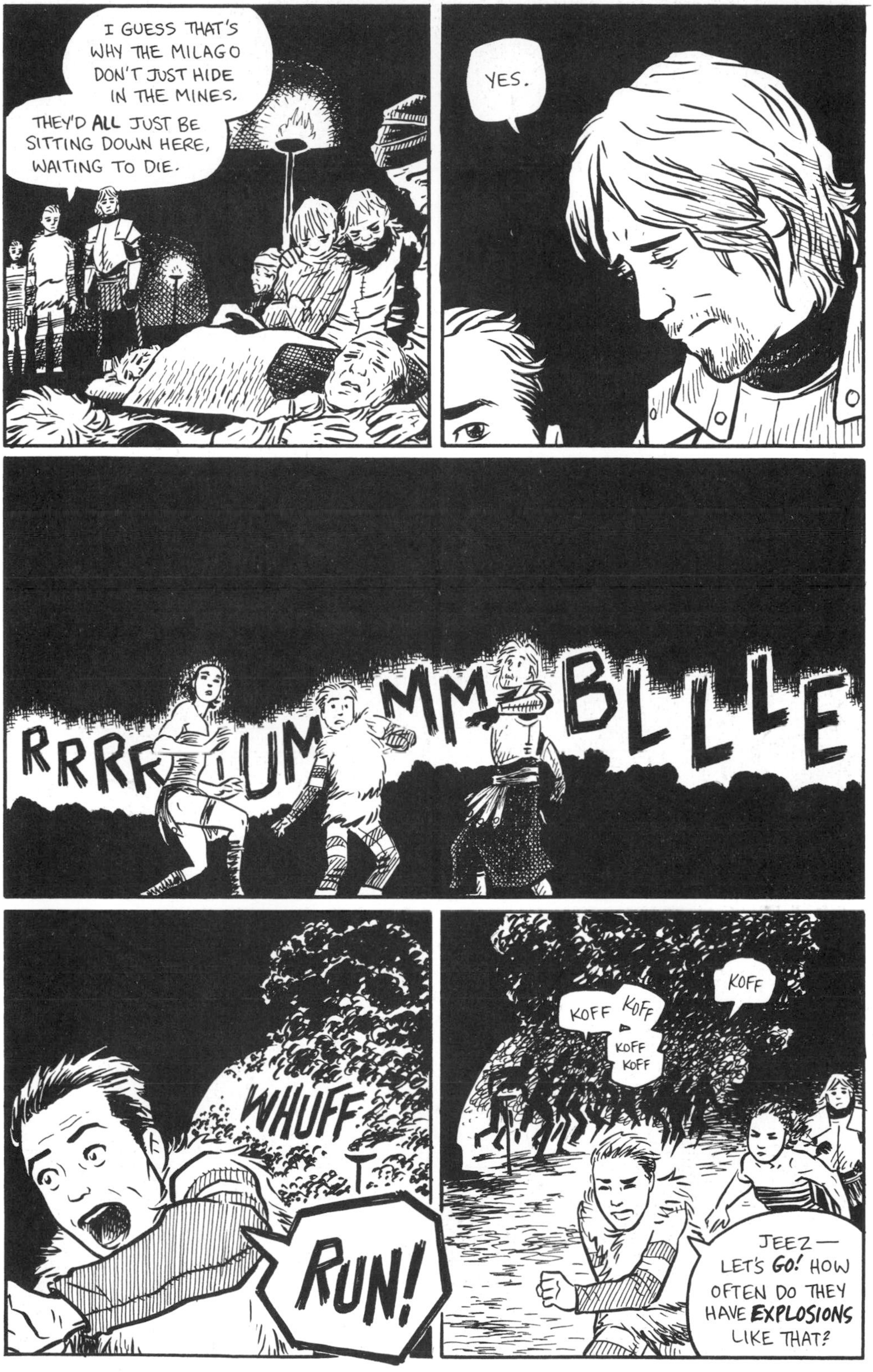
I GUESS THAT'S WHY THE MILAGO DON'T JUST HIDE IN THE MINES.
THEY'D **ALL** JUST BE SITTING DOWN HERE, WAITING TO DIE.
YES.
RRRRUMMMBLLLE
WHUFF
RUN!
KOFF
KOFF KOFF
KOFF KOFF
KOFF
JEEZ— LET'S **GO!** HOW OFTEN DO THEY HAVE **EXPLOSIONS** LIKE THAT?

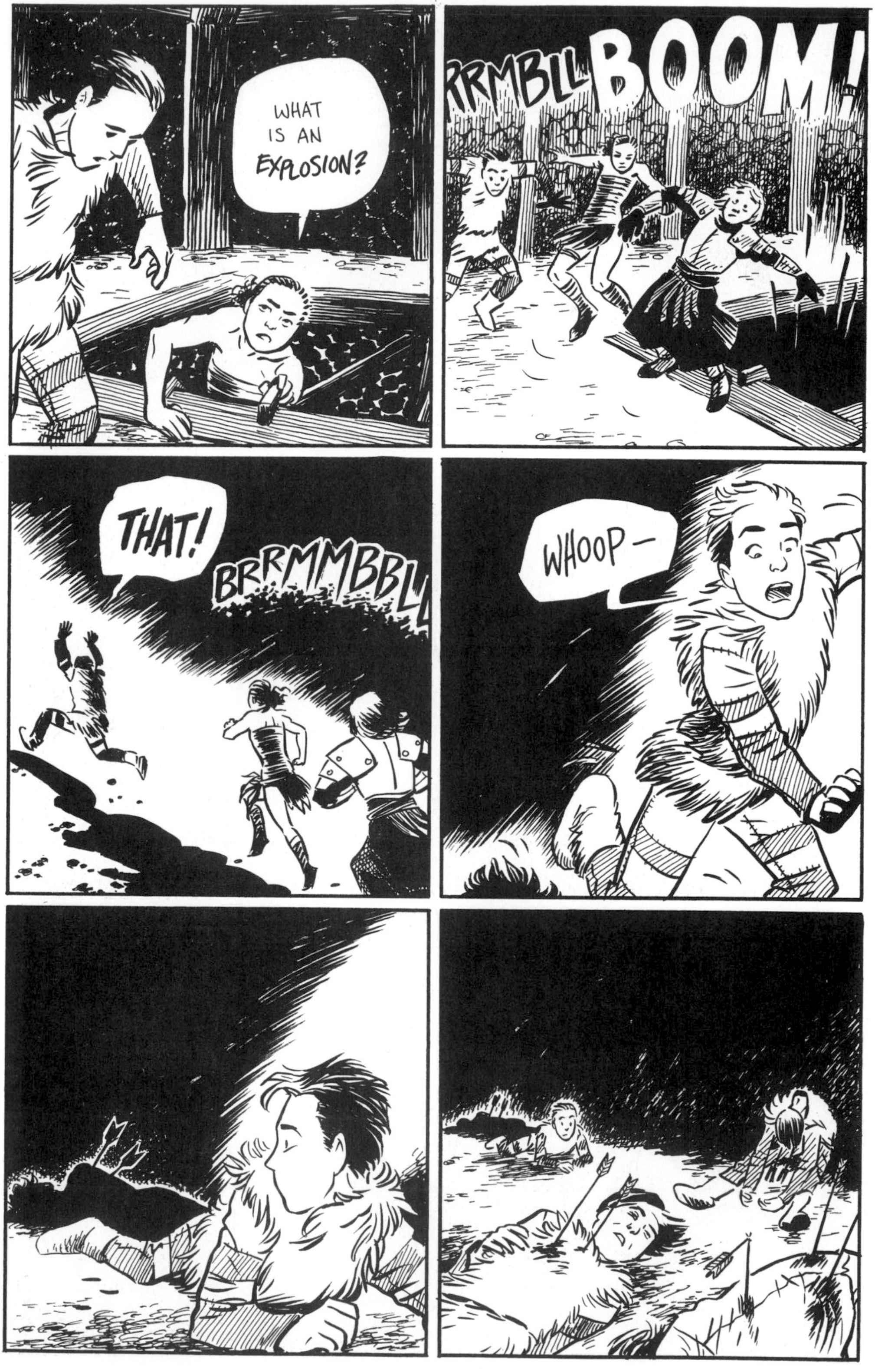
WHAT IS AN EXPLOSION?
RRMBLLL BOOM!
THAT!
BRRMMBBLL
WHOOP–

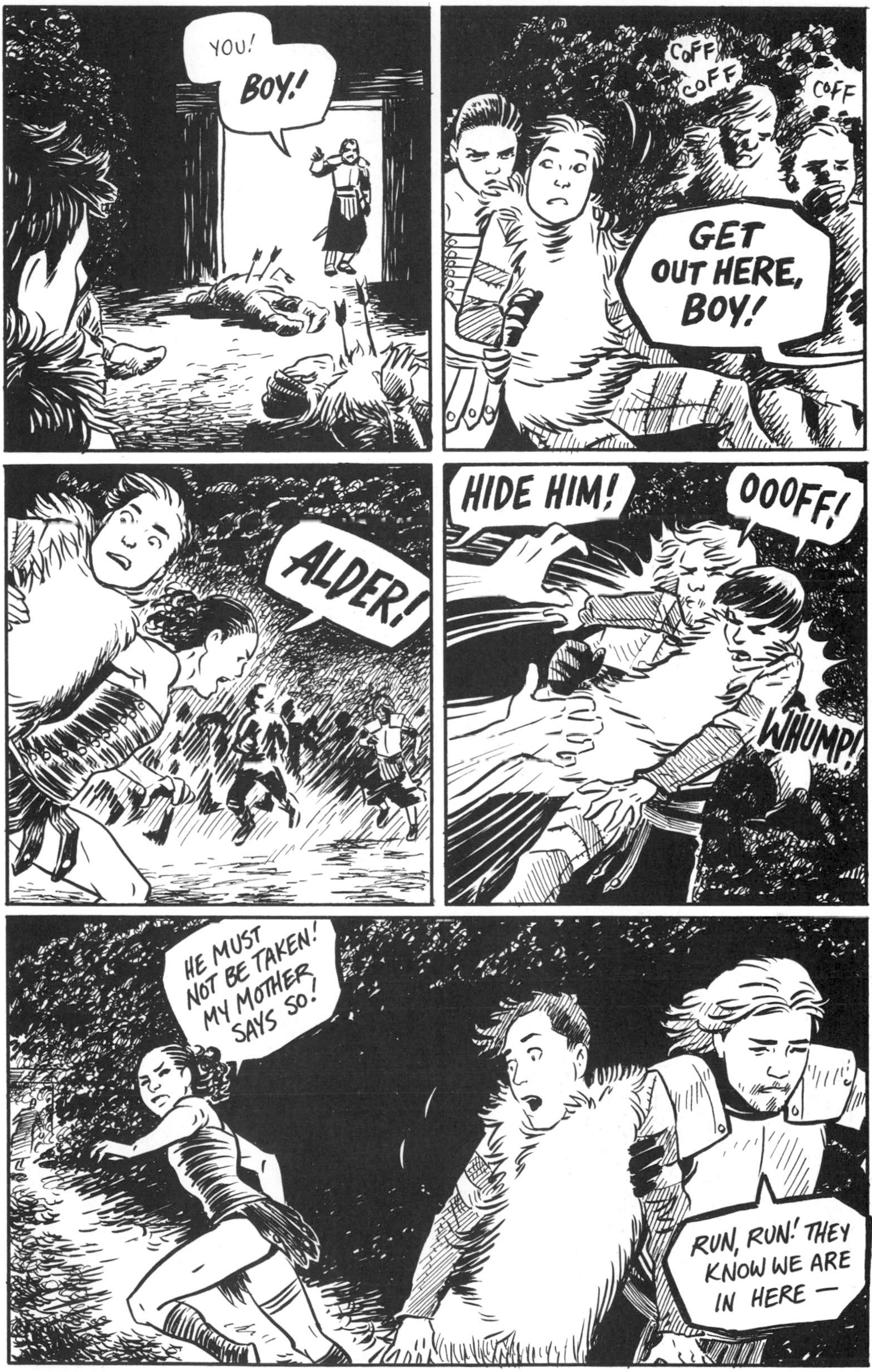
YOU!
BOY!
COFF
COFF
COFF
GET OUT HERE, BOY!
ALDER!
HIDE HIM!
OOOFF!
WHUMP!
HE MUST NOT BE TAKEN! MY MOTHER SAYS SO!
RUN, RUN! THEY KNOW WE ARE IN HERE —

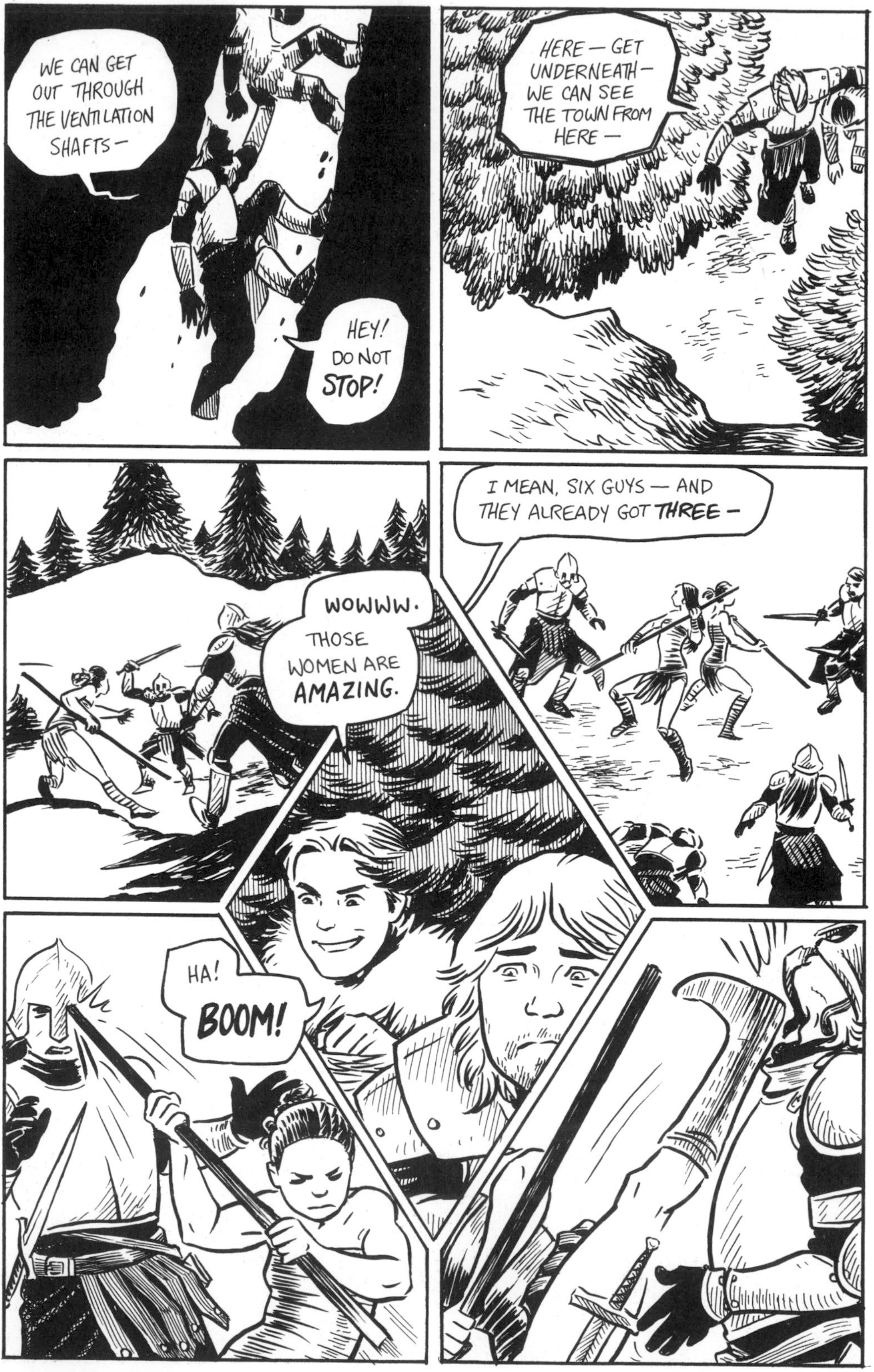
WE CAN GET OUT THROUGH THE VENTILATION SHAFTS—
HEY! DO NOT STOP!
HERE—GET UNDERNEATH—WE CAN SEE THE TOWN FROM HERE—
WOWWW. THOSE WOMEN ARE AMAZING.
I MEAN, SIX GUYS—AND THEY ALREADY GOT THREE—
HA! BOOM!

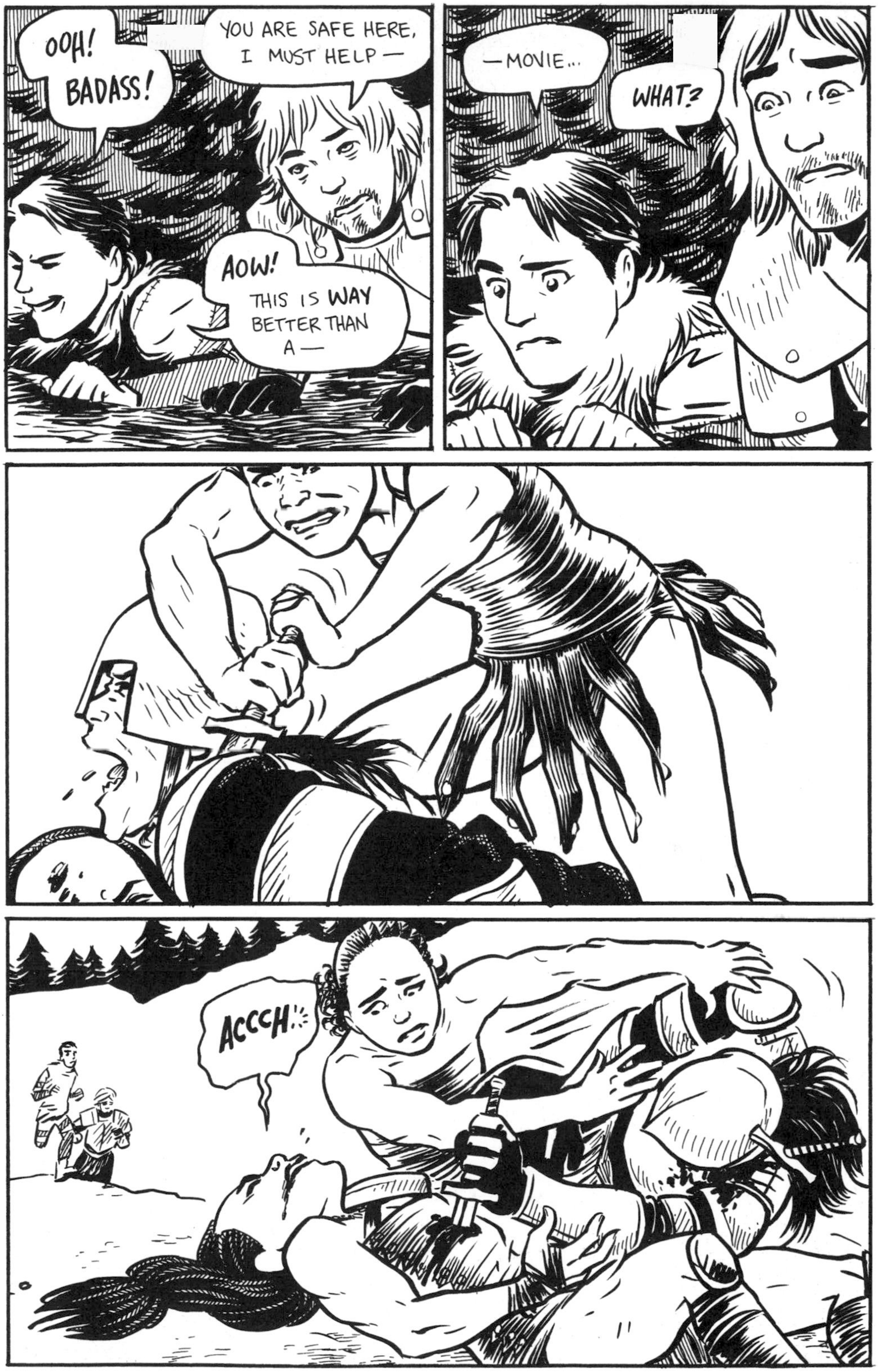
OOH! BADASS!
YOU ARE SAFE HERE, I MUST HELP—
AOW! THIS IS WAY BETTER THAN A—
—MOVIE...
WHAT?
ACCCH!

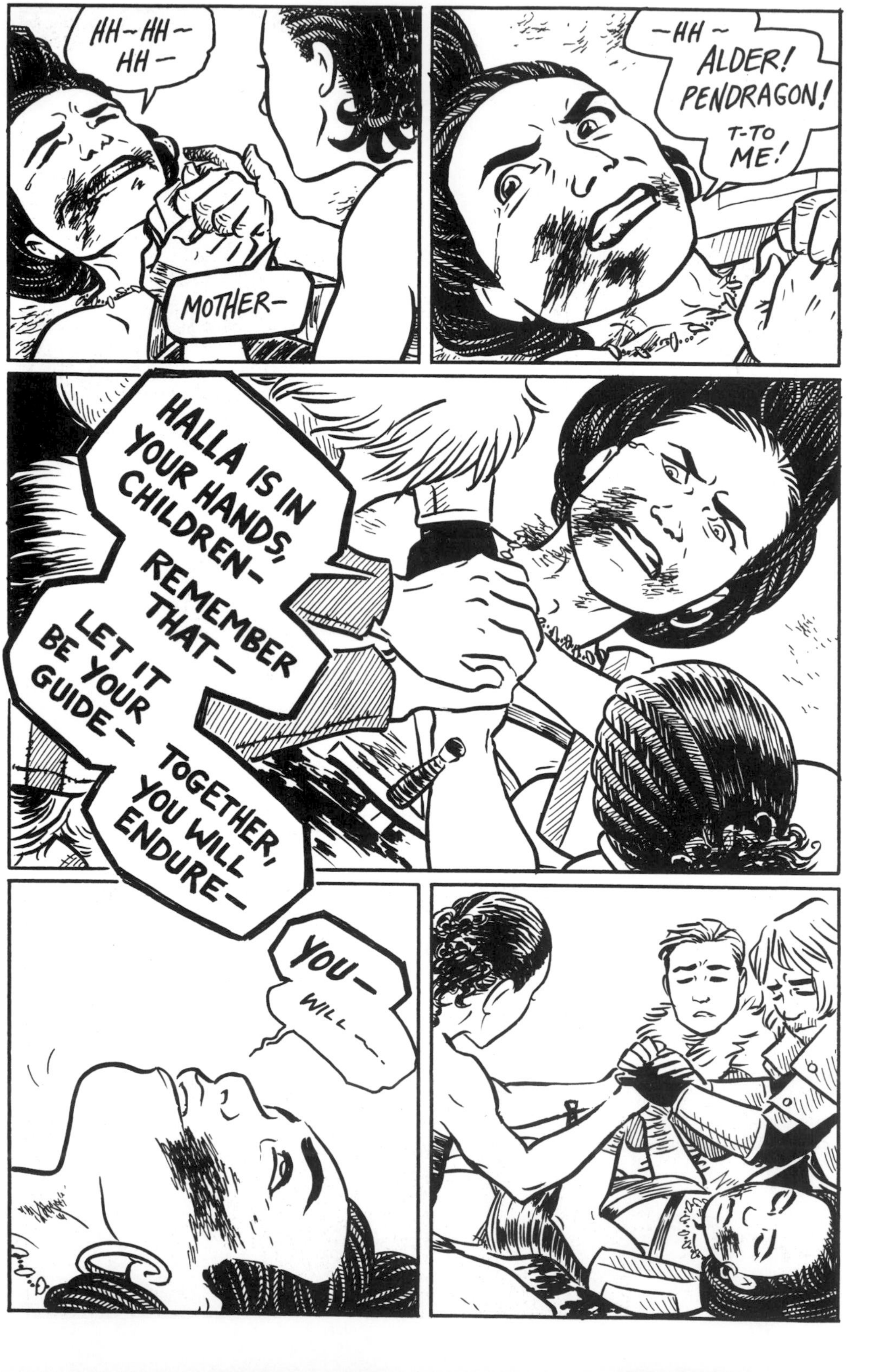
HH~HH~ HH~
MOTHER-
-HH~ ALDER! PENDRAGON!
T-TO ME!
HALLA IS IN YOUR HANDS, CHILDREN-
REMEMBER THAT-
LET IT BE YOUR GUIDE-
TOGETHER, YOU WILL ENDURE-
YOU-
WILL

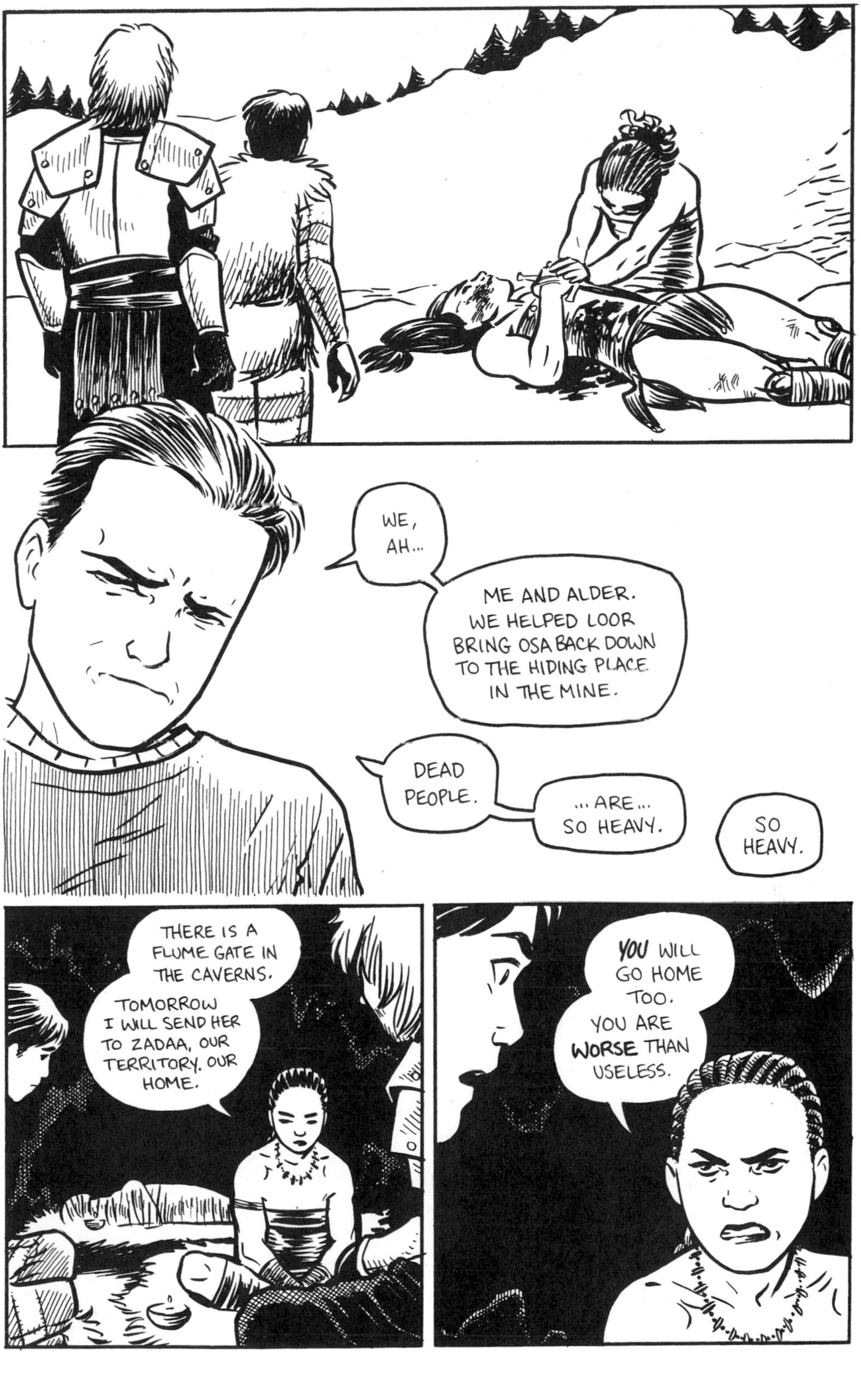
WE, AH...
ME AND ALDER. WE HELPED LOOR BRING OSA BACK DOWN TO THE HIDING PLACE IN THE MINE.
DEAD PEOPLE.
...ARE... SO HEAVY.
SO HEAVY.
THERE IS A FLUME GATE IN THE CAVERNS.
TOMORROW I WILL SEND HER TO ZADAA, OUR TERRITORY. OUR HOME.
YOU WILL GO HOME TOO. YOU ARE WORSE THAN USELESS.

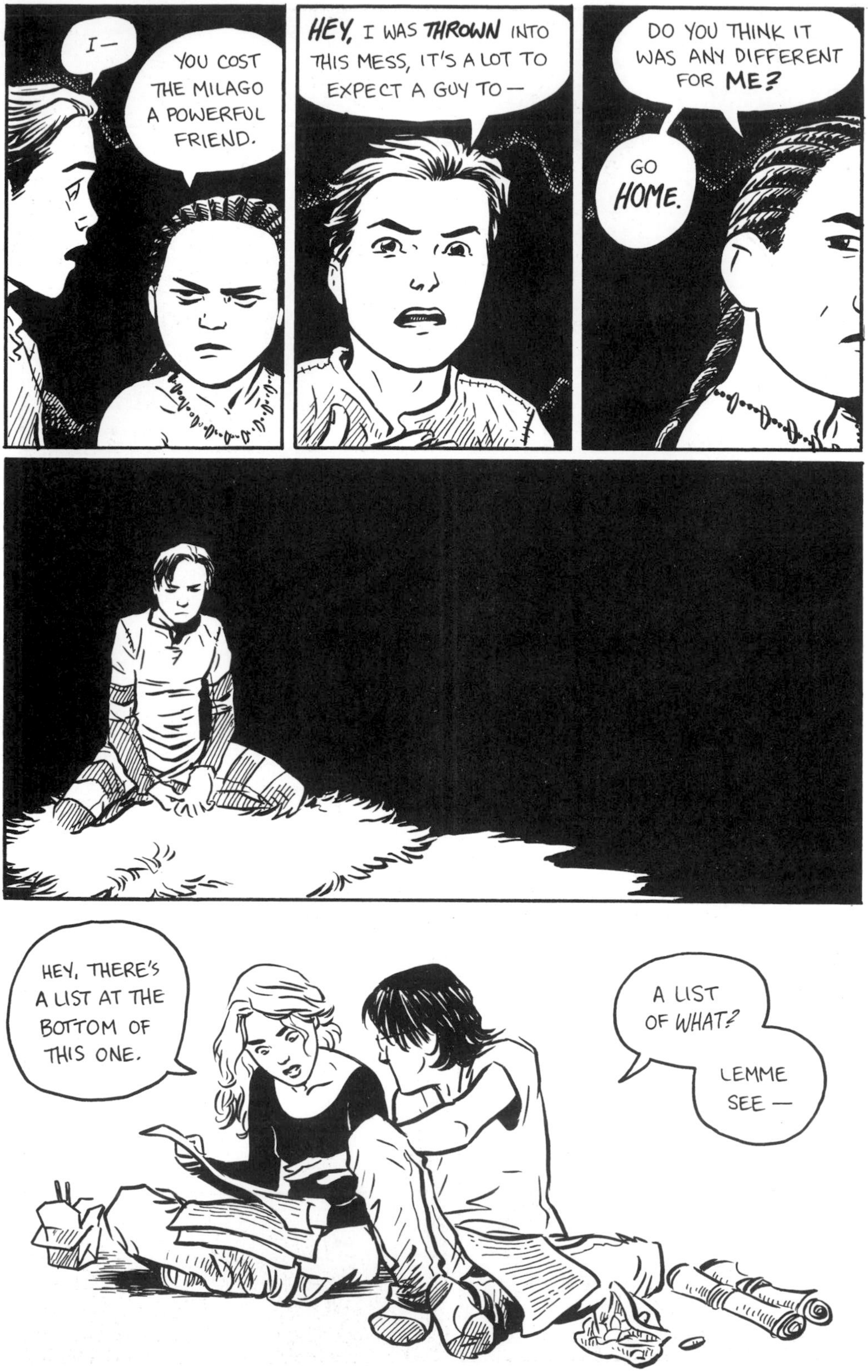
I—
YOU COST THE MILAGO A POWERFUL FRIEND.
HEY, I WAS THROWN INTO THIS MESS, IT'S A LOT TO EXPECT A GUY TO—
DO YOU THINK IT WAS ANY DIFFERENT FOR ME?
GO HOME.
HEY, THERE'S A LIST AT THE BOTTOM OF THIS ONE.
A LIST OF WHAT?
LEMME SEE—

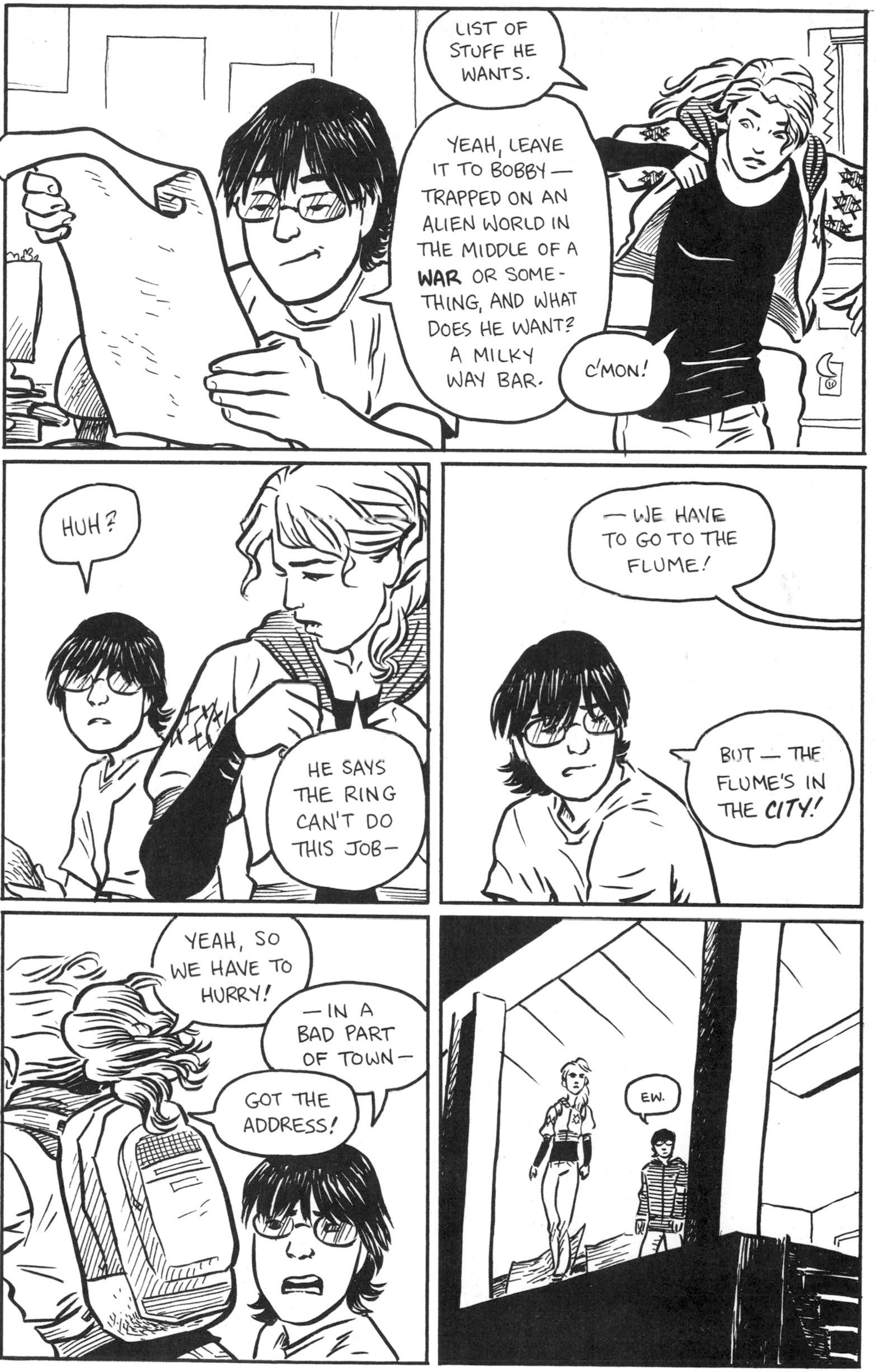
LIST OF STUFF HE WANTS.
YEAH, LEAVE IT TO BOBBY— TRAPPED ON AN ALIEN WORLD IN THE MIDDLE OF A WAR OR SOMETHING, AND WHAT DOES HE WANT? A MILKY WAY BAR.
C'MON!
HUH?
HE SAYS THE RING CAN'T DO THIS JOB—
—WE HAVE TO GO TO THE FLUME!
BUT—THE FLUME'S IN THE CITY!
YEAH, SO WE HAVE TO HURRY!
—IN A BAD PART OF TOWN—
GOT THE ADDRESS!
EW.

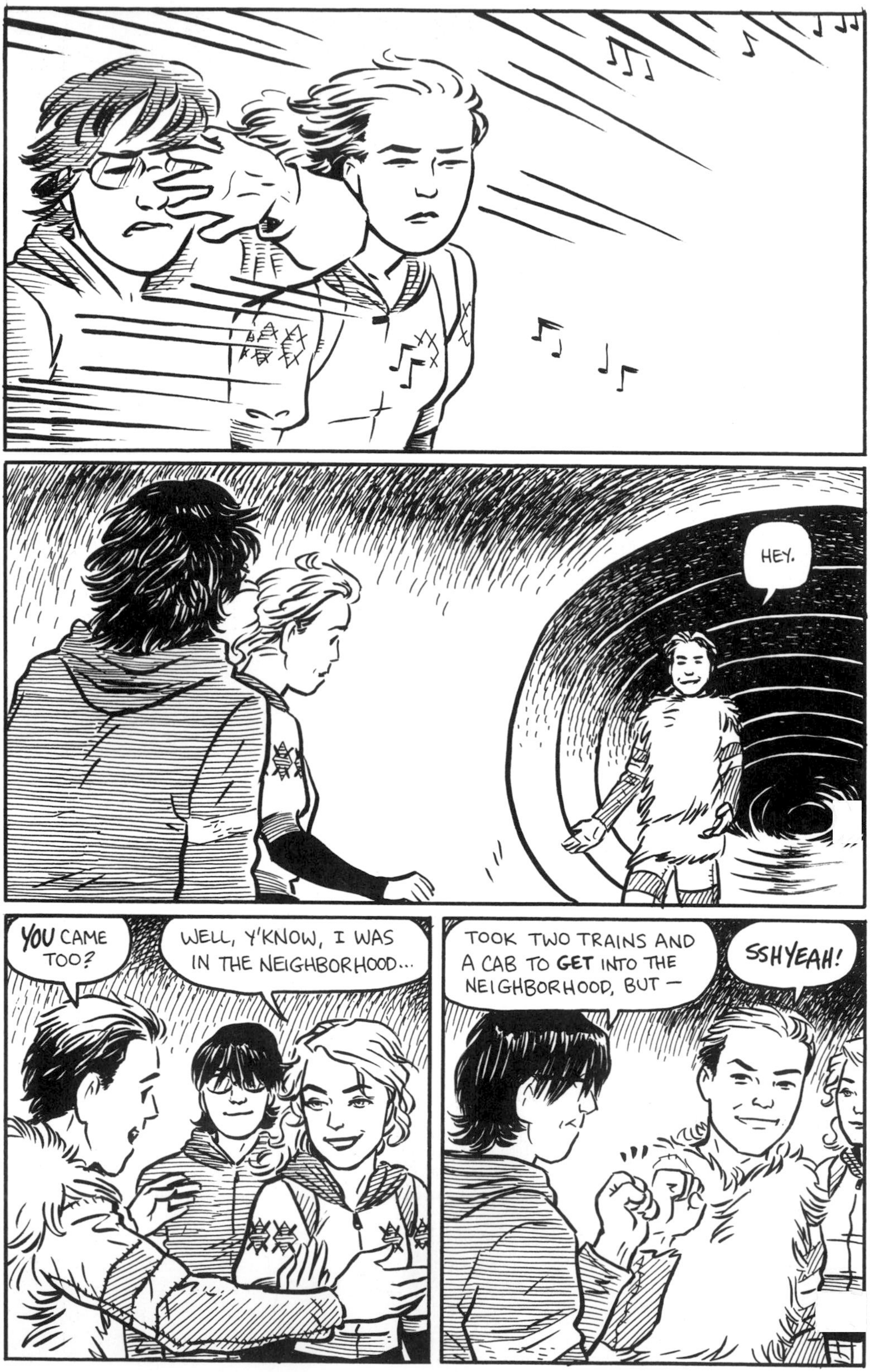
HEY.
YOU CAME TOO?
WELL, Y'KNOW, I WAS IN THE NEIGHBORHOOD...
TOOK TWO TRAINS AND A CAB TO GET INTO THE NEIGHBORHOOD, BUT —
SSHYEAH!

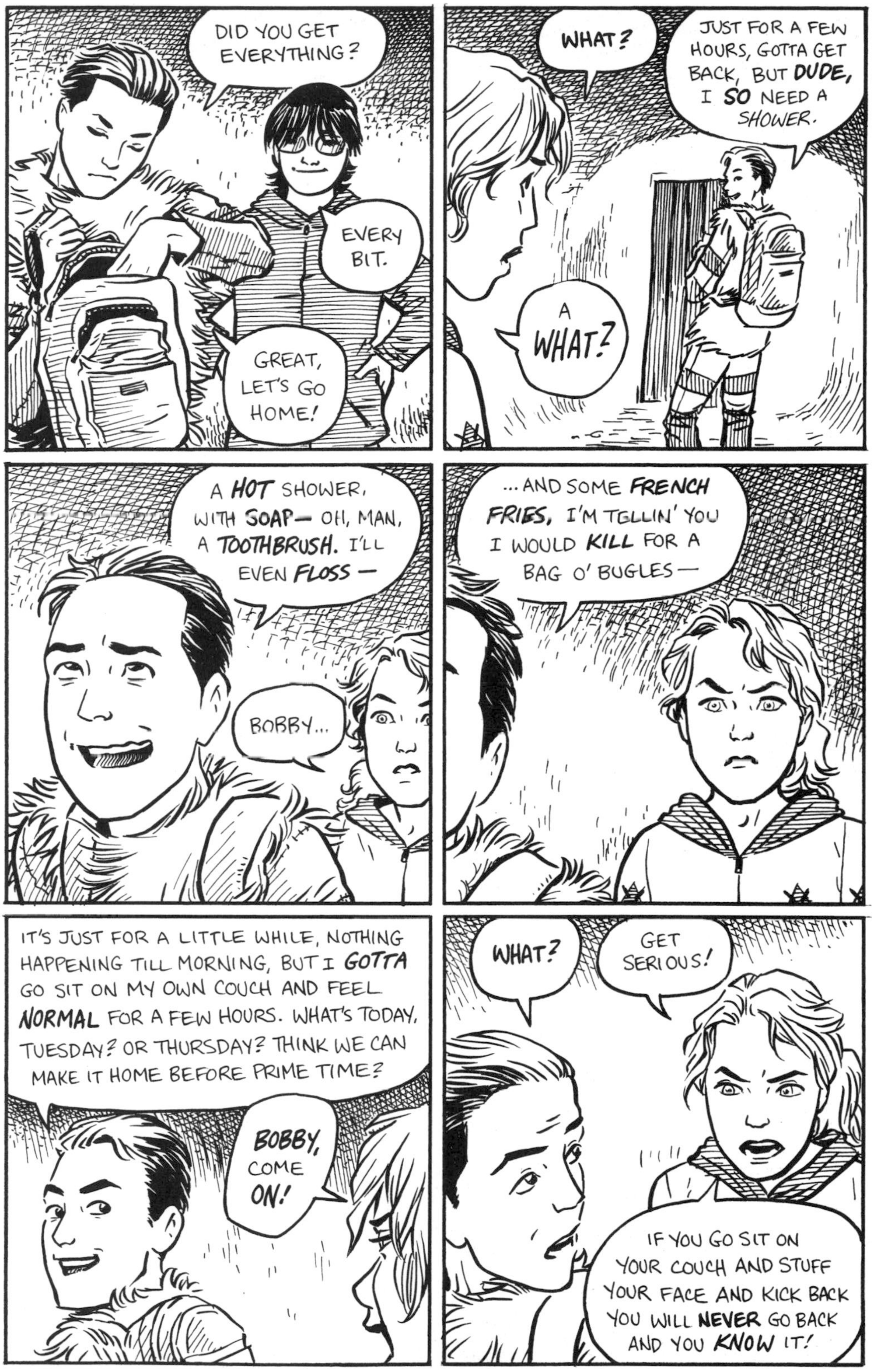

DID YOU GET EVERYTHING?
EVERY BIT.
GREAT, LET'S GO HOME!
WHAT?
JUST FOR A FEW HOURS, GOTTA GET BACK, BUT **DUDE,** I **SO** NEED A SHOWER.
A **WHAT?**
A **HOT** SHOWER, WITH **SOAP**— OH, MAN, A **TOOTHBRUSH.** I'LL EVEN **FLOSS**—
BOBBY...
...AND SOME **FRENCH FRIES,** I'M TELLIN' YOU I WOULD **KILL** FOR A BAG O' BUGLES—
IT'S JUST FOR A LITTLE WHILE, NOTHING HAPPENING TILL MORNING, BUT I **GOTTA** GO SIT ON MY OWN COUCH AND FEEL **NORMAL** FOR A FEW HOURS. WHAT'S TODAY, TUESDAY? OR THURSDAY? THINK WE CAN MAKE IT HOME BEFORE PRIME TIME?
BOBBY, COME **ON!**
WHAT?
GET SERIOUS!
IF YOU GO SIT ON YOUR COUCH AND STUFF YOUR FACE AND KICK BACK YOU WILL **NEVER** GO BACK AND YOU **KNOW** IT!

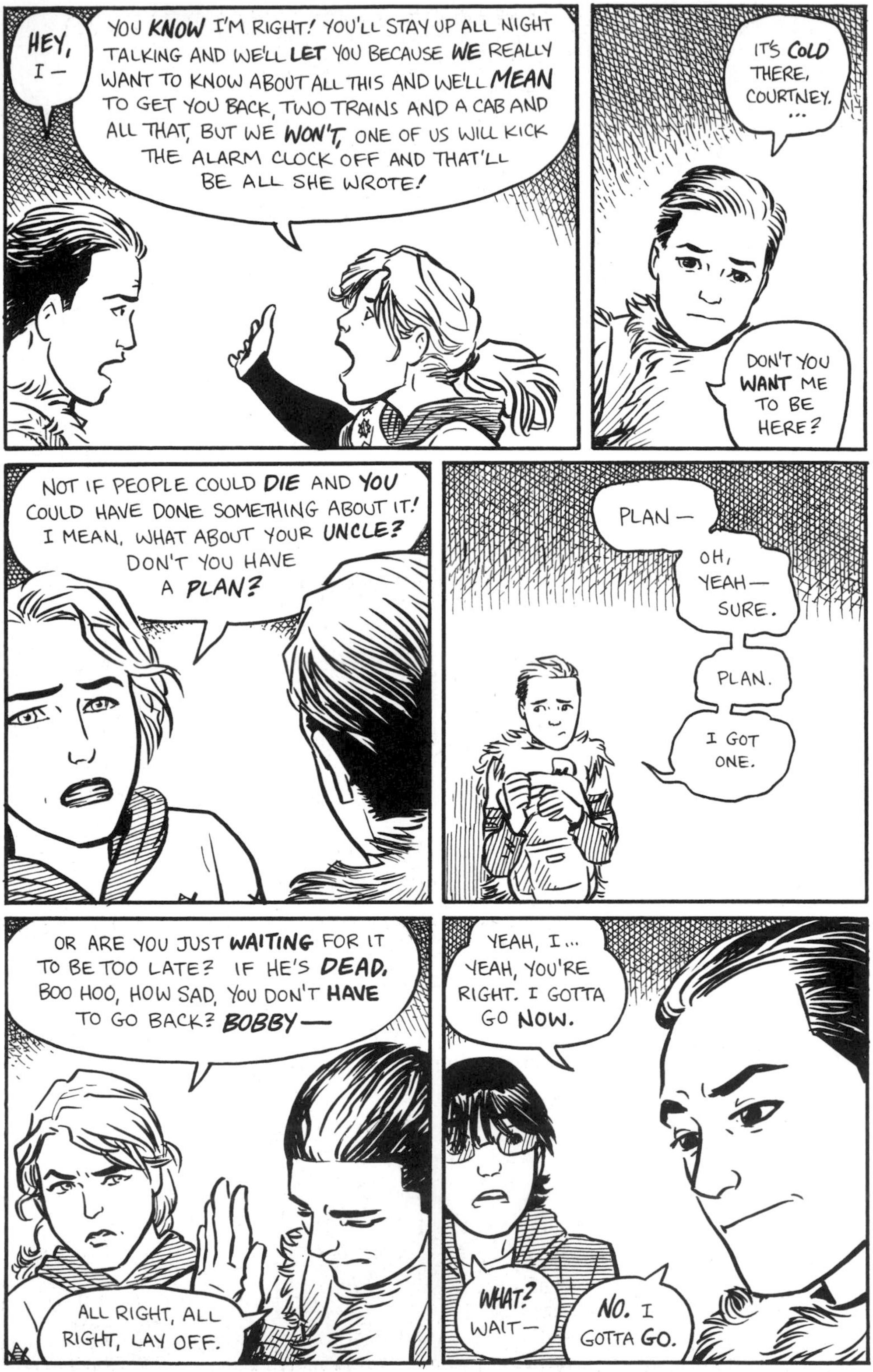
HEY, I—
YOU KNOW I'M RIGHT! YOU'LL STAY UP ALL NIGHT TALKING AND WE'LL LET YOU BECAUSE WE REALLY WANT TO KNOW ABOUT ALL THIS AND WE'LL MEAN TO GET YOU BACK, TWO TRAINS AND A CAB AND ALL THAT, BUT WE WON'T, ONE OF US WILL KICK THE ALARM CLOCK OFF AND THAT'LL BE ALL SHE WROTE!
IT'S COLD THERE, COURTNEY. ...
DON'T YOU WANT ME TO BE HERE?
NOT IF PEOPLE COULD DIE AND YOU COULD HAVE DONE SOMETHING ABOUT IT! I MEAN, WHAT ABOUT YOUR UNCLE? DON'T YOU HAVE A PLAN?
PLAN—
OH, YEAH— SURE.
PLAN.
I GOT ONE.
OR ARE YOU JUST WAITING FOR IT TO BE TOO LATE? IF HE'S DEAD, BOO HOO, HOW SAD, YOU DON'T HAVE TO GO BACK? BOBBY—
ALL RIGHT, ALL RIGHT, LAY OFF.
YEAH, I... YEAH, YOU'RE RIGHT. I GOTTA GO NOW.
WHAT? WAIT—
NO. I GOTTA GO.

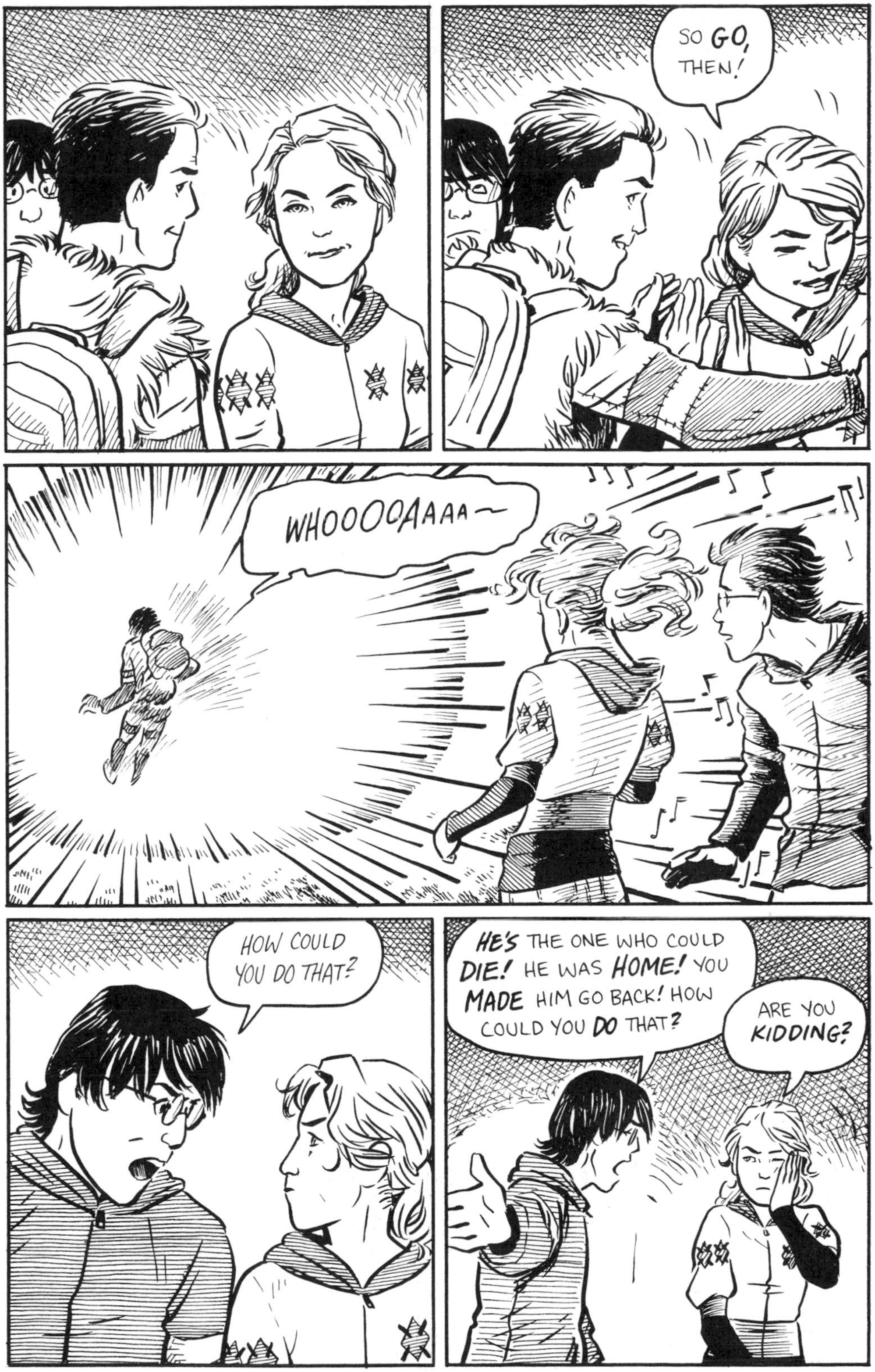
SO GO, THEN!
WHOOOOAAAA~
HOW COULD YOU DO THAT?
HE'S THE ONE WHO COULD DIE! HE WAS HOME! YOU MADE HIM GO BACK! HOW COULD YOU DO THAT?
ARE YOU KIDDING?

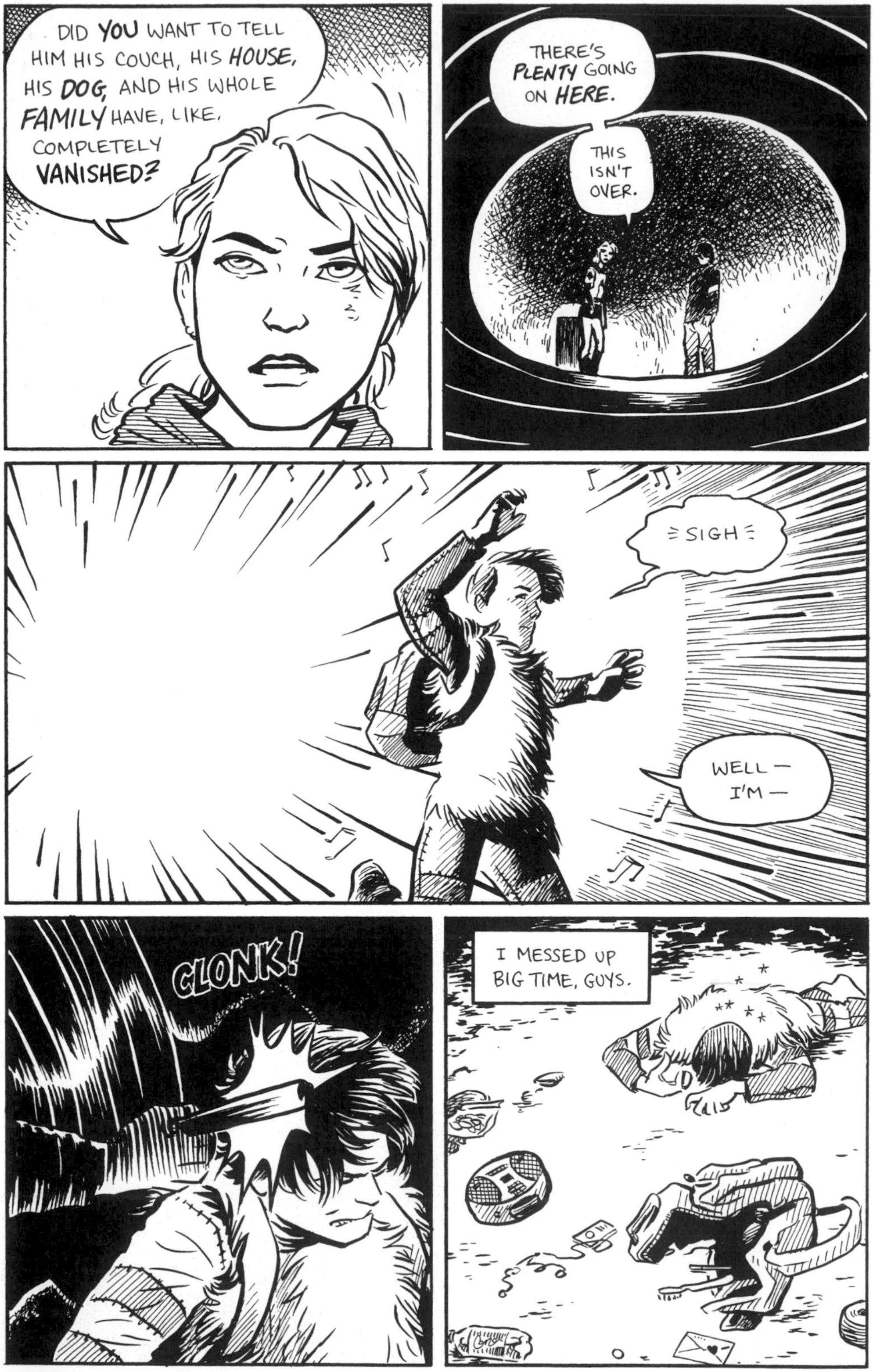
DID YOU WANT TO TELL HIM HIS COUCH, HIS HOUSE, HIS DOG, AND HIS WHOLE FAMILY HAVE, LIKE, COMPLETELY VANISHED?
THERE'S PLENTY GOING ON HERE.
THIS ISN'T OVER.
SIGH
WELL — I'M —
CLONK!
I MESSED UP BIG TIME, GUYS.

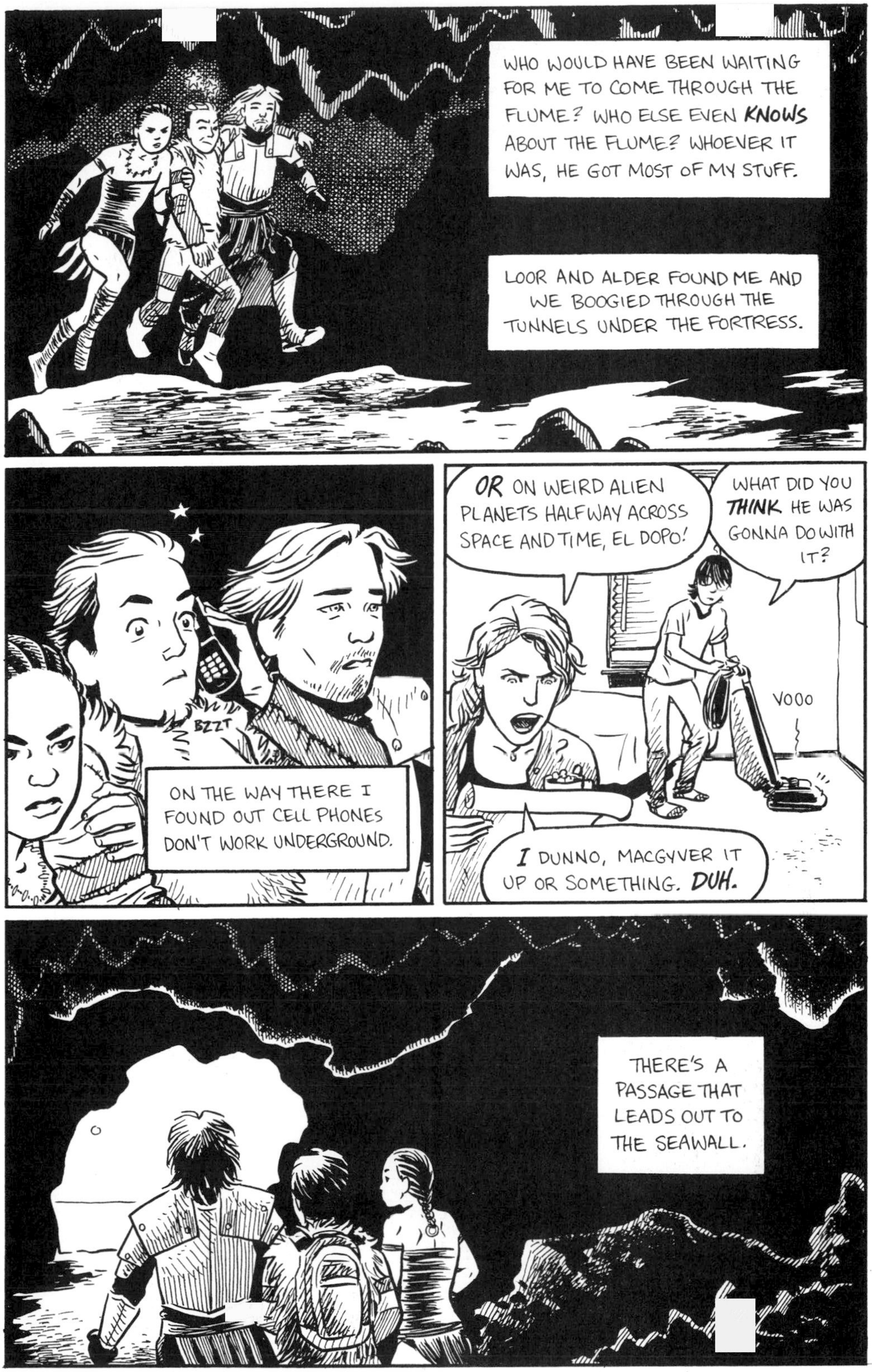
WHO WOULD HAVE BEEN WAITING FOR ME TO COME THROUGH THE FLUME? WHO ELSE EVEN KNOWS ABOUT THE FLUME? WHOEVER IT WAS, HE GOT MOST OF MY STUFF.
LOOR AND ALDER FOUND ME AND WE BOOGIED THROUGH THE TUNNELS UNDER THE FORTRESS.
BZZT
ON THE WAY THERE I FOUND OUT CELL PHONES DON'T WORK UNDERGROUND.
OR ON WEIRD ALIEN PLANETS HALFWAY ACROSS SPACE AND TIME, EL DOPO!
WHAT DID YOU THINK HE WAS GONNA DO WITH IT?
VOOO
I DUNNO, MACGYVER IT UP OR SOMETHING. DUH.
THERE'S A PASSAGE THAT LEADS OUT TO THE SEAWALL.

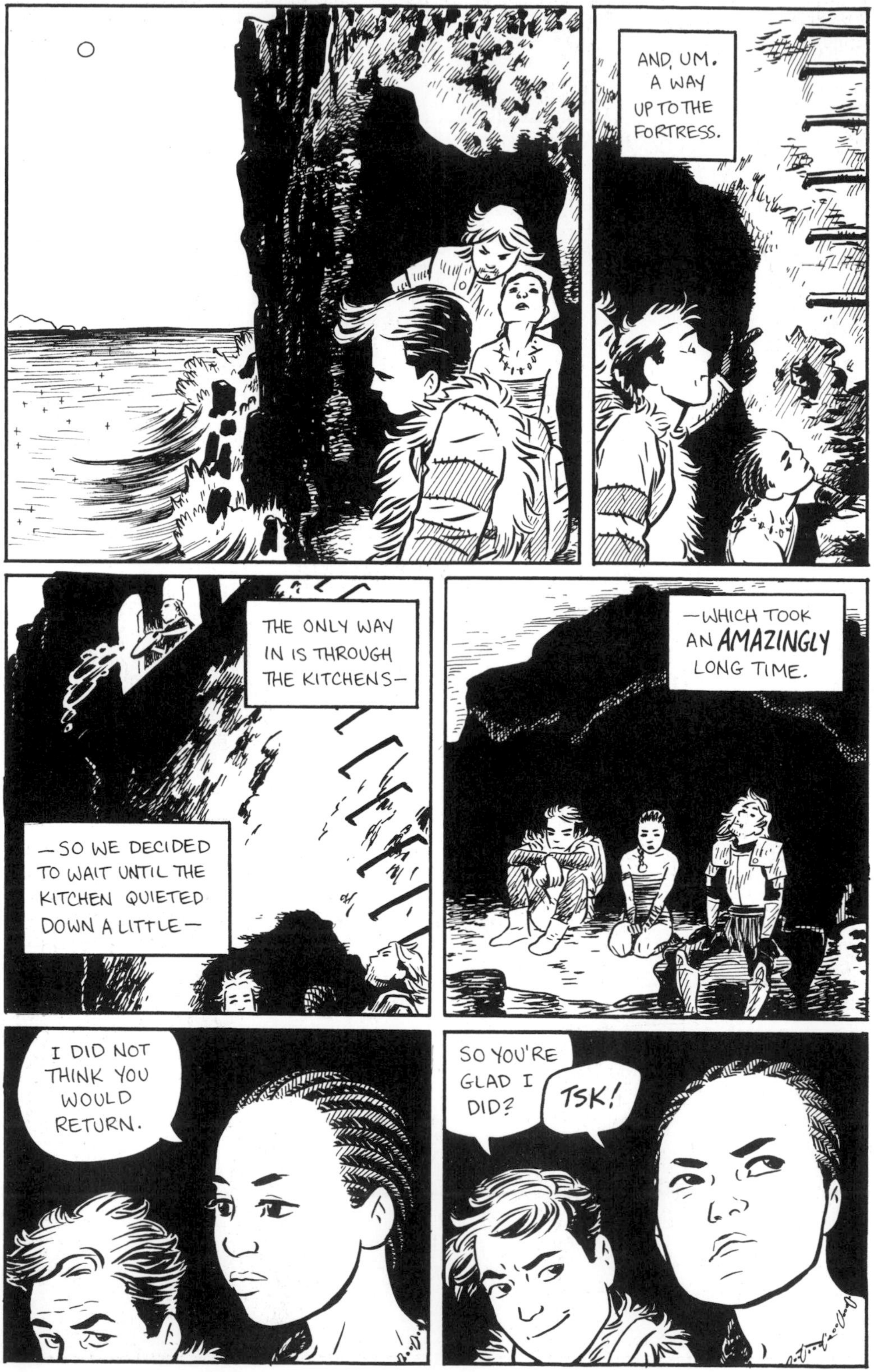
AND, UM. A WAY UP TO THE FORTRESS.
THE ONLY WAY IN IS THROUGH THE KITCHENS—
—SO WE DECIDED TO WAIT UNTIL THE KITCHEN QUIETED DOWN A LITTLE—
—WHICH TOOK AN AMAZINGLY LONG TIME.
I DID NOT THINK YOU WOULD RETURN.
SO YOU'RE GLAD I DID?
TSK!

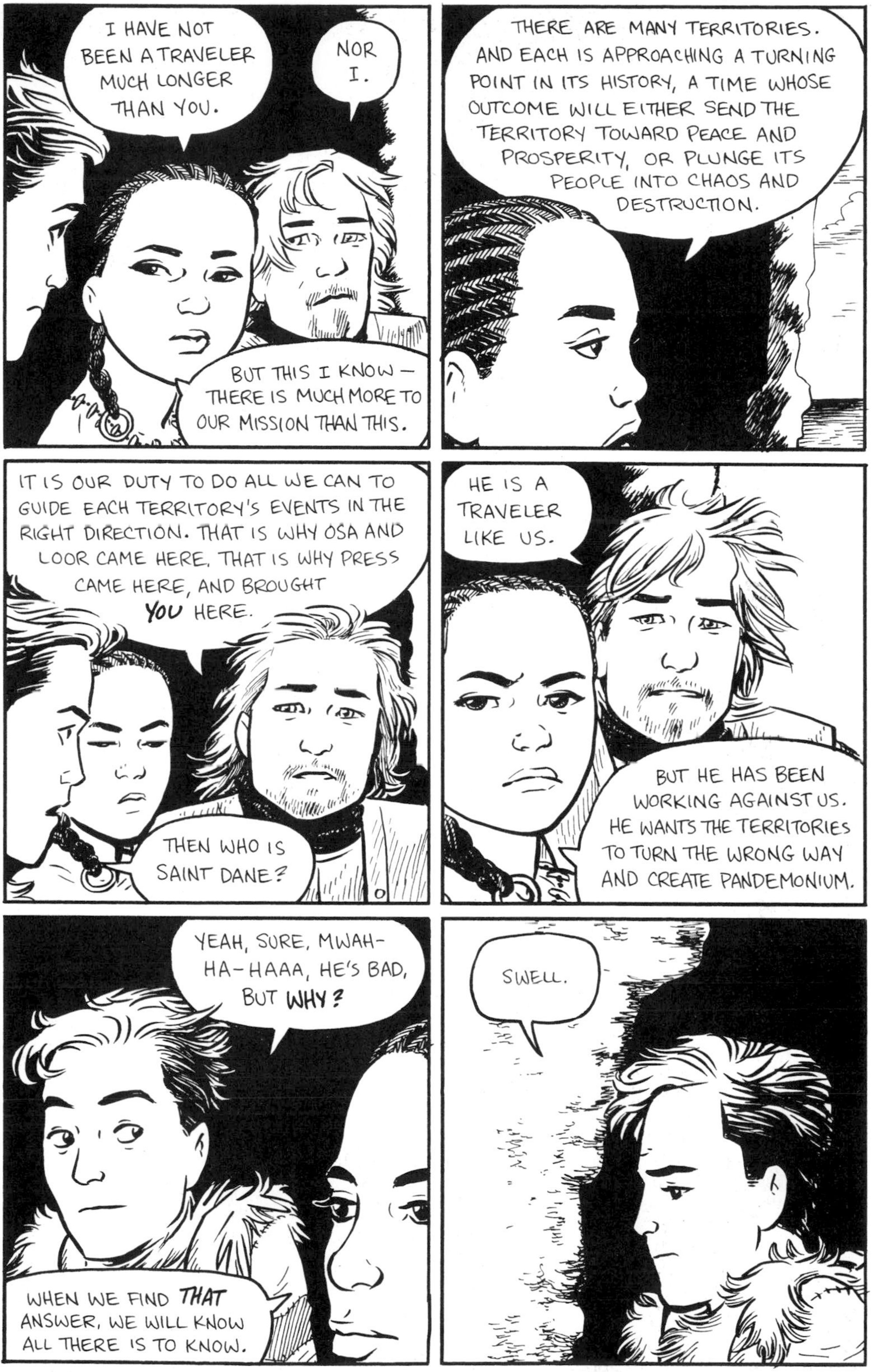
I HAVE NOT BEEN A TRAVELER MUCH LONGER THAN YOU.
NOR I.
BUT THIS I KNOW— THERE IS MUCH MORE TO OUR MISSION THAN THIS.
THERE ARE MANY TERRITORIES. AND EACH IS APPROACHING A TURNING POINT IN ITS HISTORY, A TIME WHOSE OUTCOME WILL EITHER SEND THE TERRITORY TOWARD PEACE AND PROSPERITY, OR PLUNGE ITS PEOPLE INTO CHAOS AND DESTRUCTION.
IT IS OUR DUTY TO DO ALL WE CAN TO GUIDE EACH TERRITORY'S EVENTS IN THE RIGHT DIRECTION. THAT IS WHY OSA AND LOOR CAME HERE. THAT IS WHY PRESS CAME HERE, AND BROUGHT YOU HERE.
THEN WHO IS SAINT DANE?
HE IS A TRAVELER LIKE US.
BUT HE HAS BEEN WORKING AGAINST US. HE WANTS THE TERRITORIES TO TURN THE WRONG WAY AND CREATE PANDEMONIUM.
YEAH, SURE, MWAH-HA-HAAA, HE'S BAD, BUT WHY?
WHEN WE FIND THAT ANSWER, WE WILL KNOW ALL THERE IS TO KNOW.
SWELL.

AFTER A WHILE, THE KITCHEN STAFF RAN OFF LOADED DOWN WITH FOOD, SO WE WENT IN.
THE FIRST THING YOU NOTICE ABOUT THE BEDOOWAN FORTRESS—
IT'S NICE.
I MEAN BLING BLING NICE.

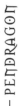

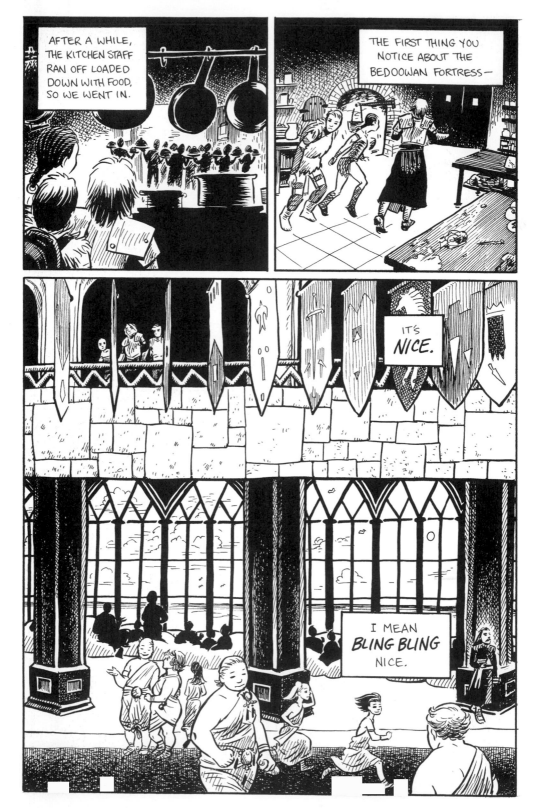

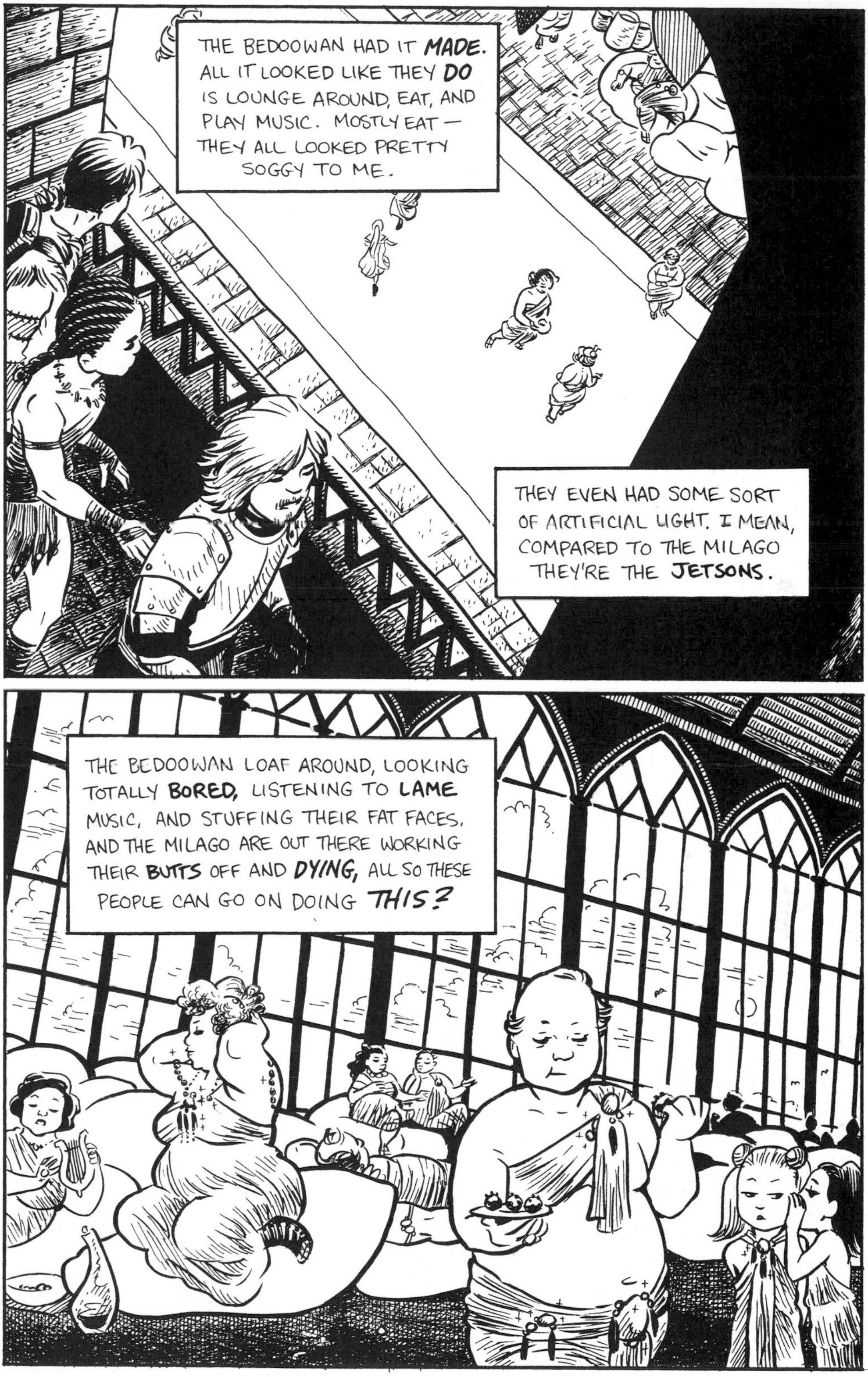

THE BEDOOWAN HAD IT **MADE**. ALL IT LOOKED LIKE THEY **DO** IS LOUNGE AROUND, EAT, AND PLAY MUSIC. MOSTLY EAT — THEY ALL LOOKED PRETTY SOGGY TO ME.
THEY EVEN HAD SOME SORT OF ARTIFICIAL LIGHT. I MEAN, COMPARED TO THE MILAGO THEY'RE THE **JETSONS**.
THE BEDOOWAN LOAF AROUND, LOOKING TOTALLY **BORED**, LISTENING TO **LAME** MUSIC, AND STUFFING THEIR FAT FACES, AND THE MILAGO ARE OUT THERE WORKING THEIR **BUTTS** OFF AND ***DYING***, ALL SO THESE PEOPLE CAN GO ON DOING ***THIS?***

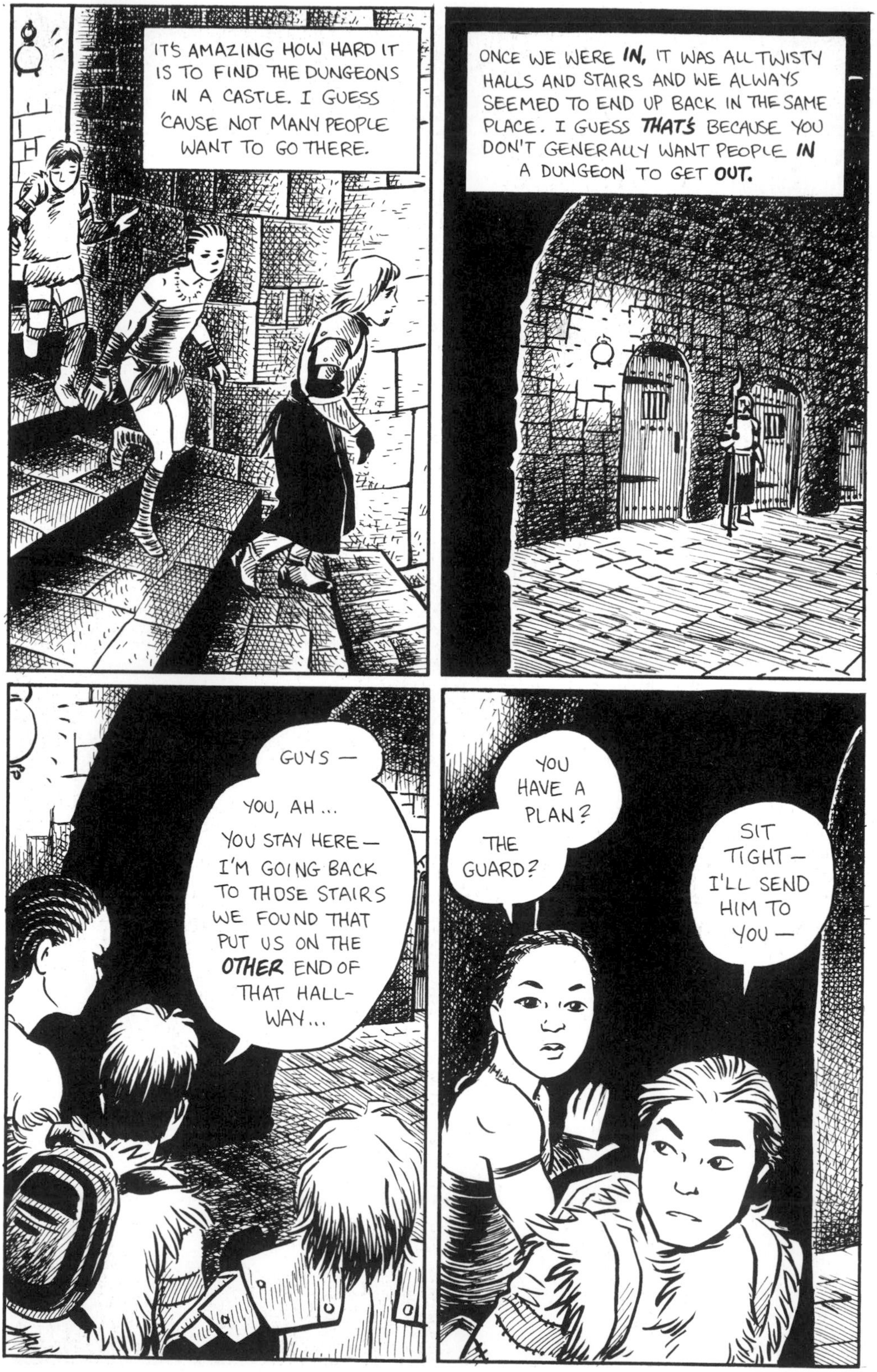
IT'S AMAZING HOW HARD IT IS TO FIND THE DUNGEONS IN A CASTLE. I GUESS 'CAUSE NOT MANY PEOPLE WANT TO GO THERE.
ONCE WE WERE **IN**, IT WAS ALL TWISTY HALLS AND STAIRS AND WE ALWAYS SEEMED TO END UP BACK IN THE SAME PLACE. I GUESS **THAT'S** BECAUSE YOU DON'T GENERALLY WANT PEOPLE **IN** A DUNGEON TO GET **OUT.**
GUYS —
YOU, AH ...
YOU STAY HERE — I'M GOING BACK TO THOSE STAIRS WE FOUND THAT PUT US ON THE **OTHER** END OF THAT HALL-WAY...
THE GUARD?
YOU HAVE A PLAN?
SIT TIGHT — I'LL SEND HIM TO YOU —

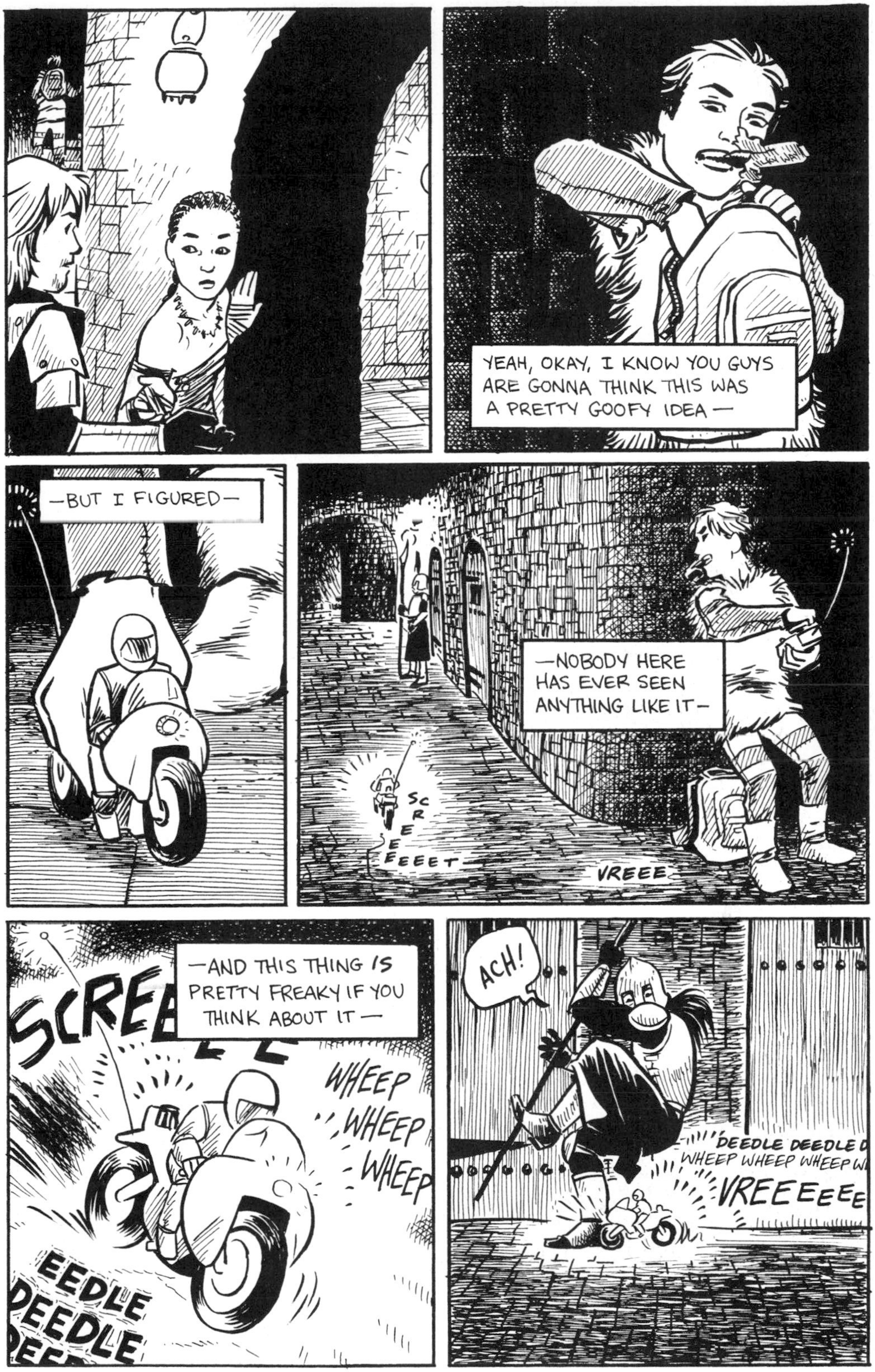
YEAH, OKAY, I KNOW YOU GUYS ARE GONNA THINK THIS WAS A PRETTY GOOFY IDEA —
—BUT I FIGURED—
—NOBODY HERE HAS EVER SEEN ANYTHING LIKE IT—
SCREEEEEET
VREEE
—AND THIS THING IS PRETTY FREAKY IF YOU THINK ABOUT IT —
SCREE
WHEEP WHEEP WHEEP
EEDLE DEEDLE
ACH!
DEEDLE DEEDLE
WHEEP WHEEP WHEEP
VREEEEEE

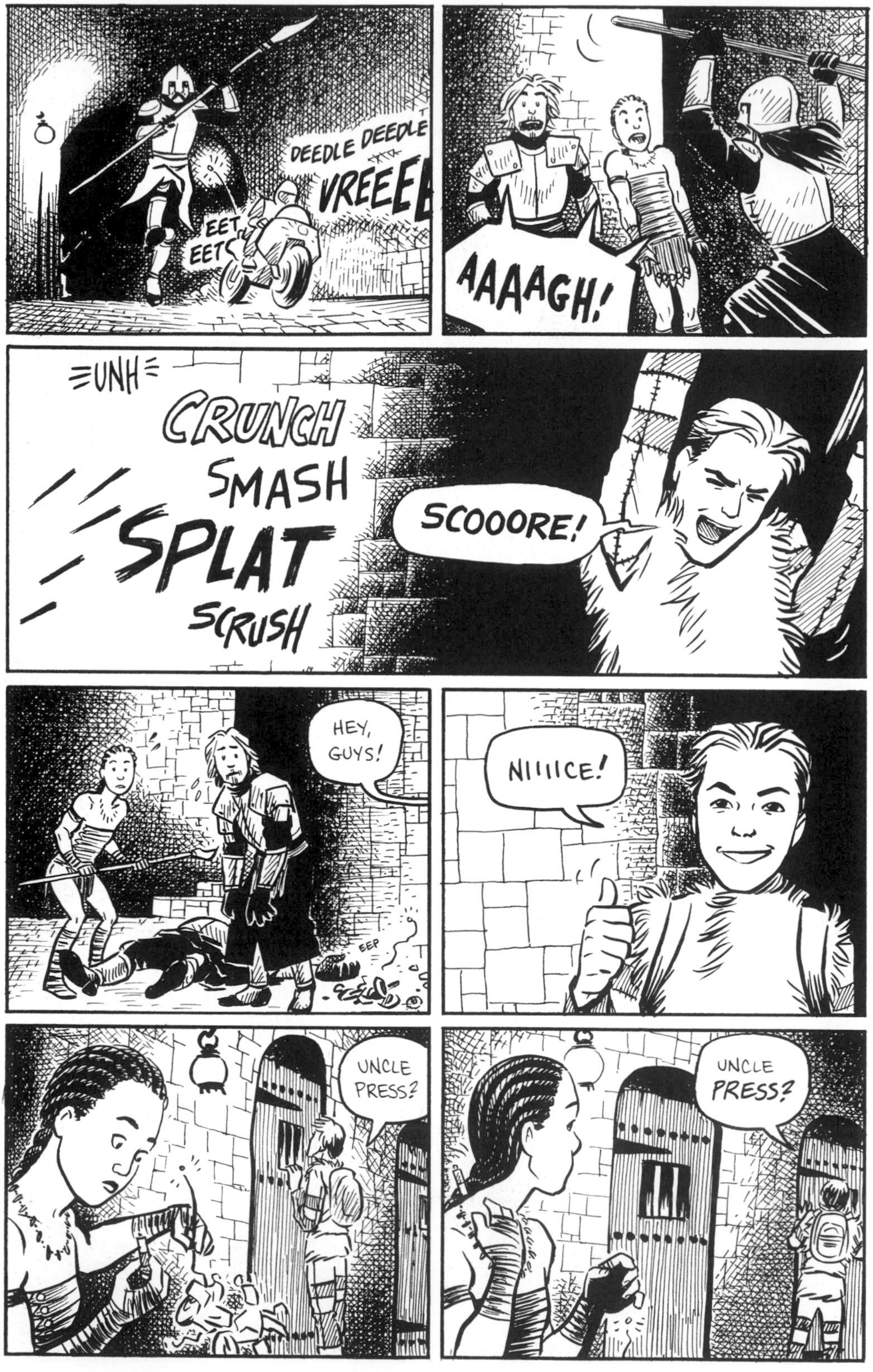
DEEDLE DEEDLE
VREEEE
EET EETS
AAAAGH!
UNH
CRUNCH
SMASH
SPLAT
SCRUSH
SCOOORE!
HEY, GUYS!
EEP
NIIIICE!
UNCLE PRESS?
UNCLE PRESS?

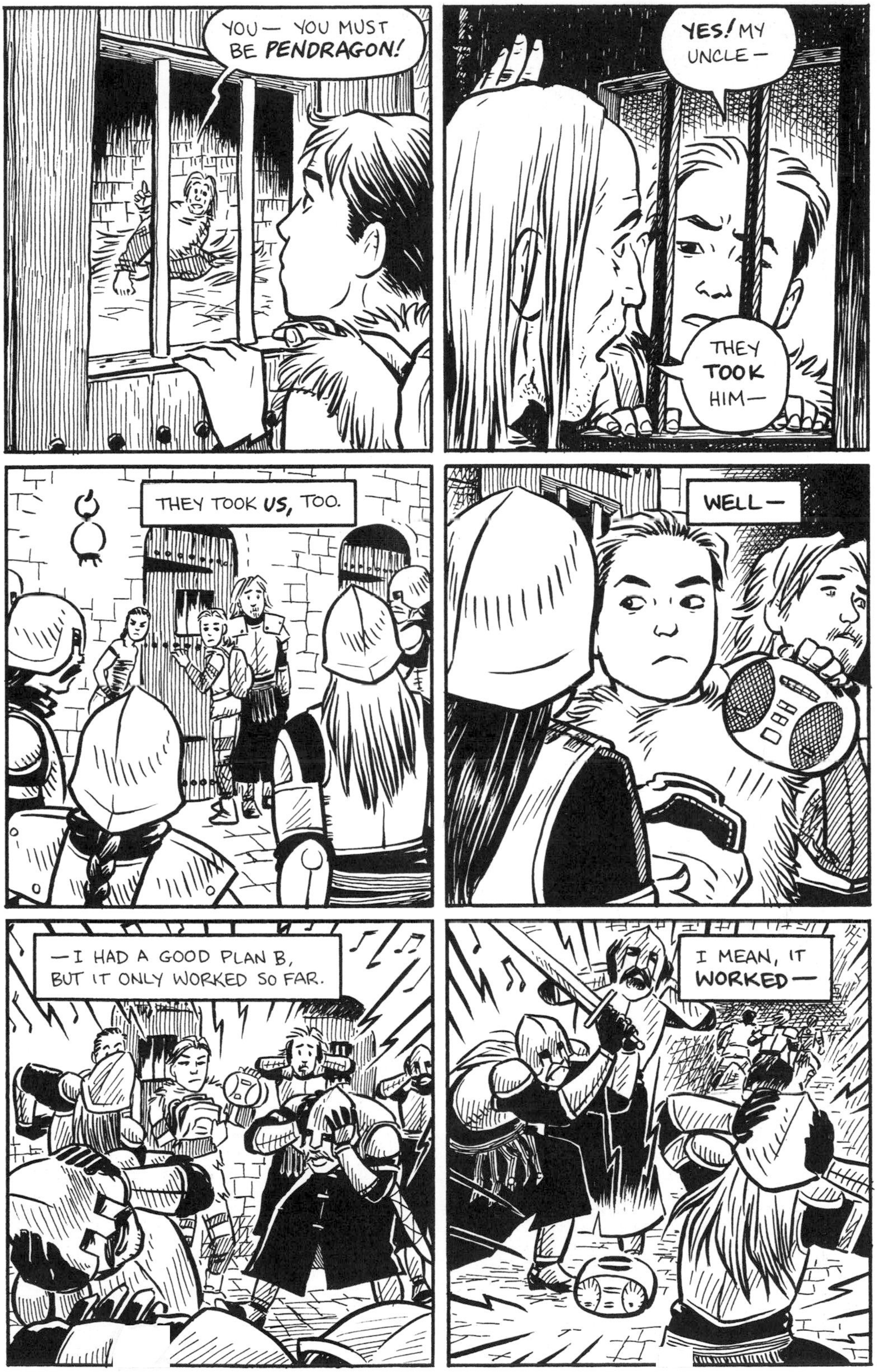

YOU— YOU MUST BE PENDRAGON!
YES! MY UNCLE—
THEY TOOK HIM—
THEY TOOK US, TOO.
WELL—
—I HAD A GOOD PLAN B, BUT IT ONLY WORKED SO FAR.
I MEAN, IT WORKED—

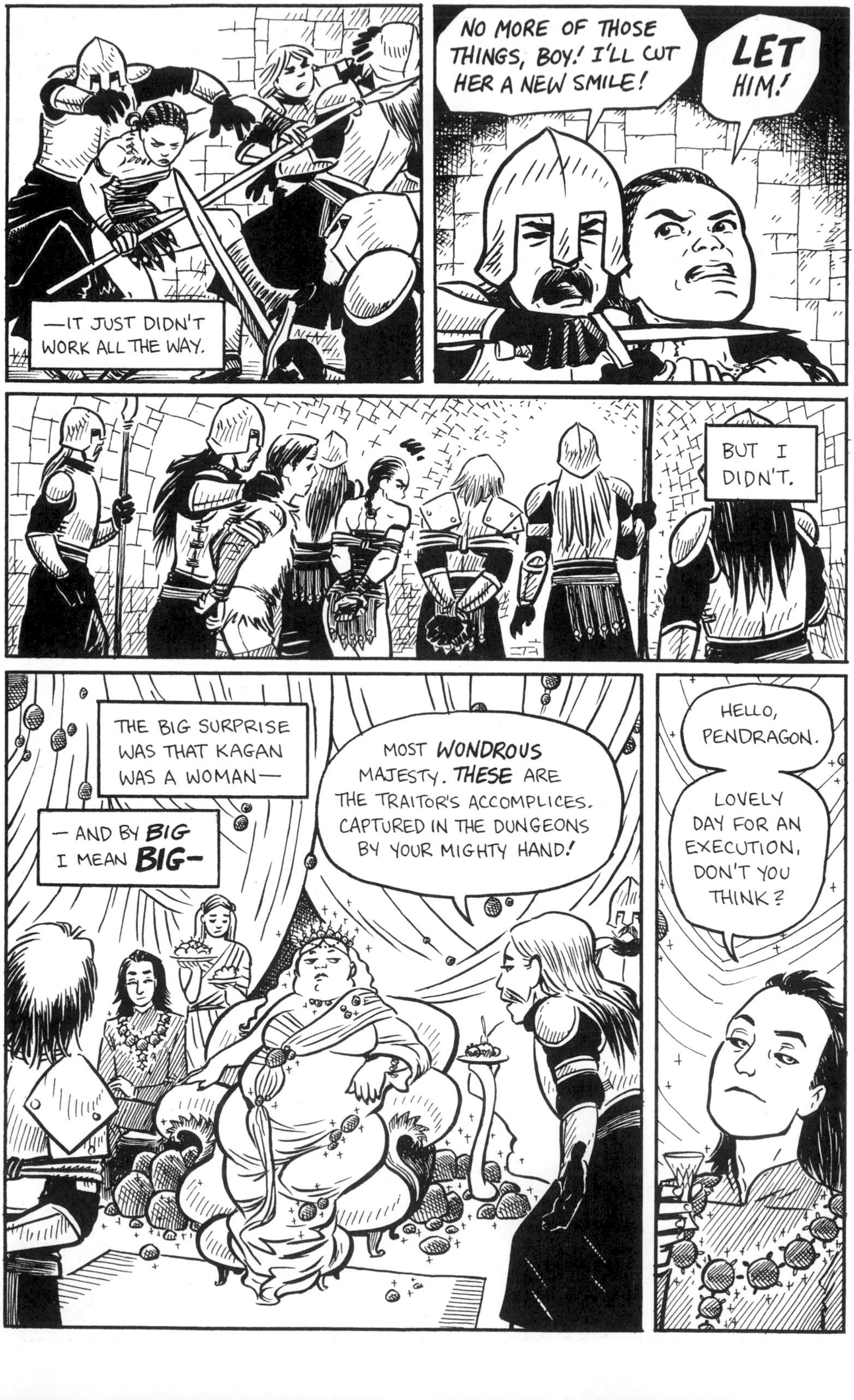
—IT JUST DIDN'T WORK ALL THE WAY.
NO MORE OF THOSE THINGS, BOY! I'LL CUT HER A NEW SMILE!
LET HIM!
BUT I DIDN'T.
THE BIG SURPRISE WAS THAT KAGAN WAS A WOMAN—
— AND BY BIG I MEAN BIG—
MOST WONDROUS MAJESTY. THESE ARE THE TRAITOR'S ACCOMPLICES. CAPTURED IN THE DUNGEONS BY YOUR MIGHTY HAND!
HELLO, PENDRAGON.
LOVELY DAY FOR AN EXECUTION, DON'T YOU THINK?

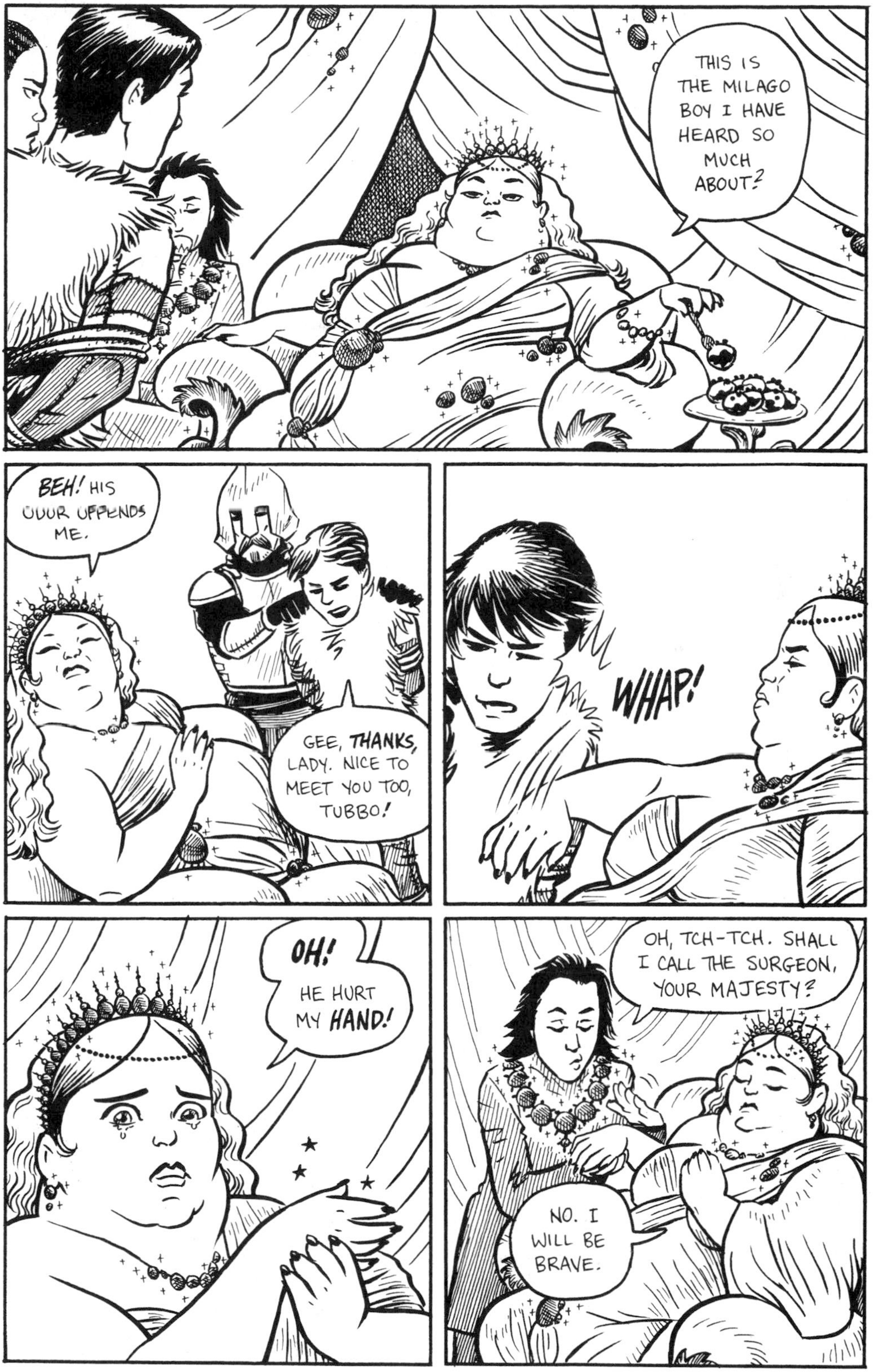
THIS IS THE MILAGO BOY I HAVE HEARD SO MUCH ABOUT?
BEH! HIS ODOR OFFENDS ME.
GEE, THANKS, LADY. NICE TO MEET YOU TOO, TUBBO!
WHAP!
OH!
HE HURT MY HAND!
OH, TCH-TCH. SHALL I CALL THE SURGEON, YOUR MAJESTY?
NO. I WILL BE BRAVE.

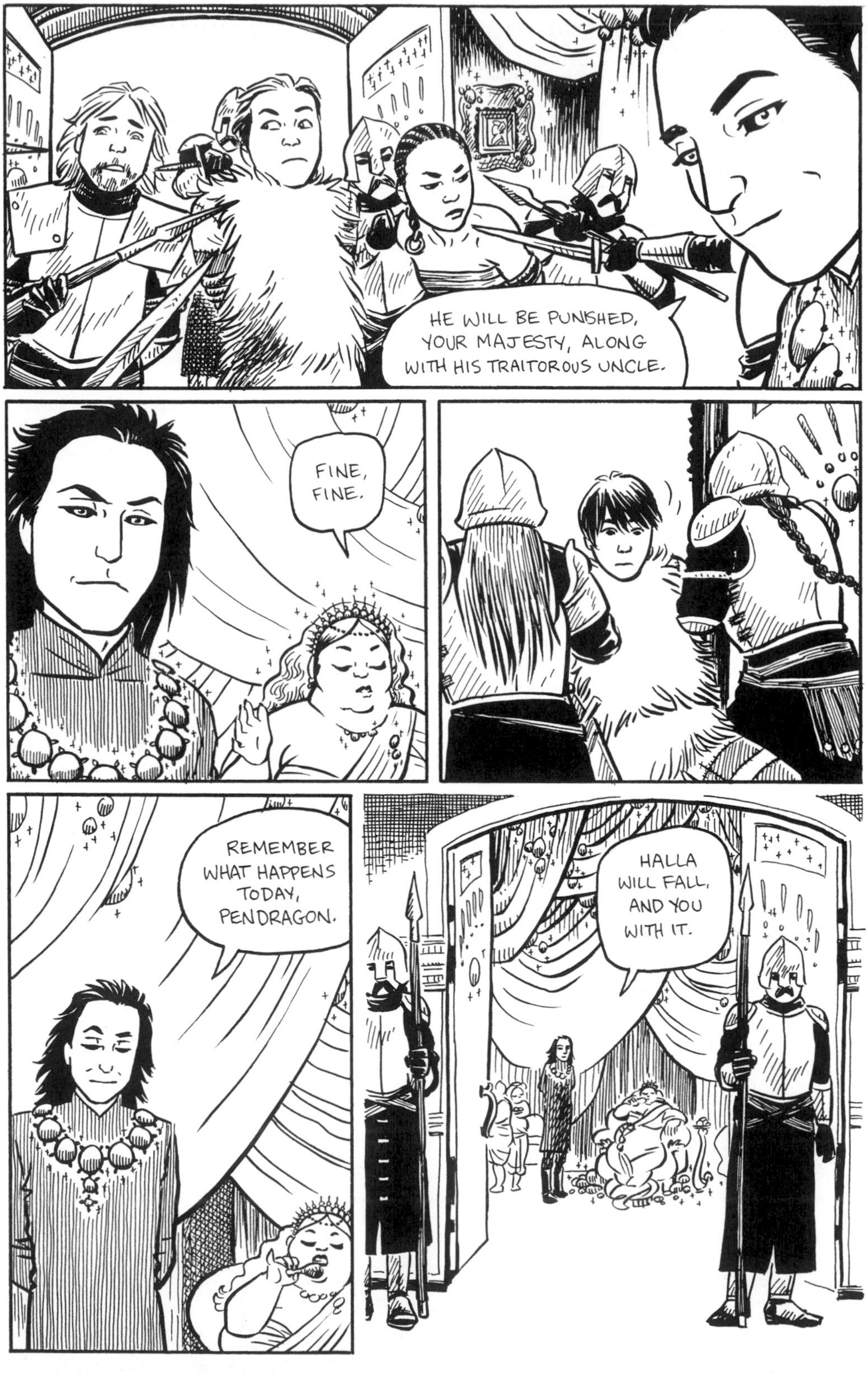
HE WILL BE PUNISHED, YOUR MAJESTY, ALONG WITH HIS TRAITOROUS UNCLE.
FINE, FINE.
REMEMBER WHAT HAPPENS TODAY, PENDRAGON.
HALLA WILL FALL, AND YOU WITH IT.

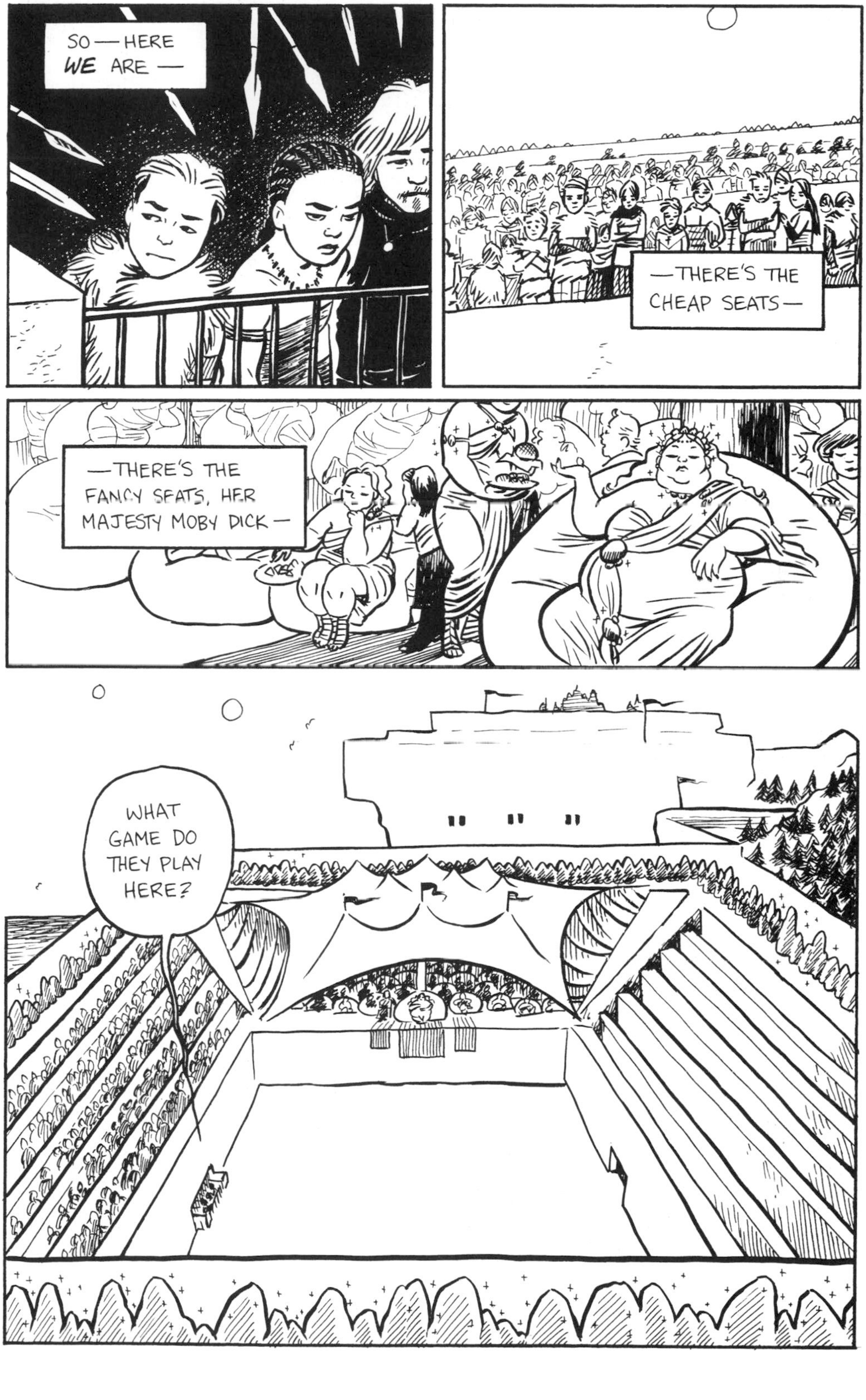
SO — HERE WE ARE —
— THERE'S THE CHEAP SEATS —
— THERE'S THE FANCY SEATS, HER MAJESTY MOBY DICK —
WHAT GAME DO THEY PLAY HERE?

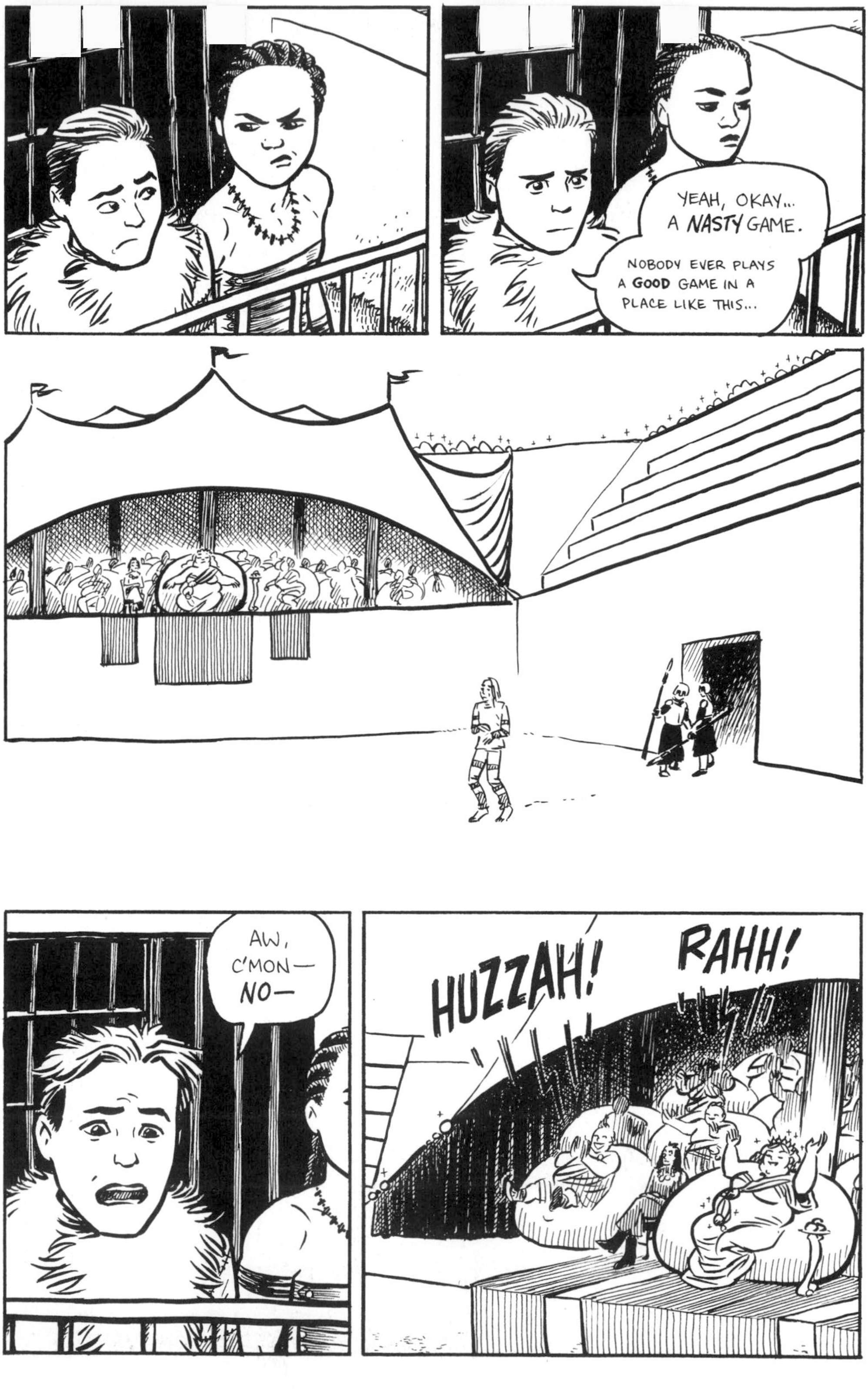
YEAH, OKAY... A NASTY GAME.
NOBODY EVER PLAYS A GOOD GAME IN A PLACE LIKE THIS...
AW, C'MON— NO—
HUZZAH!
RAHH!

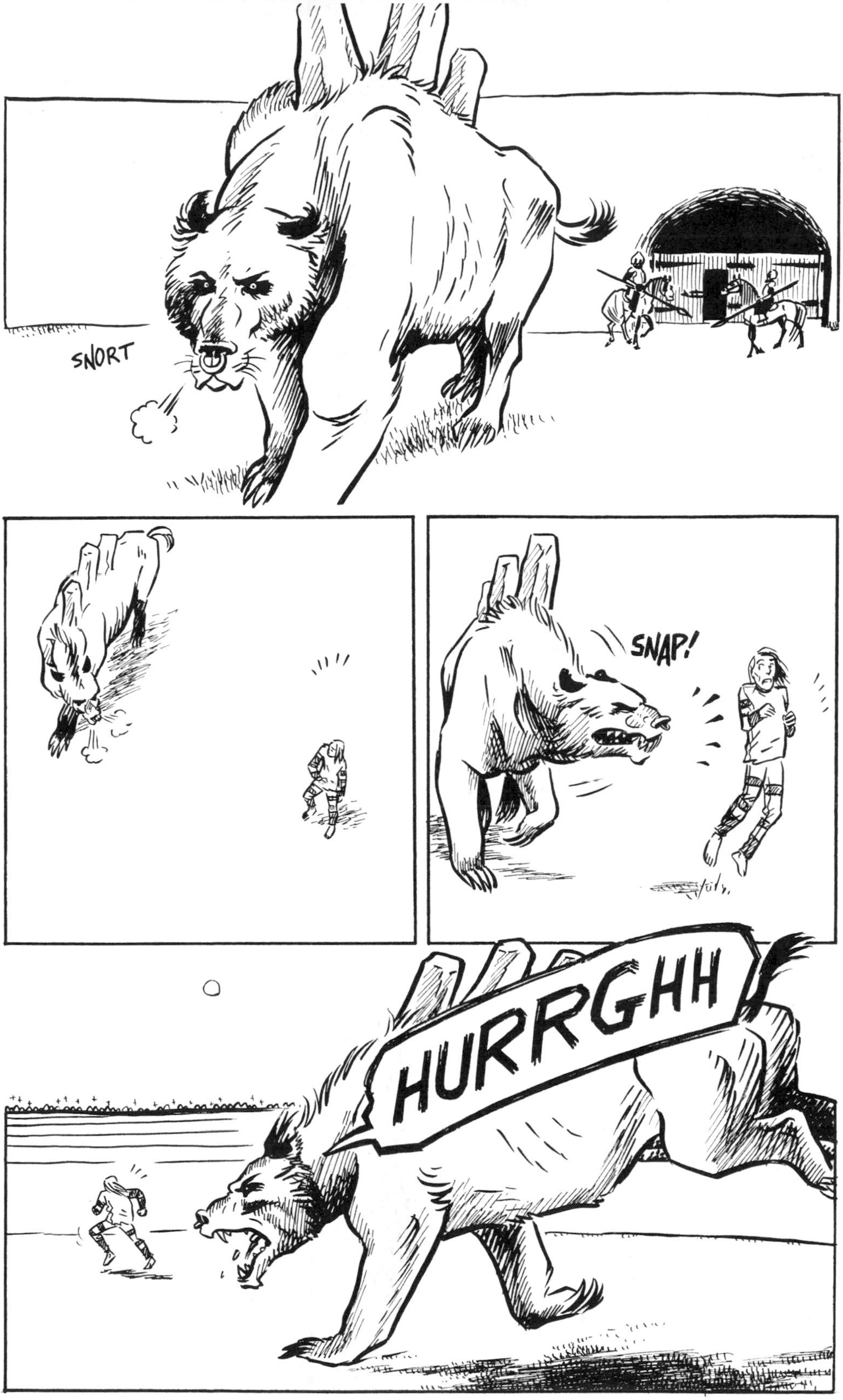
SNORT
SNAP!
HURRGHH

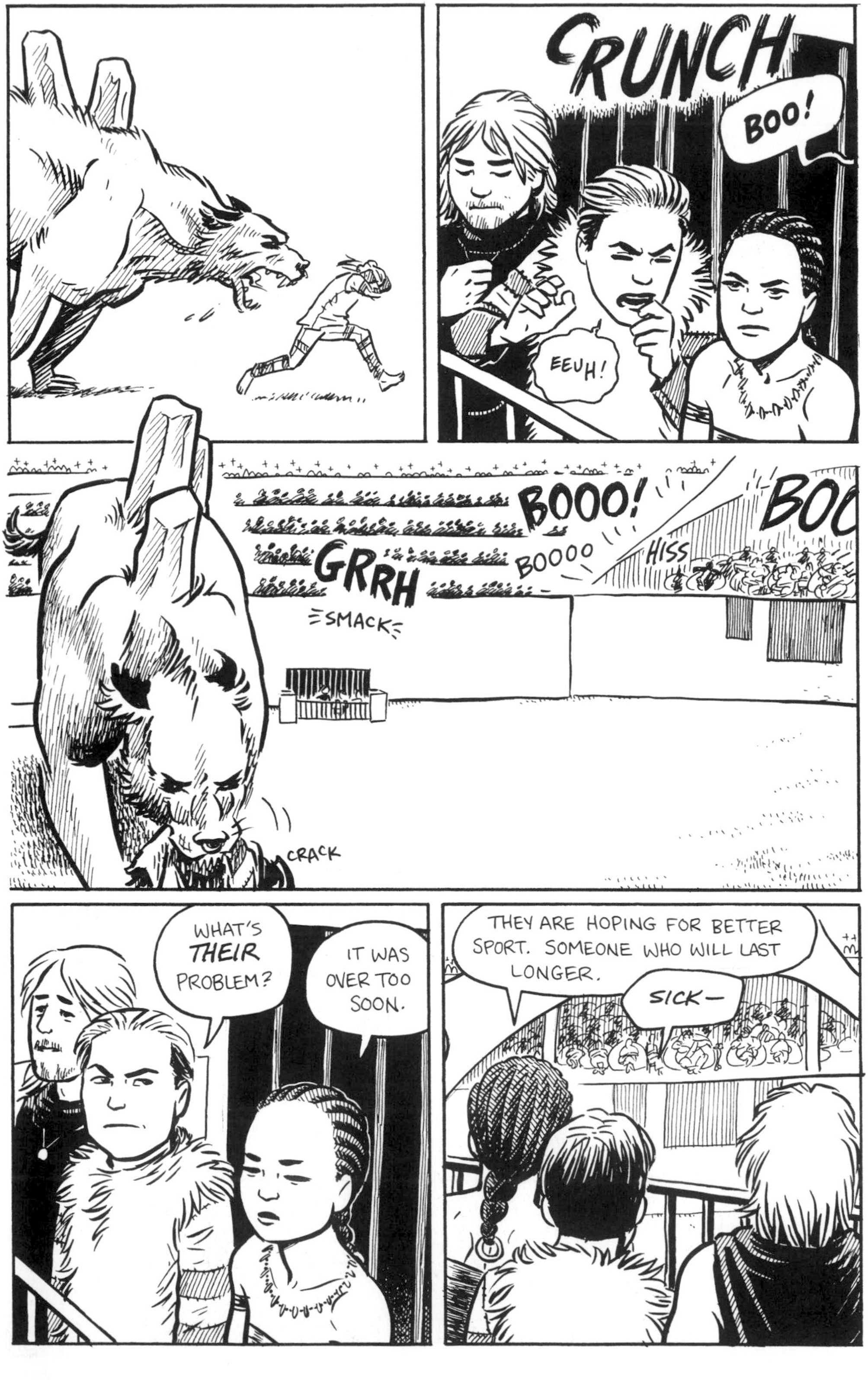
CRUNCH
BOO!
EEUH!
BOOO!
BOO
BOOOO
HISS
GRRH
SMACK
CRACK
WHAT'S THEIR PROBLEM?
IT WAS OVER TOO SOON.
THEY ARE HOPING FOR BETTER SPORT. SOMEONE WHO WILL LAST LONGER.
SICK—

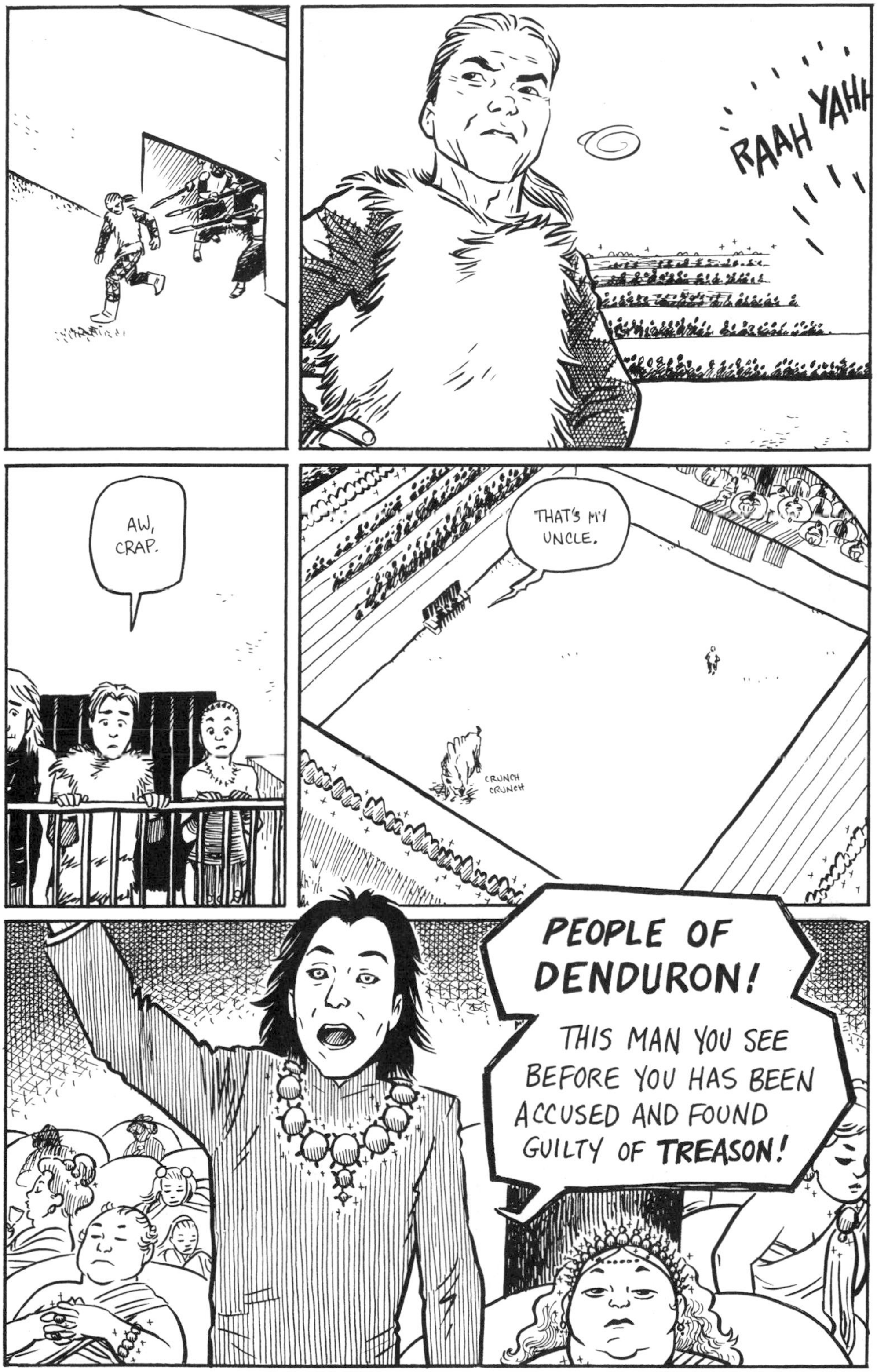
RAAH YAHH
AW, CRAP.
THAT'S MY UNCLE.
CRUNCH CRUNCH
PEOPLE OF DENDURON!
THIS MAN YOU SEE BEFORE YOU HAS BEEN ACCUSED AND FOUND GUILTY OF TREASON!

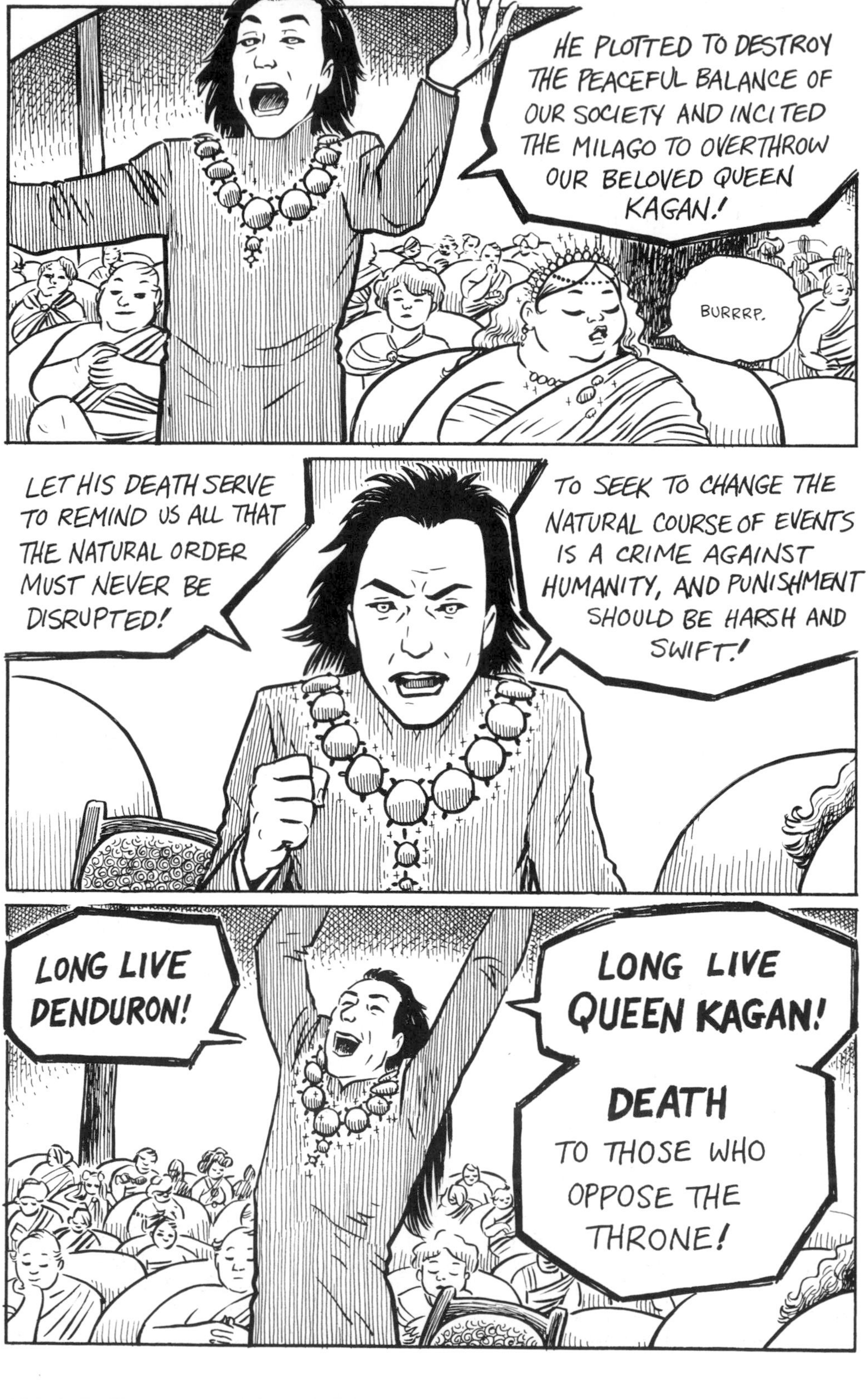
HE PLOTTED TO DESTROY THE PEACEFUL BALANCE OF OUR SOCIETY AND INCITED THE MILAGO TO OVERTHROW OUR BELOVED QUEEN KAGAN!
BURRRP.
LET HIS DEATH SERVE TO REMIND US ALL THAT THE NATURAL ORDER MUST NEVER BE DISRUPTED!
TO SEEK TO CHANGE THE NATURAL COURSE OF EVENTS IS A CRIME AGAINST HUMANITY, AND PUNISHMENT SHOULD BE HARSH AND SWIFT!
LONG LIVE DENDURON!
LONG LIVE QUEEN KAGAN!
DEATH TO THOSE WHO OPPOSE THE THRONE!

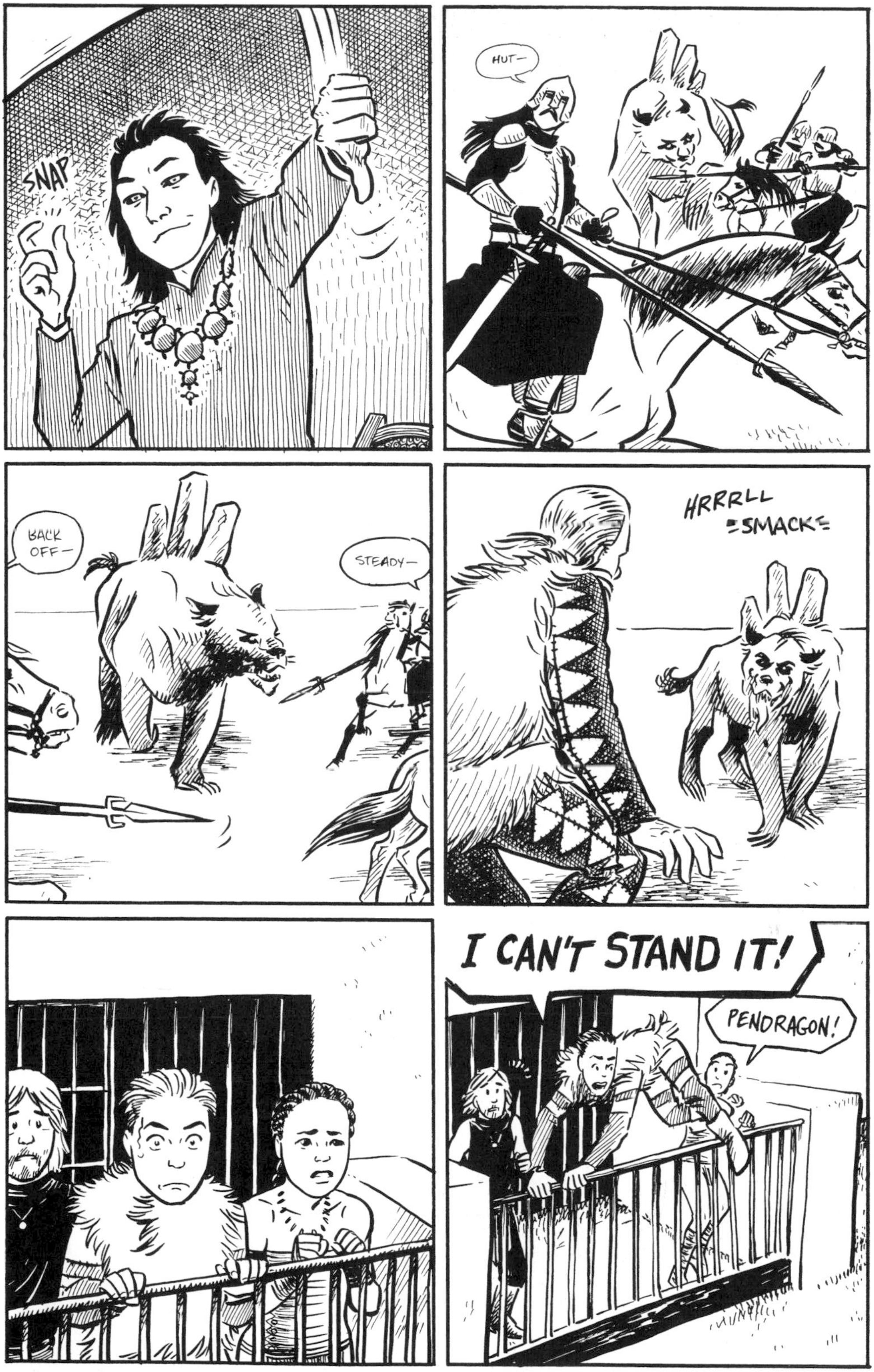
SNAP
HUT-
BACK OFF-
STEADY-
HRRRLL
SMACK
I CAN'T STAND IT!
PENDRAGON!

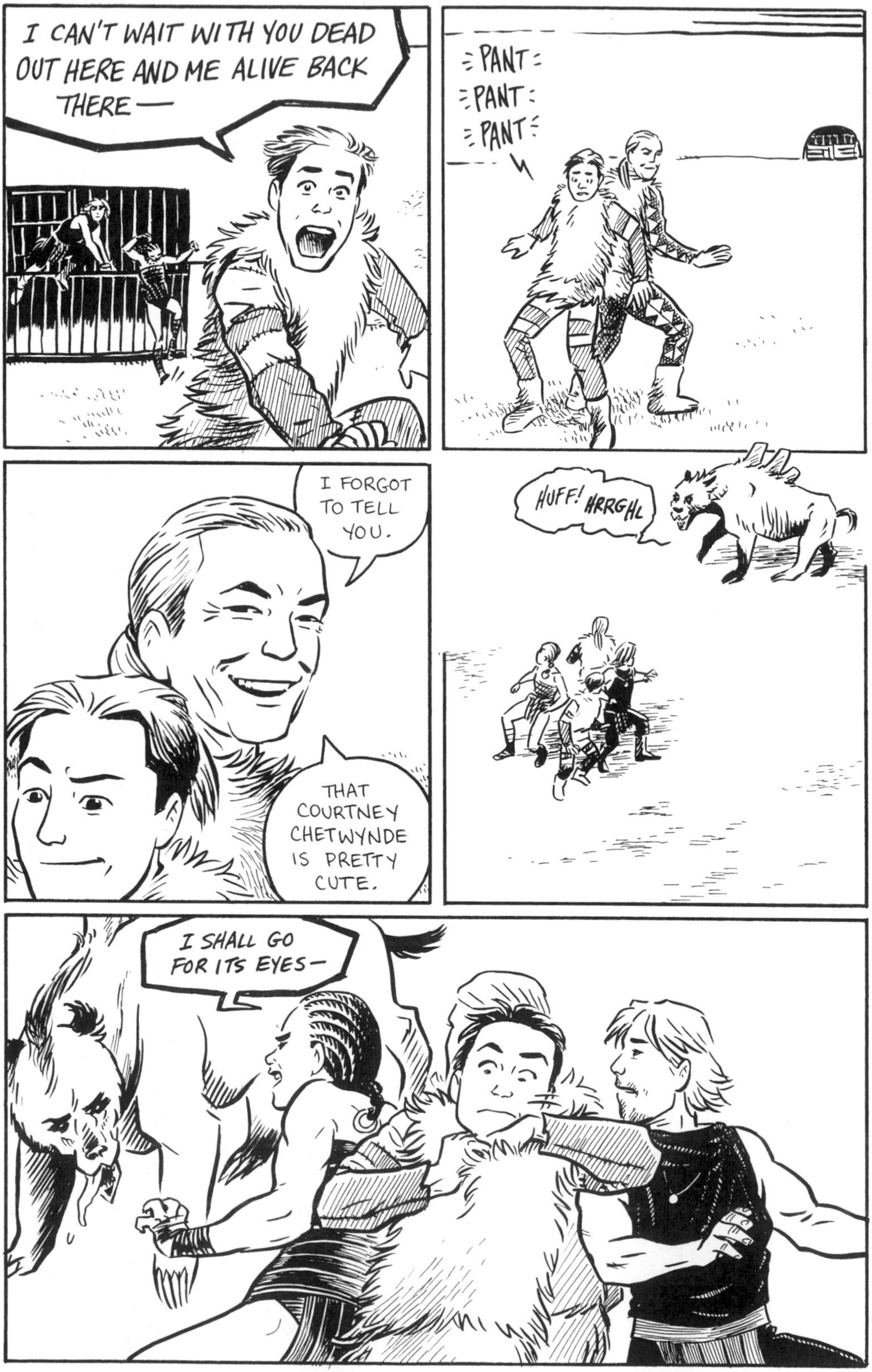
I CAN'T WAIT WITH YOU DEAD OUT HERE AND ME ALIVE BACK THERE—
PANT
PANT
PANT
I FORGOT TO TELL YOU.
THAT COURTNEY CHETWYNDE IS PRETTY CUTE.
HUFF! HRRGHL
I SHALL GO FOR ITS EYES—

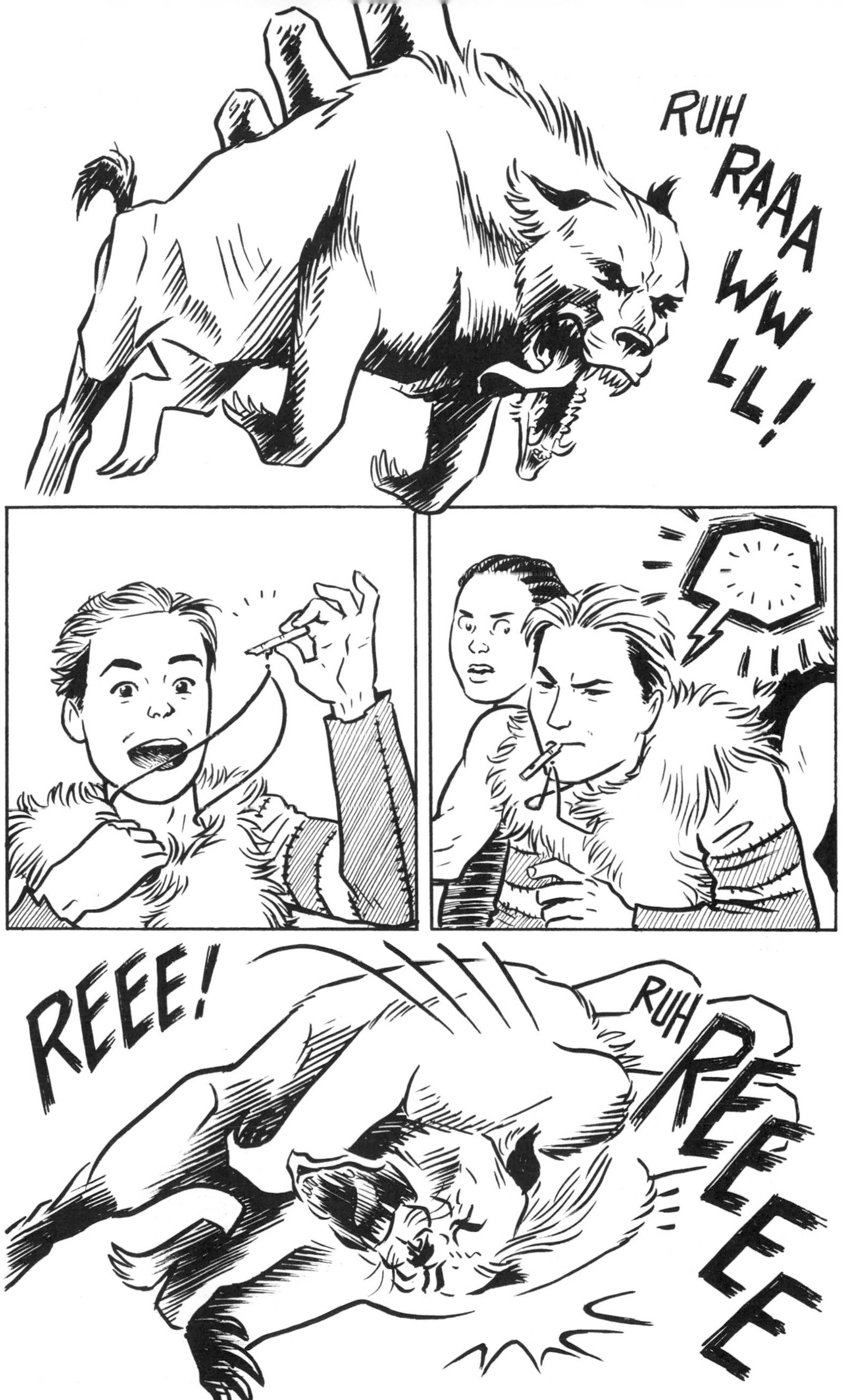
RUH RAAAWWLL!
REEE!
RUH REEEE

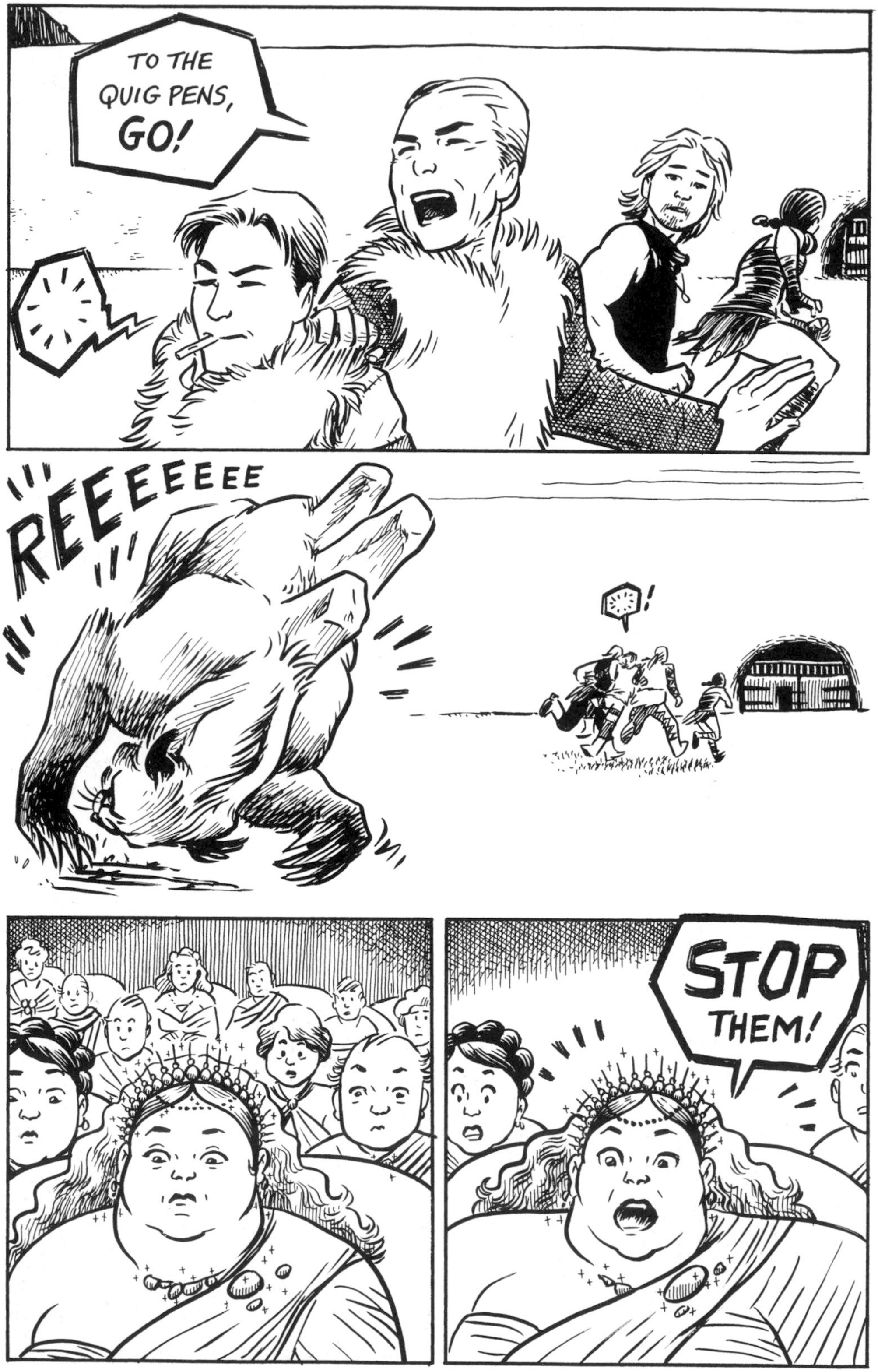
TO THE QUIG PENS, GO!
REEEEEEEE
STOP THEM!

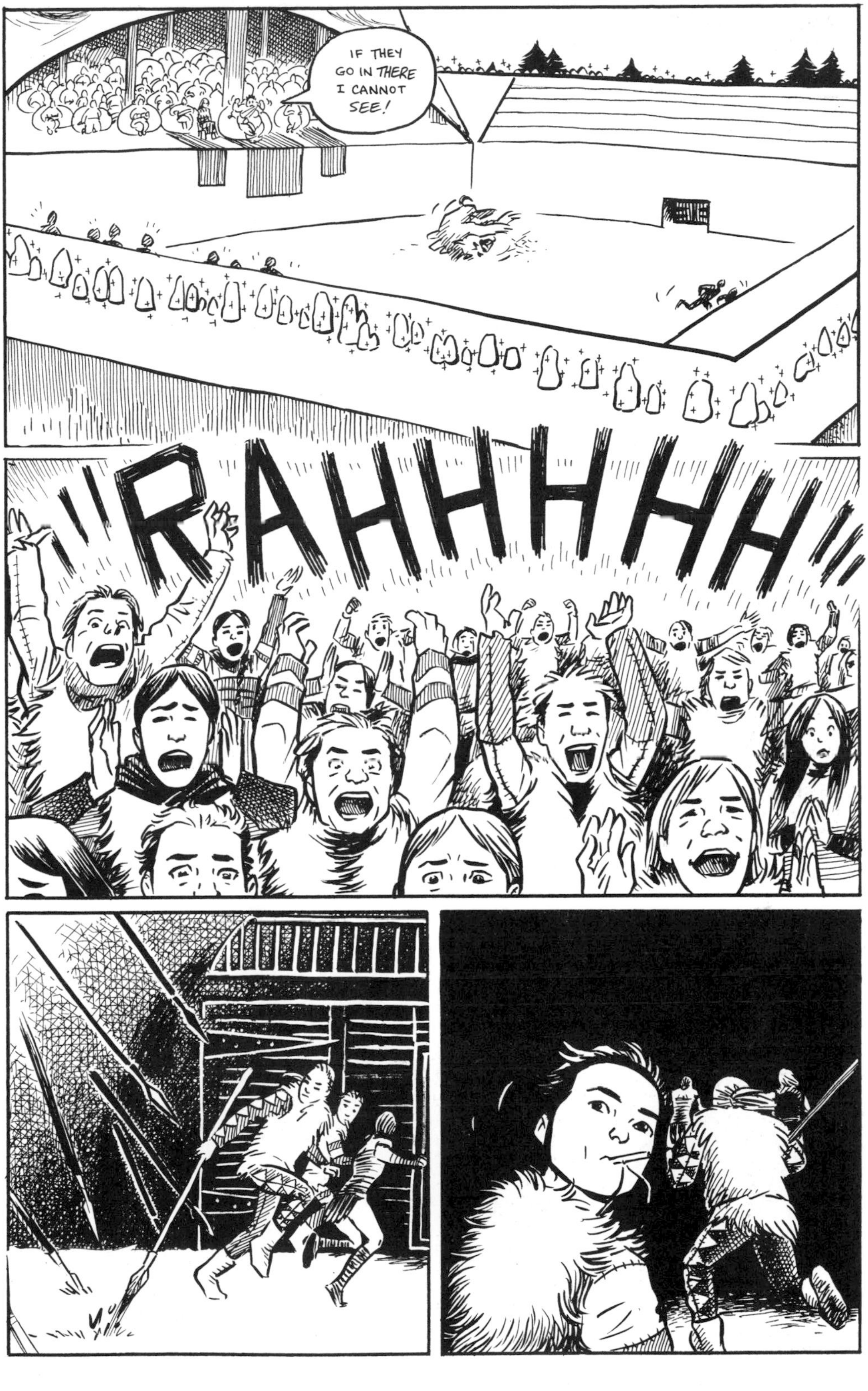
IF THEY GO IN THERE I CANNOT SEE!
"RAHHHHH"

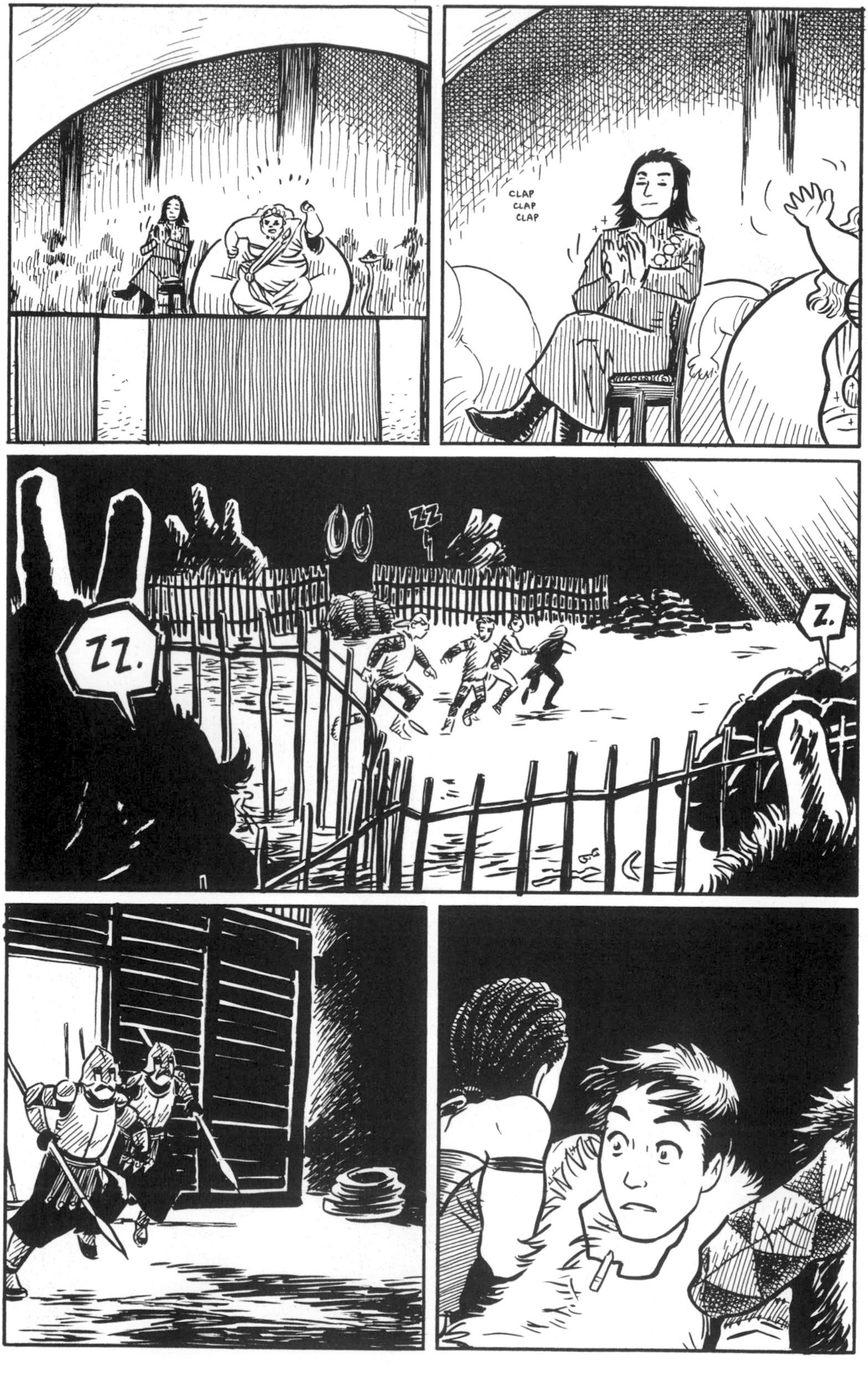
CLAP
CLAP
CLAP
ZZ.
ZZ
Z.

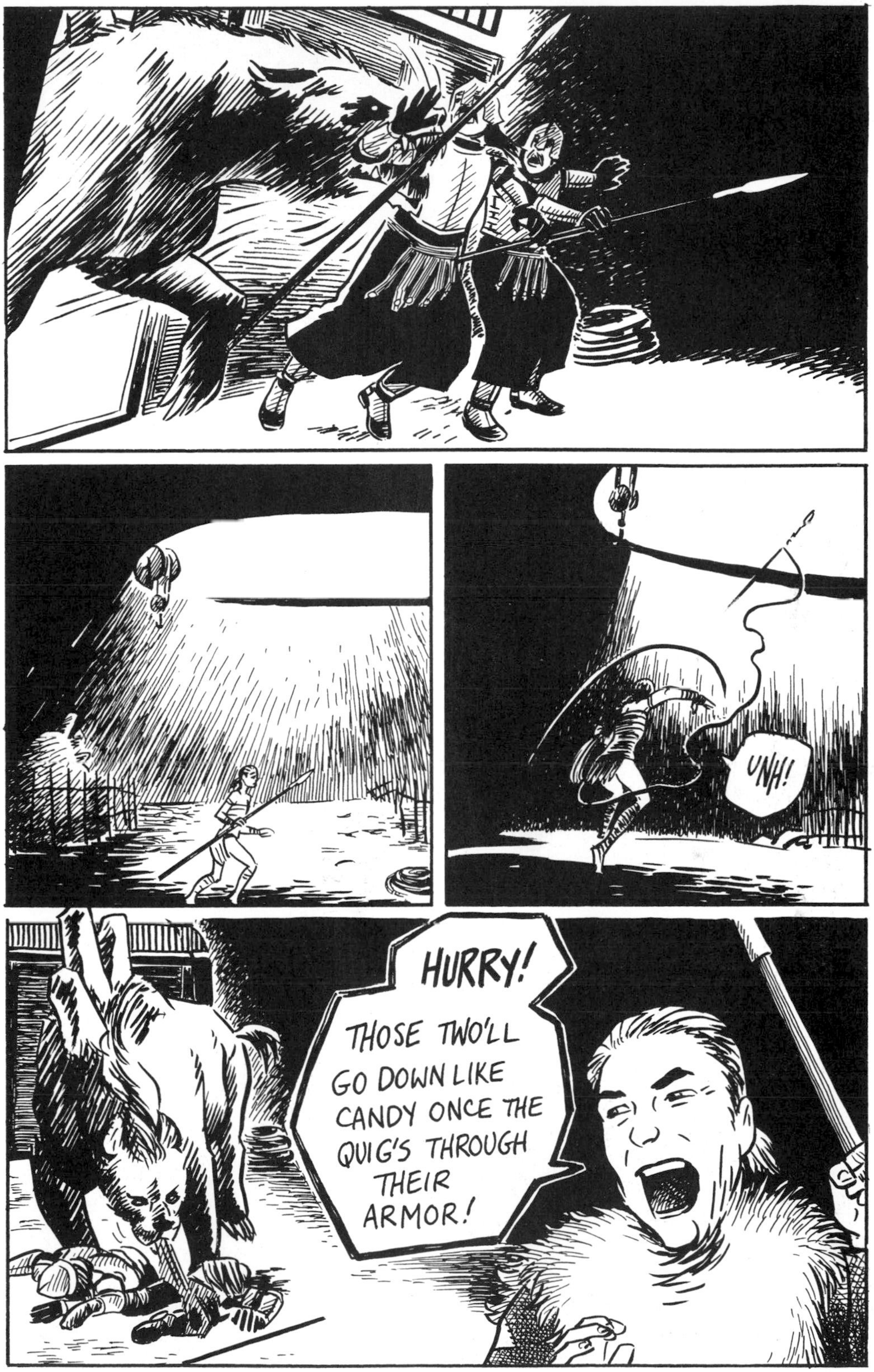
UNH!
HURRY!
THOSE TWO'LL GO DOWN LIKE CANDY ONCE THE QUIG'S THROUGH THEIR ARMOR!

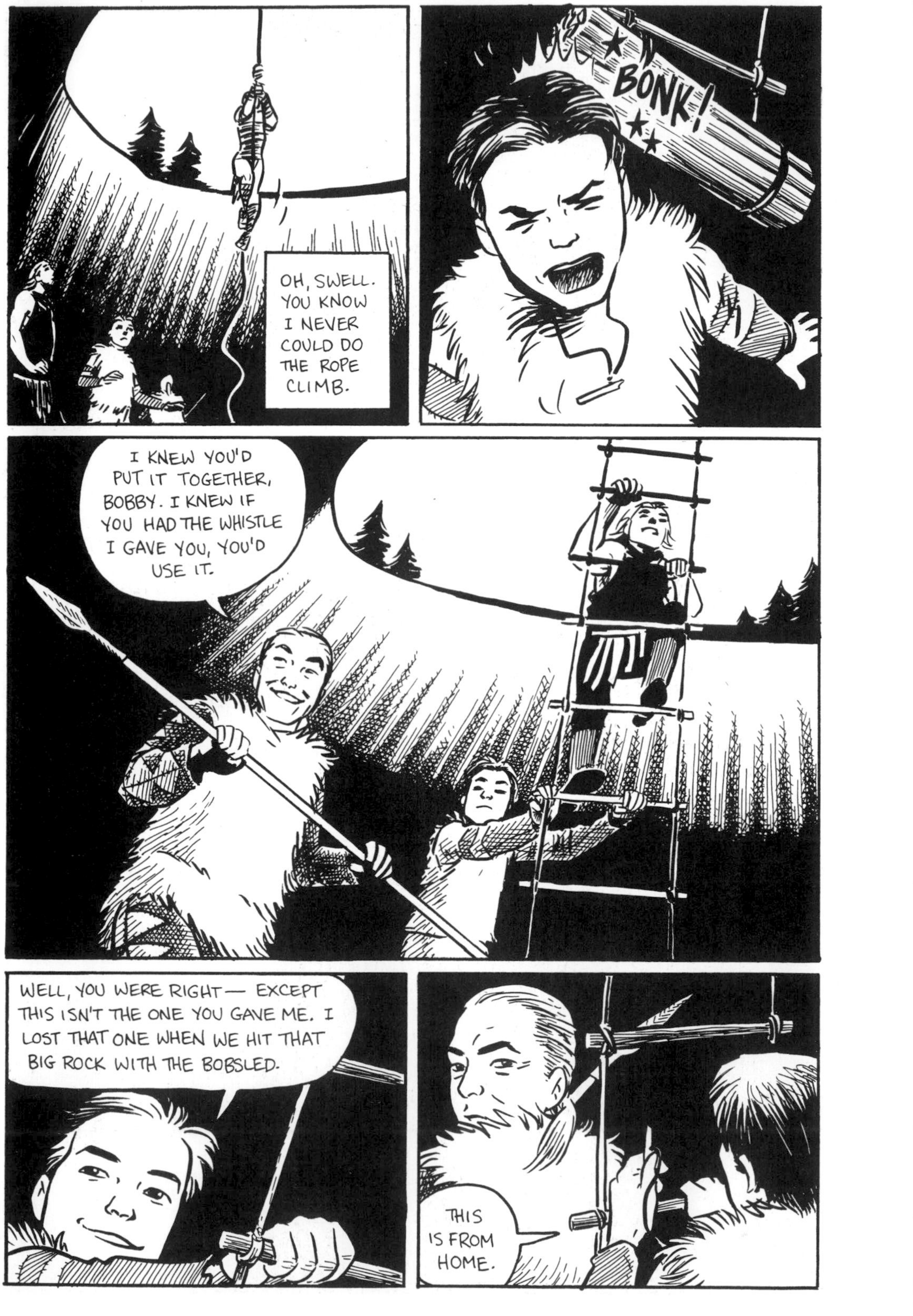
OH, SWELL. YOU KNOW I NEVER COULD DO THE ROPE CLIMB.
BONK!
I KNEW YOU'D PUT IT TOGETHER, BOBBY. I KNEW IF YOU HAD THE WHISTLE I GAVE YOU, YOU'D USE IT.
WELL, YOU WERE RIGHT— EXCEPT THIS ISN'T THE ONE YOU GAVE ME. I LOST THAT ONE WHEN WE HIT THAT BIG ROCK WITH THE BOBSLED.
THIS IS FROM HOME.

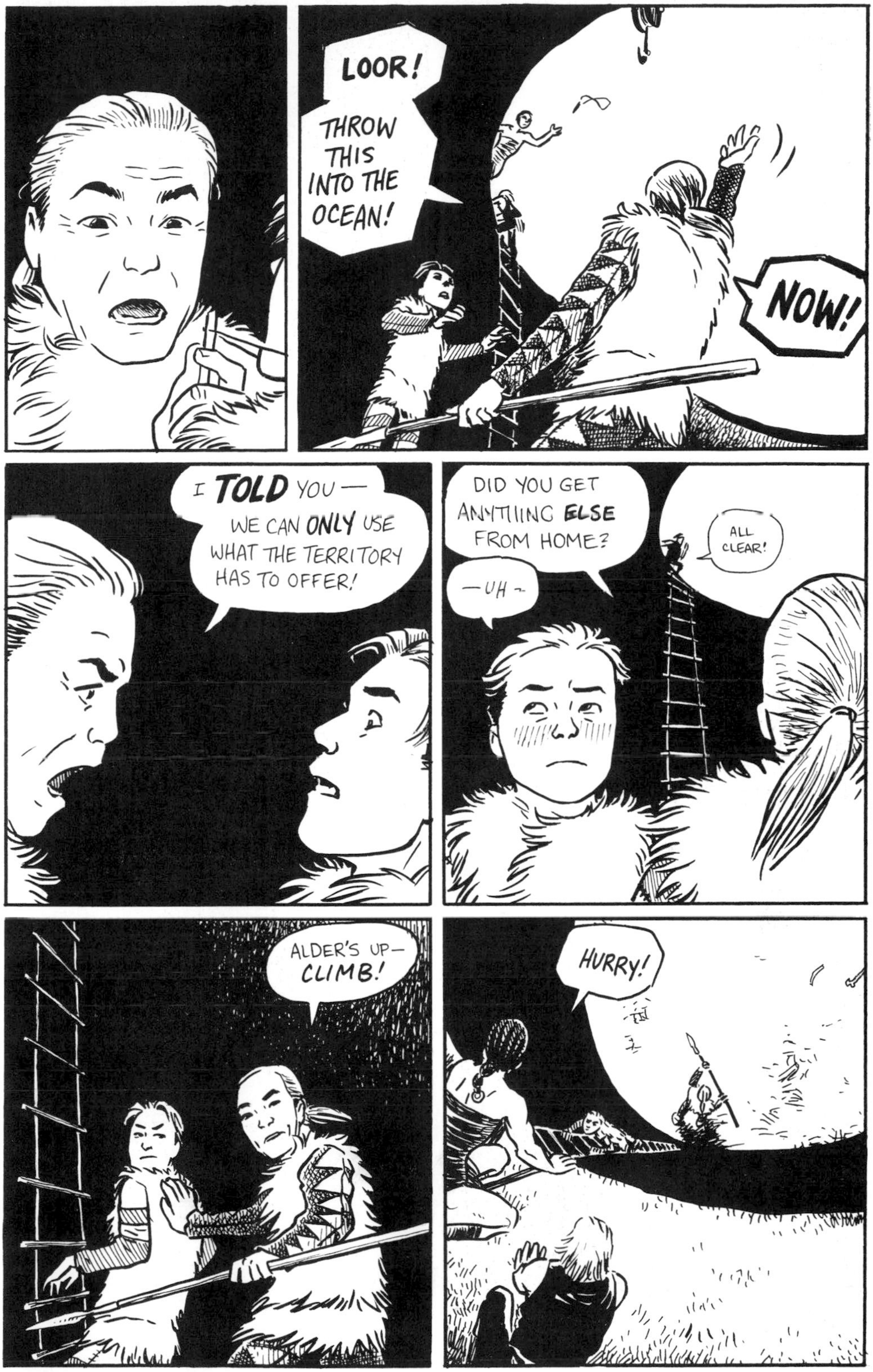
LOOR!
THROW THIS INTO THE OCEAN!
NOW!
I TOLD YOU — WE CAN ONLY USE WHAT THE TERRITORY HAS TO OFFER!
DID YOU GET ANYTHING ELSE FROM HOME?
—UH—
ALL CLEAR!
ALDER'S UP— CLIMB!
HURRY!

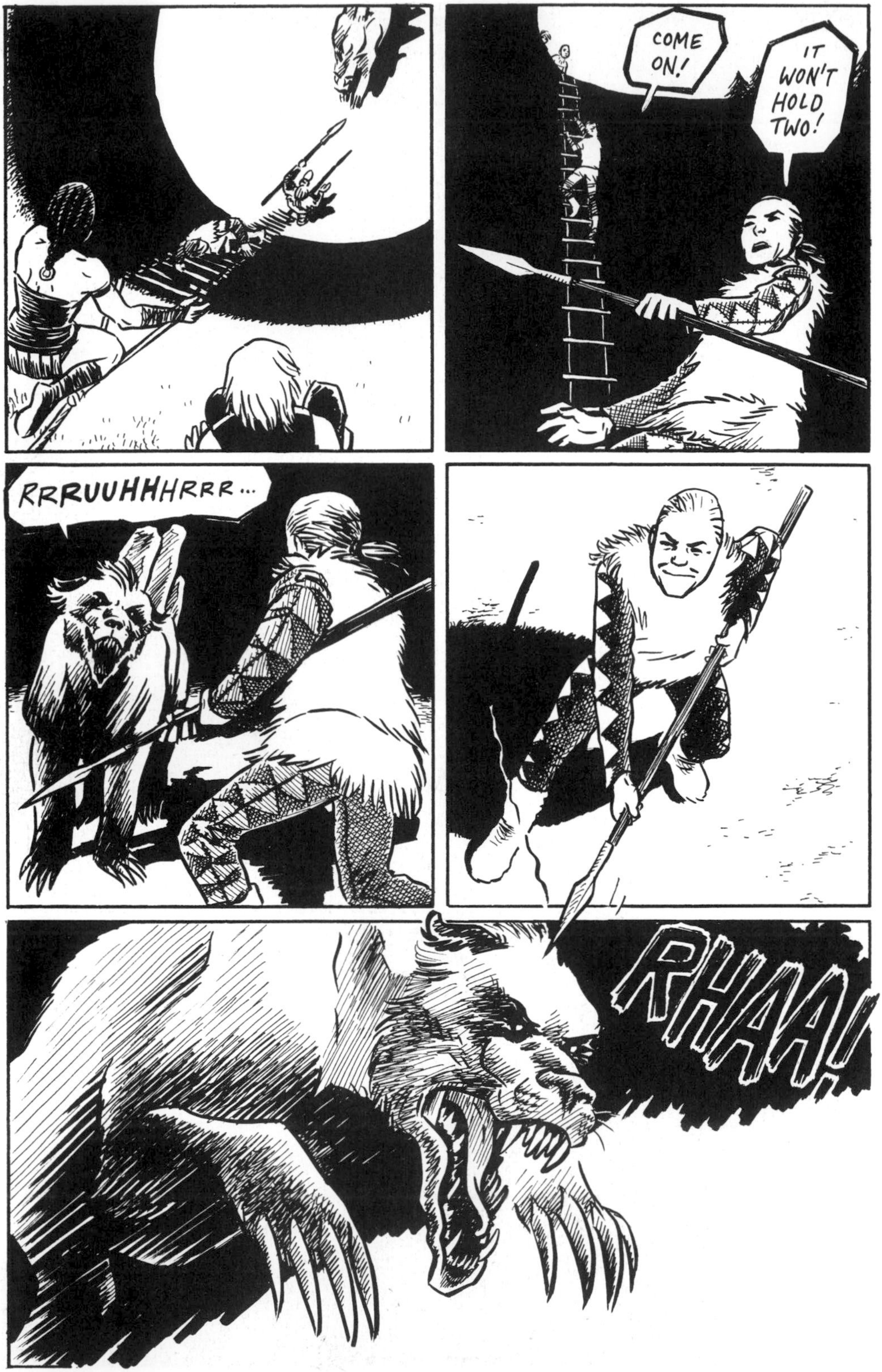
COME ON!
IT WON'T HOLD TWO!
RRRUUHHHRRR...
RHAA!

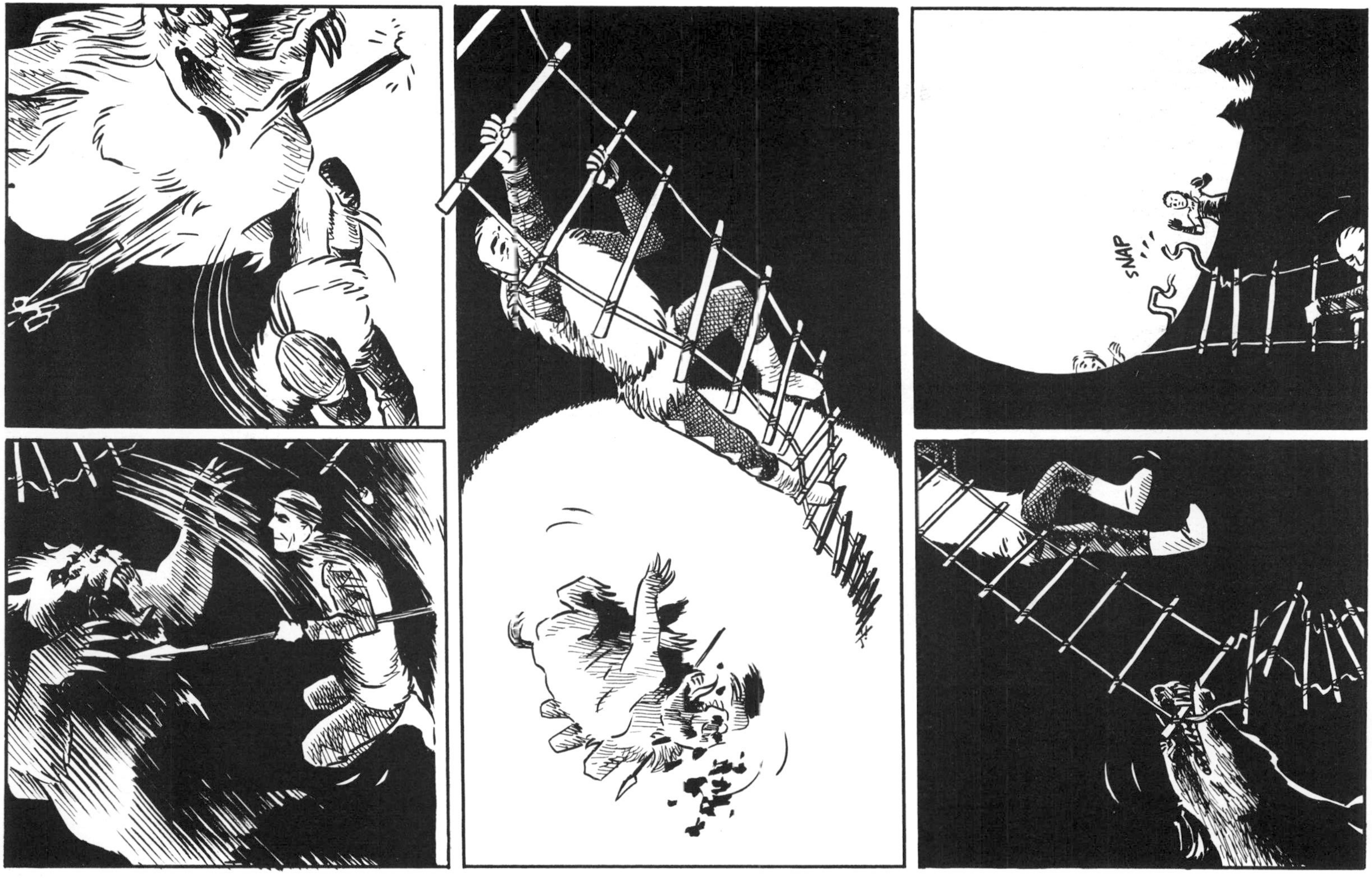
SNAP

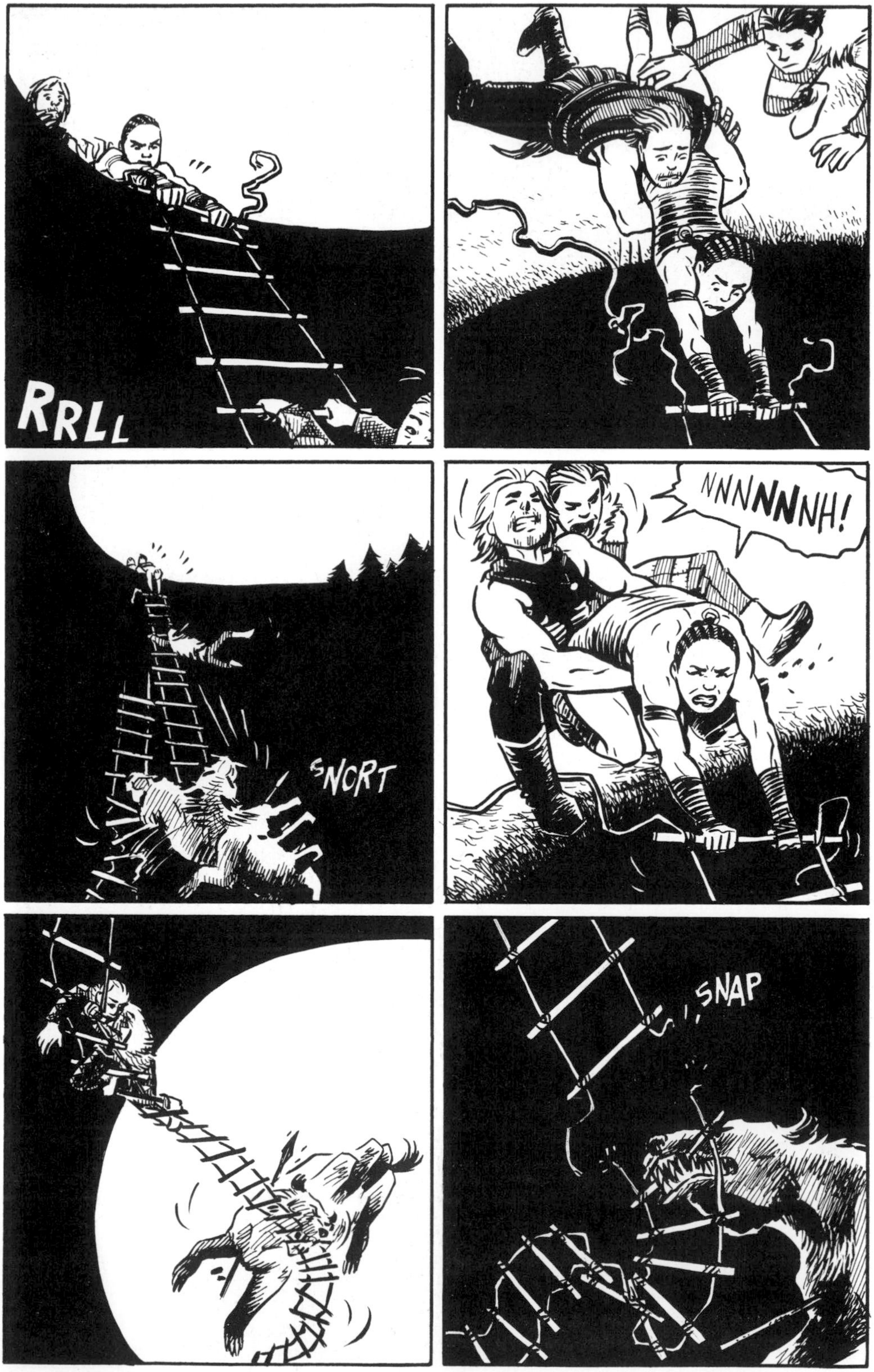
RRLL
SNORT
NNNNNNH!
SNAP

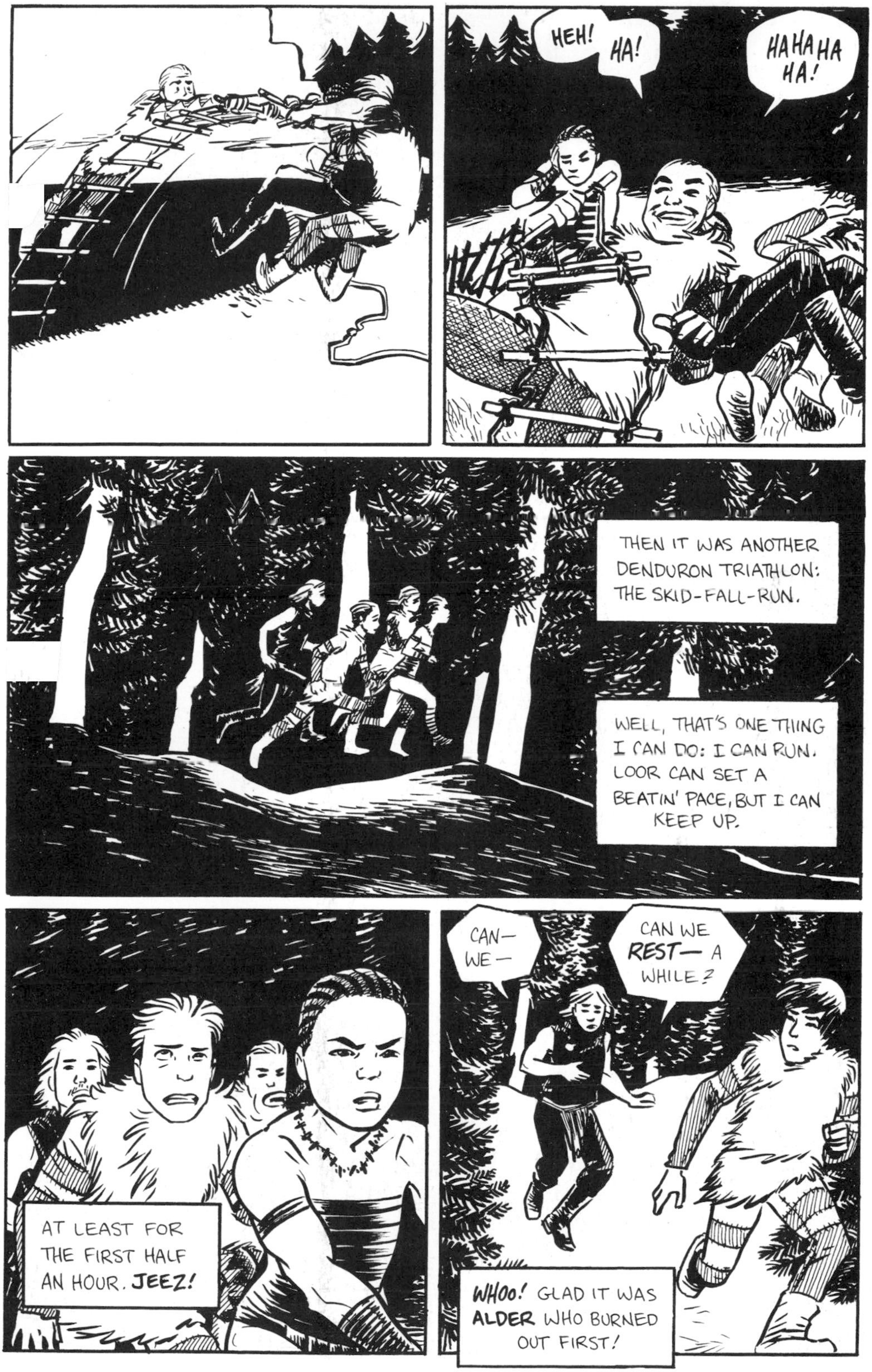
HEH!
HA!
HAHAHA HA HA!
THEN IT WAS ANOTHER DENDURON TRIATHLON: THE SKID-FALL-RUN.
WELL, THAT'S ONE THING I CAN DO: I CAN RUN. LOOR CAN SET A BEATIN' PACE, BUT I CAN KEEP UP.
AT LEAST FOR THE FIRST HALF AN HOUR. JEEZ!
CAN— WE—
CAN WE REST— A WHILE?
WHOO! GLAD IT WAS ALDER WHO BURNED OUT FIRST!

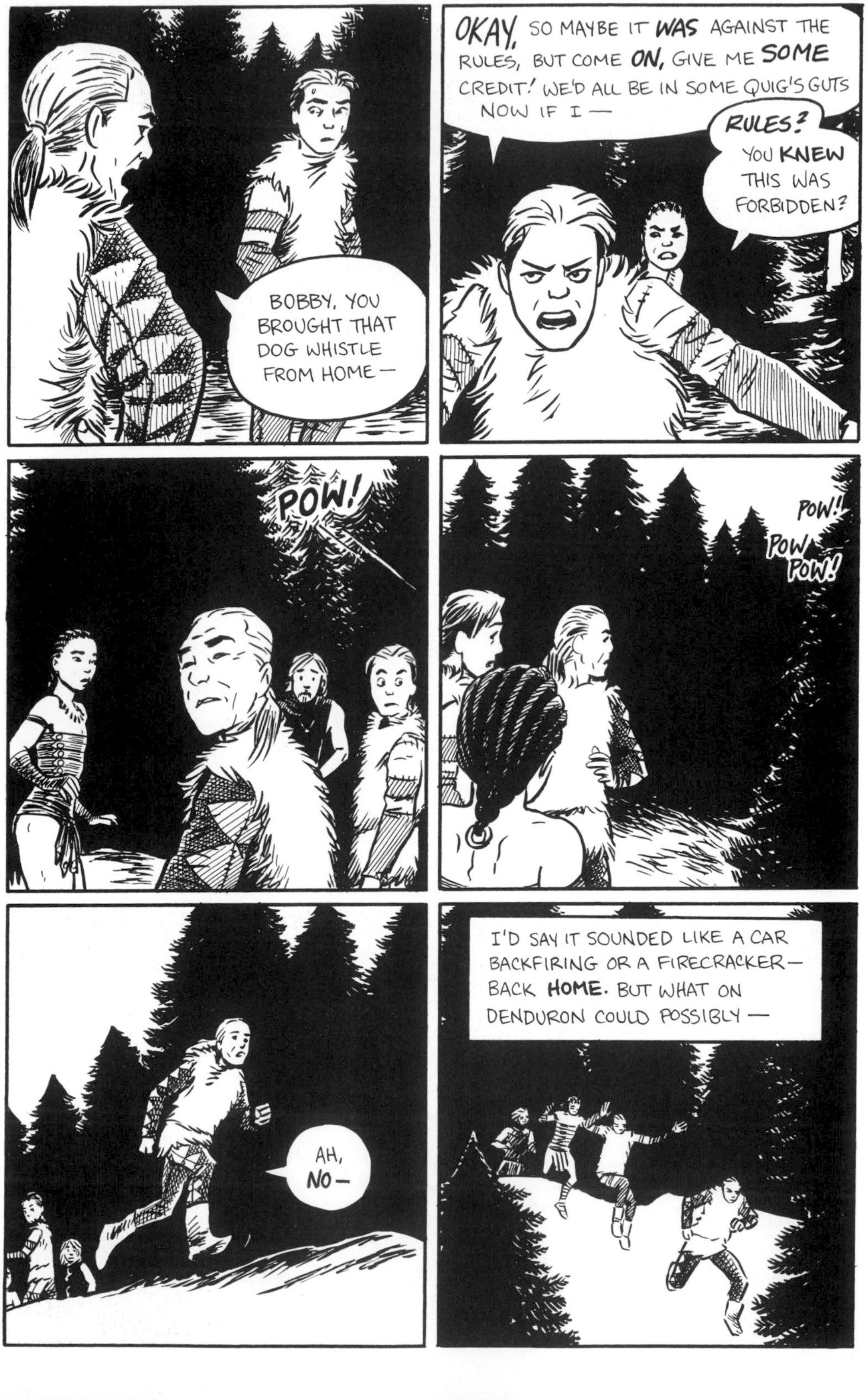
BOBBY, YOU BROUGHT THAT DOG WHISTLE FROM HOME—
OKAY, SO MAYBE IT WAS AGAINST THE RULES, BUT COME ON, GIVE ME SOME CREDIT! WE'D ALL BE IN SOME QUIG'S GUTS NOW IF I—
RULES? YOU KNEW THIS WAS FORBIDDEN?
POW!
POW!
POW
POW!
AH, NO—
I'D SAY IT SOUNDED LIKE A CAR BACKFIRING OR A FIRECRACKER— BACK HOME. BUT WHAT ON DENDURON COULD POSSIBLY—

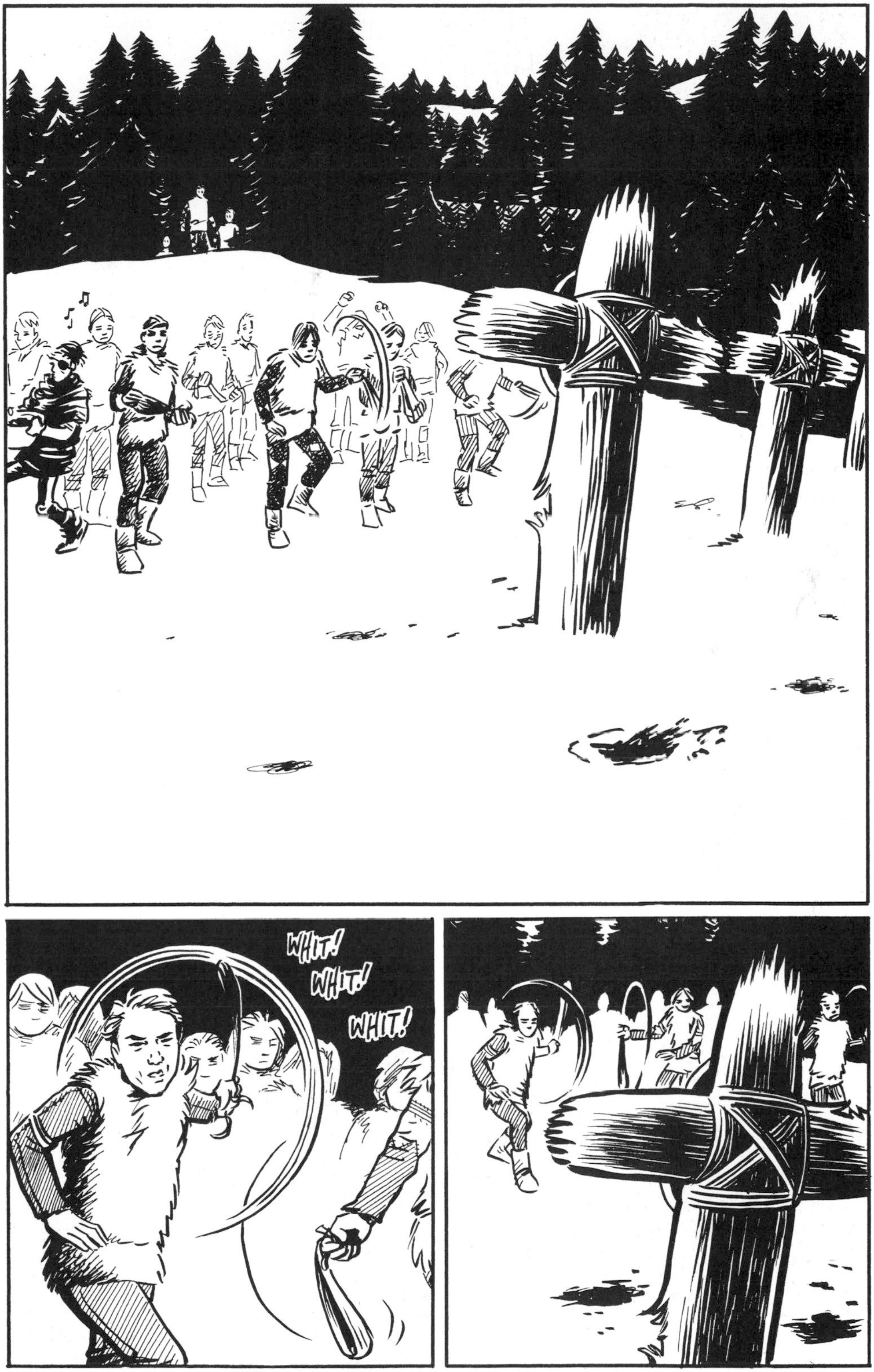
WHIT!
WHIT!
WHIT!

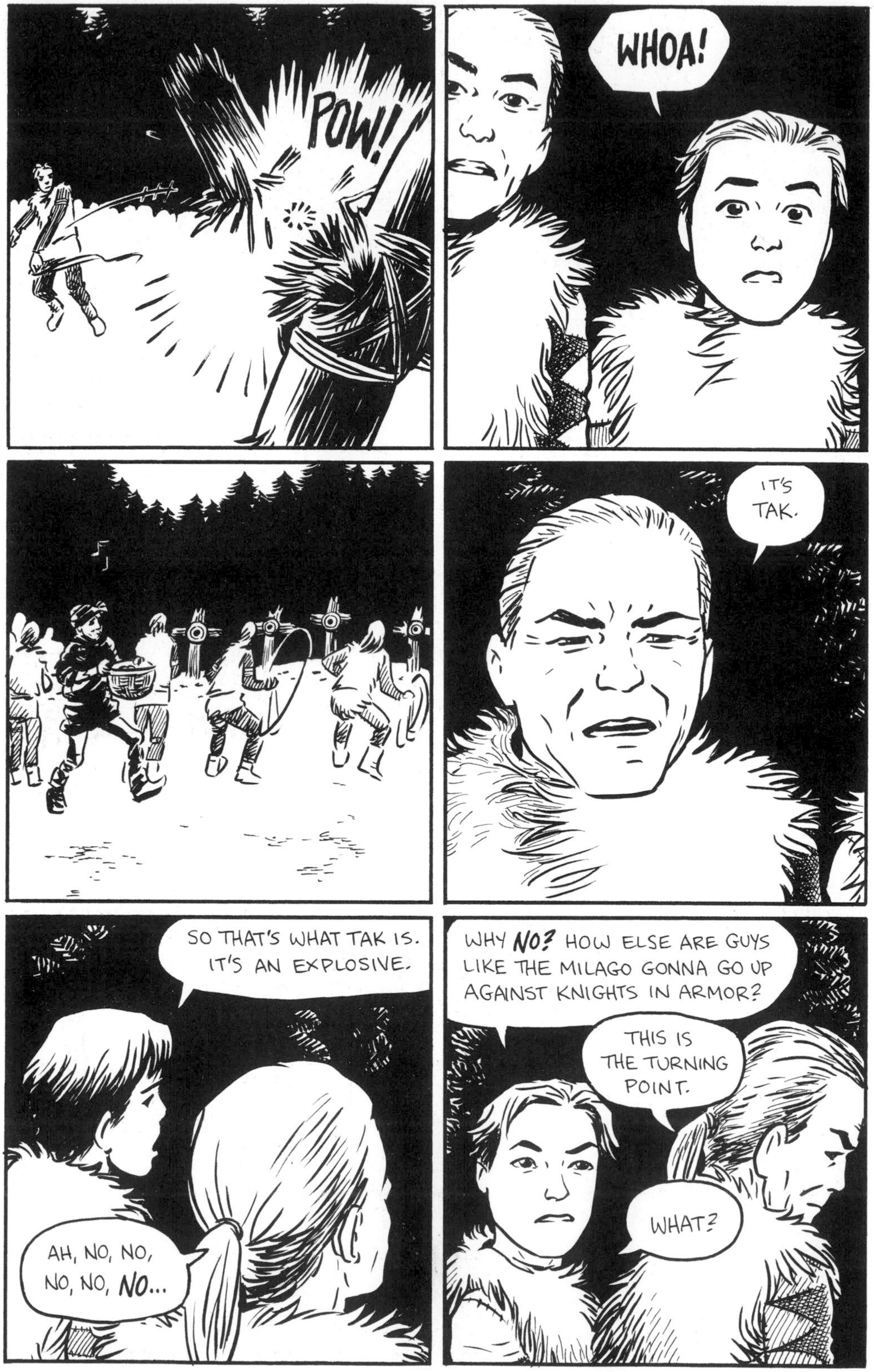
POW!
WHOA!
IT'S TAK.
SO THAT'S WHAT TAK IS. IT'S AN EXPLOSIVE.
AH, NO, NO, NO, NO, NO...
WHY NO? HOW ELSE ARE GUYS LIKE THE MILAGO GONNA GO UP AGAINST KNIGHTS IN ARMOR?
THIS IS THE TURNING POINT.
WHAT?

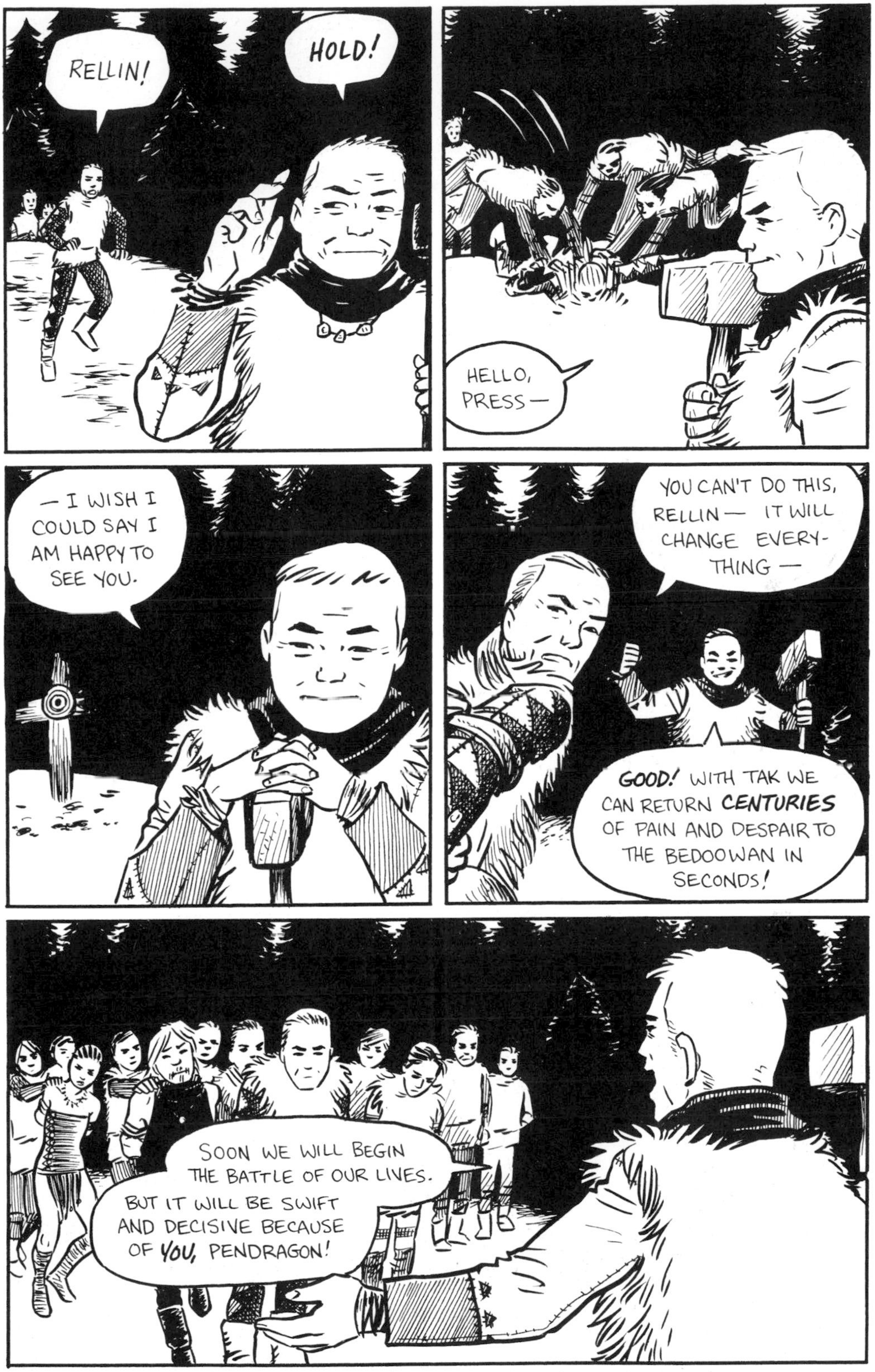
RELLIN!
HOLD!
HELLO, PRESS—
—I WISH I COULD SAY I AM HAPPY TO SEE YOU.
YOU CAN'T DO THIS, RELLIN— IT WILL CHANGE EVERY-THING—
GOOD! WITH TAK WE CAN RETURN CENTURIES OF PAIN AND DESPAIR TO THE BEDOOWAN IN SECONDS!
SOON WE WILL BEGIN THE BATTLE OF OUR LIVES.
BUT IT WILL BE SWIFT AND DECISIVE BECAUSE OF YOU, PENDRAGON!

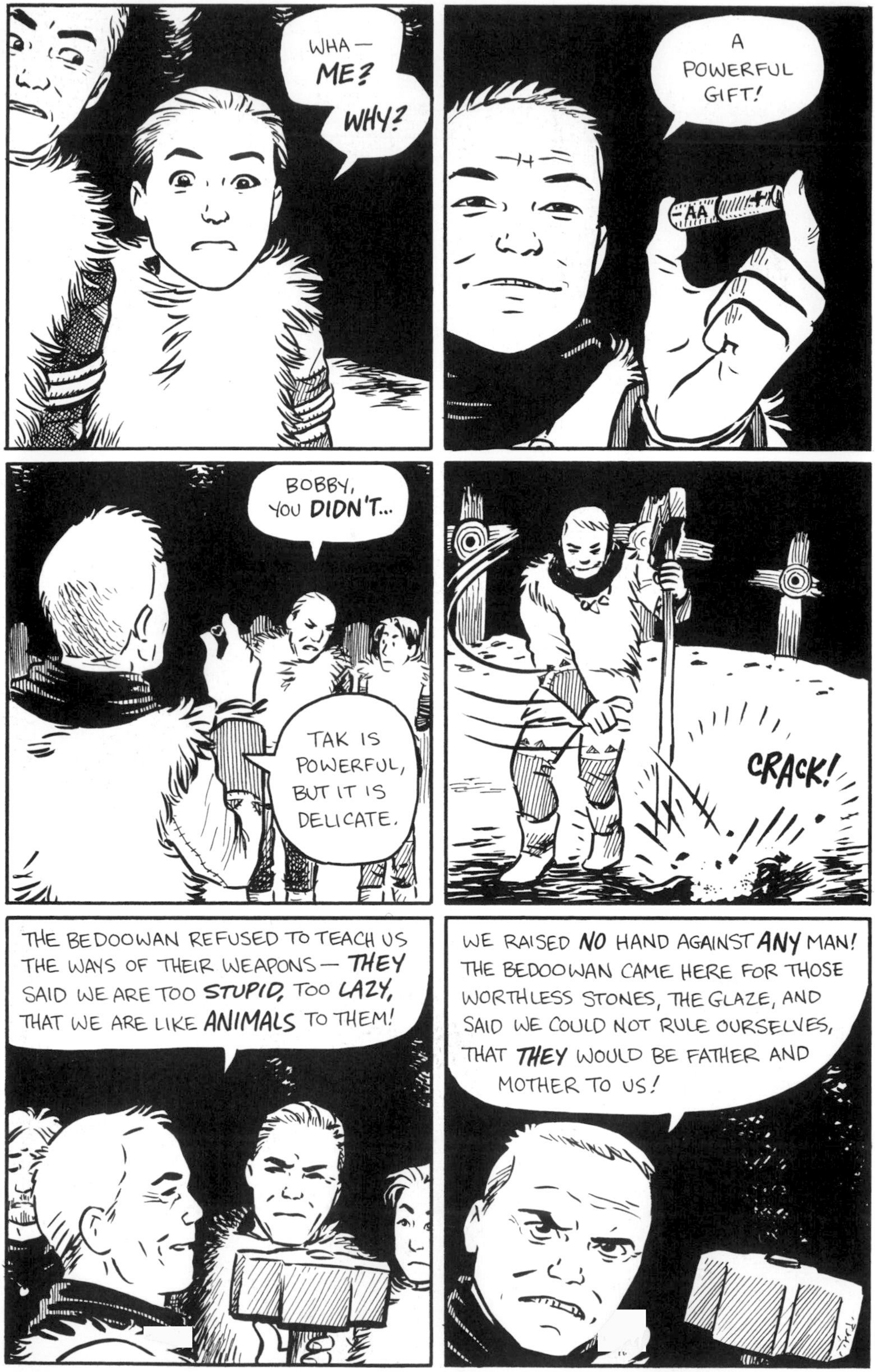
WHA— ME? WHY?
A POWERFUL GIFT!
AA
BOBBY, YOU DIDN'T...
TAK IS POWERFUL, BUT IT IS DELICATE.
CRACK!
THE BEDOOWAN REFUSED TO TEACH US THE WAYS OF THEIR WEAPONS— THEY SAID WE ARE TOO STUPID, TOO LAZY, THAT WE ARE LIKE ANIMALS TO THEM!
WE RAISED NO HAND AGAINST ANY MAN! THE BEDOOWAN CAME HERE FOR THOSE WORTHLESS STONES, THE GLAZE, AND SAID WE COULD NOT RULE OURSELVES, THAT THEY WOULD BE FATHER AND MOTHER TO US!

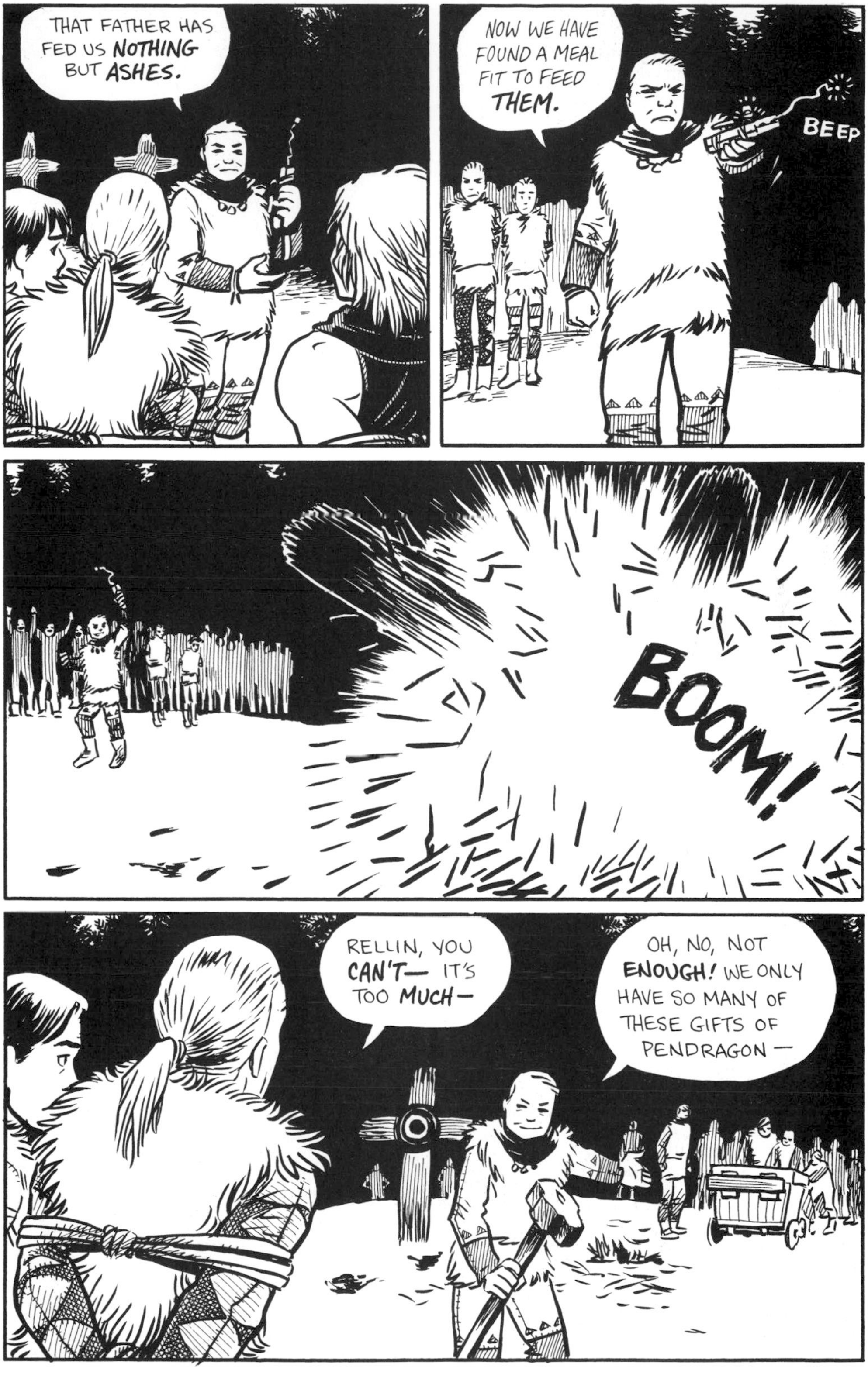
THAT FATHER HAS FED US NOTHING BUT ASHES.
NOW WE HAVE FOUND A MEAL FIT TO FEED THEM.
BEEP
BOOM!
RELLIN, YOU CAN'T— IT'S TOO MUCH—
OH, NO, NOT ENOUGH! WE ONLY HAVE SO MANY OF THESE GIFTS OF PENDRAGON—

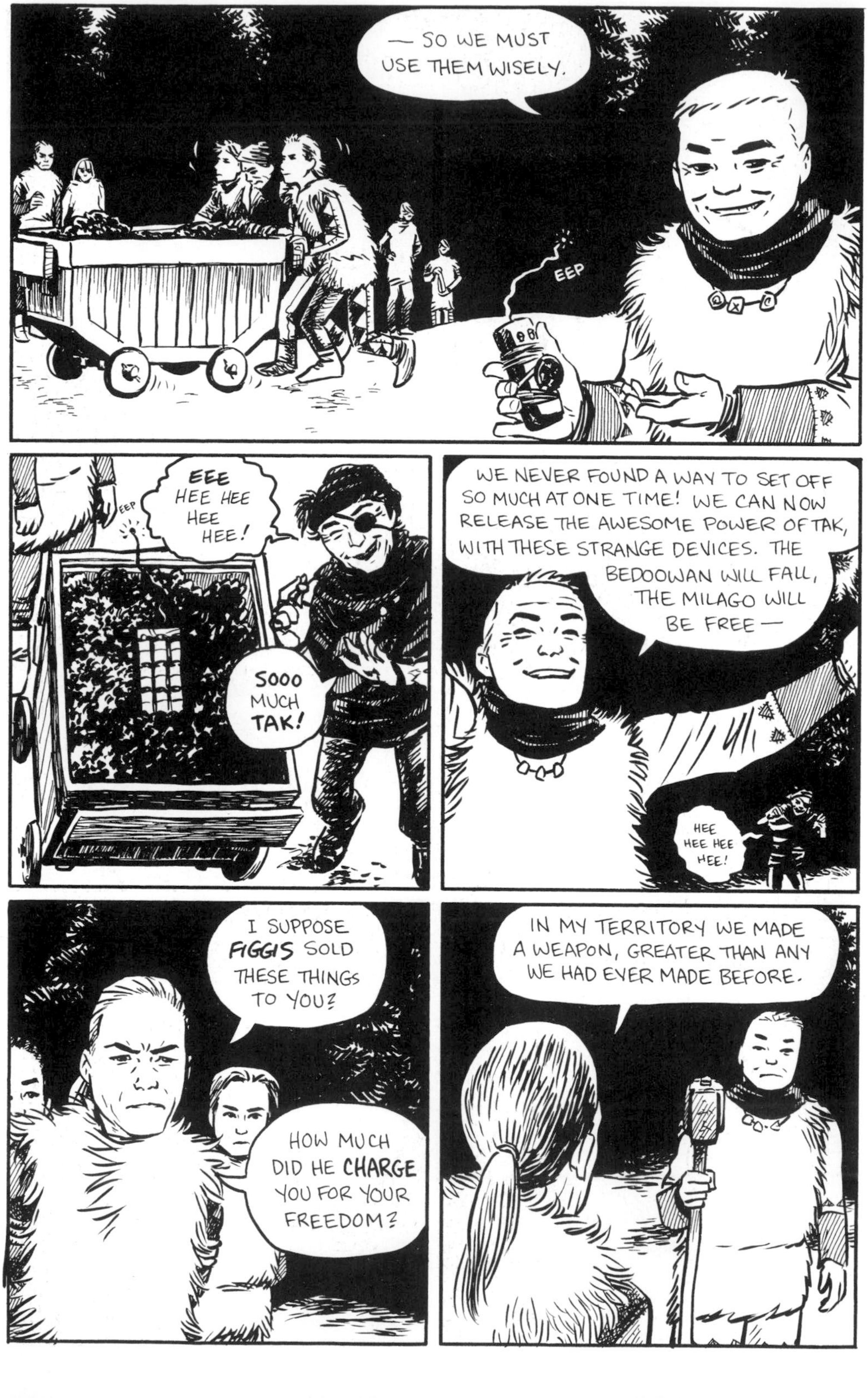
— SO WE MUST USE THEM WISELY.
EEP
EEP
EEE HEE HEE HEE HEE!
SOOO MUCH TAK!
WE NEVER FOUND A WAY TO SET OFF SO MUCH AT ONE TIME! WE CAN NOW RELEASE THE AWESOME POWER OF TAK, WITH THESE STRANGE DEVICES. THE BEDOOWAN WILL FALL, THE MILAGO WILL BE FREE —
HEE HEE HEE HEE!
I SUPPOSE FIGGIS SOLD THESE THINGS TO YOU?
HOW MUCH DID HE CHARGE YOU FOR YOUR FREEDOM?
IN MY TERRITORY WE MADE A WEAPON, GREATER THAN ANY WE HAD EVER MADE BEFORE.

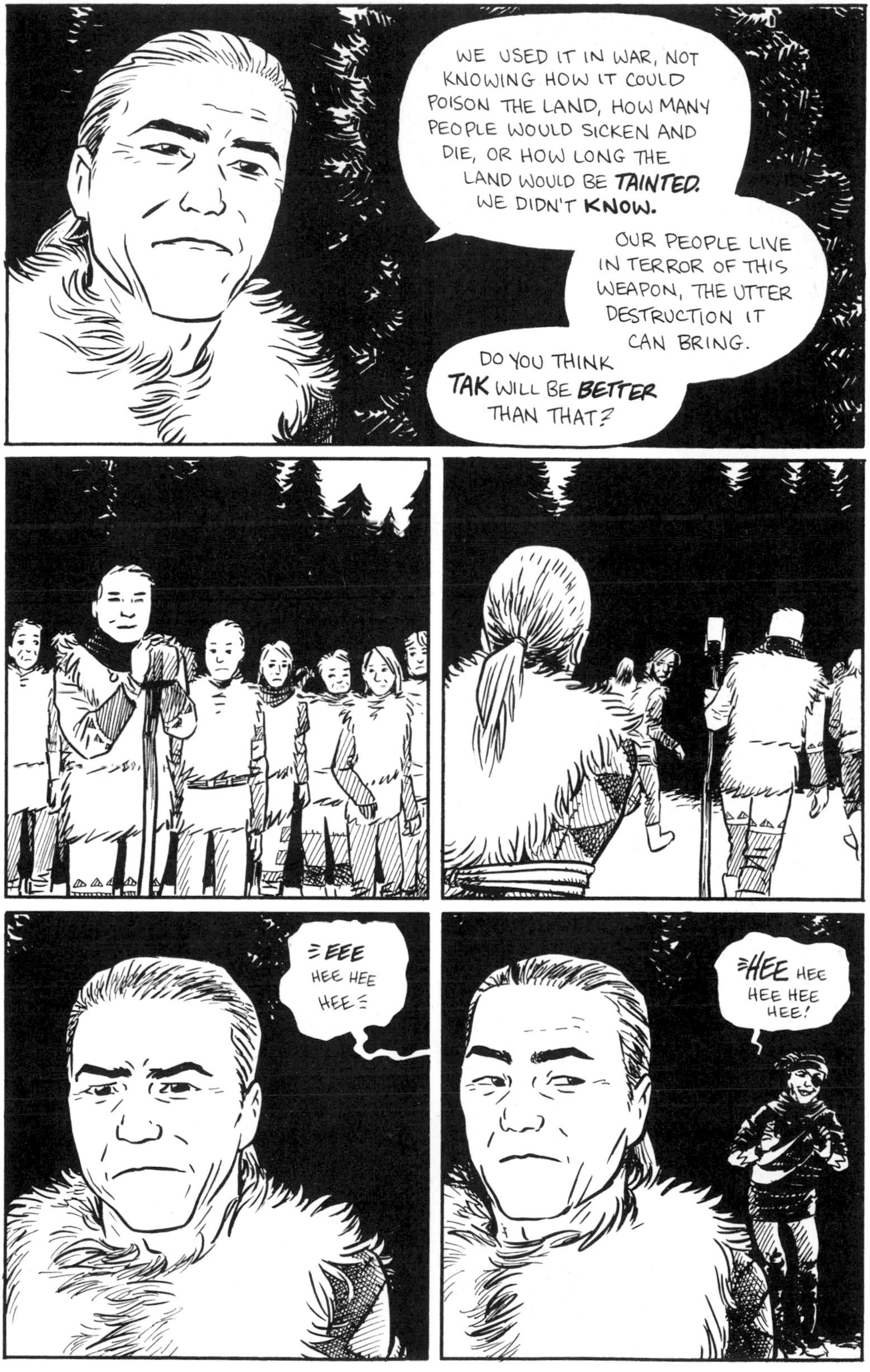
WE USED IT IN WAR, NOT KNOWING HOW IT COULD POISON THE LAND, HOW MANY PEOPLE WOULD SICKEN AND DIE, OR HOW LONG THE LAND WOULD BE TAINTED. WE DIDN'T KNOW.
OUR PEOPLE LIVE IN TERROR OF THIS WEAPON, THE UTTER DESTRUCTION IT CAN BRING.
DO YOU THINK TAK WILL BE BETTER THAN THAT?
EEE HEE HEE HEE
HEE HEE HEE HEE HEE!

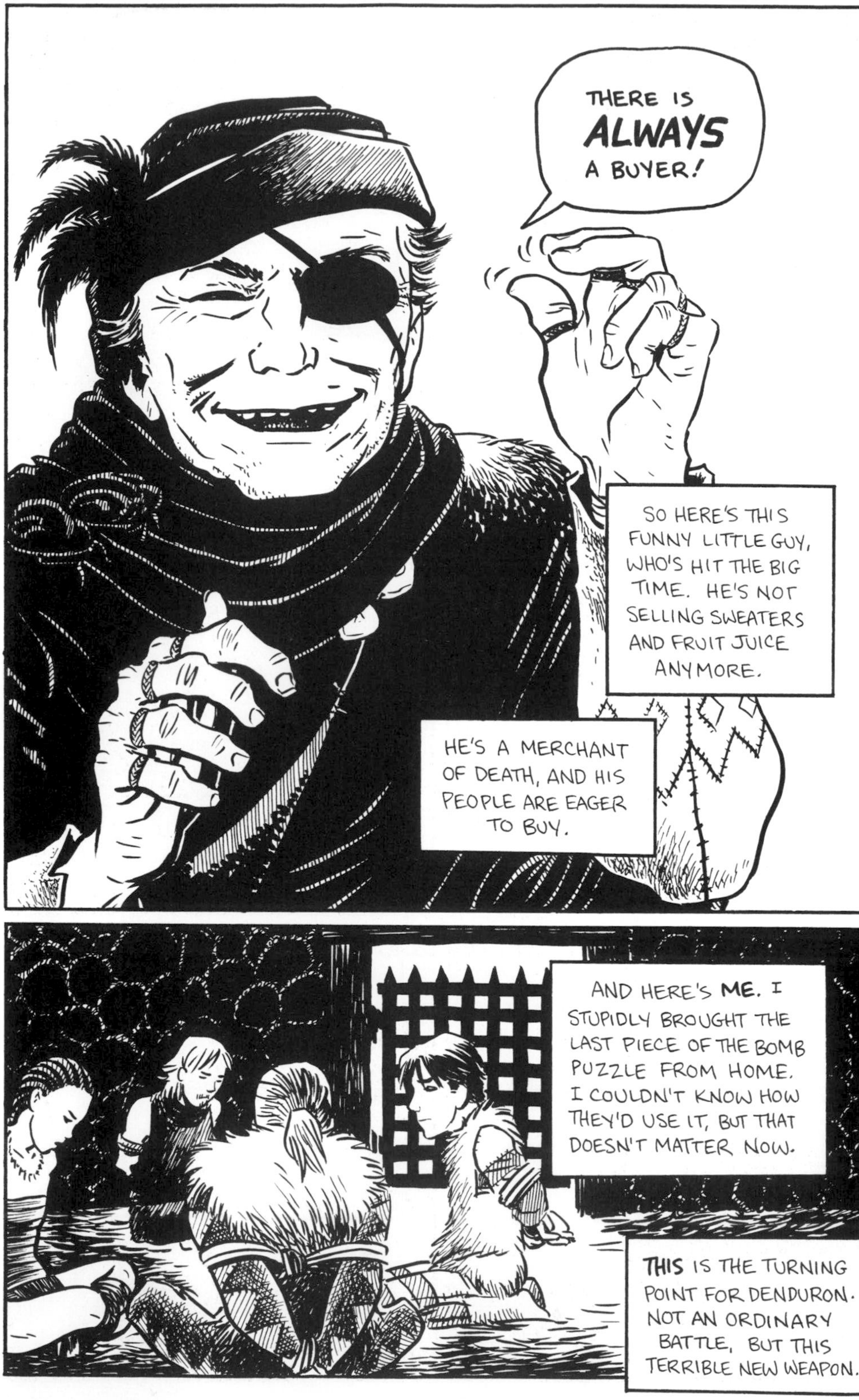
THERE IS ALWAYS A BUYER!
SO HERE'S THIS FUNNY LITTLE GUY, WHO'S HIT THE BIG TIME. HE'S NOT SELLING SWEATERS AND FRUIT JUICE ANYMORE.
HE'S A MERCHANT OF DEATH, AND HIS PEOPLE ARE EAGER TO BUY.
AND HERE'S ME. I STUPIDLY BROUGHT THE LAST PIECE OF THE BOMB PUZZLE FROM HOME. I COULDN'T KNOW HOW THEY'D USE IT, BUT THAT DOESN'T MATTER NOW.
THIS IS THE TURNING POINT FOR DENDURON. NOT AN ORDINARY BATTLE, BUT THIS TERRIBLE NEW WEAPON.

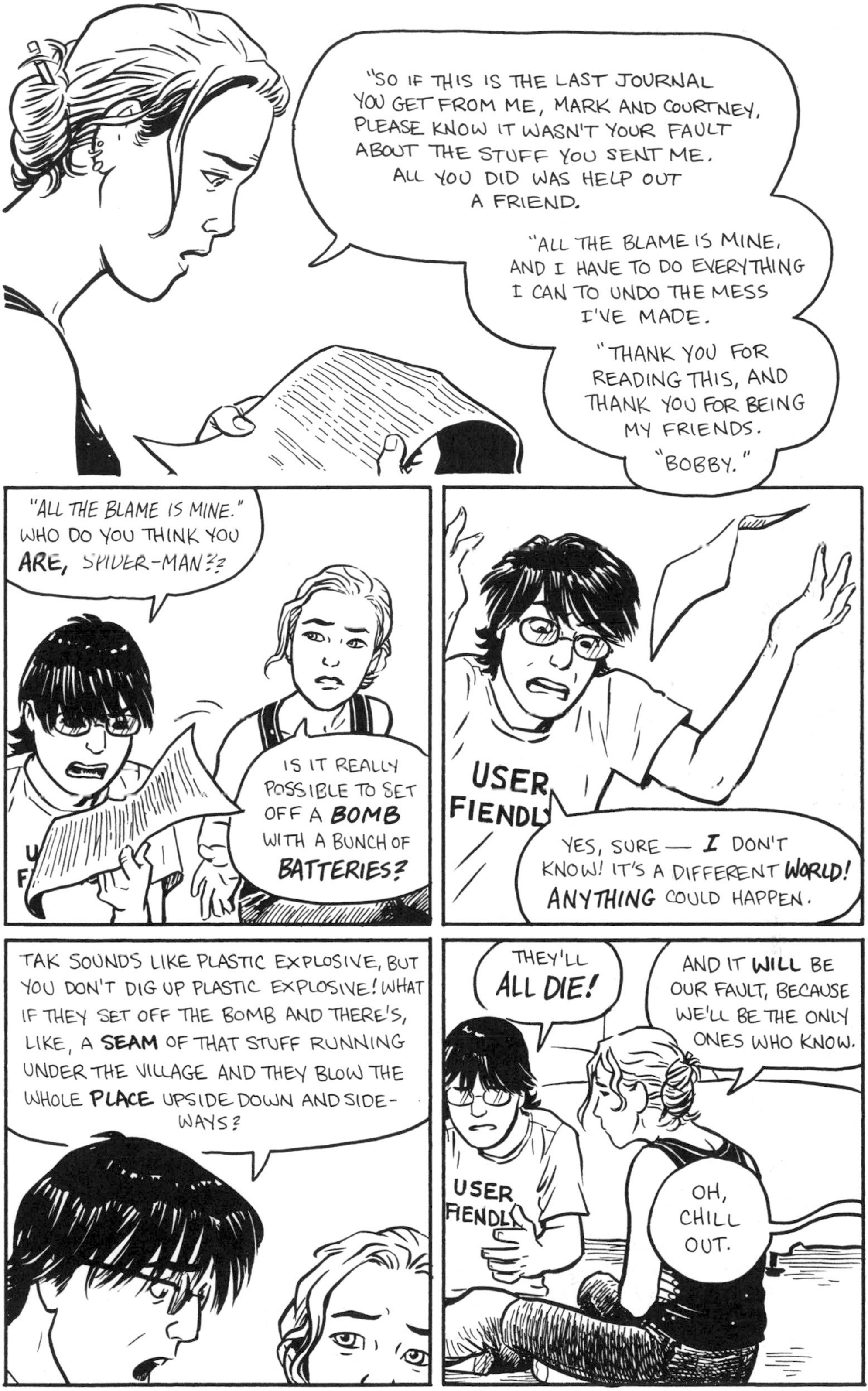
"SO IF THIS IS THE LAST JOURNAL YOU GET FROM ME, MARK AND COURTNEY, PLEASE KNOW IT WASN'T YOUR FAULT ABOUT THE STUFF YOU SENT ME. ALL YOU DID WAS HELP OUT A FRIEND.
"ALL THE BLAME IS MINE, AND I HAVE TO DO EVERYTHING I CAN TO UNDO THE MESS I'VE MADE.
"THANK YOU FOR READING THIS, AND THANK YOU FOR BEING MY FRIENDS.
"BOBBY."
"ALL THE BLAME IS MINE." WHO DO YOU THINK YOU ARE, SPIDER-MAN?!?
IS IT REALLY POSSIBLE TO SET OFF A BOMB WITH A BUNCH OF BATTERIES?
USER FIENDLY
YES, SURE — I DON'T KNOW! IT'S A DIFFERENT WORLD! ANYTHING COULD HAPPEN.
TAK SOUNDS LIKE PLASTIC EXPLOSIVE, BUT YOU DON'T DIG UP PLASTIC EXPLOSIVE! WHAT IF THEY SET OFF THE BOMB AND THERE'S, LIKE, A SEAM OF THAT STUFF RUNNING UNDER THE VILLAGE AND THEY BLOW THE WHOLE PLACE UPSIDE DOWN AND SIDEWAYS?
THEY'LL ALL DIE!
AND IT WILL BE OUR FAULT, BECAUSE WE'LL BE THE ONLY ONES WHO KNOW.
USER FIENDLY
OH, CHILL OUT.

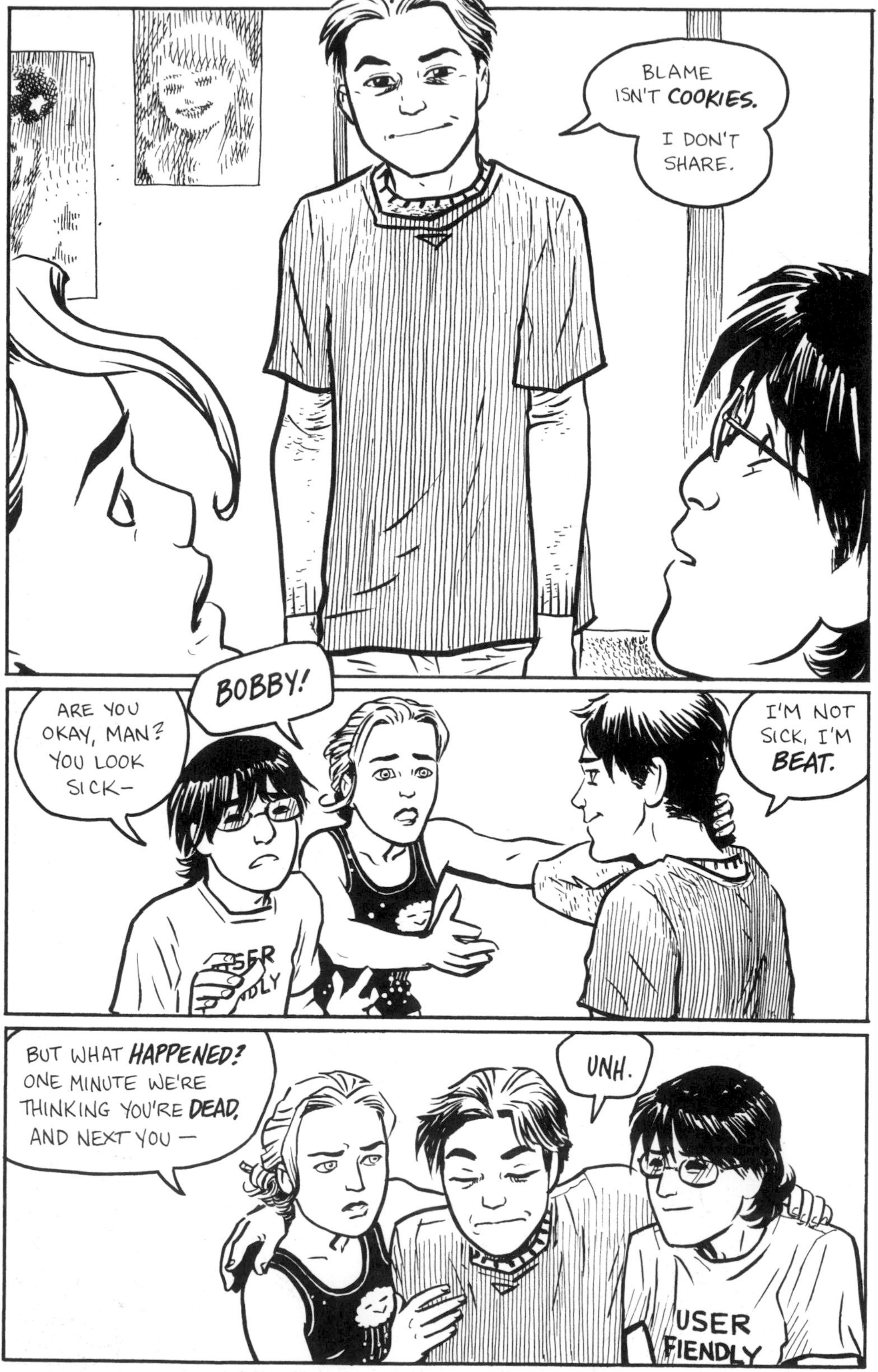
BLAME ISN'T COOKIES.
I DON'T SHARE.
ARE YOU OKAY, MAN? YOU LOOK SICK—
BOBBY!
I'M NOT SICK, I'M BEAT.
BUT WHAT HAPPENED? ONE MINUTE WE'RE THINKING YOU'RE DEAD, AND NEXT YOU—
UNH.
USER FIENDLY

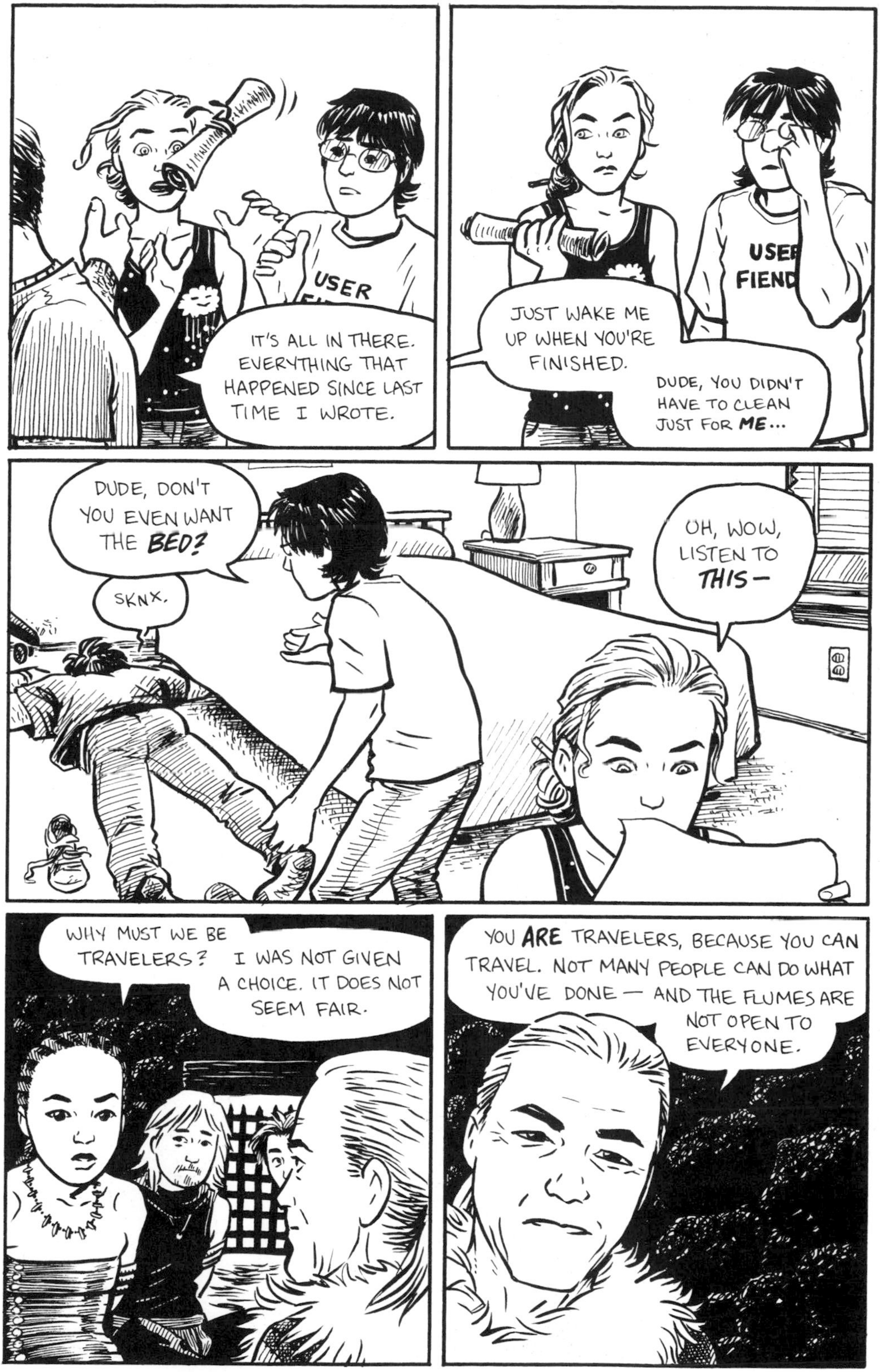
USER
IT'S ALL IN THERE. EVERYTHING THAT HAPPENED SINCE LAST TIME I WROTE.
USER FIEND
JUST WAKE ME UP WHEN YOU'RE FINISHED.
DUDE, YOU DIDN'T HAVE TO CLEAN JUST FOR **ME**...
DUDE, DON'T YOU EVEN WANT THE ***BED?***
SKNX.
OH, WOW, LISTEN TO ***THIS***—
WHY MUST WE BE TRAVELERS?
I WAS NOT GIVEN A CHOICE. IT DOES NOT SEEM FAIR.
YOU **ARE** TRAVELERS, BECAUSE YOU CAN TRAVEL. NOT MANY PEOPLE CAN DO WHAT YOU'VE DONE — AND THE FLUMES ARE NOT OPEN TO EVERYONE.

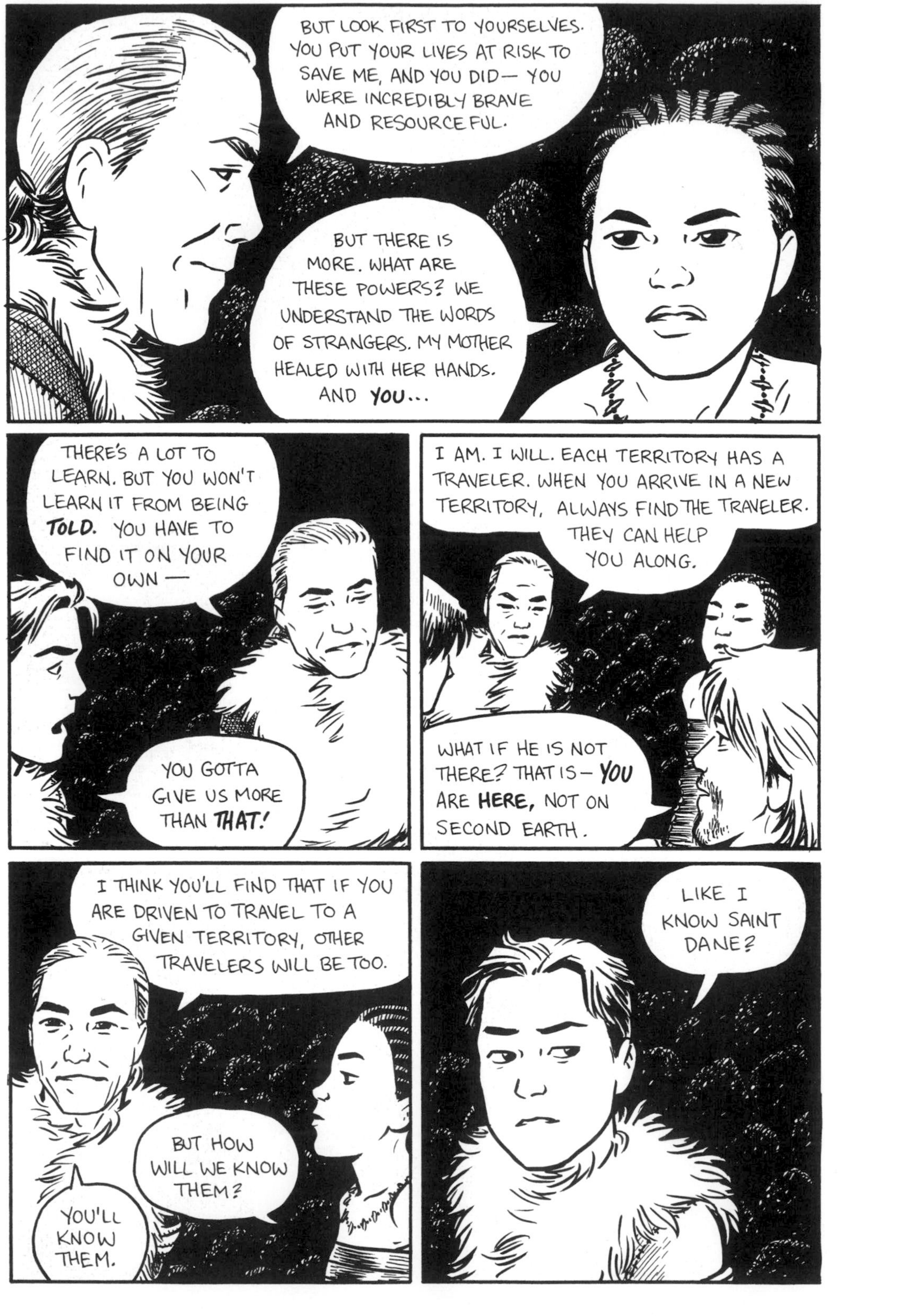
BUT LOOK FIRST TO YOURSELVES. YOU PUT YOUR LIVES AT RISK TO SAVE ME, AND YOU DID— YOU WERE INCREDIBLY BRAVE AND RESOURCEFUL.
BUT THERE IS MORE. WHAT ARE THESE POWERS? WE UNDERSTAND THE WORDS OF STRANGERS. MY MOTHER HEALED WITH HER HANDS. AND **YOU**...
THERE'S A LOT TO LEARN. BUT YOU WON'T LEARN IT FROM BEING **TOLD.** YOU HAVE TO FIND IT ON YOUR OWN—
YOU GOTTA GIVE US MORE THAN **THAT!**
I AM. I WILL. EACH TERRITORY HAS A TRAVELER. WHEN YOU ARRIVE IN A NEW TERRITORY, ALWAYS FIND THE TRAVELER.
THEY CAN HELP YOU ALONG.
WHAT IF HE IS NOT THERE? THAT IS— **YOU** ARE **HERE,** NOT ON SECOND EARTH.
I THINK YOU'LL FIND THAT IF YOU ARE DRIVEN TO TRAVEL TO A GIVEN TERRITORY, OTHER TRAVELERS WILL BE TOO.
BUT HOW WILL WE KNOW THEM?
YOU'LL KNOW THEM.
LIKE I KNOW SAINT DANE?

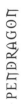

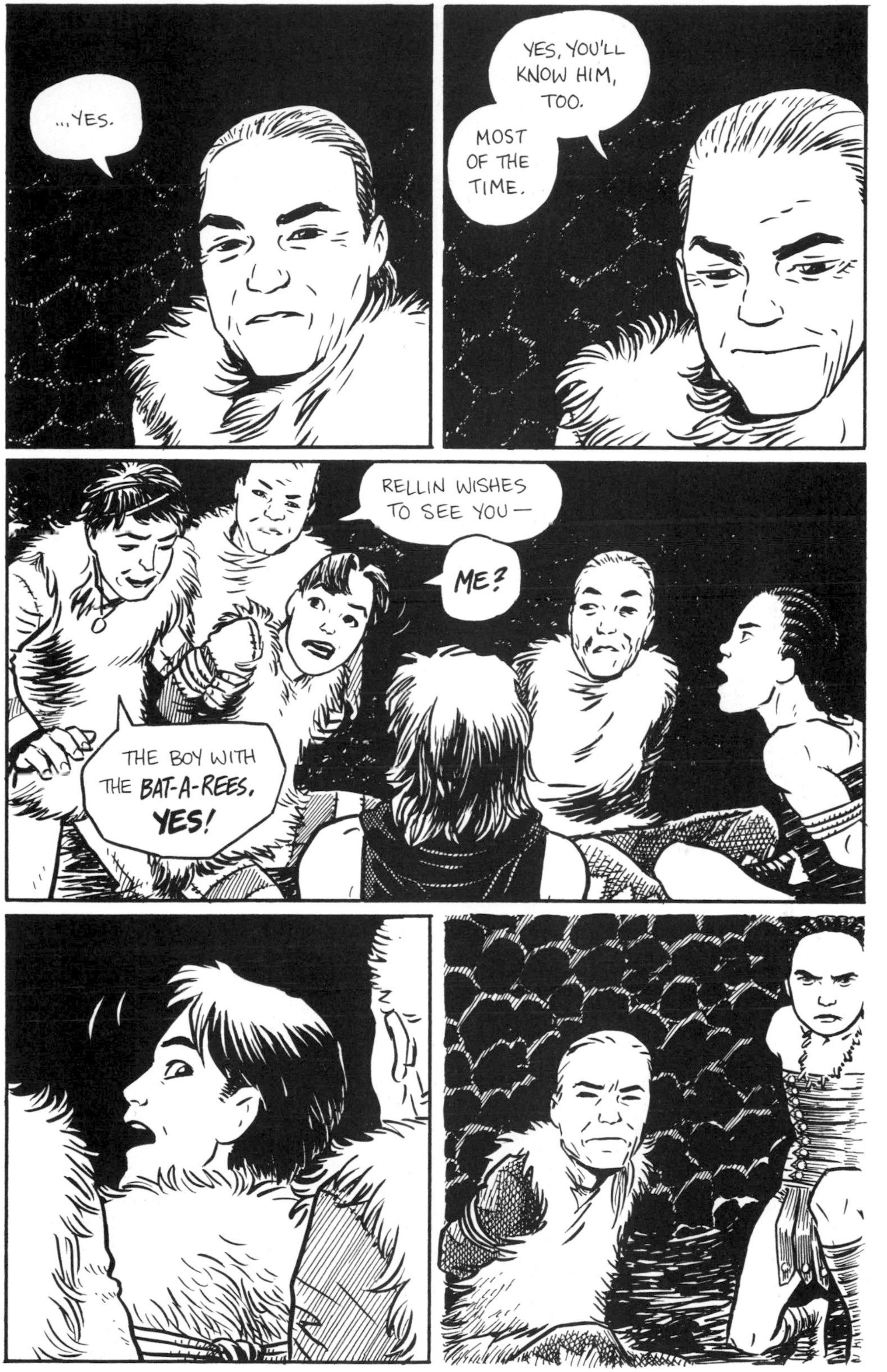
...YES.
YES, YOU'LL KNOW HIM, TOO.
MOST OF THE TIME.
RELLIN WISHES TO SEE YOU—
ME?
THE BOY WITH THE BAT-A-REES. YES!

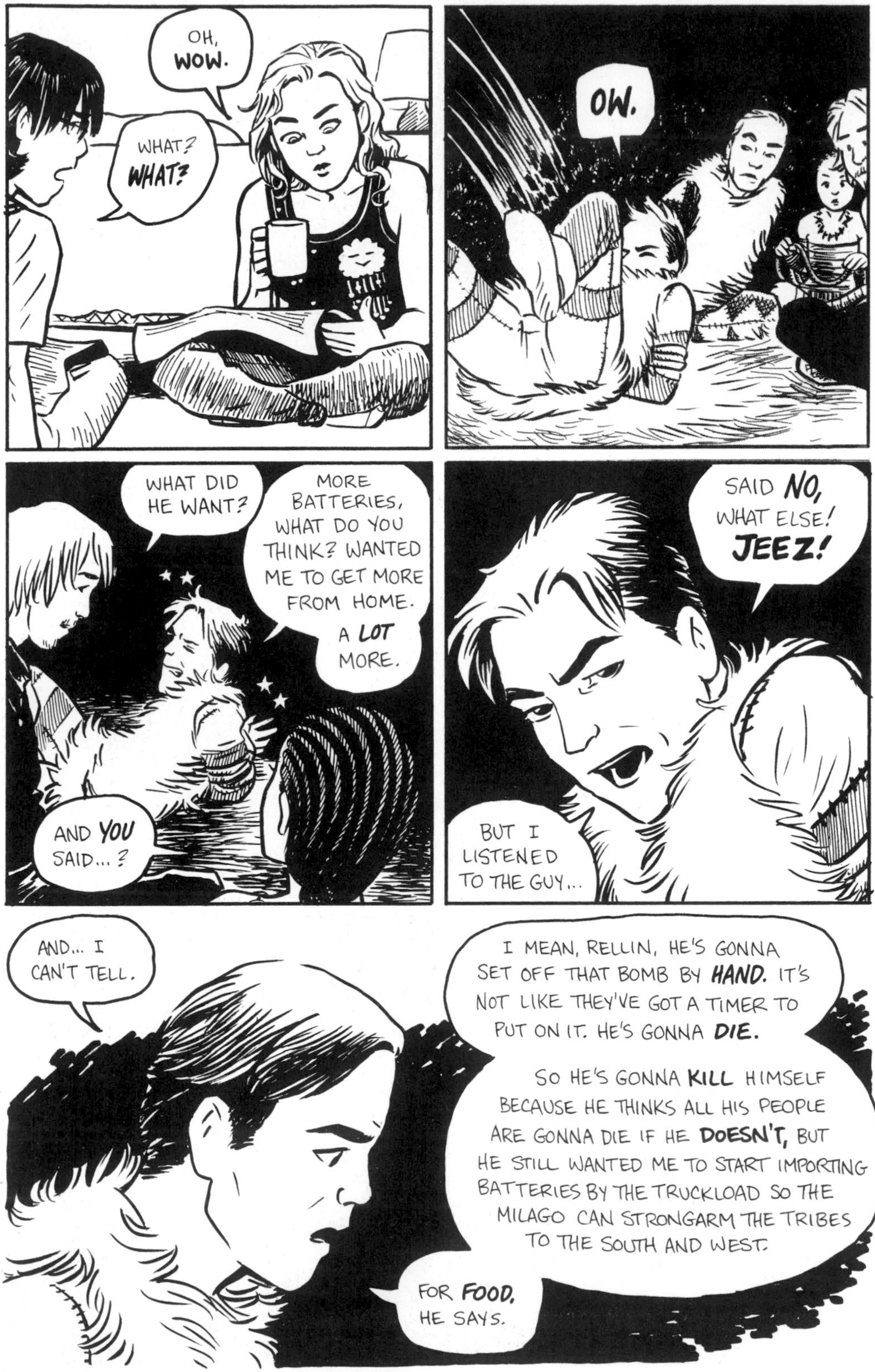
OH, WOW.
WHAT? WHAT?
OW.
WHAT DID HE WANT?
MORE BATTERIES, WHAT DO YOU THINK? WANTED ME TO GET MORE FROM HOME.
A LOT MORE.
AND YOU SAID... ?
SAID NO, WHAT ELSE! JEEZ!
BUT I LISTENED TO THE GUY...
AND... I CAN'T TELL.
I MEAN, RELLIN, HE'S GONNA SET OFF THAT BOMB BY HAND. IT'S NOT LIKE THEY'VE GOT A TIMER TO PUT ON IT. HE'S GONNA DIE.
SO HE'S GONNA KILL HIMSELF BECAUSE HE THINKS ALL HIS PEOPLE ARE GONNA DIE IF HE DOESN'T, BUT HE STILL WANTED ME TO START IMPORTING BATTERIES BY THE TRUCKLOAD SO THE MILAGO CAN STRONGARM THE TRIBES TO THE SOUTH AND WEST.
FOR FOOD, HE SAYS.

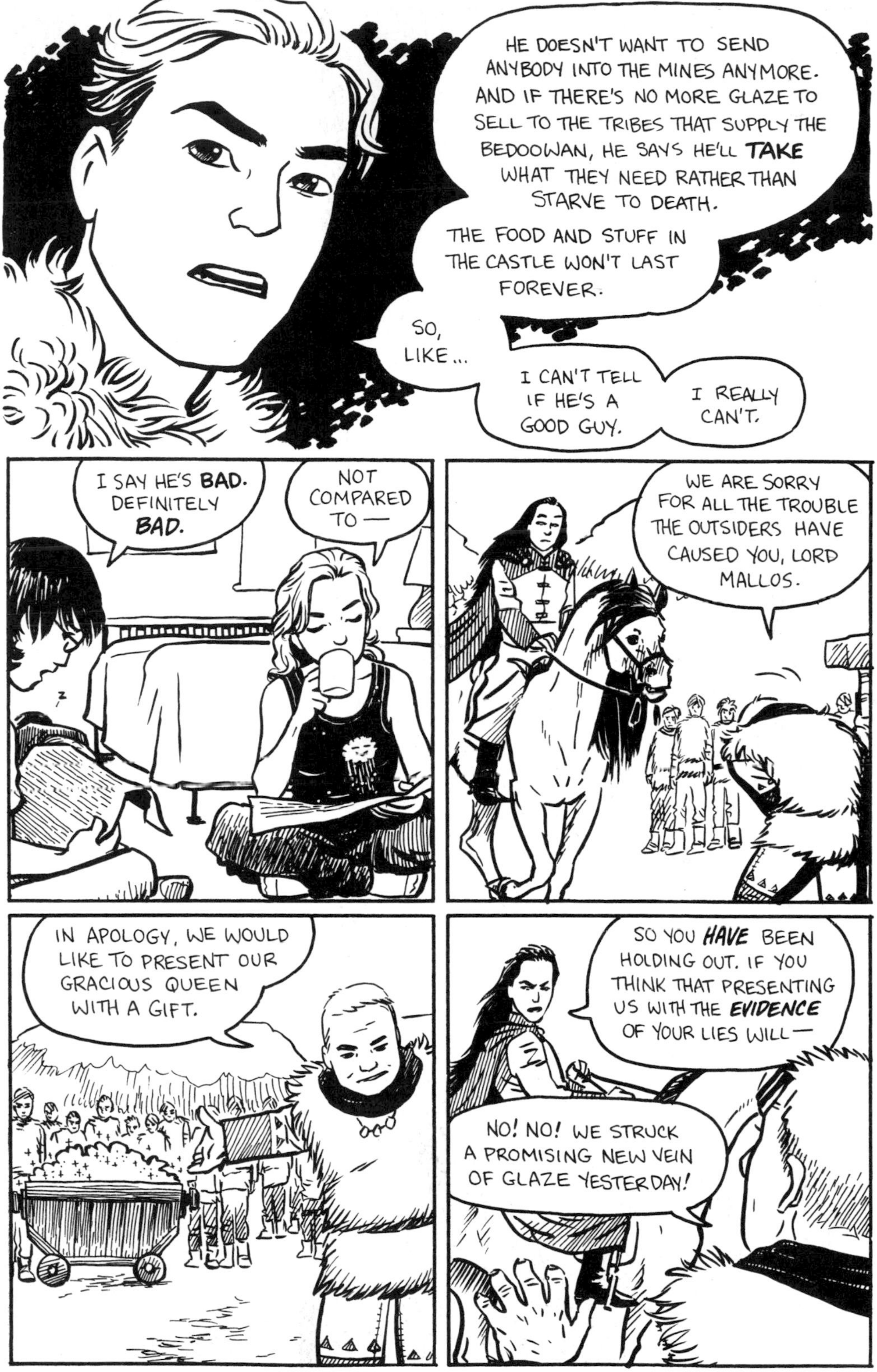

HE DOESN'T WANT TO SEND ANYBODY INTO THE MINES ANYMORE. AND IF THERE'S NO MORE GLAZE TO SELL TO THE TRIBES THAT SUPPLY THE BEDOOWAN, HE SAYS HE'LL TAKE WHAT THEY NEED RATHER THAN STARVE TO DEATH.
THE FOOD AND STUFF IN THE CASTLE WON'T LAST FOREVER.
SO, LIKE...
I CAN'T TELL IF HE'S A GOOD GUY.
I REALLY CAN'T.
I SAY HE'S BAD. DEFINITELY BAD.
NOT COMPARED TO—
WE ARE SORRY FOR ALL THE TROUBLE THE OUTSIDERS HAVE CAUSED YOU, LORD MALLOS.
IN APOLOGY, WE WOULD LIKE TO PRESENT OUR GRACIOUS QUEEN WITH A GIFT.
SO YOU HAVE BEEN HOLDING OUT. IF YOU THINK THAT PRESENTING US WITH THE EVIDENCE OF YOUR LIES WILL—
NO! NO! WE STRUCK A PROMISING NEW VEIN OF GLAZE YESTERDAY!

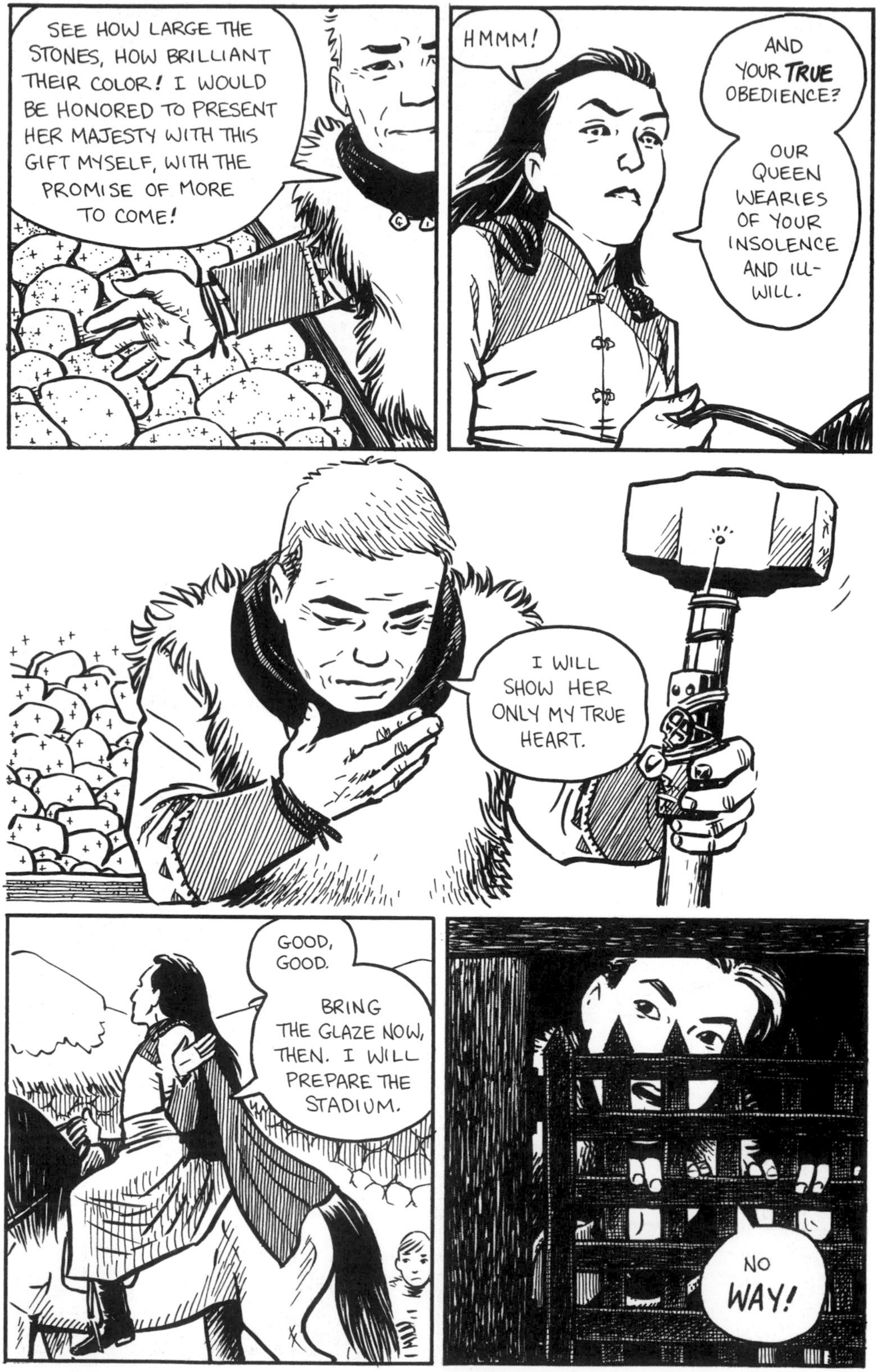
SEE HOW LARGE THE STONES, HOW BRILLIANT THEIR COLOR! I WOULD BE HONORED TO PRESENT HER MAJESTY WITH THIS GIFT MYSELF, WITH THE PROMISE OF MORE TO COME!
HMMM!
AND YOUR TRUE OBEDIENCE?
OUR QUEEN WEARIES OF YOUR INSOLENCE AND ILL-WILL.
I WILL SHOW HER ONLY MY TRUE HEART.
GOOD, GOOD.
BRING THE GLAZE NOW, THEN. I WILL PREPARE THE STADIUM.
NO WAY!

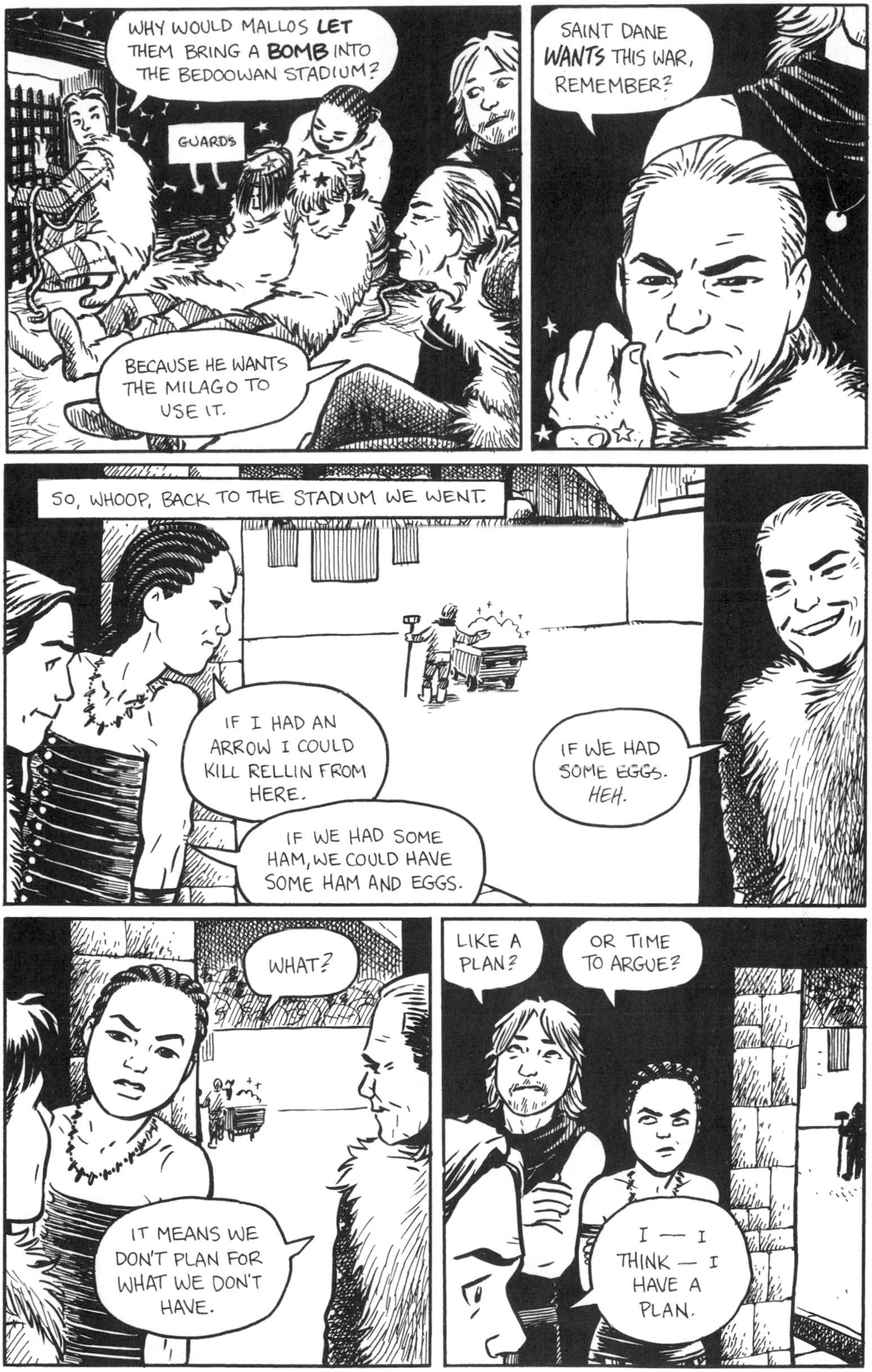
WHY WOULD MALLOS LET THEM BRING A BOMB INTO THE BEDOOWAN STADIUM?
GUARDS
BECAUSE HE WANTS THE MILAGO TO USE IT.
SAINT DANE WANTS THIS WAR, REMEMBER?
SO, WHOOP, BACK TO THE STADIUM WE WENT.
IF I HAD AN ARROW I COULD KILL RELLIN FROM HERE.
IF WE HAD SOME EGGS. HEH.
IF WE HAD SOME HAM, WE COULD HAVE SOME HAM AND EGGS.
WHAT?
IT MEANS WE DON'T PLAN FOR WHAT WE DON'T HAVE.
LIKE A PLAN?
OR TIME TO ARGUE?
I — I THINK — I HAVE A PLAN.

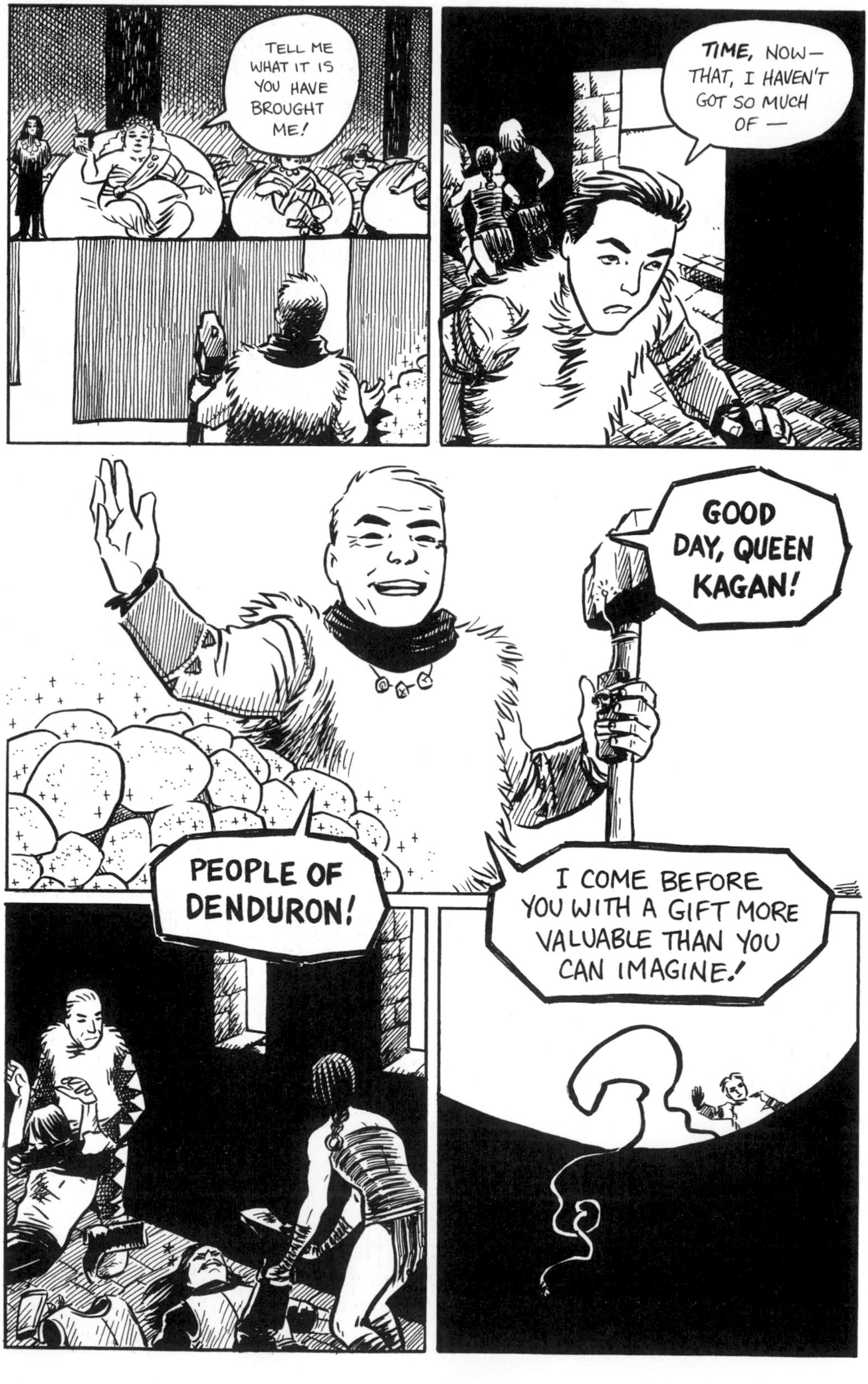
TELL ME WHAT IT IS YOU HAVE BROUGHT ME!
TIME, NOW— THAT, I HAVEN'T GOT SO MUCH OF —
GOOD DAY, QUEEN KAGAN!
PEOPLE OF DENDURON!
I COME BEFORE YOU WITH A GIFT MORE VALUABLE THAN YOU CAN IMAGINE!

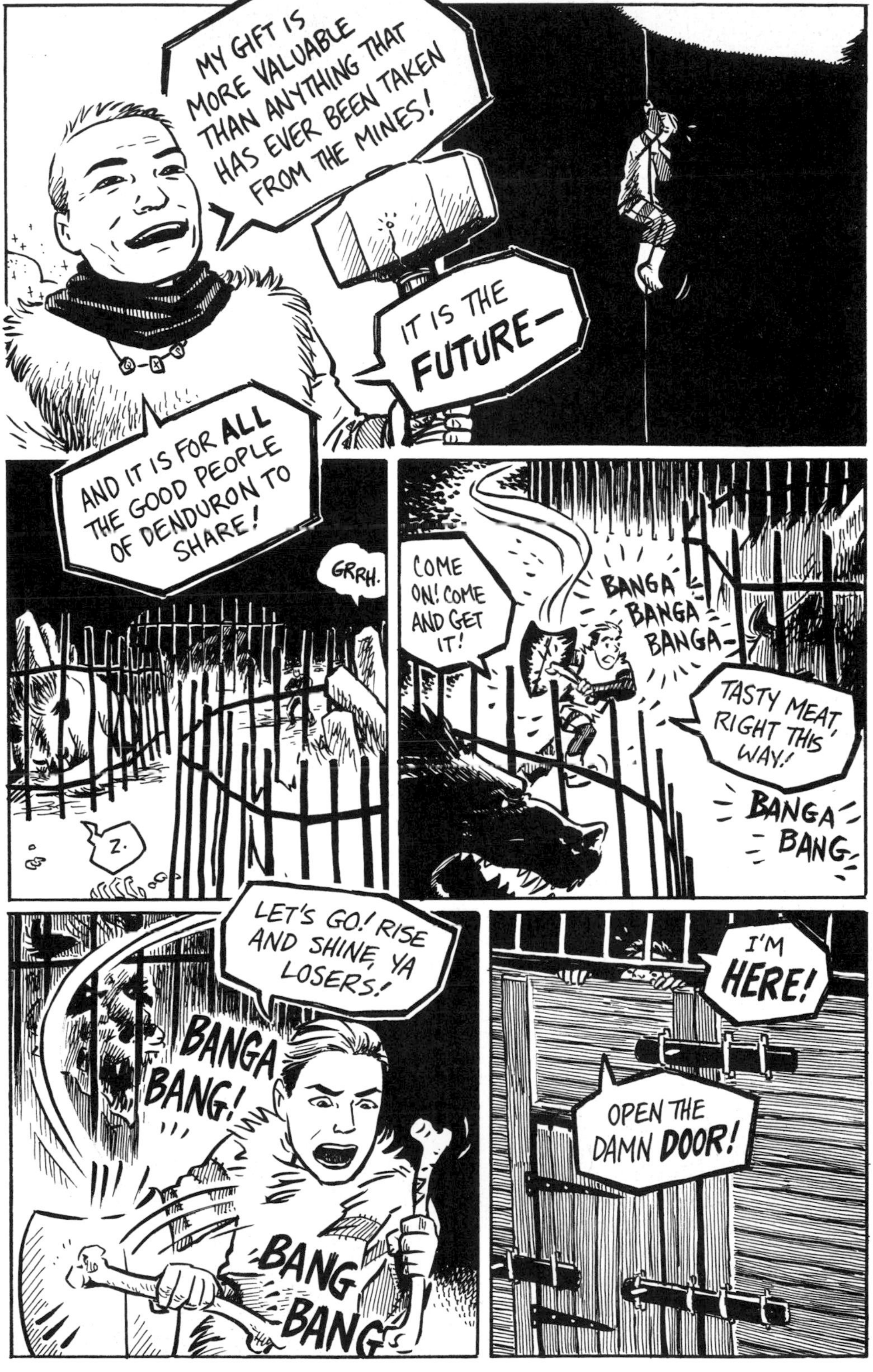
MY GIFT IS MORE VALUABLE THAN ANYTHING THAT HAS EVER BEEN TAKEN FROM THE MINES!
IT IS THE FUTURE—
AND IT IS FOR ALL THE GOOD PEOPLE OF DENDURON TO SHARE!
GRRH.
Z.
COME ON! COME AND GET IT!
BANGA BANGA BANGA
TASTY MEAT, RIGHT THIS WAY!
BANGA BANG
LET'S GO! RISE AND SHINE, YA LOSERS!
BANGA BANG!
BANG BANG
I'M HERE!
OPEN THE DAMN DOOR!

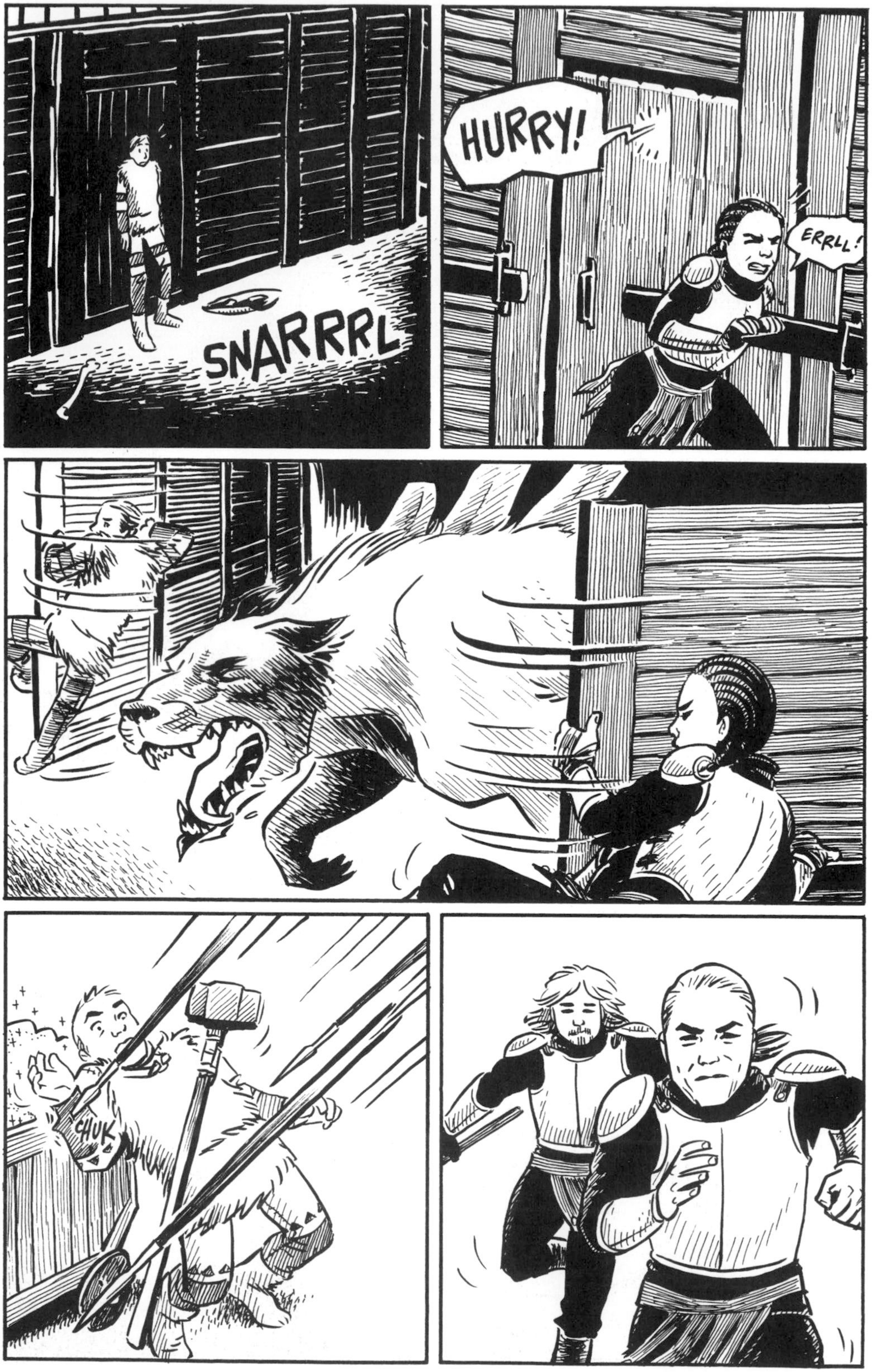
SNARRRL
HURRY!
ERRLL!
CHUK

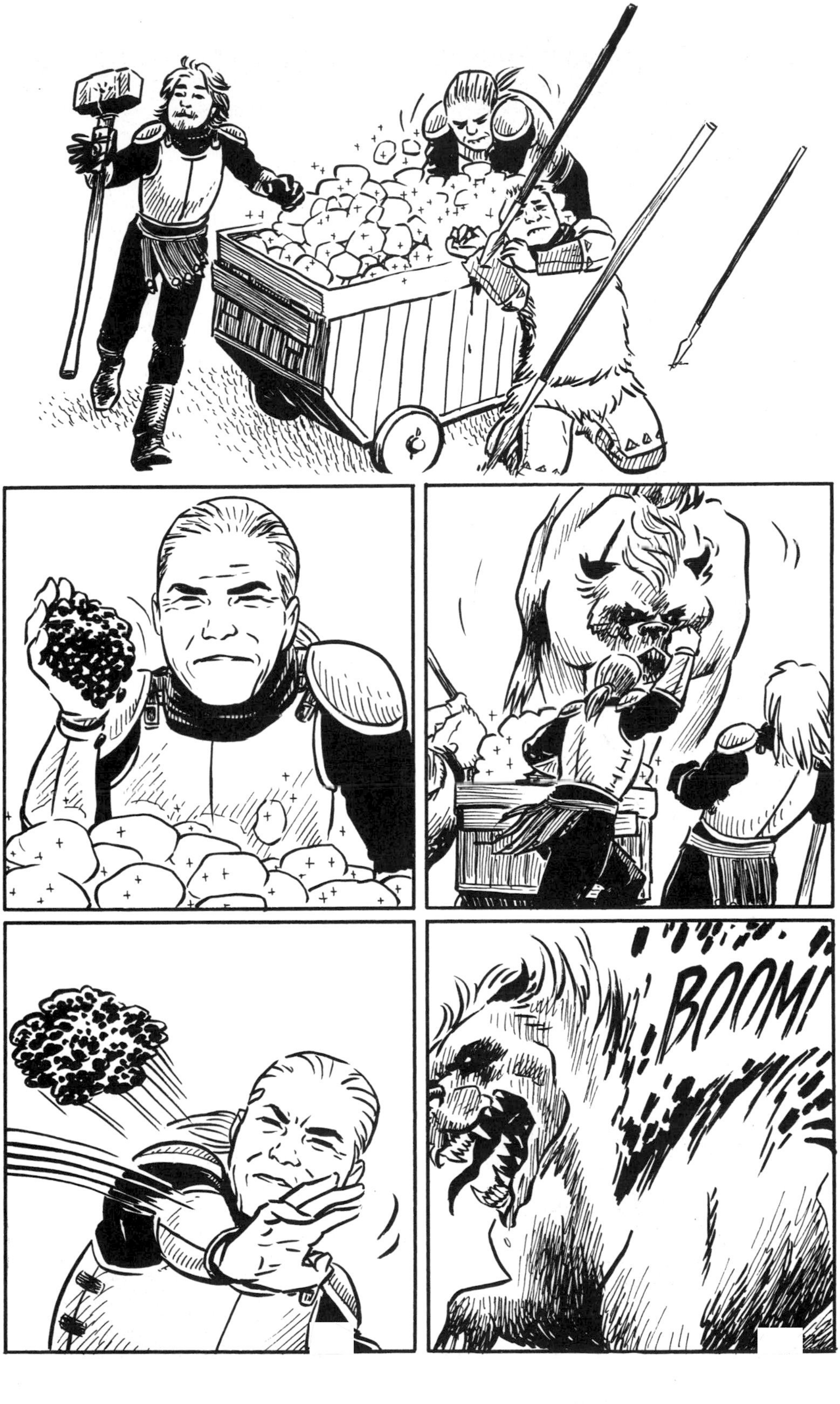
BOOM!

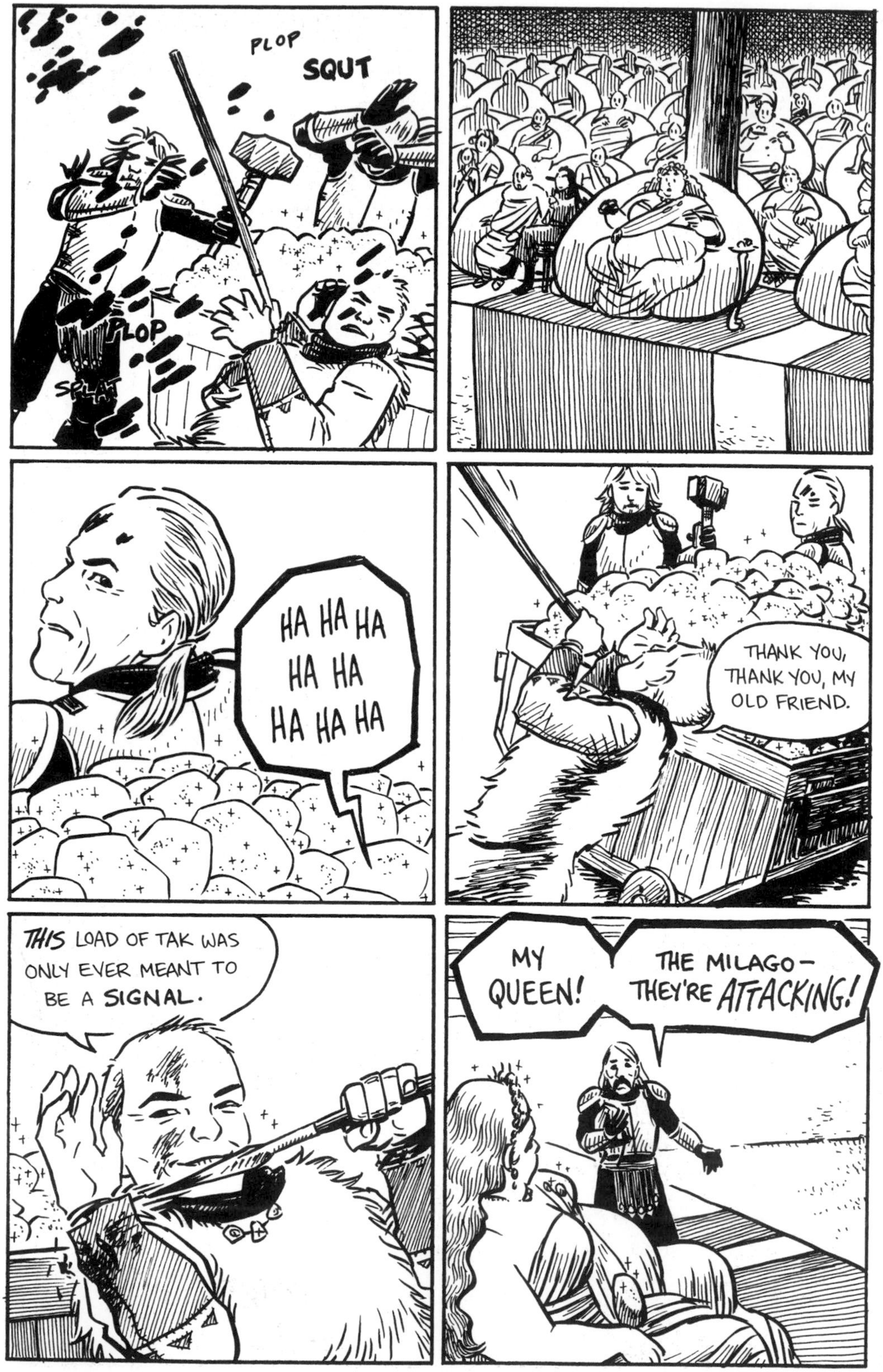
PLOP
SQUT
PLOP
SPLAT
HA HA HA HA HA HA HA HA
THANK YOU, THANK YOU, MY OLD FRIEND.
THIS LOAD OF TAK WAS ONLY EVER MEANT TO BE A SIGNAL.
MY QUEEN!
THE MILAGO— THEY'RE ATTACKING!

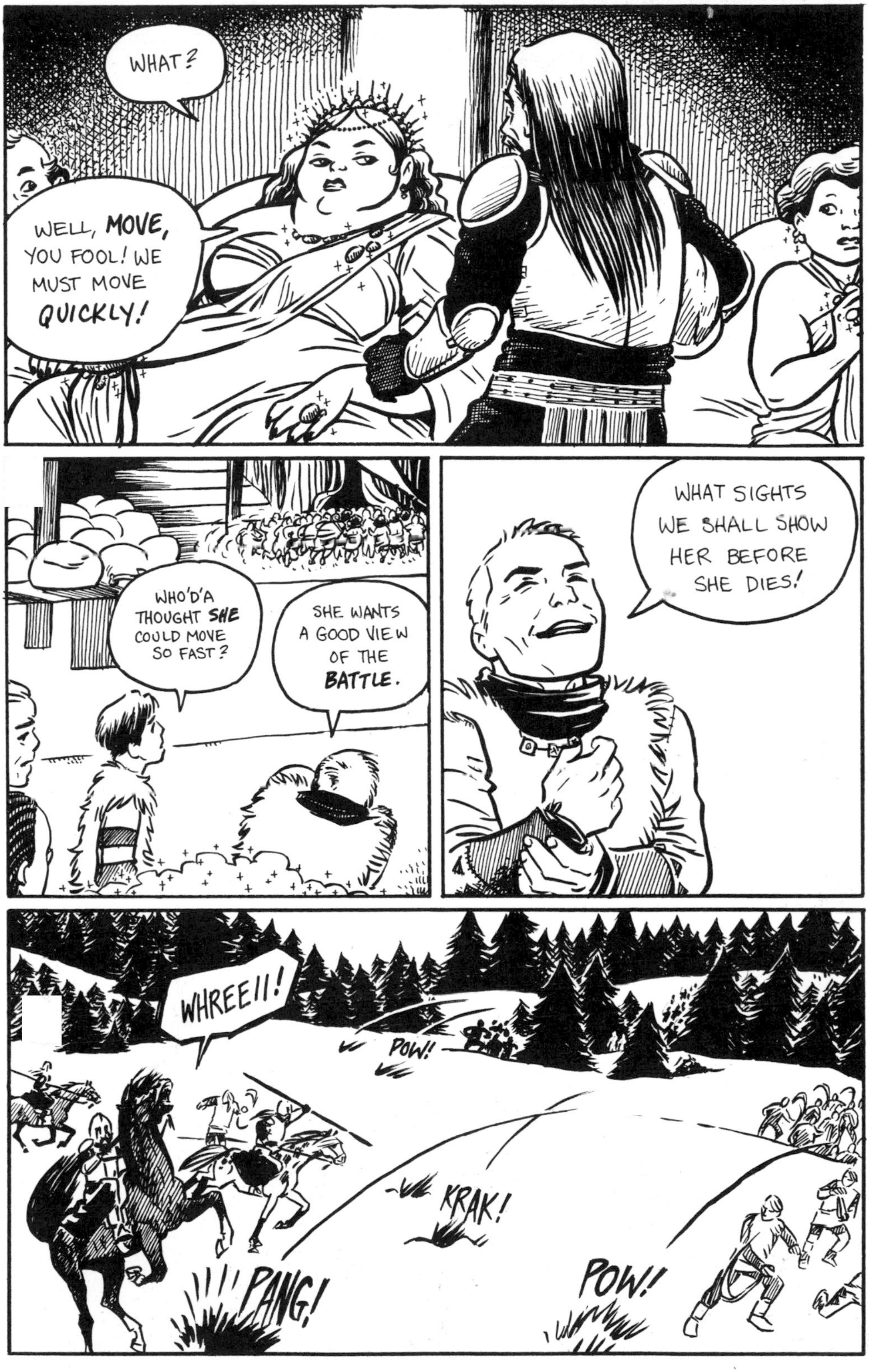
WHAT?
WELL, MOVE, YOU FOOL! WE MUST MOVE QUICKLY!
WHO'D'A THOUGHT SHE COULD MOVE SO FAST?
SHE WANTS A GOOD VIEW OF THE BATTLE.
WHAT SIGHTS WE SHALL SHOW HER BEFORE SHE DIES!
WHREE!!!
POW!
KRAK!
PANG!
POW!

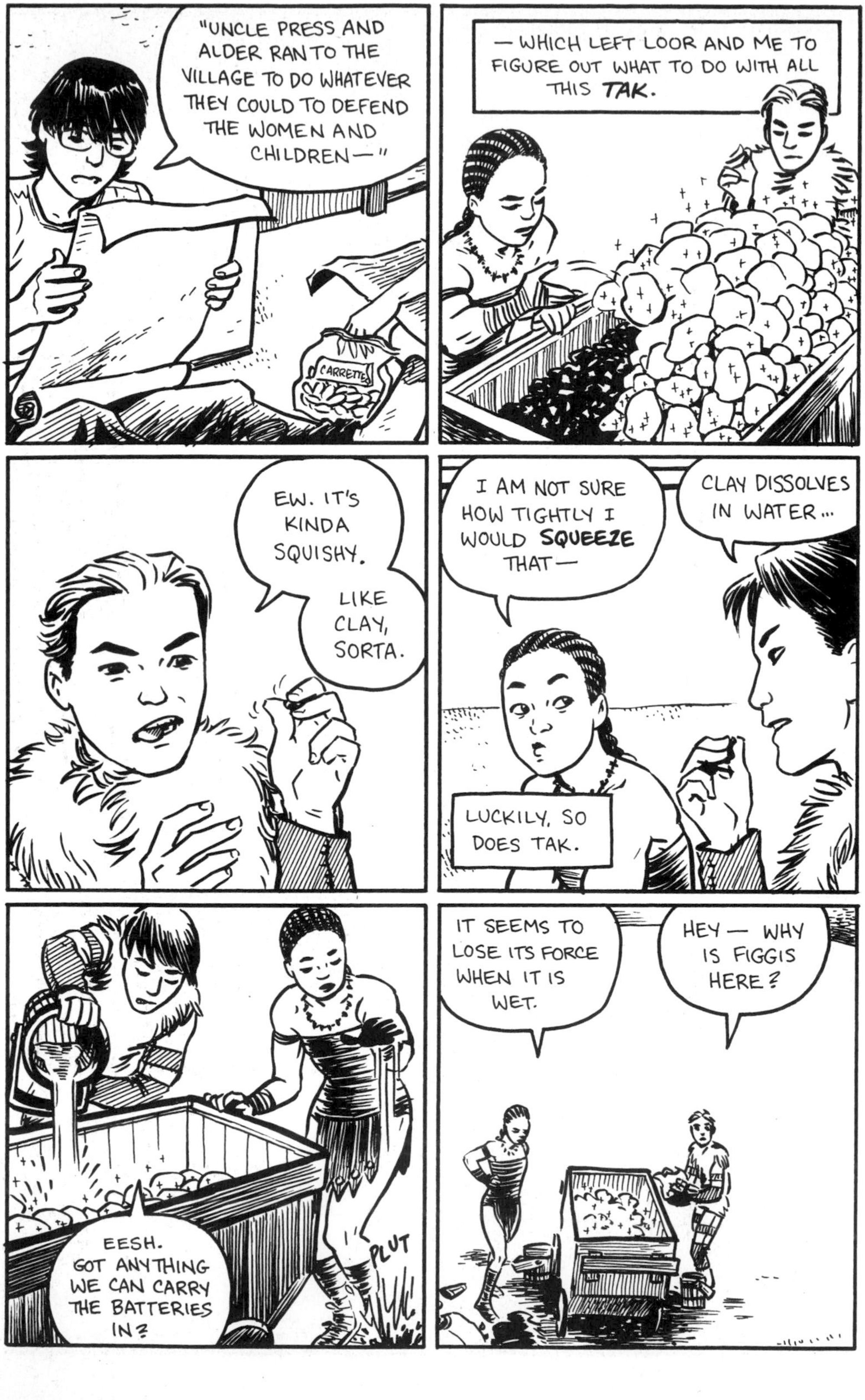
"UNCLE PRESS AND ALDER RAN TO THE VILLAGE TO DO WHATEVER THEY COULD TO DEFEND THE WOMEN AND CHILDREN—"
CARRETTES
—WHICH LEFT LOOR AND ME TO FIGURE OUT WHAT TO DO WITH ALL THIS TAK.
EW. IT'S KINDA SQUISHY.
LIKE CLAY, SORTA.
I AM NOT SURE HOW TIGHTLY I WOULD SQUEEZE THAT—
CLAY DISSOLVES IN WATER...
LUCKILY, SO DOES TAK.
EESH. GOT ANYTHING WE CAN CARRY THE BATTERIES IN?
PLUT
IT SEEMS TO LOSE ITS FORCE WHEN IT IS WET.
HEY— WHY IS FIGGIS HERE?

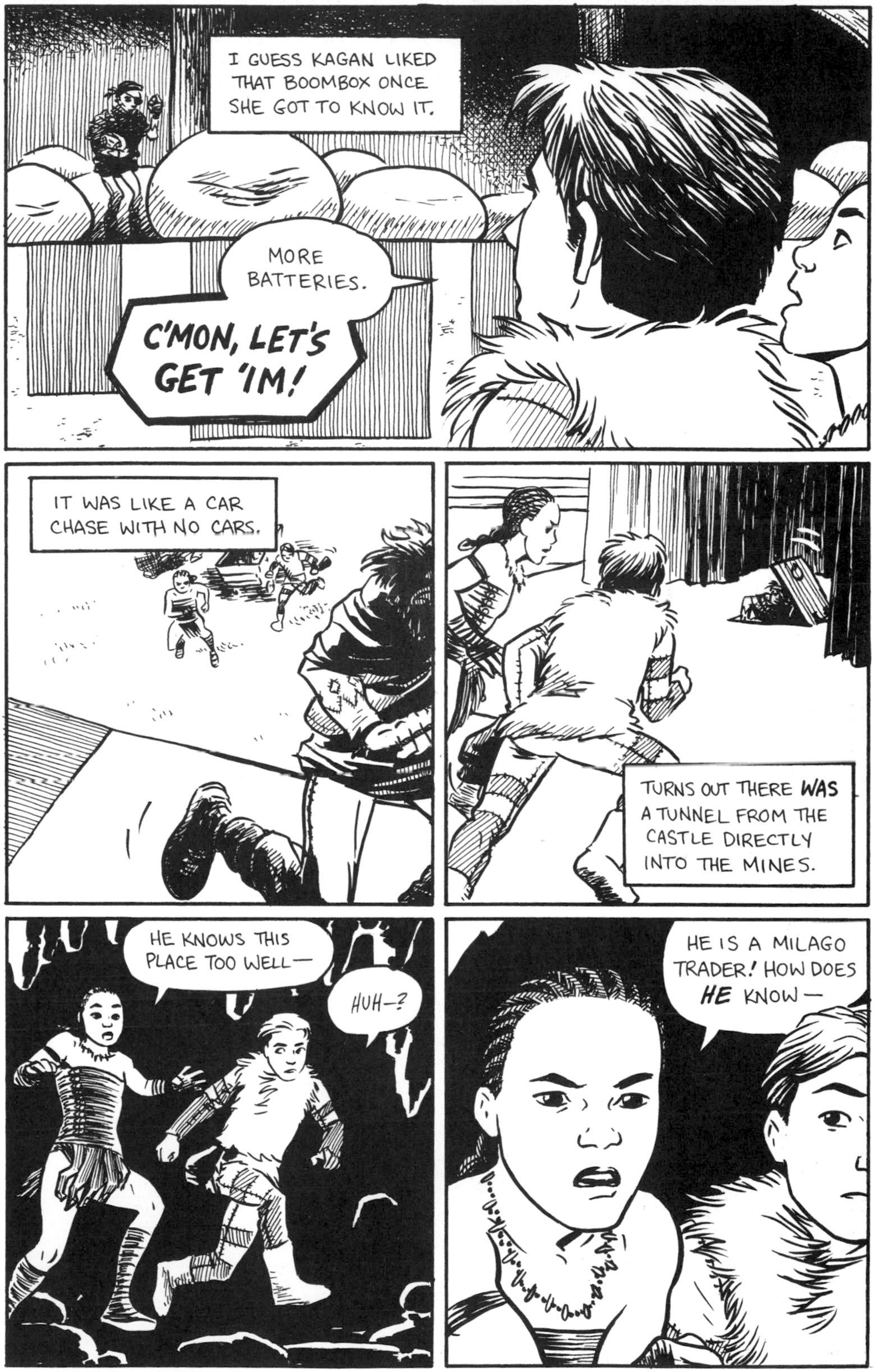

I GUESS KAGAN LIKED THAT BOOMBOX ONCE SHE GOT TO KNOW IT.
MORE BATTERIES.
C'MON, LET'S GET 'IM!
IT WAS LIKE A CAR CHASE WITH NO CARS.
TURNS OUT THERE WAS A TUNNEL FROM THE CASTLE DIRECTLY INTO THE MINES.
HE KNOWS THIS PLACE TOO WELL—
HUH—?
HE IS A MILAGO TRADER! HOW DOES HE KNOW—

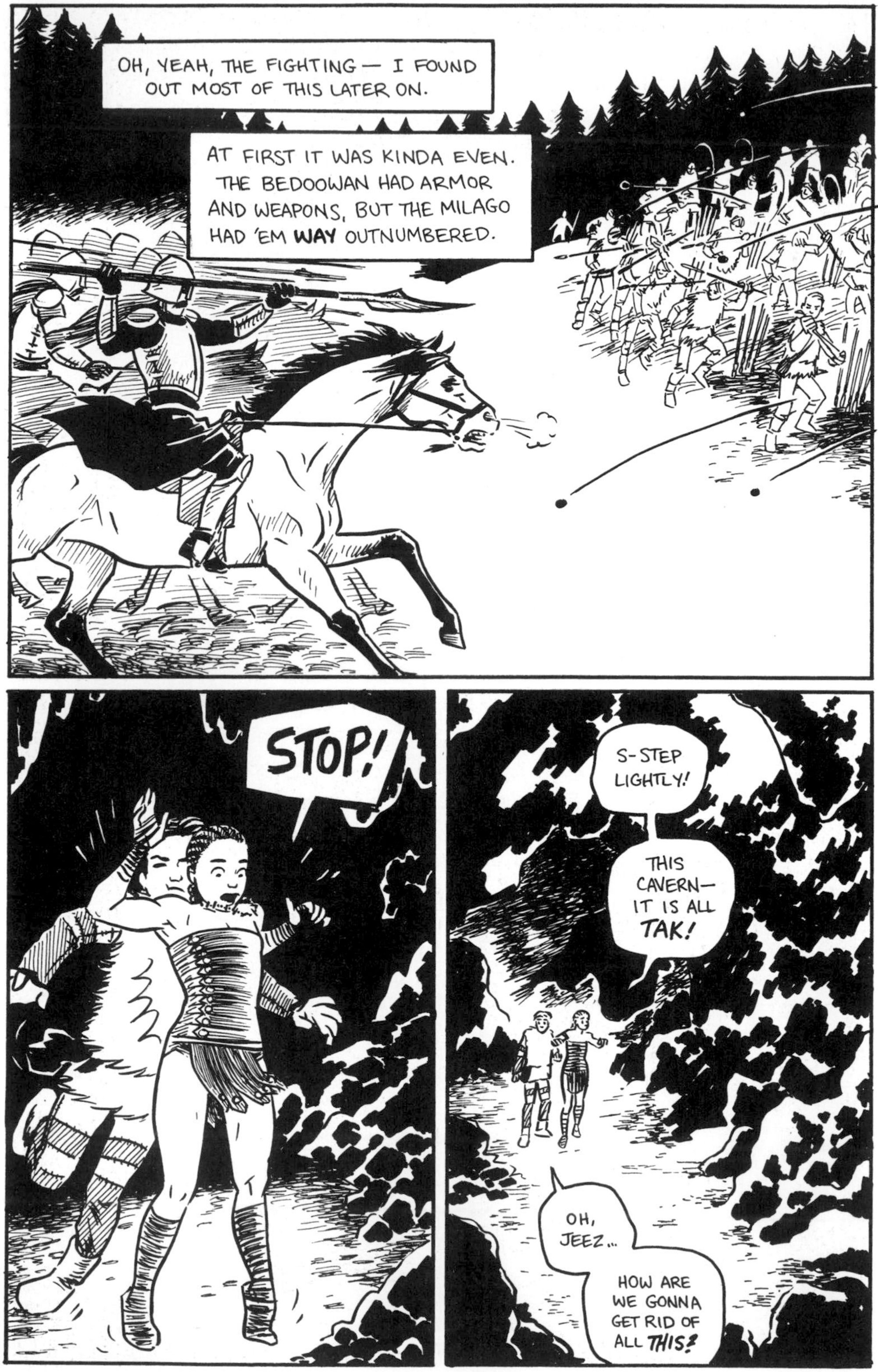
OH, YEAH, THE FIGHTING — I FOUND OUT MOST OF THIS LATER ON.
AT FIRST IT WAS KINDA EVEN. THE BEDOOWAN HAD ARMOR AND WEAPONS, BUT THE MILAGO HAD 'EM **WAY** OUTNUMBERED.
STOP!
S-STEP LIGHTLY!
THIS CAVERN— IT IS ALL **TAK!**
OH, JEEZ...
HOW ARE WE GONNA GET RID OF ALL **THIS?**

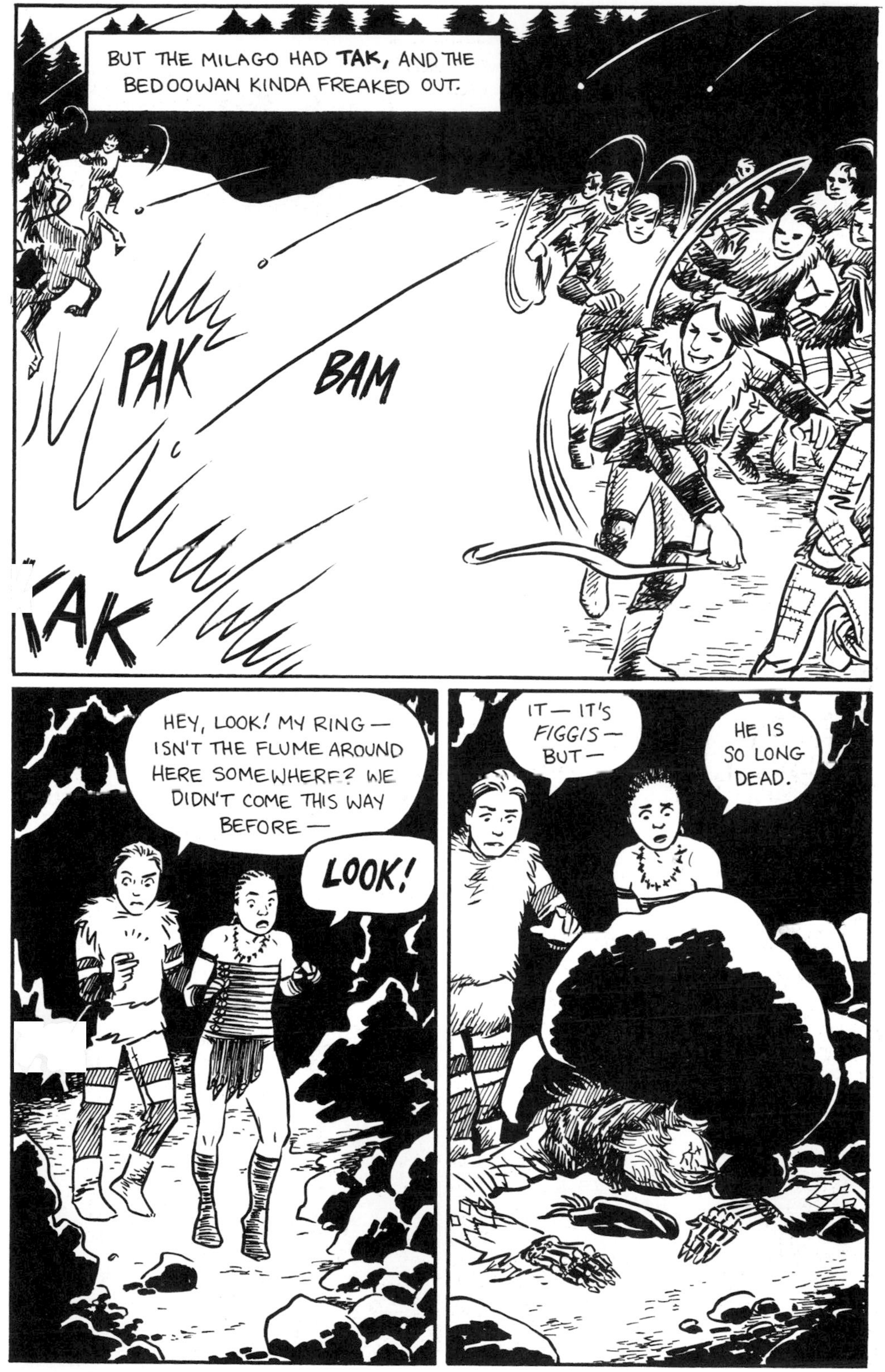
BUT THE MILAGO HAD TAK, AND THE BEDOOWAN KINDA FREAKED OUT.
PAK
BAM
AK
HEY, LOOK! MY RING— ISN'T THE FLUME AROUND HERE SOMEWHERE? WE DIDN'T COME THIS WAY BEFORE—
LOOK!
IT— IT'S FIGGIS— BUT—
HE IS SO LONG DEAD.

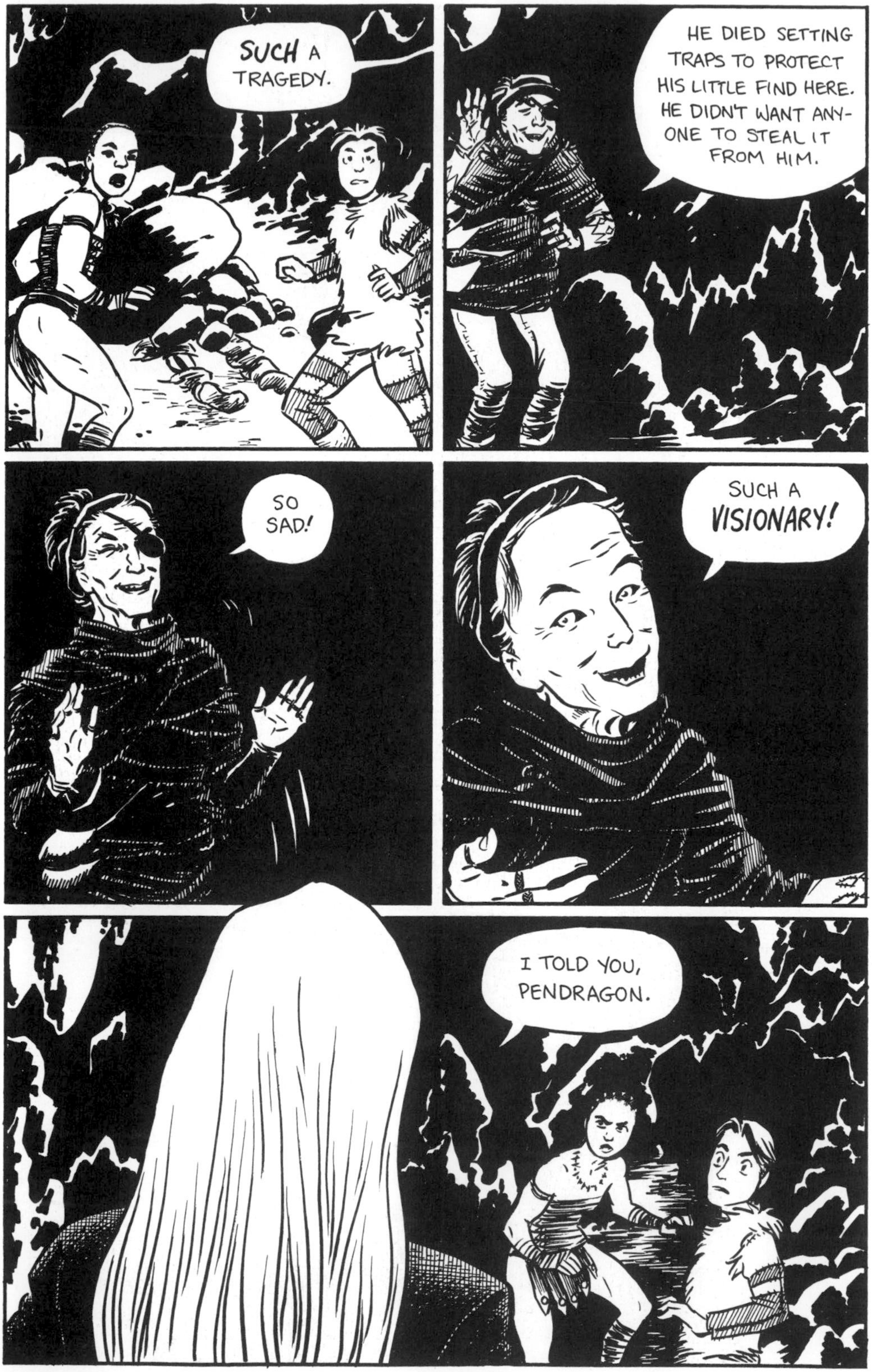
SUCH A TRAGEDY.
HE DIED SETTING TRAPS TO PROTECT HIS LITTLE FIND HERE. HE DIDN'T WANT ANY-ONE TO STEAL IT FROM HIM.
SO SAD!
SUCH A VISIONARY!
I TOLD YOU, PENDRAGON.

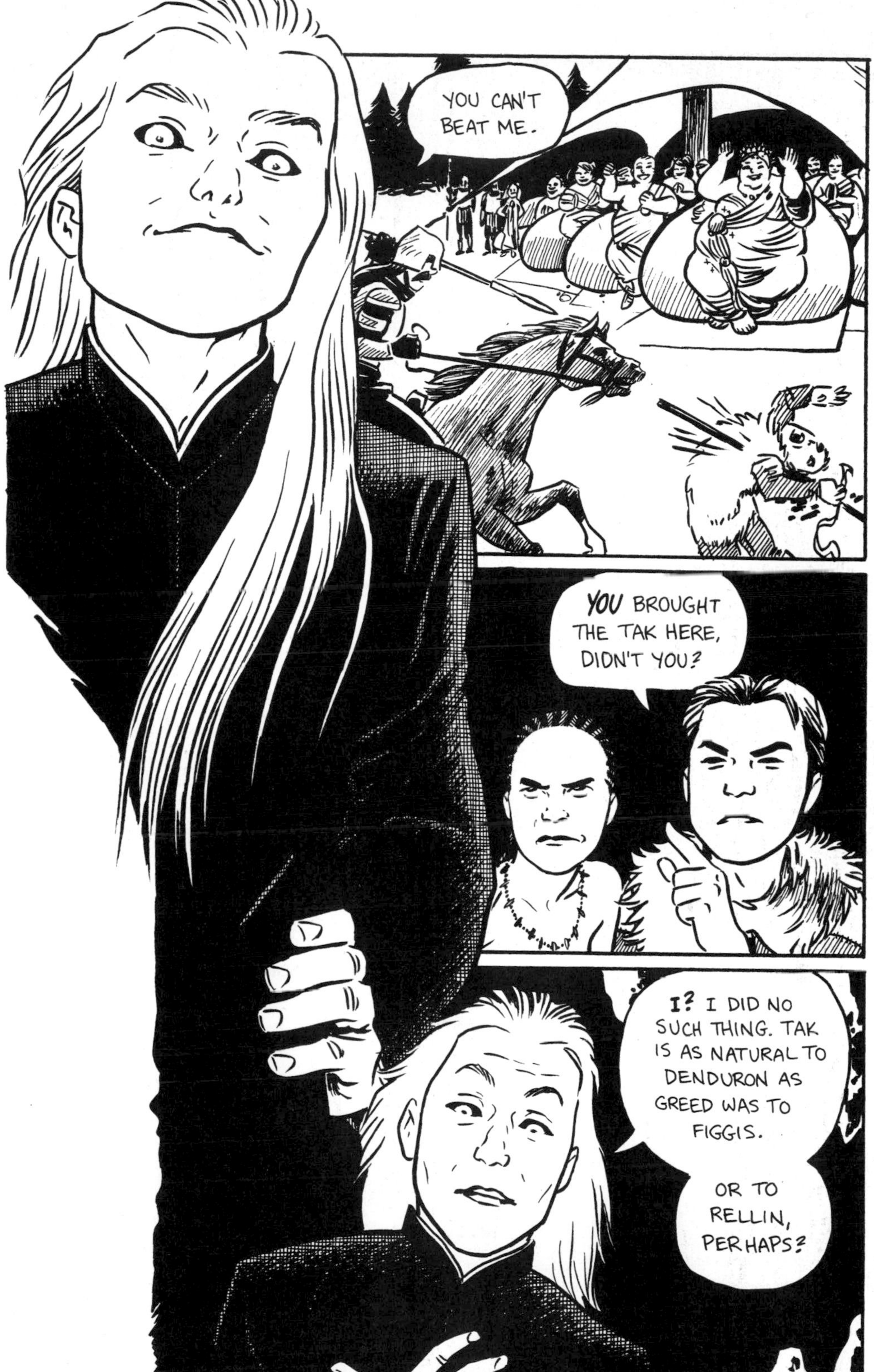
YOU CAN'T BEAT ME.
YOU BROUGHT THE TAK HERE, DIDN'T YOU?
I? I DID NO SUCH THING. TAK IS AS NATURAL TO DENDURON AS GREED WAS TO FIGGIS.
OR TO RELLIN, PERHAPS?

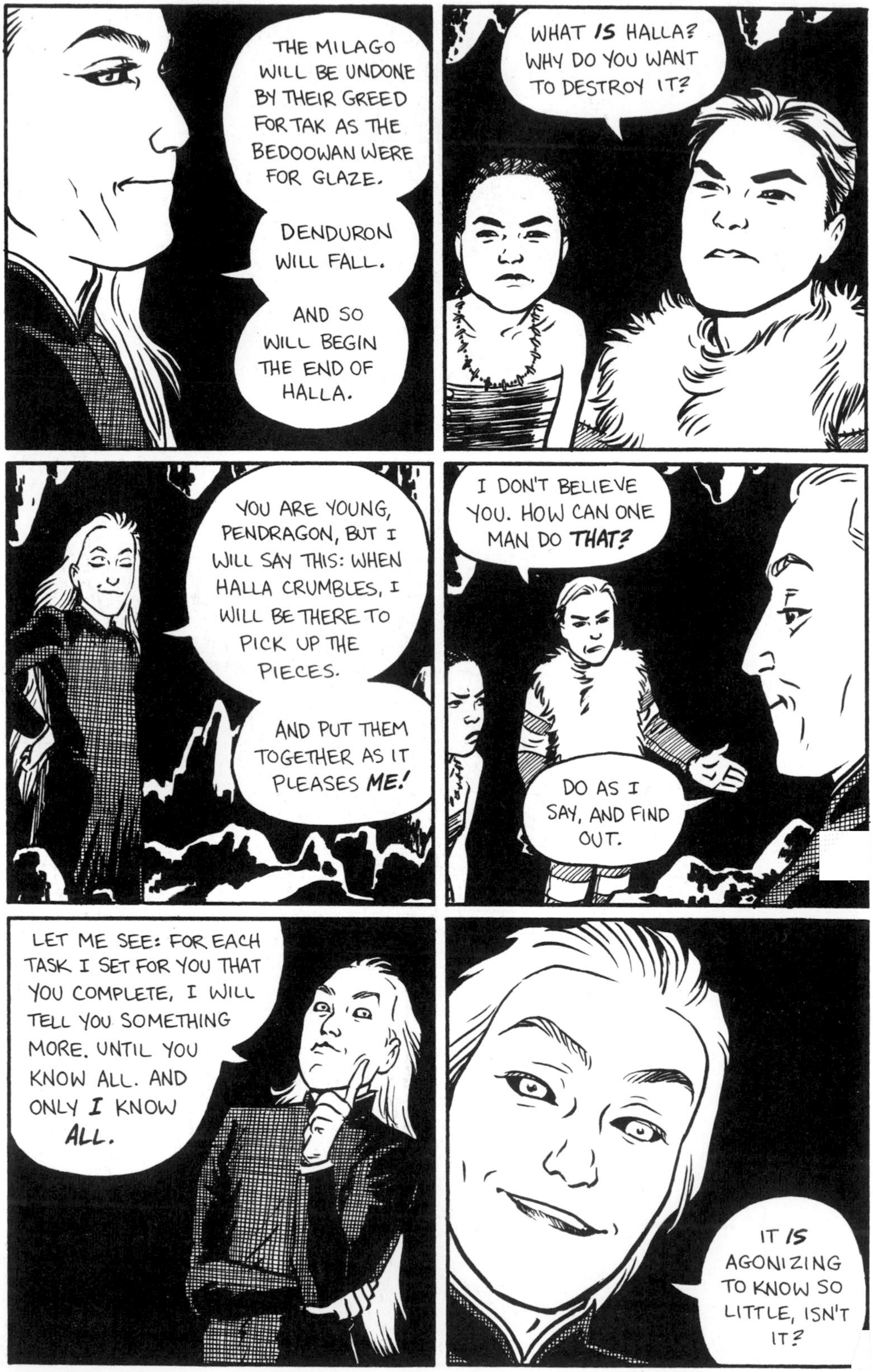
THE MILAGO WILL BE UNDONE BY THEIR GREED FOR TAK AS THE BEDOOWAN WERE FOR GLAZE.
DENDURON WILL FALL.
AND SO WILL BEGIN THE END OF HALLA.
WHAT *IS* HALLA? WHY DO YOU WANT TO DESTROY IT?
YOU ARE YOUNG, PENDRAGON, BUT I WILL SAY THIS: WHEN HALLA CRUMBLES, I WILL BE THERE TO PICK UP THE PIECES.
AND PUT THEM TOGETHER AS IT PLEASES **ME!**
I DON'T BELIEVE YOU. HOW CAN ONE MAN DO **THAT?**
DO AS I SAY, AND FIND OUT.
LET ME SEE: FOR EACH TASK I SET FOR YOU THAT YOU COMPLETE, I WILL TELL YOU SOMETHING MORE. UNTIL YOU KNOW ALL. AND ONLY *I* KNOW **ALL.**
IT *IS* AGONIZING TO KNOW SO LITTLE, ISN'T IT?

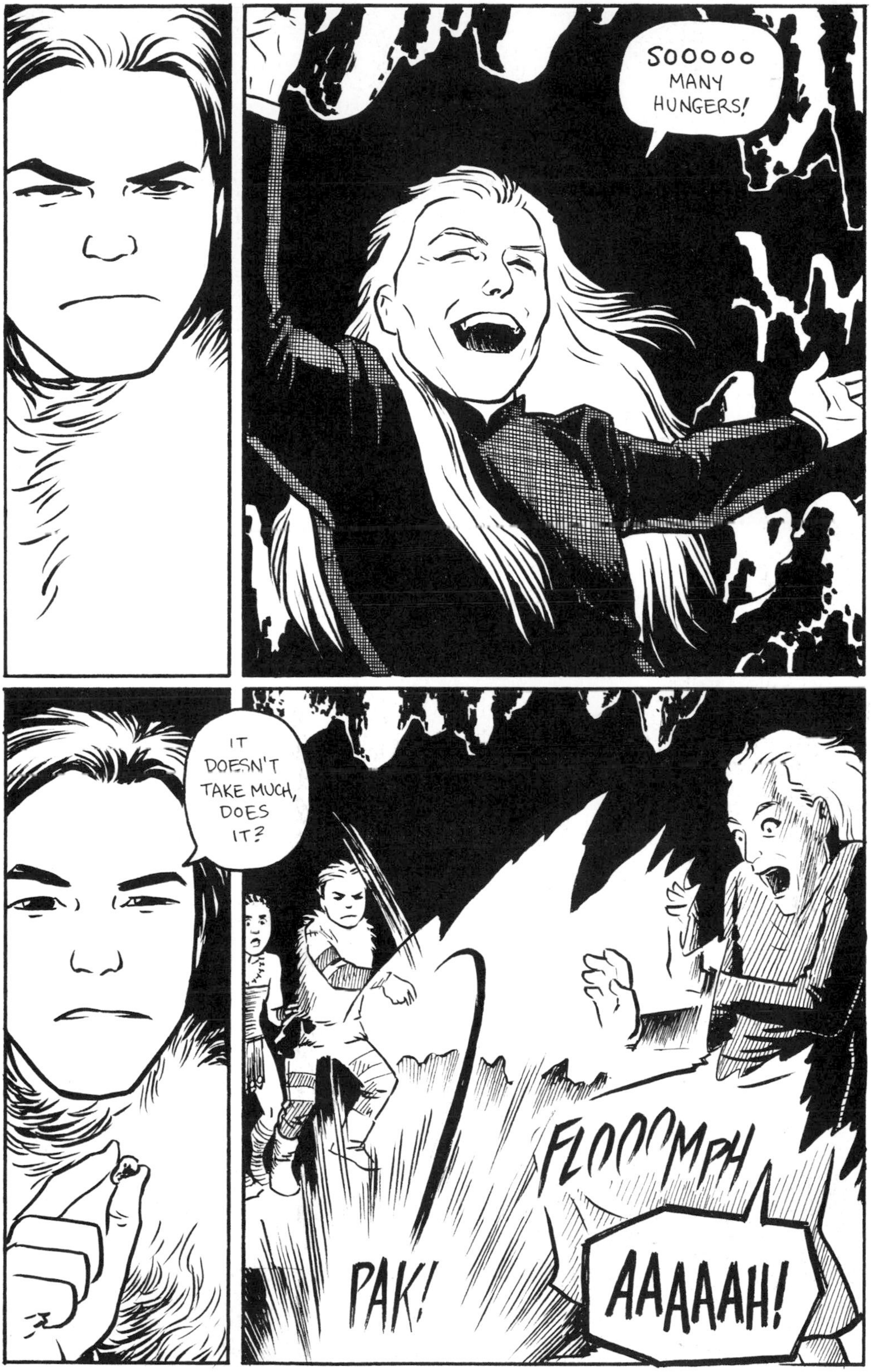
SOOOOO MANY HUNGERS!
IT DOESN'T TAKE MUCH, DOES IT?
FLOOOMPH
PAK!
AAAAAH!

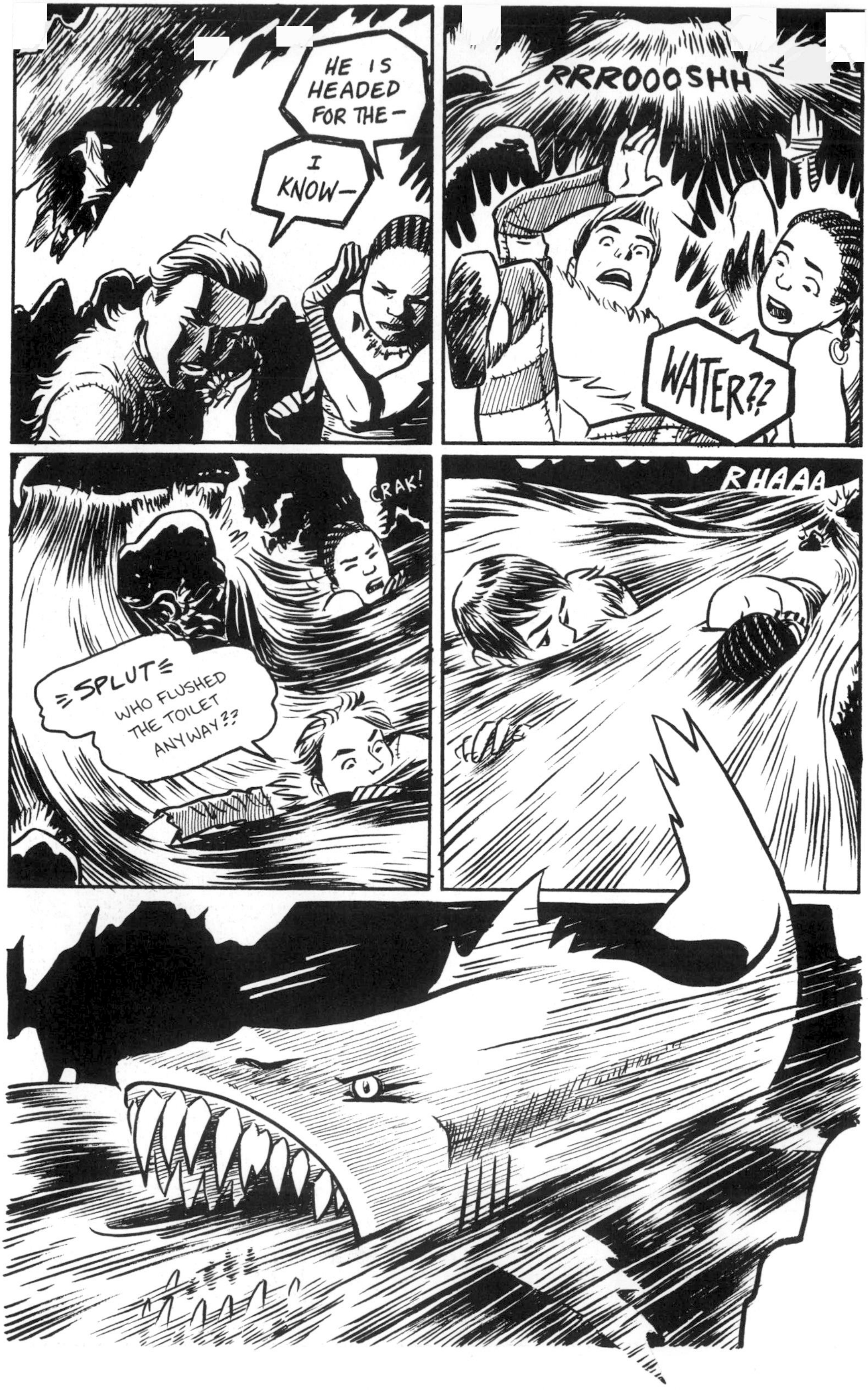
HE IS HEADED FOR THE—
I KNOW—
RRROOOSHH
WATER??
CRAK!
SPLUT
WHO FLUSHED THE TOILET ANYWAY??
RHAAA

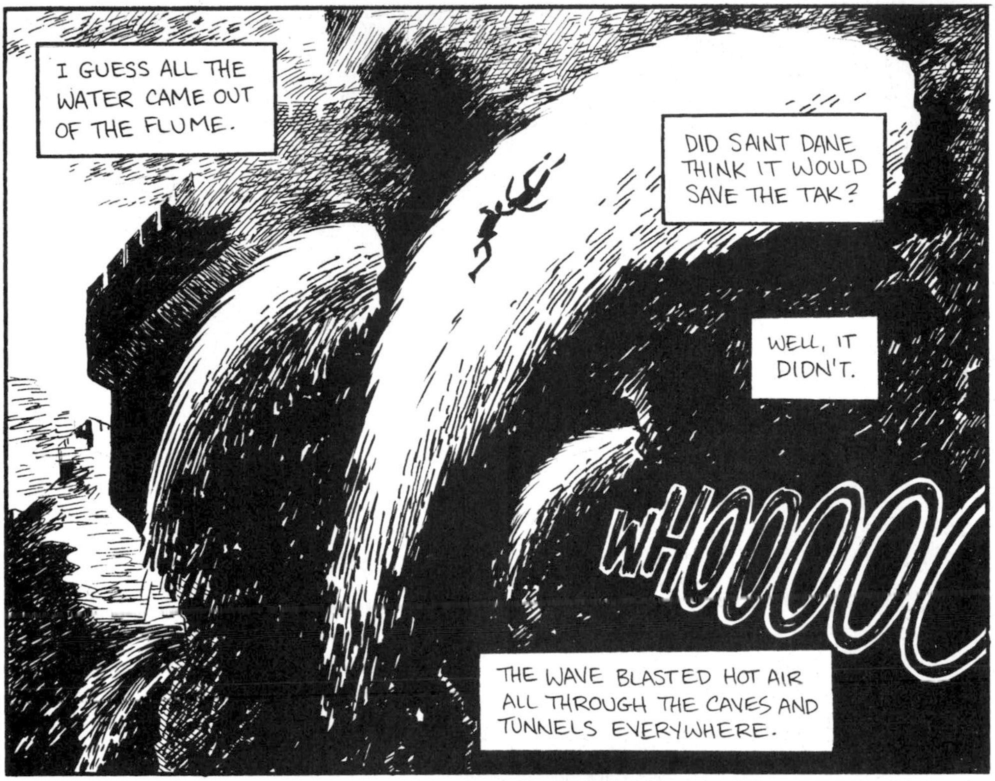
I GUESS ALL THE WATER CAME OUT OF THE FLUME.
DID SAINT DANE THINK IT WOULD SAVE THE TAK?
WELL, IT DIDN'T.
WHOOOOO
THE WAVE BLASTED HOT AIR ALL THROUGH THE CAVES AND TUNNELS EVERYWHERE.

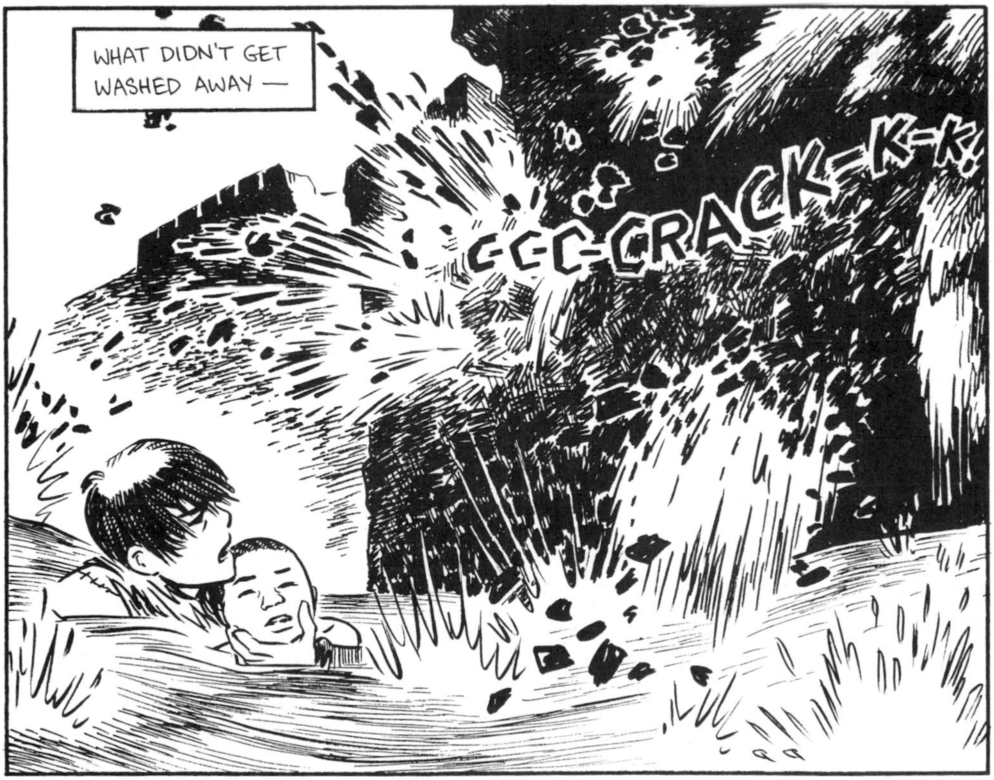
WHAT DIDN'T GET WASHED AWAY —
C-C-C-CRACK-K-K!

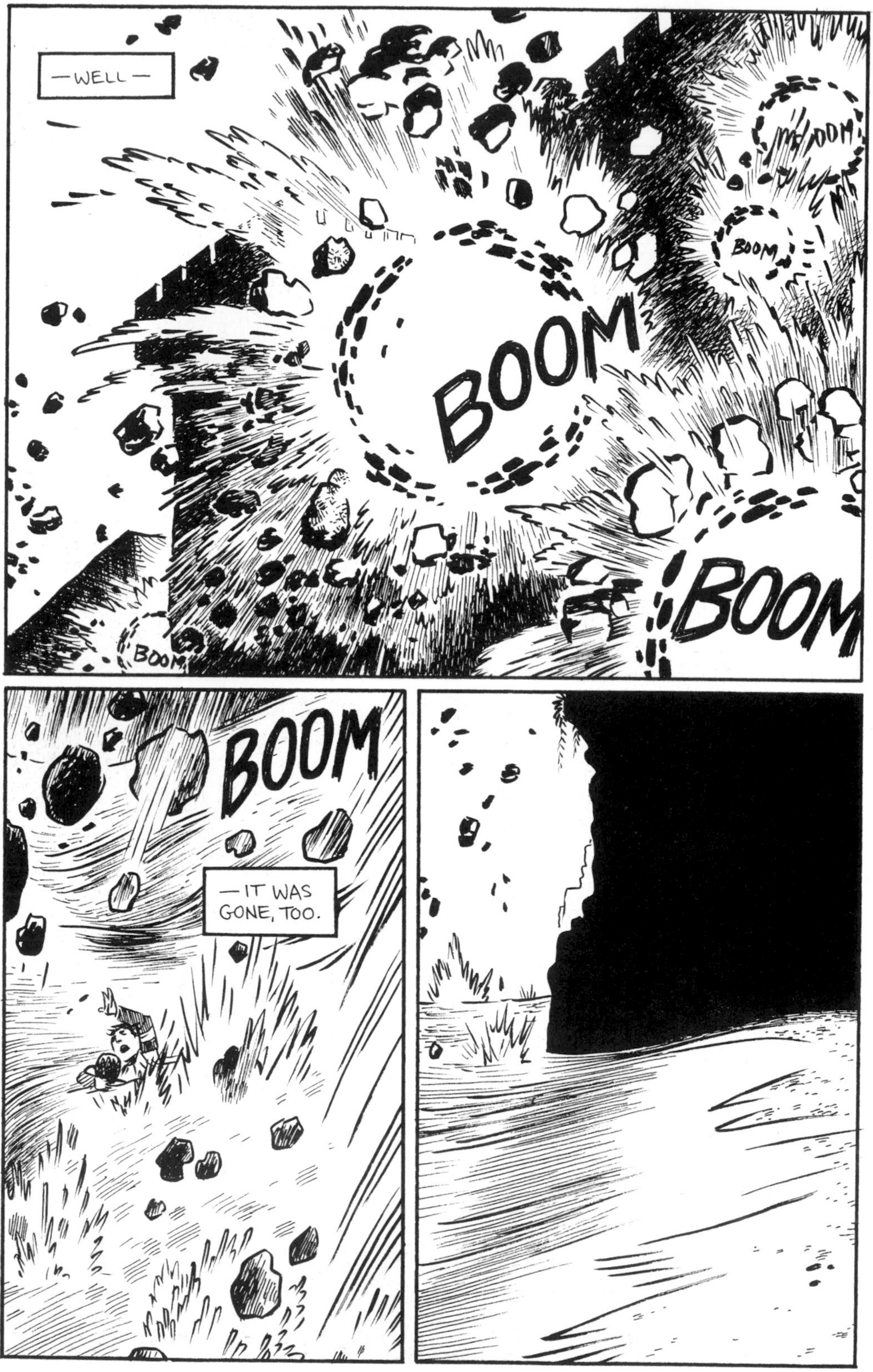
—WELL—
BOOM
BOOM
BOOM
BOOM
BOOM
BOOM
—IT WAS GONE, TOO.

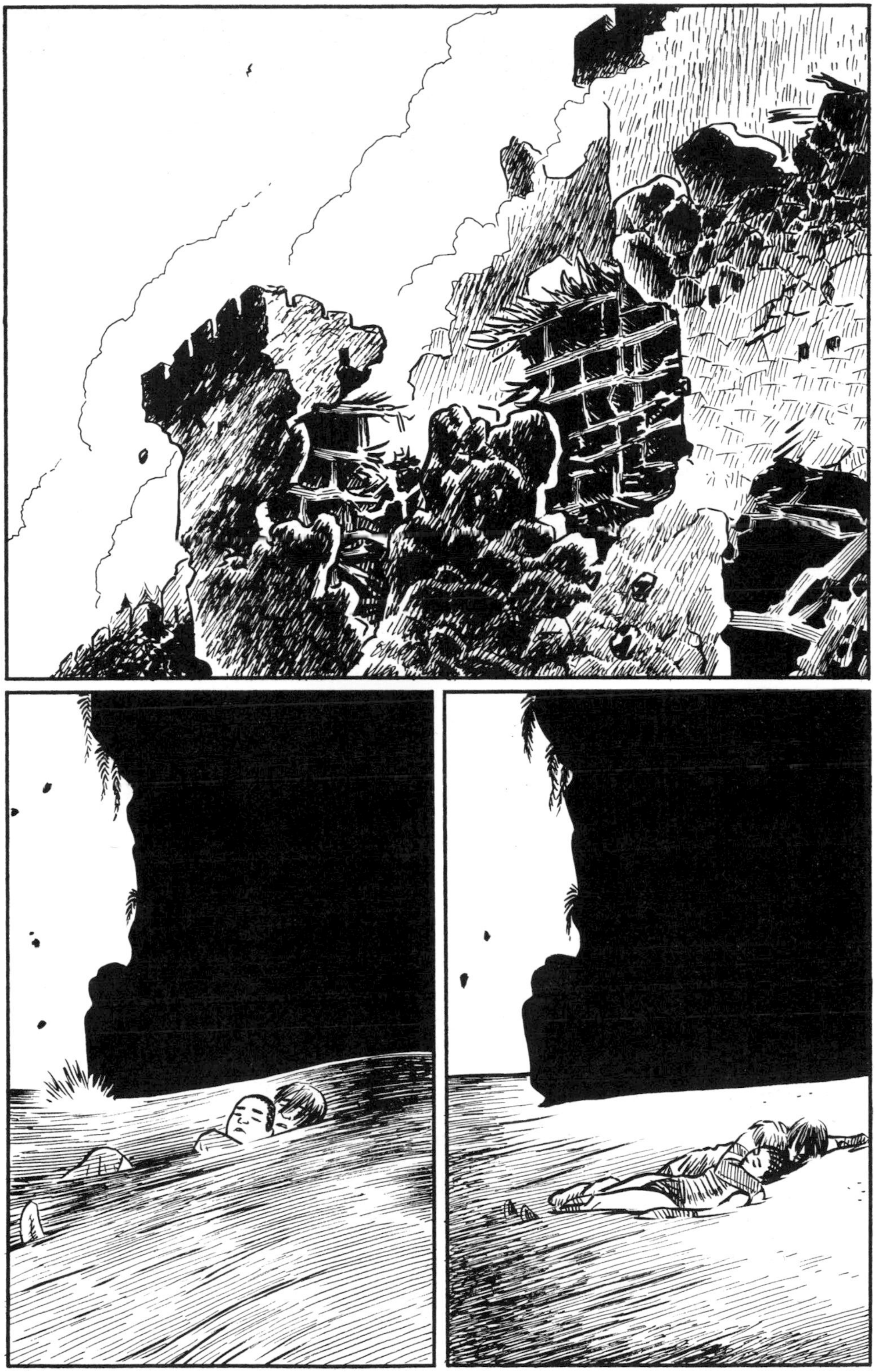

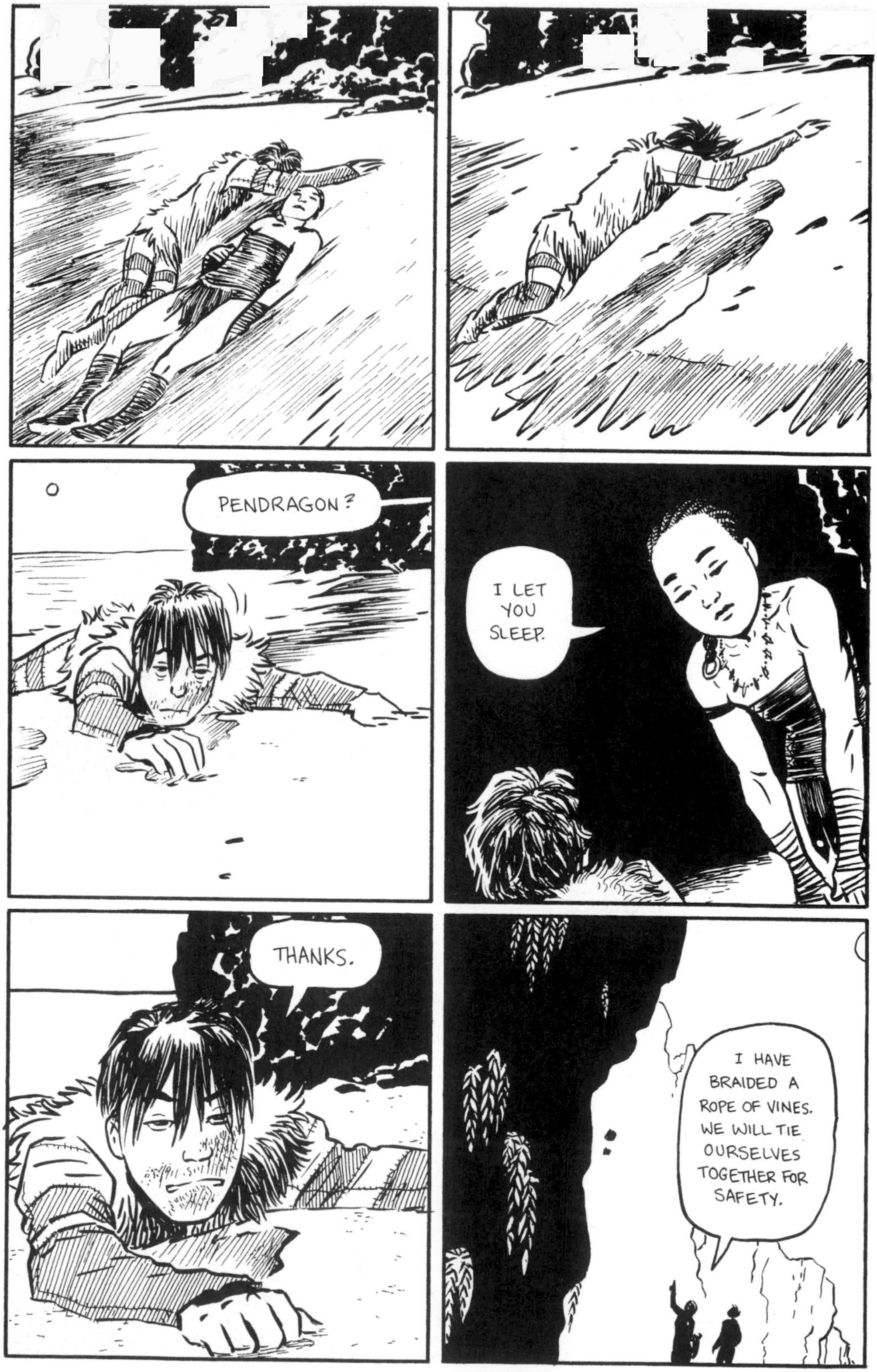
PENDRAGON?
I LET YOU SLEEP.
THANKS.
I HAVE BRAIDED A ROPE OF VINES. WE WILL TIE OURSELVES TOGETHER FOR SAFETY.

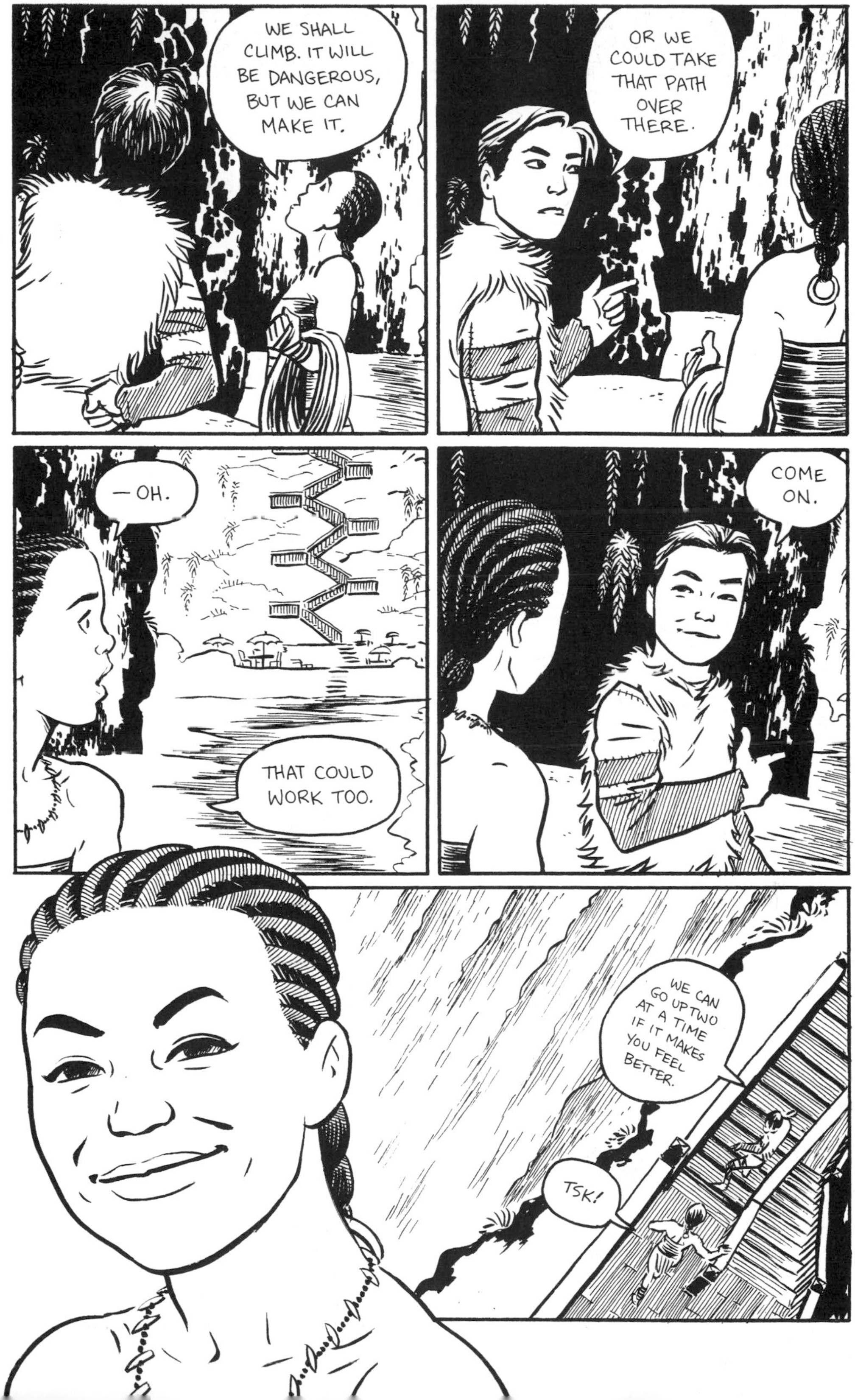
WE SHALL CLIMB. IT WILL BE DANGEROUS, BUT WE CAN MAKE IT.
OR WE COULD TAKE THAT PATH OVER THERE.
—OH.
THAT COULD WORK TOO.
COME ON.
WE CAN GO UP TWO AT A TIME IF IT MAKES YOU FEEL BETTER.
TSK!

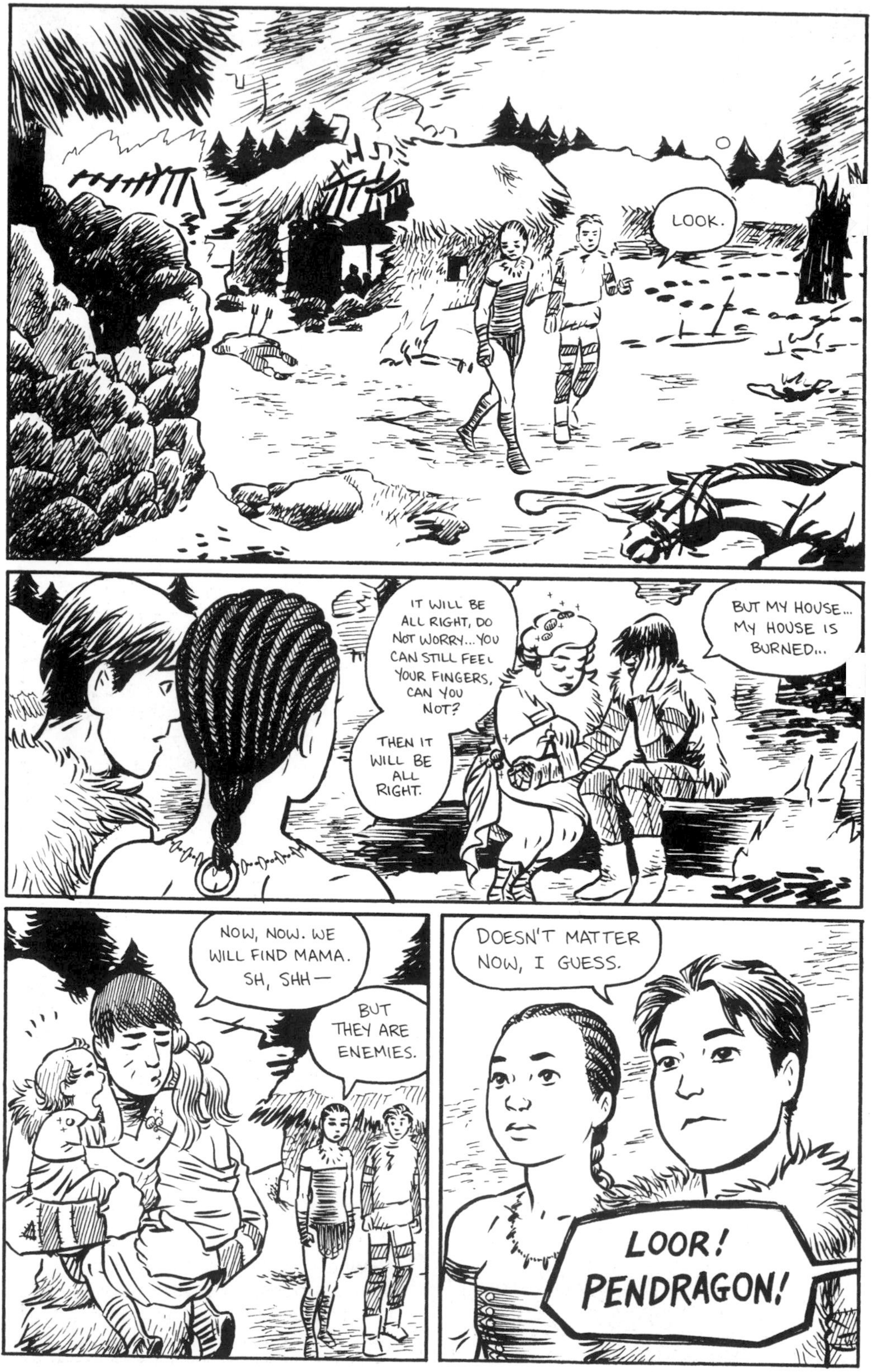
LOOK.
IT WILL BE ALL RIGHT, DO NOT WORRY... YOU CAN STILL FEEL YOUR FINGERS, CAN YOU NOT?
THEN IT WILL BE ALL RIGHT.
BUT MY HOUSE... MY HOUSE IS BURNED...
NOW, NOW. WE WILL FIND MAMA. SH, SHH—
BUT THEY ARE ENEMIES.
DOESN'T MATTER NOW, I GUESS.
LOOR! PENDRAGON!

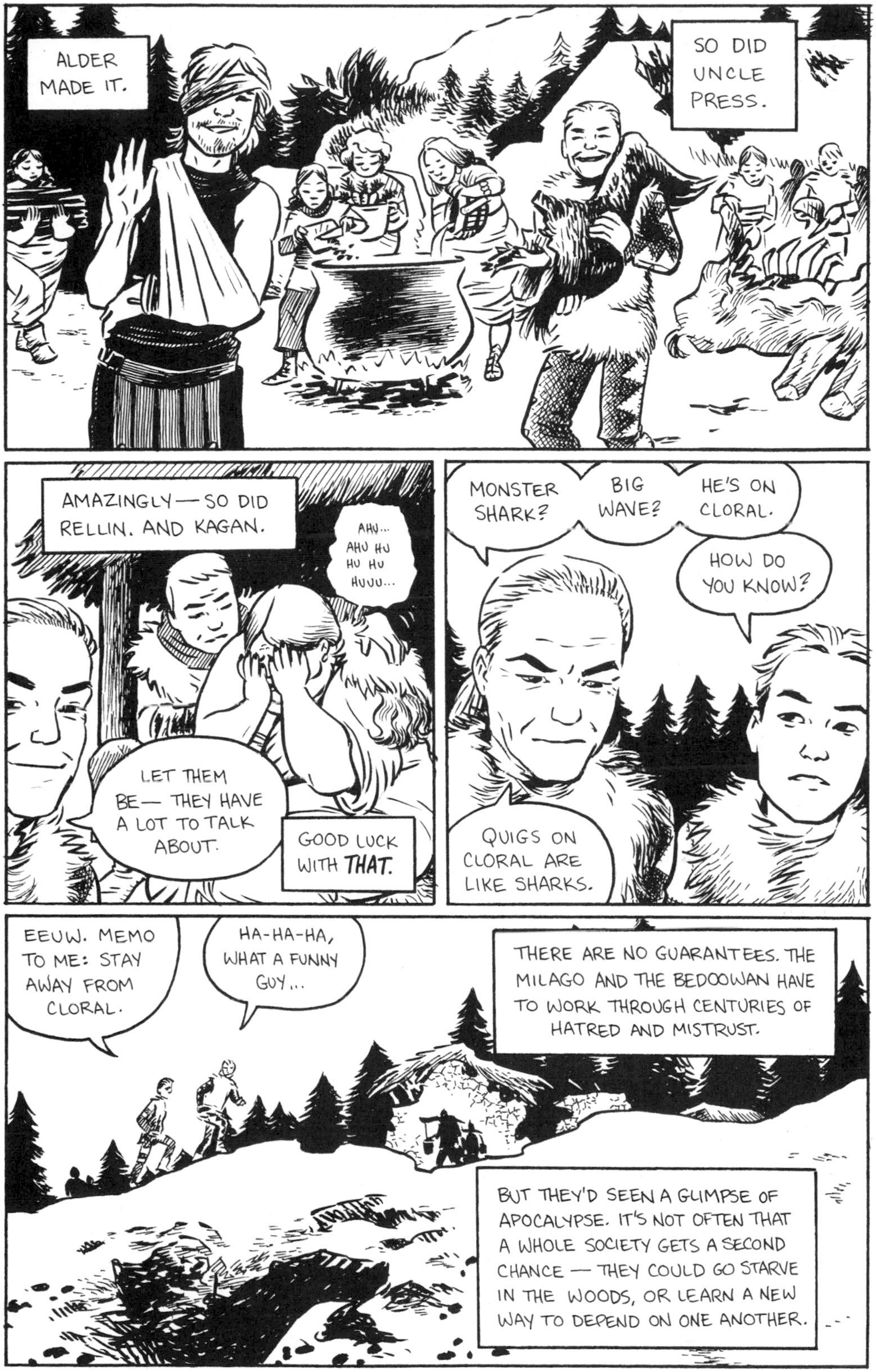
ALDER MADE IT.
SO DID UNCLE PRESS.
AMAZINGLY— SO DID RELLIN. AND KAGAN.
AHU... AHU HU HU HU HUUU...
LET THEM BE— THEY HAVE A LOT TO TALK ABOUT.
GOOD LUCK WITH THAT.
MONSTER SHARK?
BIG WAVE?
HE'S ON CLORAL.
HOW DO YOU KNOW?
QUIGS ON CLORAL ARE LIKE SHARKS.
EEUW. MEMO TO ME: STAY AWAY FROM CLORAL.
HA-HA-HA, WHAT A FUNNY GUY...
THERE ARE NO GUARANTEES. THE MILAGO AND THE BEDOOWAN HAVE TO WORK THROUGH CENTURIES OF HATRED AND MISTRUST.
BUT THEY'D SEEN A GLIMPSE OF APOCALYPSE. IT'S NOT OFTEN THAT A WHOLE SOCIETY GETS A SECOND CHANCE — THEY COULD GO STARVE IN THE WOODS, OR LEARN A NEW WAY TO DEPEND ON ONE ANOTHER...

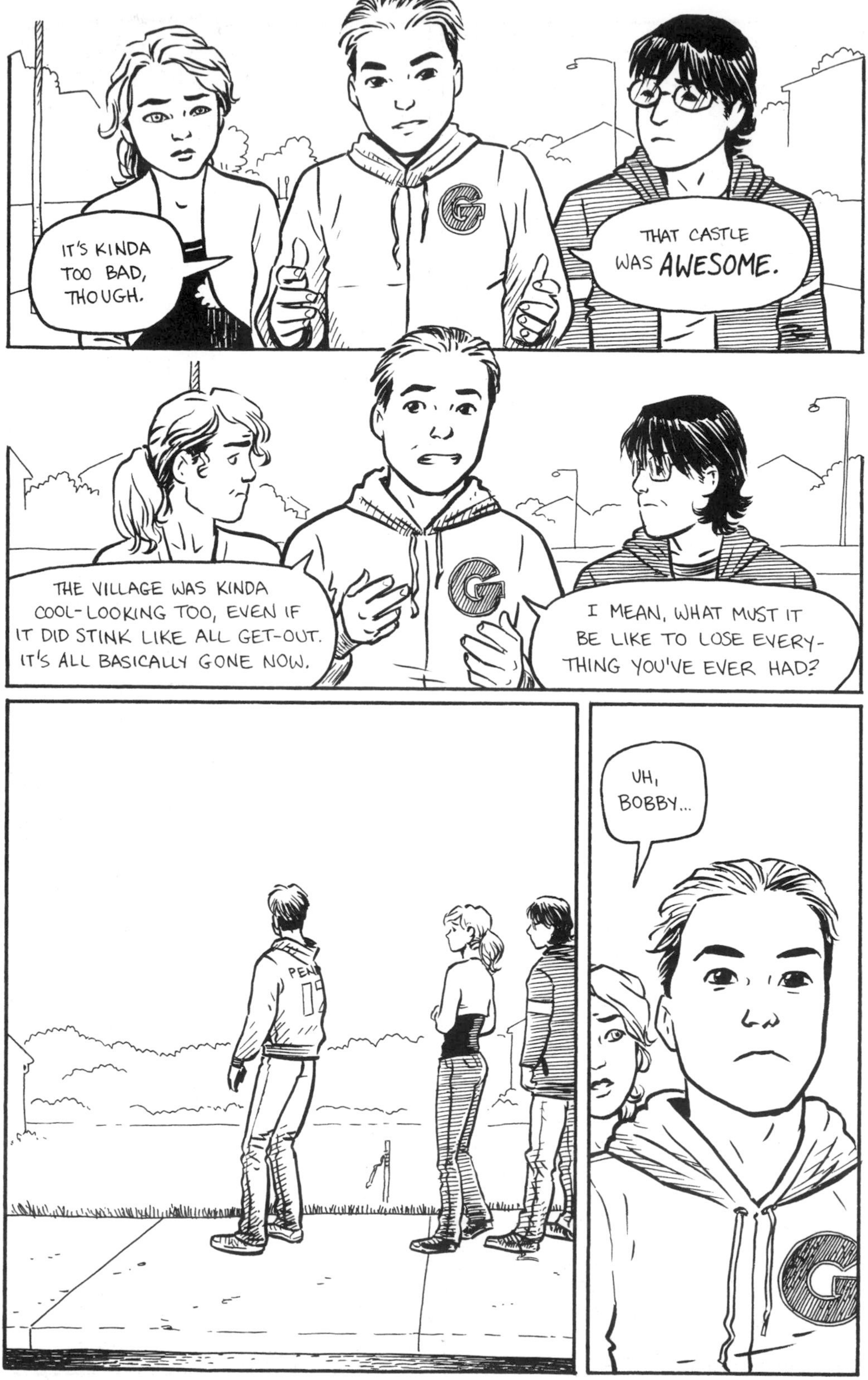
IT'S KINDA TOO BAD, THOUGH.
THAT CASTLE WAS AWESOME.
THE VILLAGE WAS KINDA COOL-LOOKING TOO, EVEN IF IT DID STINK LIKE ALL GET-OUT. IT'S ALL BASICALLY GONE NOW.
I MEAN, WHAT MUST IT BE LIKE TO LOSE EVERYTHING YOU'VE EVER HAD?
UH, BOBBY...

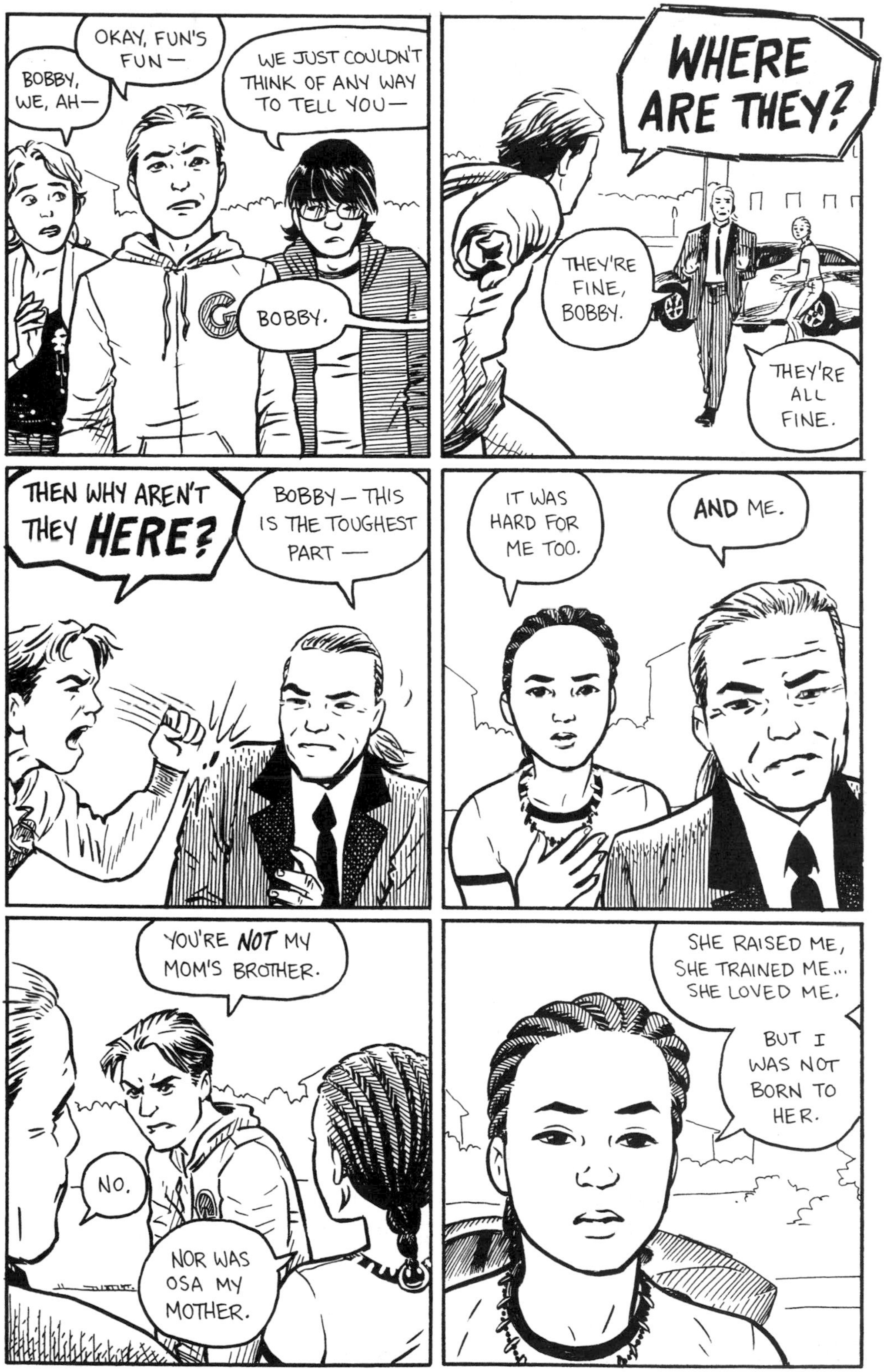
BOBBY, WE, AH—
OKAY, FUN'S FUN—
WE JUST COULDN'T THINK OF ANY WAY TO TELL YOU—
BOBBY.
WHERE ARE THEY?
THEY'RE FINE, BOBBY.
THEY'RE ALL FINE.
THEN WHY AREN'T THEY HERE?
BOBBY—THIS IS THE TOUGHEST PART—
IT WAS HARD FOR ME TOO.
AND ME.
YOU'RE NOT MY MOM'S BROTHER.
NO.
NOR WAS OSA MY MOTHER.
SHE RAISED ME, SHE TRAINED ME... SHE LOVED ME.
BUT I WAS NOT BORN TO HER.

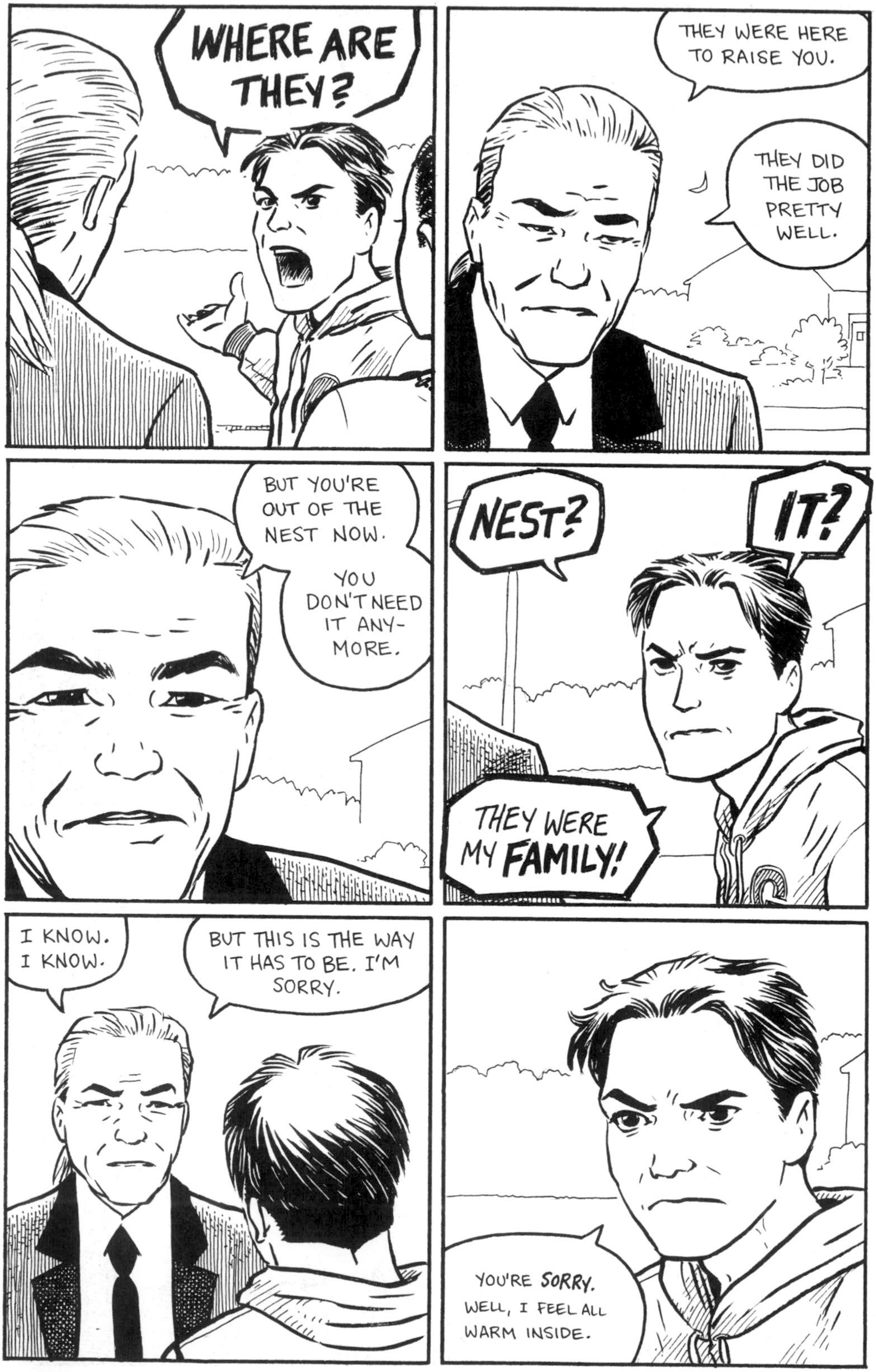
WHERE ARE THEY?
THEY WERE HERE TO RAISE YOU.
THEY DID THE JOB PRETTY WELL.
BUT YOU'RE OUT OF THE NEST NOW.
YOU DON'T NEED IT ANY-MORE.
NEST?
IT?
THEY WERE MY FAMILY!
I KNOW. I KNOW.
BUT THIS IS THE WAY IT HAS TO BE. I'M SORRY.
YOU'RE SORRY. WELL, I FEEL ALL WARM INSIDE.

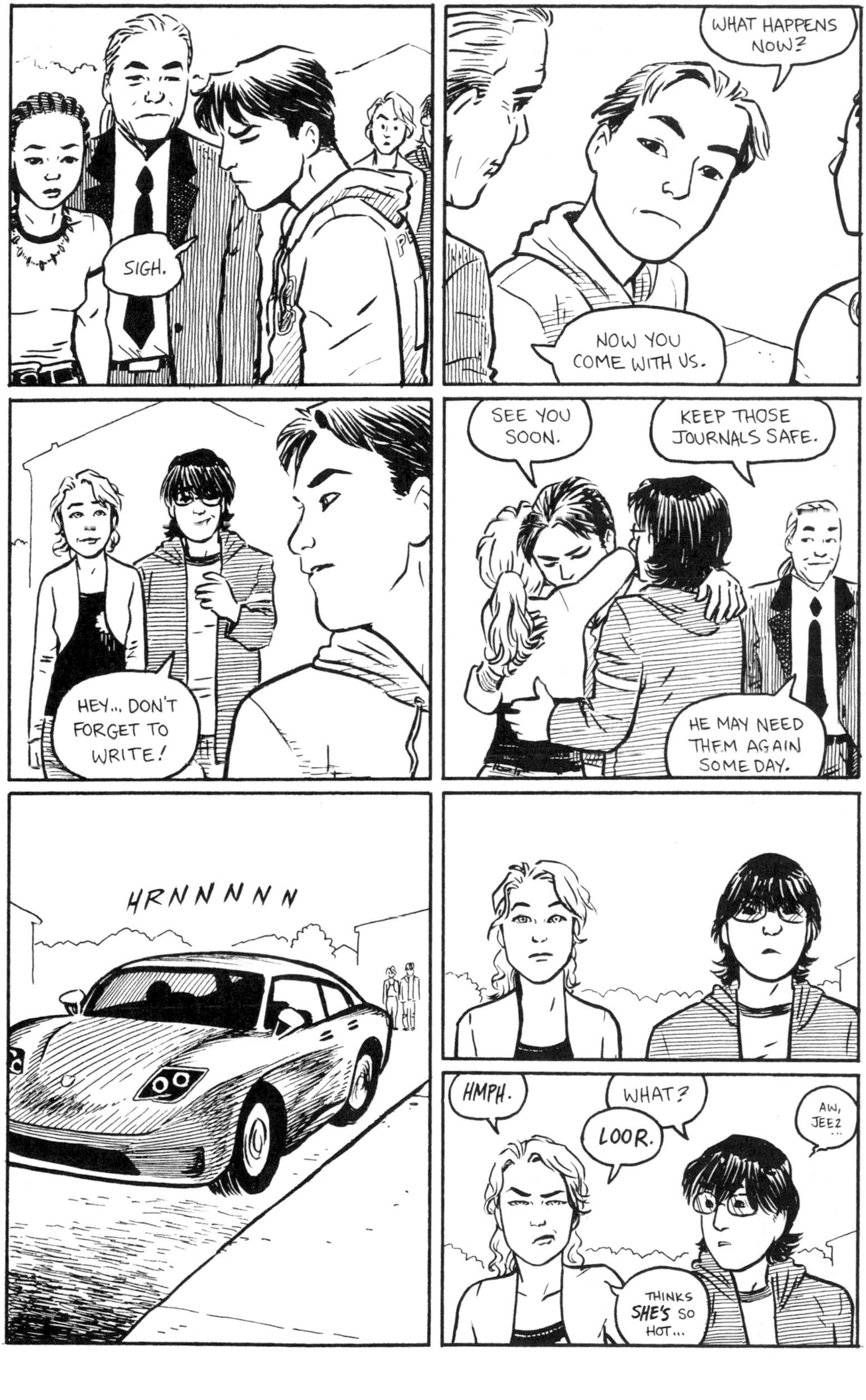
SIGH.
WHAT HAPPENS NOW?
NOW YOU COME WITH US.
HEY... DON'T FORGET TO WRITE!
SEE YOU SOON.
KEEP THOSE JOURNALS SAFE.
HE MAY NEED THEM AGAIN SOME DAY.
HRNNNNNN
HMPH.
WHAT?
LOOR.
AW, JEEZ...
THINKS SHE'S SO HOT...

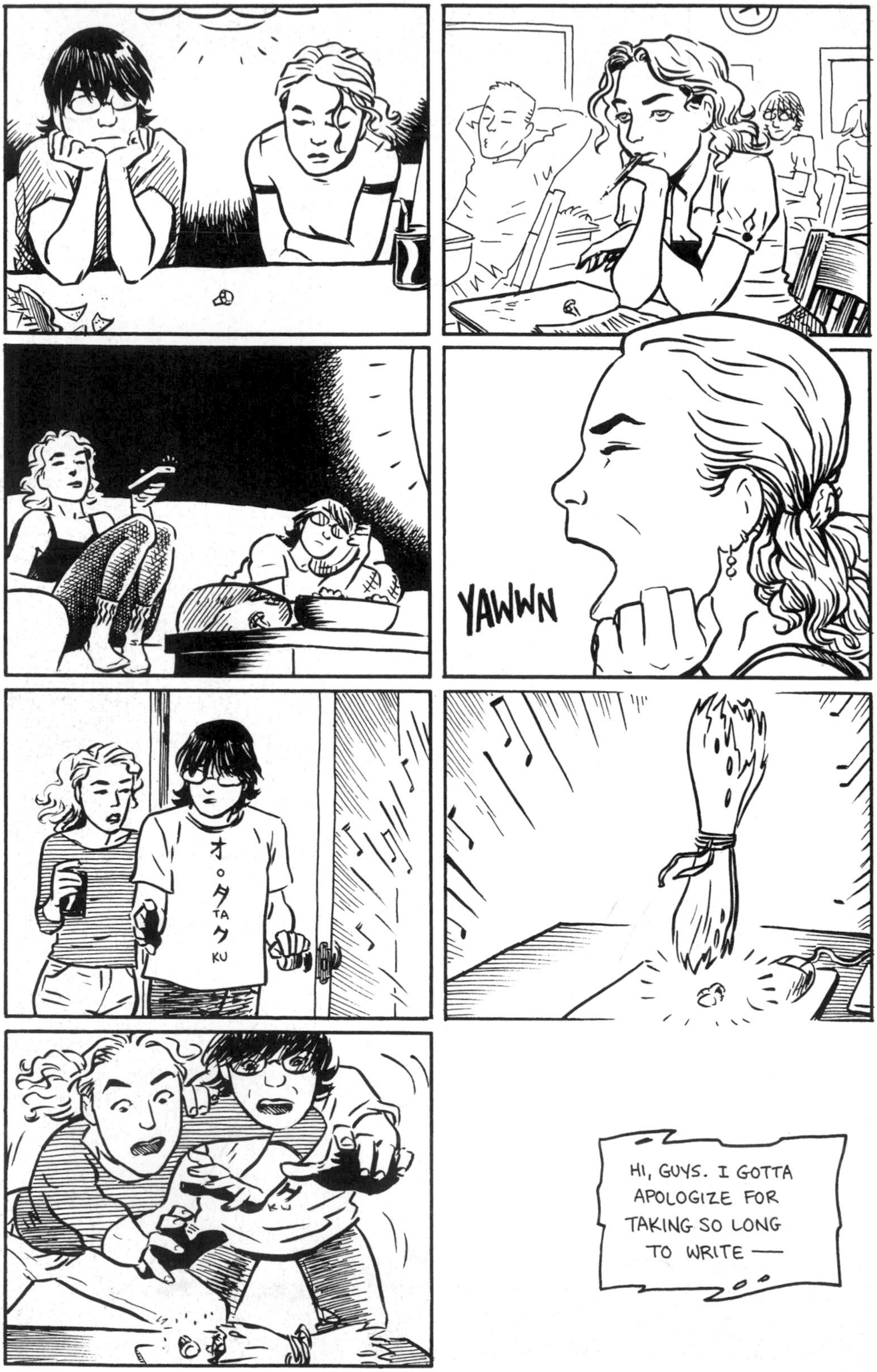
YAWWN
HI, GUYS. I GOTTA APOLOGIZE FOR TAKING SO LONG TO WRITE —

PENDRAGON

Bobby Pendragon is a seemingly normal fourteen-year-old boy. He has a family, a home, and a possible new girlfriend. But something happens to Bobby that changes his life forever.

HE IS CHOSEN TO DETERMINE
THE COURSE OF HUMAN EXISTENCE.

Pulled away from the comfort of his family and suburban home, Bobby is launched into the middle of an immense, interdimensional conflict involving racial tensions, threatened ecosystems, and more. It's a journey of danger and discovery for Bobby, and his success or failure will do nothing less than determine the fate of the world. . . .

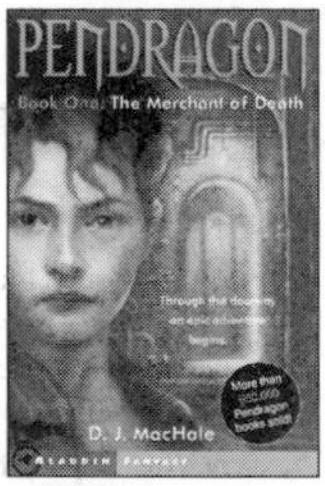
PENDRAGON
Book One: The Merchant of Death
D. J. MacHale

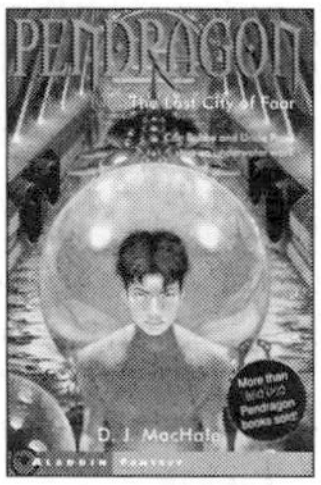
PENDRAGON
D. J. MacHale

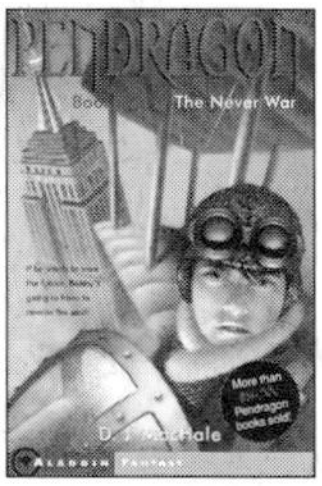
PENDRAGON
The Never War

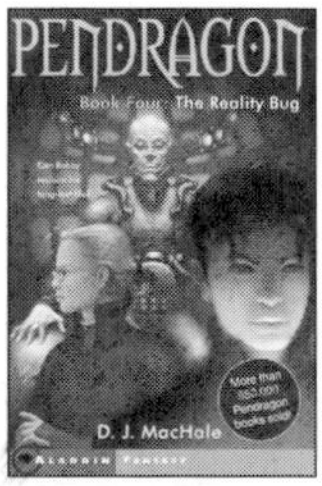
PENDRAGON
The Reality Bug
D. J. MacHale

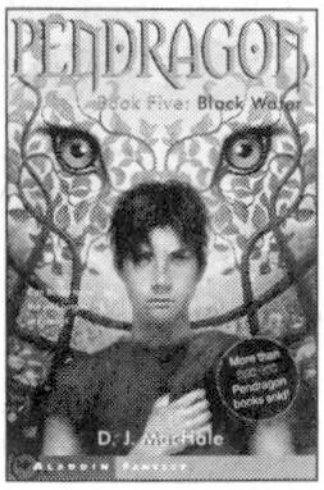
PENDRAGON
Book Five: Black Water

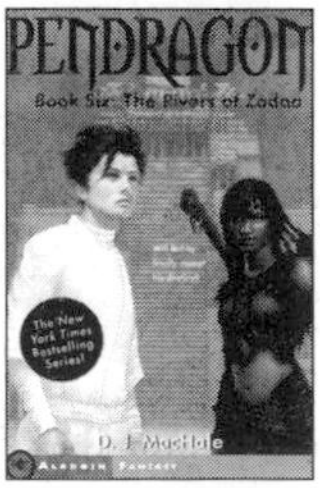
PENDRAGON
Book Six: The Rivers of Zadaa

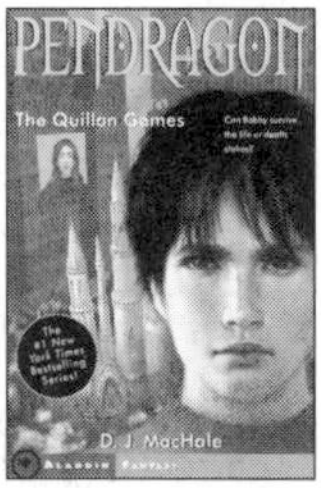
PENDRAGON
The Quillan Games
D. J. MacHale

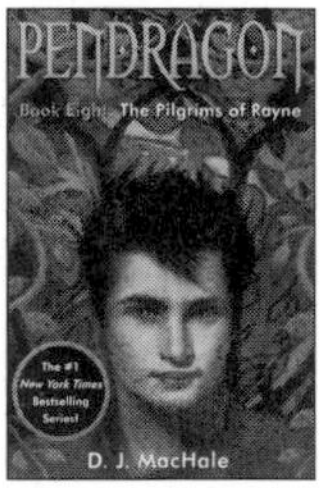
PENDRAGON
The Pilgrims of Rayne
D. J. MacHale

On sale now: Book Nine: *Raven Rise*

From Aladdin Paperbacks and Simon & Schuster Books for Young Readers